THE MYSTERIOUS BENEDICT SOCIETY

Written By Trenton Lee Stewart

Illustrations By Carson Ellis

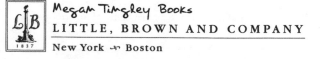

Megan Tingley Books

LITTLE, BROWN AND COMPANY

New York • Boston

Little, Brown and Company

Hachette Book Group USA
1271 Avenue of the Americas, New York, NY 10020
Visit our Web site at www.lb-kids.com

First Edition: March 2007

Library of Congress Cataloging-in-Publication Data
Stewart, Trenton Lee.
The mysterious Benedict Society / by Trenton Lee Stewart ; illustrated by Carson
Ellis. — 1st ed.
    p. cm.
Summary: After passing a series of mind-bending tests, four children are selected to
go on a secret mission that requires them to go undercover at the Learning Institute
for the Very Enlightened, where the only rule is that there are no rules.
ISBN-13: 978-0-316-05777-6
ISBN-10: 0-316-05777-0
[1. Adventure and adventurers — Fiction.   2. Schools — Fiction.   3. Science
fiction.]   I. Ellis, Carson, 1975- ill.   II. Title.
PZ7.S8513My   2007
[Fic] — dc22

                                                                2006009925

10 9 8 7 6 5 4 3 2 1

Q-MT

Printed in the United States of America

The text was set in Janson Text.

For Elliot
— T.L.S.

Contents

Pencils, Erasers, and Disqualification

In a city called Stonetown, near a port called Stonetown Harbor, a boy named Reynie Muldoon was preparing to take an important test. It was the second test of the day — the first had been in an office across town. After that one he was told to come here, to the Monk Building on Third Street, and to bring nothing but a single pencil and a single rubber eraser, and to arrive no later than one o'clock. If he happened to be late, or bring two pencils, or forget his eraser, or in any other way deviate from the instructions, he would not be allowed to take the test, and that would be that. Reynie, who very much wanted to take it, was careful to follow the instructions. Curiously enough, these were the only ones given. He was not told how to *get* to the Monk Building, for example, and had found it necessary to ask directions to the nearest bus stop, acquire a schedule from a dishonest bus driver who tried to trick him into paying for it, and walk several blocks to catch the Third Street bus. Not that any of this was difficult for Reynie Muldoon. Although he was only eleven years old, he was quite used to figuring things out for himself.

From somewhere across the city, a church bell struck the half hour. Twelve-thirty. He still had a while to wait. When he'd checked the doors of the Monk Building at noon, they were locked. So Reynie had bought a sandwich at a deli stand and sat down on this park bench to eat. A tall building in Stonetown's busiest district must surely have many offices inside, he thought. Locked doors at noon seemed a little peculiar. But then, what *hadn't* been peculiar about this whole affair?

To begin with, there was the advertisement. A few days before, Reynie had been reading the newspaper over breakfast at the Stonetown Orphanage, sharing sections with his tutor, Miss Perumal. (As Reynie had already completed all the textbooks on his own, even those for high school students, the orphanage director had assigned him a special tutor while the other children went to class. Miss Perumal didn't quite know what to do with Reynie, either, but she was intelligent and kind, and in their time together they had grown fond of sharing the morning newspaper over breakfast and tea.)

The newspaper that morning had been filled with the usual headlines, several of them devoted to what was commonly called the Emergency: Things had gotten desperately out of control, the headlines reported; the school systems, the budget, the pollution, the crime, the weather . . . why, everything, in fact, was a complete mess, and citizens everywhere were clamoring for a major — no, a *dramatic* — improvement in government. "Things must change NOW!" was the slogan plastered on billboards all over the city (it was a very old slogan), and although Reynie rarely watched television, he knew the Emergency was the main subject of the news programs every day, as it had been for years. Naturally, when Reynie and Miss Perumal first met, they had discussed the Emergency at great length. Finding themselves quite in agreement about politics, however, they soon found such conversation boring and decided to drop the subject. In general, then, they talked about the other news stories, those that varied day to day, and afterward they amused themselves by reading the advertisements. Such was the case on that particular morning when Reynie's life had so suddenly taken a turn.

"Do you care for more honey with your tea?" Miss Perumal had asked — speaking in Tamil, a language she was teaching him — but before Reynie could answer that of *course* he wanted more honey, the advertisement caught Miss Perumal's eye, and she exclaimed, "Reynie! Look at this! Would you be interested?"

Miss Perumal sat across the table from him, but Reynie, who had no trouble reading upside down, quickly scanned the advertisement's bold-printed words: "ARE YOU A GIFTED CHILD LOOKING FOR SPECIAL OPPORTUNITIES?" How odd, he thought. The question was addressed directly to children, not to their parents. Reynie had never known his parents, who died when he was an infant, and it pleased him to read a notice that seemed to take this possibility into account. But still, how odd. How many children read the newspaper, after all? Reynie did, but he had always been alone in this, had always been considered an oddball. If not for Miss Perumal he might even have given it up by now, to avoid some of the teasing.

"I suppose I might be interested," he said to Miss Perumal, "if you think I would qualify."

Miss Perumal gave him a wry look. "Don't you play games with me, Reynie Muldoon. If you aren't the most talented child I've ever known, then I've never known a child at all."

There were to be several sessions of the test administered over the weekend; they made plans for Reynie to attend the very first session. Unfortunately, on Saturday Miss Perumal's mother fell ill and Miss Perumal couldn't take him. This was a real disappointment to Reynie, and not just because of the delay. He always looked forward to Miss Perumal's company — her laughter, her wry expressions, the stories she told (often in Tamil) of her childhood in India, even the occasional sighs she made when she didn't think he was aware. They were gentle and lilting, these sighs, and despite their melancholy Reynie loved to hear them. Miss Perumal sighed when she was feeling sad for him, he knew — sad to see him teased by the other children, sad the poor boy had lost his parents — and Reynie wished he hadn't worried her, but he did like knowing she cared. She was the only one who did (not counting Seymore, the orphanage cat, with whom Reynie spent the day in the reading room — and *he* only wanted to be petted). Quite apart from his eagerness to take the special test, Reynie simply missed Miss Perumal.

He was hopeful, then, when Mr. Rutger, the orphanage director, informed him late that evening that Miss Perumal's mother was considerably improved. Reynie was in the reading room again, the only place in the orphanage where he could be assured of solitude (no one else ever ventured into it) and freedom from persecution. At dinner, an older boy named Vic Morgeroff had tormented Reynie for using the word "enjoyable" to describe the book he was reading. Vic thought it too fancy a word to be proper, and soon had gotten the entire table laughing and saying "enjoyable" in mocking tones until Reynie had finally excused himself without dessert and retreated here.

"Yes, she's much better, much better," said Mr. Rutger, through a mouthful of cheesecake. He was a thin man with a thin face, and his cheeks positively bulged as he chewed. "Miss Perumal just telephoned with the news. She asked for *you*, but as you were not to be found in the dining hall, and I was in the middle of dinner, I took the message for you."

"Thank you," said Reynie with a mixture of relief and disappointment. Cheesecake was his favorite dessert. "I'm glad to hear it."

"Indeed, nothing like health. Absolutely nothing like it. Best thing for anyone," said Mr. Rutger, but here he paused in his chewing, with an unpleasant worried expression upon his face, as if he thought perhaps there had been an insect in his food. Finally he swallowed, brushed the crumbs from his waistcoat, and said, "But see here, Reynie, Miss Perumal mentioned a *test* of some sort. 'Special opportunities,' she said. What is this all about? This isn't about attending an advanced school, is it?"

They had been through this before. Reynie had repeatedly asked permission to apply elsewhere, but Mr. Rutger had insisted Reynie would fare better here, with a tutor, than at an advanced school. "Here you are comfortable," Mr. Rutger had told him more than once. And more than once Reynie had thought, *Here I'm alone.* But in the end Mr. Rutger had his way, and Miss Perumal was hired. It had proved a blessing — Reynie would never complain about Miss Perumal. Still, he had often wondered what life might have been like at a school where the other students didn't find him so odd.

"I don't know, sir," Reynie said, his hopefulness slipping into dejection. He wished Miss Perumal hadn't mentioned the test, though of course she must have felt obliged to. "We just wanted to see what it was about."

Mr. Rutger considered this. "Well, no harm in seeing what things are about, I suppose. I should like to know what it's about myself. In fact, why don't you prepare a report for me when you return? Say, ten pages? No hurry, you can turn it in tomorrow evening."

"Tomorrow evening?" said Reynie. "Does that mean I'm taking the test?"

"I thought I told you," said Mr. Rutger with a frown. "Miss Perumal will come for you first thing in the morning." He took out an embroidered handkerchief and blew his nose with great ferocity. "And now, Reynie, I believe I'll leave you to your reading. This dusty room is a hardship on my sinuses. Be a good man and run a feather duster over the shelves before you leave, will you?"

After hearing this news, Reynie could hardly return to his reading. He flailed about with the feather duster and went straight to bed, as if doing so would hasten the morning's arrival. Instead it lengthened his night, for he was far too eager and anxious to sleep. *Special opportunities,* he kept thinking, over and over again. He would have been thrilled to get a crack at plain old *regular* opportunities, much less special ones.

Just before dawn he rose quietly, got ready with the lights off so as not to disturb his roommates (they often snarled at him for reading in bed at night, even when he used a tiny pen light under the covers), and hurried down to the kitchen. Miss Perumal was already waiting for him — she had been too excited to sleep, as well, and had arrived early. The kettle was just beginning to whistle on the stove, and Miss Perumal, with her back to him, was setting out cups and saucers.

"Good morning, Miss Perumal," he said froggily. He cleared his throat. "I was glad to hear your mother's doing better."

"Thank you, Reynie. Would you —" Miss Perumal turned then, took one look at him, and said, "You'll not make a good impression dressed like that, I'm afraid. One mustn't wear striped pants with a checkered shirt, Reynie. In fact, I believe those must belong to a roommate — they're at least a size too big. Also, it appears that one of your socks is blue and the other purple."

Reynie looked down at his outfit in surprise. Usually he was the least noticeable of boys: He was of average size, of an average pale complexion, his brown hair was of average length, and he wore average clothes. This morning, though, he would stand out in a crowd — unless it happened to be a crowd of clowns. He grinned at Miss Perumal and said, "I dressed this way for luck."

"*Luckily* you won't *need* luck," said Miss Perumal, taking the kettle from the stove. "Now please go change, and this time turn on your light — never mind how your roommates grumble — so that you may have better luck choosing your clothes."

When Reynie returned Miss Perumal told him that she had a long errand to run. Her mother had been prescribed new medicine and a special diet, and Miss Perumal must go shopping for her. So it was agreed that she would take him to the test and pick him up when it was over. After a light breakfast (neither of them wanted more than toast), yet well before anyone else in the orphanage had risen, Miss Perumal drove him across the sleepy city to an office building near Stonetown Bay. A line of children already stood at the door, all of them accompanied by their parents, all fidgeting nervously.

When Miss Perumal moved to get out of the car, Reynie said, "I thought you were dropping me off."

"You don't think I would just leave you here without investigating first, do you?" replied Miss Perumal. "The notice didn't even list a telephone number for questions. It's a bit out of the ordinary, don't you think?"

So Reynie took his place at the end of the line while Miss Perumal went inside the building to speak with someone. It was a long line, and Reynie wondered how many special opportunities were available. Perhaps only a very few — perhaps they would all be given out before he even reached the door. He was growing anxious at this idea when a friendly man ahead of him turned and said, "Don't worry, son, you haven't long to wait. All the children are to go inside together in a few minutes. They made the announcement just before you arrived."

Reynie thanked him gratefully, noticing as he did so that a

number of parents were casting grumpy looks at the man, apparently disliking the notion of being friendly to competitors. The man, embarrassed, turned away from Reynie and said nothing else.

"Very well," said Miss Perumal when she returned, "everything is set. You may call me on their telephone when you've finished the test. Here is the number. If I'm not back by then, simply call a taxi and Mr. Rutger will pay the fare. You can tell me all about it this afternoon."

"Thanks so much for everything, Miss Perumal," said Reynie, earnestly taking her hand.

"Oh, Reynie, you silly child, don't look so grateful," said Miss Perumal. To Reynie's surprise, there were tears on her cheeks. "It's nothing at all. Now give your poor tutor a hug. I imagine my services won't be needed after this."

"I haven't passed it yet, Miss Perumal!"

"Oh, stop being silly," she said, and after squeezing him tightly, Miss Perumal dabbed her eyes with a handkerchief, walked determinedly to her car, and drove away just as the children were ushered into the building.

It was a curious test. The first section was rather what Reynie would have expected — one or two questions regarding octagons and hexagons, another devoted to bushels of this and kilograms of that, and another that required calculating how much time must pass before two speeding trains collided. (This last question Reynie answered with a thoughtful frown, noting in the margin that since the two trains were approaching each other on an empty stretch of track, it was likely the engineers would recognize the impending disaster and apply their brakes, thus avoiding the collision altogether.)

Reynie raced through these questions and many like them, then came to the second section, whose first question was: "Do you like to watch television?"

This certainly was not the sort of question Reynie had expected. It was only a question of preference. Anyway, of *course* he liked to watch television — *everybody* liked to watch television. As he started to mark down the answer, however, Reynie hesitated. Well, did he really? The more he thought about it, the more he realized that he didn't, in fact, like to watch television at all. I really *am* an oddball, he thought, with a feeling of disappointment. Nonetheless, he answered the question truthfully: NO.

The next question read: "Do you like to listen to the radio?" And again, Reynie realized that he did not, although he was sure everyone else did. With a growing sense of isolation, he answered the question: NO.

The third question, thankfully, was less emotional. It read: "What is wrong with this statement?" How funny, Reynie thought, and marking down his answer he felt somewhat cheered. "It isn't a statement at all," he wrote. "It's a question."

The next page showed a picture of a chessboard, upon which all the pieces and pawns rested in their starting positions, except for a black pawn, which had advanced two spaces. The question read: "According to the rules of chess, is this position possible?" Reynie studied the board a moment, scratched his head, and wrote down his answer: YES.

After a few more pages of questions, all of which Reynie felt confident he had answered correctly, he arrived at the test's final question: "Are you brave?" Just reading the words quickened Reynie's heart. Was he brave? Bravery had never been required of him, so how could he tell? Miss Perumal would say he was: She would point out how cheerful he tried to be despite feeling lonely, how patiently he withstood the teasing of other children, and how he was always eager for a challenge. But these things only showed that he was good-natured, polite, and very often bored. Did they really show that he was brave? He didn't think so. Finally he gave up trying to decide and simply wrote, "I hope so."

He laid down his pencil and looked around. Most of the other children were also finishing the test. At the front of the room, munching rather loudly on an apple, the test administrator was keeping a close eye on them to ensure they didn't cheat. She was a thin woman in a mustard-yellow suit, with a yellowish complexion, short-cropped, rusty-red hair, and a stiff posture. She reminded Reynie of a giant walking pencil.

"Pencils!" the woman suddenly called out, as if she'd read his thoughts.

The children jumped in their seats.

"Please lay down your pencils now," the pencil woman said. "The test is over."

"But I'm not finished!" one child cried. "That's not fair!"

"I want more time!" cried another.

The woman's eyes narrowed. "I'm sorry you haven't finished, children, but the test is over. Please pass your papers to the front of the room, and remain seated while the tests are graded. Don't worry, it won't take long."

As the papers were passed forward, Reynie heard the boy behind him snicker and say to his neighbor, "If they couldn't finish *that* test, they shouldn't even have come. Like that chess question — who could have missed it?"

The neighbor, sounding every bit as smug, replied, "They were trying to trick us. Pawns can only move one space at a time, so of *course* the position wasn't possible. I'll bet some stupid kids didn't know that."

"Ha! You're just lucky you didn't miss it yourself! Pawns *can* move two spaces — on their very first move, they can. But whether it moved one space or two is beside the point. Don't you know that white always moves first? The *black* pawn couldn't have moved yet at all! It's so simple. This test was for babies."

"Are you calling me a baby?" growled the other.

"You boys there!" snapped the pencil woman. "Stop talking!"

Reynie was suddenly anxious. Could he possibly have answered that question wrong? And what about the other questions? Except for the odd ones about television and bravery, they had seemed easy, but perhaps he was such a strange bird that he had misunderstood everything. He shook his head and tried not to care. If he wanted to prove himself brave, after all, he had better just stop worrying. If he must return to his old routine at the orphanage, at least he had Miss Perumal. What did it matter if he was different from other children? Everyone got teased from time to time — he was no different in *that* respect.

Reynie told himself this, but his anxious feeling didn't fade.

After all the tests had been turned in, the pencil woman stepped out of the room, leaving the children to bite their nails and watch the clock. Only a few minutes passed, however, before she returned and announced, "I shall now read the names of children admitted into the second phase of the test."

The children began to murmur. A second phase? The advertisement hadn't mentioned a second phase.

The woman continued, "If your name is called, you are to report to the Monk Building on Third Street no later than one o'clock, where you will join children from other sessions who also passed the test." She went on to lay out the rules about pencils, erasers, and disqualification. Then she popped a handful of peanuts into her mouth and chewed ferociously, as if she were starving.

Reynie raised his hand.

"Mm-yes?" the woman said, swallowing.

"Excuse me, you say to bring only one pencil, but what if the pencil lead breaks? Will there be a pencil sharpener?"

Again the boy behind Reynie snickered, this time muttering: "What makes him so sure he'll be taking that test? She hasn't even called the names yet!"

It was true — he should have waited until she'd called the names. He must have seemed very arrogant. Cheeks burning, Reynie ducked his head.

The pencil woman answered, "Yes, if a sharpener should become necessary, one will be provided. Children are *not* to bring their own, understood?" There was a general nodding of heads, after which the woman clapped the peanut grit from her hands, took out a sheet of paper, and continued, "Very well, if there are no other questions, I shall read the list."

The room became very quiet.

"Reynard Muldoon!" the woman called. Reynie's heart leaped.

There was a grumble of discontent from the seat behind him, but as soon as it passed, the room again grew quiet, and the children waited with bated breath for the other names to be called. The woman glanced up from the sheet.

"That is all," she said matter-of-factly, folding the paper and tucking it away. "The rest of you are dismissed."

The room erupted in outcries of anger and dismay. "Dismissed?" said the boy behind Reynie. *"Dismissed?"*

As the children filed out the door — some weeping bitterly, some stunned, some whining in complaint — Reynie approached the woman. For some reason, she was hurrying around the room checking the window locks. "Excuse me. Miss? May I please use your telephone? My tutor said —"

"I'm sorry, Reynard," the woman interrupted, tugging unsuccessfully on a closed window. "I'm afraid there isn't a telephone."

"But Miss Perumal —"

"Reynard," the woman said with a smile, "I'm sure you can make do without one, can't you? Now, if you'll excuse me, I must sneak out the back door. These windows appear to have been painted shut."

"Sneak out? But why?"

"I've learned from experience. Any moment now, some of these children's parents will come storming in to demand explanations. Unfortunately, I have none to give them. Therefore, off I go. I'll see you this afternoon. Don't be late!"

And with that, away she went.

It had been a strange business indeed, and Reynie had a suspicion it was to grow stranger still. When the distant church bell struck the quarter hour, Reynie finished his sandwich and rose from the park bench. If the doors to the Monk Building weren't open by now, he would try to find another way in. At this point, it would hardly surprise him to discover he must enter the building through a basement window.

As he mounted the steps to the Monk Building's broad front plaza, Reynie saw two girls well ahead of him, walking together toward the front doors. Other test-takers, he guessed. One girl, who seemed to have green hair — though perhaps this was a trick of the light; the sun shone blindingly bright today — was carelessly flinging her pencil up into the air and catching it again. Not the best idea, Reynie thought. And sure enough, even as he thought it, the girl missed the pencil and watched it fall through a grate at her feet.

For a moment the other girl hesitated, as if she might try to help. Then she checked her watch. In only a few minutes it would be one o'clock. "Sorry about your pencil — it's a shame," she said, but already her sympathetic expression was fading. Clearly it had occurred to her that with the green-haired girl unable to take the test, there would be less competition. With a spreading smile, she hurried across the plaza and through the front doors of the Monk Building, which had finally been unlocked.

The metal grate covered a storm drain that ran beneath the plaza, and the unfortunate girl was staring through it, down into darkness, when Reynie reached her. Her appearance was striking — indeed, even startling. She had coal-black skin; hair so long she could have tied it around her waist (and yes, it truly was green); and an extraordinarily puffy white dress that gave you the impression she was standing in a cloud.

"That's rotten luck," Reynie said. "To drop your pencil here, of all places."

The girl looked up at him with hopeful eyes. "You don't happen to have an extra one, do you?"

"I'm sorry. I was told to bring —"

"I know, I know," she interrupted. "Only one pencil. Well, that was *my* only pencil, and a fat lot of good it will do me down in that drain." She stared wistfully through the grate a moment, then looked up at Reynie as if surprised to see him still standing there. "What are you waiting for? The test starts any minute."

"I'm not going to leave you here without a pencil," Reynie said. "I was surprised your friend did."

"Friend? Oh, that other girl. She's not my friend — we just met at the bottom of the steps. I didn't even know her name. For that matter, I don't know yours, either."

"Reynard Muldoon. You can call me Reynie."

"Okay, Reynie, nice to meet you. I'm Rhonda Kazembe. So now that we're friends and all that, how do you intend to get my pencil back? We'd better hurry, you know. One minute late and we're disqualified."

Reynie took out his own pencil, a new yellow #2 that he'd sharpened to a fine point that morning. "Actually," he said, "we'll just share this one." He snapped the pencil in two and handed her the sharpened end. "I'll sharpen my half and we'll both be set. Do you have your eraser?"

Rhonda Kazembe was staring at her half of the pencil with a mixture of gratitude and surprise. "That would never have occurred to me," she said, "breaking it like that. Now, what did you say? Oh, yes, I have my eraser."

"Then let's get going, we only have a minute," Reynie urged.

Rhonda held back. "Hold on, Reynie. I haven't properly thanked you."

"You're welcome," he said impatiently. "Now let's go!"

Still she resisted. "No, I *really* want to thank you. If it weren't for you, I couldn't have taken this test, and do you want to know something?" Glancing around to be sure they were alone, Rhonda whispered, "I have the answers. I'm going to make a perfect score!"

"What? How?"

"No time to explain. But if you sit right behind me, you can look over my shoulder. I'll hold up my test a bit to make it easier."

Reynie was stunned. How in the world could this girl have gotten her hands on the answers? And now she was offering to help him cheat! He was briefly tempted — he wanted desperately to learn about those special opportunities. But when he imagined returning to tell Miss Perumal of his success, hiding the fact that he'd cheated, he knew he could never do it.

"No, thank you," he said. "I'd rather not."

Rhonda Kazembe looked amazed, and Reynie once again felt the weight of loneliness upon him. If it was unpleasant to feel so different from the other children at Stonetown Orphanage, how much worse was it to be seen as an oddball by a green-haired girl wearing her own personal fog bank?

"Okay, suit yourself," Rhonda said as the two of them started for the front doors. "I hope you know what you're in for."

Reynie was in too much of a hurry to respond. He had no idea what he was in for, of course, but he certainly wanted to find out.

⌣∴⌣

Inside the Monk Building, conspicuously posted signs led them down a series of corridors, past a room where a handful of parents waited anxiously, and at last into a room crowded with children in desks. Except for the unusual silence, the room was just like any schoolroom, with a chalkboard at the front and a teacher's desk upon which rested a pencil sharpener, a ruler, and a sign that said: NO TALKING. IF YOU ARE CAUGHT TALKING IT WILL BE ASSUMED YOU ARE CHEATING. Only two seats remained empty, one behind the other. To guarantee he wouldn't be tempted to cheat, Reynie chose the one in front. A clock on the wall struck one just as Rhonda Kazembe dropped into the desk behind him.

"That was close," she said.

"There will be no talking!" boomed the pencil woman, who entered just then, slamming the door behind her. She strode briskly to the front of the room, carrying a tall stack of papers and a jar of pickles. "If any child is caught cheating, then he or she will be executed —"

The children gasped.

"I'm sorry, did I say executed? I meant to say *escorted*. Any child caught cheating will be *escorted* from the building at once. Now then, are you all relaxed? It's important to be relaxed when taking such an extremely difficult test as this, especially considering how long it is and how very little time you'll have to complete it."

In the back of the room someone groaned in distress.

"You there!" shouted the pencil woman, pointing her finger. Every head in the room swiveled to see who had groaned.

It was the same girl who had abandoned Rhonda Kazembe on the plaza. Under the savage stare of the pencil woman, the girl's face went pasty pale, like the underbelly of a dead fish. "I said no talking," the woman barked. "Do you wish to leave now?"

"But I only groaned!" the girl protested.

The pencil woman frowned. "Do you mean to suggest that saying, 'But I only groaned!' doesn't count as talking?"

The girl, frightened and perplexed, could hardly muster a shake of the head.

"Very well, let this be a warning to you. To *all* of you. From this moment on there will be no talking, period. Now then, are there any questions?"

Reynie raised his hand.

"Reynard Muldoon, you have a question?"

Reynie held up his broken pencil and made a pencil-sharpening motion with the other hand.

"Very well, you may use the pencil sharpener on my desk."

Reynie hustled forward, sharpened his pencil — he felt all eyes upon him as he ground away, checked the tip, and ground away again — and hurried back to his seat. As he did so, he noticed Rhonda Kazembe slipping a tiny piece of paper from the sleeve of her cloud-dress: the list of test answers. She was taking quite a risk, Reynie thought, but he had no chance to reflect on it further, as the pencil woman now launched into the rest of her speech.

"You shall have one hour to complete this test," she barked, "and you must follow these directions exactly. First, write your name at the top of the test. Second, read all the questions and answers carefully. Third, choose the correct answers by circling the appropriate letter. Fifth, bring the completed test to me. Sixth, return to your seat and wait until all the tests have been graded, at which time I will announce the names of those who pass."

The children were shifting uneasily in their seats. What had happened to the fourth step? The pencil woman had skipped from third to fifth. The children looked at one another, not daring to speak. What if the fourth step was important? Reynie was waiting, hoping someone else would raise a hand for a change. When no one did, he timidly raised his own.

"Yes, Reynard?"

He pointed to his mouth.

"Yes, you may speak. What is your question?"

"Excuse me, but what about the fourth step?"

"There is no fourth step," she replied. "Any other questions?"

Utterly baffled now, the children held their tongues.

"To pass this test," the pencil woman went on, "you must correctly answer every question, by which I mean *every* question. If you skip even one question, or answer one incorrectly, you will fail the test."

"No problem," whispered Rhonda Kazembe from behind Reynie.

The pencil woman's eyes darted to their side of the room. She stared hard at Reynie, whose mouth went dry. Why on earth didn't Rhonda keep her mouth closed? Was she *trying* to get them thrown out?

"You may begin the test as soon as you receive it," said the pencil woman, turning away at last, and Reynie resisted the urge to sigh with relief — even a sigh might disqualify him.

Besides, what relief he felt didn't last long: The pencil woman had begun handing out the tests.

The first child to receive one was a tough-looking boy in a baseball cap who eagerly grabbed it, looked at the first question, and burst into tears. The girl behind him looked at her test, rubbed her eyes as if they weren't working properly, then looked again. Her head wobbled on her neck.

"If you begin to feel faint," said the pencil woman, moving on to the next child, "place your head between your knees and take deep breaths. If you think you may vomit, please come to the front of the room, where a trash can will be provided."

Down the row she went, distributing the tests. The crying boy had begun flipping through the test now — there appeared to be several pages — and with each new page his sobs grew louder and more desperate. When he reached the end, he began to wail.

"I'm afraid loud weeping isn't permitted," said the pencil woman. "Please leave the room."

The boy, greatly relieved, leaped from his desk and raced to the door, followed at once by two other children who hadn't received the test yet but were terrified now to see it. The pencil woman closed the door.

"If any others flee the room in panic or dismay," she said sternly, "please remember to close the door behind you. Your sobs may disturb the other test-takers."

She continued handing out the test. Child after child received it with trembling fingers, and child after child, upon looking at the questions, turned pale, or red, or a subtle shade of green. By the time the pencil woman dropped the pages upon his desk, dread was making Reynie's stomach flop like a fish. And for good reason — the questions were impossible. The very first one read:

The territories of the Naxcivan Autonomous Republic and the Nagorno-Karabakh region are disputed by what two countries?

A. Bhutan, which under the 1865 Treaty of Sinchulu ceded border land to Britain; and Britain, which in exchange for that land provided Bhutan an annual subsidy, and under whose influence Bhutan's monarchy was established in 1907.

B. Azerbaijan, whose territory in 1828 was divided between Russia and Persia by the Treaty of Turkmenchay; and Armenia, a nation founded after the destruction of the Seleucid Empire some two thousand years ago, likewise incorporated into Russia by the aforementioned treaty.

C. Vanuatu, which having been administered (until its independence) by an Anglo-French Condominium, retains both French and English as official languages (in addition to Bislama, or Bichelama); and Portugal, whose explorer Pedro Fernandez de Quiros became in 1606 the first European to discover the islands Vanuatu comprises.

Although there were two more answers to choose from, Reynie didn't read them. If every question was like this one, he had absolutely no hope of passing. A quick glance at the next few questions did nothing to encourage him. If anything, they got worse. And this was only the first page! All around him children were shivering, sighing, grinding their teeth. Reynie felt like joining them. So much for those special opportunities. Back to the orphanage he would go, where no one — not even good Miss Perumal — knew what to do with him. It had been a nice idea, but apparently he did not have what it took.

Even so, he wasn't ready to leave. He had yet to follow the directions, and because he was determined not to quit until he had at least *tried*, he proceeded to follow them now. Dutifully he wrote his name atop the first page — that was the first step. *Well, you've accomplished that much*, he thought. The second step was to read all the questions and answers carefully. Reynie took a deep breath. There were forty questions in all. Just reading them would take him most of the hour. It didn't help that the pencil woman now sat eating pickles — they were especially crisp ones, too — as she watched the children struggle.

The second question wanted to know where the common vetch originated and to what family it belonged. Reynie had no idea what a common vetch was, and the possible answers offered no helpful clue — it might be an antelope, a bird, a rodent, or a vine. Reynie went on to the third question, which had to do with subatomic particles called fermions and an Indian physicist named Satyendranath Bose. The fourth question asked which church was built by the emperor Justinian to demonstrate his superiority to the late Theodoric's Ostrogothic successors. On and on the questions went. To his credit, Reynie recognized the names of a few places, a few mathematic principles, and one or two important historical figures, but it wouldn't do him any good. He would be lucky to answer a single question correctly, much less all of them.

When he was exactly halfway through the test (he was on question twenty, regarding the difference between parataxis and hypotaxis), Reynie heard Rhonda Kazembe rise from the desk behind him. Was she already *finished*? Well, of course! She had all the answers. Reynie grimaced in irritation, and as Rhonda stepped forward to turn in her test, the other children gasped in amazement. But the pencil woman seemed not the least bit suspicious. If anything, she was absorbed in Rhonda's bizarre appearance and hardly glanced at the test as she took it.

Reynie had a sudden insight: Rhonda was calling attention to herself *on purpose*. It was a trick. No one would suspect her of cheating, because who in her right mind would make such a spectacle of herself if she intended to cheat? The green hair (it must be a wig), the poofy dress, the whispering — they were all meant to distract. Most people would assume that if a child intended to cheat, then surely she would call as little attention to herself as possible, would be as quiet as a mouse and as plain as wallpaper. Reynie had to hand it to Rhonda: She might not be smart enough to pass the test, but she was clever enough to get away with cheating on it. He felt a pang of jealousy. Now Rhonda would move on to experience those special opportunities, while Reynie would mope his way back to the orphanage, defeated.

As Rhonda passed by him on the way to her desk, she winked and let fall a tiny slip of paper. It drifted down like a feather and settled lightly upon Reynie's desk. The test answers. Reynie peeked over at the pencil woman, but she hadn't noticed — she was busy grading Rhonda's test now, making check mark after check mark and nodding her head. So the answers were indeed the right ones. And here they sat on his desk.

If he'd felt tempted before, when he'd had no idea how hard the test would be, that temptation was nothing compared to now. No matter that he'd resisted, no matter that he'd chosen this seat precisely to avoid this situation, here he was, staring at a slip of paper that contained the key to his hopes. All he had to do was turn it over and look at the answers. The other children were too busy sniffling and biting their fingernails to notice, and if he hurried, he might even copy the answers down before the pencil woman looked up again. She had finished grading Rhonda's paper and was concentrating on the nearly empty jar of pickles, trying to fish out the last one. Reynie stared a long moment at the paper, sorely tempted.

Then he reached out and flicked it from his desk and onto the floor.

What good would those opportunities do him if he wasn't qualified to be given them? And where was the pleasure in cheating? If he couldn't pass fairly, he didn't want to pass. He thought this — and mostly believed it — and felt his spirits boosted by the decision. But even so, a few seconds passed before he could tear his eyes from the paper on the floor. *All right*, he told himself, returning to the test. *Get a move on, Reynie, and don't look back. There's no time to waste.*

Indeed there wasn't, as a glance at the wall clock confirmed. Less than half an hour remained, and Reynie had more than half the test yet to read. He finished reading about parataxis and hypotaxis (they either had something to do with writing or else with futuristic transportation, but he couldn't decide which), and moved on to question twenty-one, which read: "After the fall of the Russian Empire, when a failed attempt to create a Transcaucasian Republic with Georgia and Armenia led to the creation of the country Azerbaijan (which currently disputes with Armenia the territories of the Naxcivan

Autonomous Republic and the Nagorno-Karabakh region), from what key powers did Azerbaijan . . ."

Reynie stopped. Something about the question seemed awfully familiar — so familiar that he felt pressed to think about it. Hadn't he seen those names before?

Flipping back to the beginning of the test, Reynie read the very first question again: "The territories of the Naxcivan Autonomous Republic and the Nagorno-Karabakh region are disputed by what two countries?" He blinked, hardly believing his eyes. Armenia and Azerbaijan. The answer to question one lay hidden in question *twenty-one*. This wasn't a test of knowledge at all — it was a puzzle!

Reynie looked at question twenty-two, which began: "Despite having originated in Europe, the vine known as the common vetch (a member of the pea family), is widely . . ." There it was! The answer to question two! With mounting excitement, Reynie read the next one, and sure enough, although the question itself made no mention of subatomic particles or Indian physicists, there was a long discussion of them in answer D. Not only were all the answers buried in the test, he realized, they were listed *in order*. Number one's answer was found in number twenty-one (and vice versa), number two's answer was found in number twenty-two, and so on, all the way up to number forty, which cleared up the mystery of parataxis and hypotaxis raised in question twenty.

Reynie was so delighted he nearly leaped from his desk and cheered. Still, he couldn't spare even a moment to congratulate himself — time was running short. Eagerly he set to the task of finding the correct answers. This took a good while, as it was necessary to flip back and forth between pages and read a great deal of text, and in the end it took Reynie almost exactly one hour to finish the test. He had only just circled the last answer, placed his test on the pencil woman's desk, and looked around at the other children (some were furiously circling numbers at random, hoping to get lucky; and some were not to be seen at all, having crept out of the room in bleak despair), when the pencil woman shouted: "Pencils! Time's up, children. Lay down your pencils, please."

After a certain amount of blubbering and wiping away tears, the children stacked their tests on top of Reynie's and returned to their seats. In exhausted silence they waited as the pencil woman flipped through the tests. This took but a minute — she had only to look at the first question, after all. When she came to Reynie's at the bottom of the stack, she ran through the pages, making checkmarks and nodding.

"Nice work," Rhonda whispered from behind him. "You managed it on your own." She seemed genuinely pleased that he hadn't cheated, despite having encouraged him to do just that. She certainly was a strange one.

"I shall read now the names of those who passed the test," announced the pencil woman. "If your name is called you will advance to the third stage of testing, so please remain seated and await further instructions. Those whose names are not called are free to go."

Reynie's ears perked up. There was a *third* stage?

The pencil woman cleared her throat, but this time she didn't bother looking at the paper in front of her. "Reynard Muldoon!" she called out.

On her way out of the room, she added, "That is all."

Reynie, alone in the room now, was trying to make sense of what had happened. Why hadn't Rhonda Kazembe's name been called? Was it because she cheated? Did she have the wrong answers, after all? And where did she *get* those answers in the first place? It was all very mysterious, and not the least intriguing was Rhonda's behavior when she was dismissed along with the others: "Well, best of luck, kid," she'd chirped, playfully mussing his hair and scudding from the room in her cloud-dress, apparently not the slightest bit confused or disappointed that she hadn't passed.

Reynie's musings were interrupted by the pencil woman poking her head in through the doorway: "We've finally gotten rid of the other children, Reynard. Had to give them consolation doughnuts and hugs and whatnot. Only a few more minutes now to wait." She was already withdrawing again when Reynie called after her.

"Excuse me! Miss, uh — Miss? I'm sorry, you never told us your name."

"That's fine, Reynard," she said, stepping into the room. "You've nothing to be sorry for." Reynie waited for her to give her name. Instead she simply wiped doughnut crumbs from her lips and said, "You had a question?"

"Oh, yes. May I please telephone Miss Perumal, my tutor? No one has any idea where I am. I'm afraid she'll be worried."

"Very good of you, Reynard, but don't worry. We've already called Miss Perumal, so all is taken care of." The pencil woman began once again to retreat.

"Miss? Excuse me, Miss?"

She stopped. "Yes, what is it now, Reynard?"

"Forgive me for asking this, Miss. I wouldn't ask if it weren't important, but . . . well, you wouldn't happen to be lying to me, would you?"

"*Lying* to you?"

"I'm sorry to ask it. But, you know, you did tell Miss Perumal this morning that I could use your phone, and then later you told me there *was* no phone. So you see why I'm concerned. It's just that I don't want Miss Perumal to worry."

The pencil woman seemed unperturbed. "That's a perfectly reasonable question, Reynard. A perfectly reasonable question." She gave him an approving nod and made as if to leave.

"Miss, but you didn't answer my question!"

The woman scratched her head, and Reynie began to suspect that she was either a little daft or a little deaf. After a moment, however, she said, "I suppose you want the truth?"

"Yes, please!"

"The truth is I haven't called Miss Perumal, but I will do so immediately. In fact, I was *about* to call her when you asked me if I had called her yet. Does this satisfy you?"

Reynie hardly knew what to say. He didn't wish to offend the woman, but he could hardly trust her now, and it was more important to know that Miss Perumal's mind was at ease. "I'm sorry, Miss, but may I please just call her myself? I'll only take a minute."

The pencil woman smiled. When she spoke this time her voice was quite gentle, and she looked Reynie in the eyes. "You are very good to be so concerned about Miss Perumal. What would you say if I told you that I *have* in fact called her already? No, don't answer that. You won't believe me. How about this? I'll relay her message to you: 'Do you see now that you didn't need luck? I'm glad you wore matching socks.' That is what she told me to tell you. Are you satisfied?"

Before Reynie could make up his mind how to answer, she slipped out of the room, leaving him to puzzle over her mystifying behavior. The message from Miss Perumal was obviously real, so why hadn't she told him in the first place?

As he pondered this, he heard footsteps in the hall, followed by a timid knock at the half-open door. A young boy's face appeared in the doorway. "Hello," the boy said, adjusting his spectacles, "is this where I'm supposed to wait?" He spoke so softly that Reynie had to strain to hear him.

"I have no idea. It's where *I'm* supposed to wait, though, so maybe it is. You're welcome to join me, if you like. I'm Reynie Muldoon."

"Oh," the boy said uncertainly. "My name is Sticky Washington. I'm just wondering if this is the right place. The yellow lady told me to come down the hall and sit with some-one named Reynard."

"That's me," Reynie said. "People call me Reynie for short." He put out his hand, and after a moment's hesitation Sticky Washington came and shook it.

Sticky was a notably skinny boy (which Reynie suspected was how he got his nickname — he was thin as a stick) with light brown skin the very color of the tea that Miss Perumal made each morning. He had big, nervous eyes like a horse's, and, for some odd reason, a perfectly smooth bald head. His tiny wire-rimmed spectacles gave him the distinguished look of a scholar. A fidgety scholar, though: He seemed quite shy, or at the very least anxious. Well, why shouldn't he be anxious, if he'd been through what Reynie had been through today?

"Are you here for the third test?" Reynie asked.

Sticky nodded. "I've been waiting all day. I had to be here at nine o'clock this morning, and the test was over at ten. Since then I've just been sitting around in an empty room. Lucky I had a pear with me or I might have starved. I think all the other children got doughnuts. Why didn't *we* get doughnuts?"

"I wondered the same thing. Were you the only one who passed, then?"

"The first test, no. A little girl passed it, too, but I haven't seen her since yesterday. Maybe they told her to come at a different time — they've had tests here all day. Was there an extremely small girl in your group, about half our size?"

Reynie shook his head. He would have remembered anyone so tiny.

"Maybe she's coming later. Anyway, as for the second test,
yes: I was the only one who passed. Which surprised me because —" Sticky stopped himself with a glance at the doorway. He opened his mouth to continue, thought better of it,
and at last pretended to notice something on the ceiling, as if
he hadn't been about to say anything at all. Obviously he had
a secret. Reynie had a sudden suspicion what it was.

"Because there was a girl who cheated?"

Sticky's eyes widened. "How did you know?"

"The same thing happened to me. I think it's a trick of
some kind. Tell me, this girl didn't happen to drop her pencil
on the way into the building, did she? Out on the plaza?"

"Yes! I couldn't believe anybody would take such a chance.
We were only allowed to bring one pencil, you know."

"What did you do?"

"I tried to help her. A few other kids said they were sorry
but they didn't want to be late, and one boy even laughed. I
felt awfully sorry for her, so I had her hold onto my feet and
lower me down through the grate. She was strong as a bear
and had no trouble doing it, and I'm so skinny I fit right
through the bars. It was terrifying, though, I don't mind ad-
mitting it, hanging upside down, scrabbling around in the
dark. I think something even nibbled at my finger, but maybe
I imagined it. I can get a little mixed up when I'm scared."

"You were lucky to find her pencil," Reynie observed. "It
was pitch-black down in that drain."

"Oh, no, I *didn't* find it. But you know what she did? She
hauled me back up through the grate and said, 'Oh well,

never mind. I have an extra one.' And she pulled another pencil right out of her sleeve! Can you believe it? Why she would let me go down into that awful drain when she had an extra pencil, I can't imagine. Then, to top it off, she offered me the answers to the test, to repay me for trying to help her. Apparently they didn't do her any good, though. I'm glad I refused."

"Me, too," Reynie said. "I think refusing was part of the test. If we'd cheated, they would have known it, and I doubt either one of us would be here."

From his shirt pocket Sticky took out a thin piece of cotton cloth and polished his spectacles with it. "If you're right, it's a little creepy that they're tricking us like that." He put the glasses back on and blinked his big, nervous eyes. "But I shouldn't complain. They were very nice to let me continue to the third stage even though I missed a few questions. Very generous of them —"

"Wait a minute," Reynie said. "How could you possibly have missed any? Did you circle the wrong letters by accident?"

Sticky seemed embarrassed. He shuffled his feet as he spoke. "Oh, well, I suppose the questions were easy for you, but for me they were rather difficult. Time ran out before I could answer the last three, so I had to just circle some answers and hope I'd get lucky. I didn't, of course. But as I said, they were very forgiving."

Reynie couldn't believe what he was hearing. "You mean you *knew* the answers to those questions?"

Sticky grew more dejected with Reynie's every question. Tears brimmed in his eyes as he said, "Well, yes, I suppose I do look rather stupid, don't I? I look like a person who doesn't know any answers. I understand that."

Reynie interrupted him. "No, no! I didn't mean that! I meant that I'm surprised *anybody* knew the answers. One or two, maybe, but certainly not all of them."

Sticky brightened, smiling shyly and straightening his back. "Oh! Well, yes, I suppose I do know a lot of things. That's why people started calling me Sticky, because everything I read sticks in my head."

"It's perfectly amazing," Reynie said. "You must read more than anybody I've ever met. But listen, once you figured out the test was a puzzle, why didn't you just solve it that way? It would have saved time — you could have finished it."

"A puzzle?"

"You didn't notice that the answers were all right there in the test?"

"I *did* notice that a lot of information was repeated," Sticky reflected, "but I didn't really pay attention to it. I was concentrating too hard on getting the answers right. That question on colloidal suspensions really had me sweating, I can tell you, and as I said, when I'm anxious I can get mixed up." After a pause, he sighed and added, "I tend to get anxious a lot."

Reynie laughed. "Well, you didn't know it was a puzzle, and I didn't know any of the answers, but we're both here now. We'd make a good team."

"You think so?" said Sticky. He grinned. "Yes, I suppose we would."

The boys waited there for some time, discussing the curiosities of the day. Sticky was more relaxed now, and soon the two of them grew comfortable together, joking and laughing like old friends. Sticky couldn't stop giggling about Rhonda Kazembe's crazy getup, and Reynie smiled until his face hurt when Sticky told him more about hanging upside down in the storm drain. ("My shoes started to slip off in her hands," Sticky recounted, "and for a second I thought she was going to take them and leave me down there under the grate. I panicked and started wriggling like crazy — I think it was all she could do to pull me back up without dropping me!")

Then Reynie told Sticky about the pencil woman's sneakiness regarding the phone call to Miss Perumal.

Instead of laughing, as Reynie had expected, Sticky slipped back into his nervous behavior. He began polishing his spectacles again, even though he'd just done it minutes before. "Oh, yes," he said. "Yes, I tried to call my parents, too. Same thing happened. But in the end it was fine. She called them. Nothing to worry about."

Reynie nodded politely. He saw perfectly well that Sticky was trying to hide something. Maybe he hadn't thought of calling his parents and felt guilty about it now? But Reynie decided not to press him on the matter — Sticky seemed uncomfortable enough as it was.

"So where do you live?" he asked, to change the subject.

This only made Sticky polish all the harder. Perhaps he simply disliked personal questions. "Well," he began. He cleared his throat. "Well —"

Just then the door flew wide open, and a girl raced into the room carrying a bucket. She was extremely quick: One moment she was bursting through the door, golden-blond hair flying out behind her like a horse's mane, and the next she was standing right beside them. Sticky leaped back in alarm.

"What's the matter?" he cried.

"What's the matter with you?" the girl replied calmly.

"Well . . . what were you running from?"

"From? I wasn't running *from* anything. I was running *to* this room. Old Yellow Suit told me to come down here and wait with you two, so here I am. My name's Kate Wetherall."

Sticky was breathing hard and casting glances at the door, as if a lion might fly in next, so it fell to Reynie to introduce them. "I'm Reynie Muldoon and this is Sticky Washington," he said, shaking her hand and immediately regretting it — her grip was so strong it was like getting his fingers caught in a drawer. (Sticky noticed Reynie's pained expression and quickly thrust his own hands into his pockets.) Rubbing his tender knuckles, Reynie went on, "I think the question is why you were running instead of walking."

"Why not? It's faster. Now I'm here with you boys instead of trudging along the empty hallway, and it's much better, isn't it? You seem like nice fellows. So why do they call you Sticky?" She touched Sticky's arm. "You don't *feel* sticky."

"It's a long story," Sticky said, regaining his composure.

"Let's have it, then," Kate said.

So Sticky told her about his name, and then Kate revealed that she had always wanted a nickname herself. "I've tried to get people to call me The Great Kate Weather Machine," she said, "but nobody ever goes along with it. I don't suppose you boys would call me that, would you?"

"It does seem a bit awkward for a nickname," Reynie said mildly. "It takes a long time to say."

"I suppose it does," Kate admitted, "but not if you speak very quickly."

"Let us think about it," said Sticky.

Kate nodded, agreeing. She seemed pleasant enough. She had very bright, watery blue eyes, a fair complexion, and rosy cheeks, and was unusually tall and broad-shouldered for a twelve-year-old. (She announced her age right away, for children consider their ages every bit as important as their names. In return she learned that the boys were eleven.) But what Reynie was most curious about was her bucket. It was a good, solid metal bucket, painted fire-engine red. As they were talking, Kate unfastened her belt, slipped it through the bucket handle, and fastened the belt again so that the bucket hung at her hip. From the way she did this, it was obvious she'd done it a thousand times. Reynie was fascinated. Finally he asked her what it was for.

She gave him a quizzical look. "What kind of person doesn't know what a bucket's for? It's for carrying things, silly."

"Yes, I know *that*," Reynie said, "but why do you have one with you? Most people don't carry buckets around for no particular reason."

"That's true," Kate reflected. "I've often noticed that, but I can't understand why. I can't imagine not having a bucket. How else am I to tote my things?"

"What things?" asked Sticky, who, like Reynie, was trying to sneak a peek at the bucket's contents.

"I'll show you," Kate said, and began removing things from the bucket. First came a Swiss Army knife, a flashlight, a pen light, and a bottle of extra-strength glue, which Kate examined to be sure its lid was tightly closed. Then she produced a bag of marbles, a slingshot, a spool of clear fishing twine, one pencil and one eraser, a kaleidoscope, and a horseshoe magnet, which she yanked with some effort from the metal bucket. "I've been through dozens of these," she said, holding the magnet up for them to admire. "This is the strongest I've found." Finally she showed them a length of slender nylon rope coiled around the bottom and sides of the bucket.

"That's a lot of stuff to carry," Sticky remarked.

"It's all useful," Kate said, putting her things away again. "Take this morning, for example. Some crazy-looking girl dropped her pencil down a storm drain out on the plaza —"

Reynie and Sticky looked at each other.

"— and if I didn't have my bucket with me," Kate continued, "she'd have been up a creek without a paddle." A thoughtful expression came over her face. "Hmm, a paddle would be great to have. But no, I suppose it would be too big to haul around. Still, it *would* come in handy sometimes —"

"Did you help Rhonda get her pencil back?" Reynie asked.

"Of course I did. I just . . . now wait a minute. How did you know her name?"

"Finish your story," Reynie said. "We'll tell you later."

So Kate told them how she had pried up the edge of the metal grate with a screwdriver on her Swiss Army knife. After dragging the grate aside, she tied her rope to a nearby bench and lowered herself into the drain, using her flashlight to find the pencil in the darkness.

"It had rolled down into a crack," she explained, "about ten and a half inches deep, so I put a drop of glue on the end of some fishing twine — that's why it pays to have a pen light, too, you know, so you can hold it in your mouth and point it when you need both hands for something like putting glue on twine. Anyway, I poked the twine down into the crack until it reached the pencil. Gave the glue a few seconds to dry, then pulled it right out. I couldn't have done any of that without my bucket, now could I?"

"Weren't you afraid?" Sticky asked. He'd been terrified himself and didn't want to be the only one.

"Of what? Getting wet? It was perfectly dry down there. We haven't had rain for days."

Something about Kate's story had caught Reynie's attention. "How did you know that crack was ten and a half inches deep?" he said. "I don't see a tape measure in your bucket."

"Oh, I can always tell distances and weights and that sort of thing," said Kate with a shrug. She glanced around. "For example, just by looking at it I can tell this room is twenty-two feet long and sixteen feet wide."

Sticky, irritated that Kate hadn't been frightened in the dark drain, was inclined to be skeptical. "Are you sure?"

"Of course I'm sure."

"Let's measure," said Reynie, fetching the ruler from the pencil woman's desk.

The room was twenty-two feet long and sixteen feet wide.

Impressed, Reynie whistled, and Sticky said, "Not bad."

"Okay, back to your story," Reynie said. "Did Rhonda offer to help you cheat on the test?"

Kate's eyes narrowed suspiciously. "You sure seem to know a lot about it. Were you spying on me somehow? If you were, then I guess you know I called her a loon."

"We weren't spying, but that's what I figured," Reynie said. "So I take it you solved the puzzle? Unless, of course, you knew all the answers."

Kate snorted. "Who in the world could possibly know the answers to a test like that?"

"Sticky did," said Reynie.

It was Kate's turn to be impressed. "Not bad," she said,

and Sticky ducked his head shyly. "Now what's this about a puzzle?"

Once again Reynie and Sticky looked at each other.

"But if you didn't know about that," said Sticky, "how did you pass?"

"I *didn't* pass. Nobody in my session did. To tell you the truth, I think the only reason they let me stick around was because I helped Old Yellow Suit out of a tight spot."

Of course the boys wanted to hear what had happened, and Kate was happy to oblige them.

"After the test was over," she said, "Old Yellow Suit took us down the hall to give everybody doughnuts and tell the parents that she was sorry but that they had to go now, thanks for coming, that sort of thing. Some of the parents were furious. One started shouting how this was some kind of trick, and another demanded to know what these tests were all about, and Old Yellow Suit started glancing toward the exit. I could tell she was nervous, but a few people stood between her and the door, and she was trapped.

"I felt sorry for her, you know, because I figured she was only doing her job, whatever it is, and at least she'd given me something interesting to do today, so I decided to help her out. While the grown-ups were all yelling, and the other kids were making themselves sick on doughnuts, I whipped out my Army knife screwdriver and took off the doorknob. Then I pointed and yelled, 'There's the man behind all this! That's him in the corner!' And everybody turned and pushed against one another to see — except Old Yellow Suit, of course, who made a beeline for the exit. As soon as she was out, I turned off the light and closed the door, and the two of us ran off down the hall. We had a good head start, because it was dark in the room now, and they kept reaching for the doorknob and not finding it. Finally someone turned on the light, and I suppose they all came flying out like angry hornets, but by then we were hiding in a closet.

"After we heard the last person leave, Old Yellow Suit smiled at me and said, 'I believe you should stay for the next stage of testing.' And so here I am."

"Amazing!" Reynie said.

"I can't believe it!" cried Sticky. "You're a hero!"

"Oh good grief," Kate said, frowning with embarrassment. "It was no big deal. Anybody could have done it. Now, I've told you *my* story, so you have to tell me yours. How did you know about Rhonda Kazembe? And what's all this about the test being a puzzle?"

Before they could answer her, the pencil woman poked her head into the room and said, "It's time for the third test, children. Please report immediately to Room 7-B." Then she disappeared again.

"Where in the world is Room 7-B?" Sticky said, exasperated. "She never tells us where anything *is*. It took me half the night to find the Monk Building."

"I'm sure we can find it easily enough," Reynie said, but privately he was thinking about Sticky's words — "half the night." What was Sticky doing in the city alone at night? Where were his parents?

"You'd better fill me in quick," Kate said. "You know Old Yellow Suit isn't particularly patient."

"You're right," Reynie said. "We'll tell you on the way."

And with that, the three new friends went in search of Room 7-B.

SQUARES and ARROWS

The room was on the seventh floor, as Reynie had suspected. The door had no sign on it, but after roaming the empty hallways and looking at all the other door signs (there was a 7-A, a 7-C, a 7-D, and a 7-E), they returned to the unmarked door, upon which Kate knocked boldly. After a pause, she knocked again, still more loudly. This happened several times before they got a response — which, as it happened, came not from beyond the door, but from directly behind them.

"That's enough with the knocking," said a deep voice, quite close.

The children whirled around in surprise.

Before them stood a tall man in a weatherbeaten hat, a weatherbeaten jacket, weatherbeaten trousers, and weather-beaten boots. His ruddy cheeks were dark with whisker stubble, while his hair (what little peeked from beneath his hat) was yellow as flax. If not for the alertness in his ocean-blue eyes, he would resemble, more than anything, a scarecrow that had come down from its stake. On top of all this, the man's expression was profoundly sad. All the children noticed this at once. Reynie was so struck by it that instead of saying hello, he asked, "Are you all right, sir?"

"I'm afraid not," the man said. "But that's neither here nor there. Are you ready to begin the next test?"

"But we haven't even met yet!" Kate said, sticking out her hand. "My name's Kate Wetherall, though my friends call me —" She glanced at the boys, who looked at her doubtfully. "Well, my friends call me Kate."

The man shook Kate's hand, somewhat reluctantly. Even his handshake seemed sad — he hardly squeezed at all. The boys introduced themselves and the man sadly shook their hands, too. "There," he said. "We've met. Now —"

"But you haven't given us *your* name," Kate insisted.

The man sighed, considering this. "Call me Milligan," he said at last.

"Is that your first name or your last name?"

"Just Milligan. And no more questions. We have to proceed. Now, which of you is George?"

Kate scowled. She was getting very impatient with this man. "Weren't you listening? Our names are Sticky, Reynie, and Kate!"

Sticky cleared his throat. "Uh, well, actually, my name is George. Sticky's my nickname."

"Your name is George Washington?" Kate said. "Like the president? The father of our country?"

"It isn't that unusual," Sticky said defensively. "You don't have to tease me about it."

"Take it easy, pal," said Kate. "I wasn't teasing you." Clearly Sticky was a bit touchy about his name.

"Sticky or George, whichever it is," said Milligan. "You're to go first. Step through that door now and shut it behind you."

Sticky's eyes grew wide. "I have to go in alone?"

"It's all right. It's only a test. The others will be with you soon."

"Good luck, Sticky," Reynie said, clapping him on the shoulder. "I'm sure you'll do fine!"

"Go, Sticky!" said Kate.

Sticky removed his spectacles, polished them, and replaced them. After a moment's consideration, he removed them and began polishing again. There seemed to be a speck on the lens he couldn't remove.

"Quit stalling," Milligan said. "Nothing's going to harm you in that room."

At last Sticky nodded, settled his glasses on his nose, tucked away his polishing cloth, and passed through the door. Milligan closed it behind him and went away without a word.

"How do you like that?" Kate said. "He didn't even tell us what to do, or how long it would take, or anything."

"Big surprise," said Reynie.

Soon Milligan came back and announced that it was

Reynie's turn. He gave no hint about what had happened to Sticky.

"See you on the other side," said Kate. "Wherever that is."

Reynie took a deep breath and went in, the door closing behind him. He found himself in an empty room. On the opposite wall, above another closed door, hung a large sign that read: CROSS THE ROOM WITHOUT SETTING FOOT ON A BLUE OR BLACK SQUARE.

Reynie looked down. On the cement floor just inside the door, where he now stood, was a large red circle. On the other side of the room, by the opposite door, was another red circle. Between these circles the floor resembled a giant checkerboard, with alternating rectangles of blue, black, and yellow. Reynie studied the pattern. There was far more blue and black than yellow. So much more, in fact, that he soon realized it would be impossible to cross the room without stepping on blue or black. The yellow parts were so widely scattered that he doubted even a kangaroo could hop from one to the other. He looked at the sign again, and after a moment's consideration, he laughed and shook his head. Then he strode confidently across the room, into the other red circle, and out the far door.

Sticky and Milligan stood waiting for him beyond the door. They had been watching him secretly through tiny holes in the wall. Sticky looked confused and started to ask Reynie something, but Milligan shushed him. "You boys can watch, but you must be quiet," he said. He went away to tell Kate it was her turn.

Moments later they saw Kate step boldly into Room 7-B. After reading the sign, she studied the floor, considering whether she might manage to leap from yellow to yellow. At last she shook her head, rejecting the idea. Next she looked from one door to the other, gauging the distance. Then, taking the length of rope from her bucket, she fashioned a loop at the end, and with one expert throw lassoed the doorknob at the far side of the room. Fastening the other end to the doorknob behind her, she pulled the rope tight, knotted it securely, and climbed up. "Now, if I only had that paddle," she said aloud to herself as she walked along the rope, "I could hold it out in front of me for balance."

Indeed, a paddle might have helped, for halfway across the room she nearly fell (the boys caught their breath), but after wobbling back and forth and wheeling her arms around, she recovered. After a few more careful steps, she hopped down into the other red circle.

"Wow!" Sticky whispered. "She did it!"

But before Kate could join the boys, Milligan appeared and took her back to the starting point to try again, this time without her rope, which he informed her would be returned upon completion of the test.

"That's hardly fair," Sticky whispered. "Nobody told her she couldn't use a rope."

Kate, meanwhile, was removing all the items from her bucket and stuffing them into her pockets. When she'd finished, her pockets bulging ridiculously, she unscrewed the handle from her bucket and tucked it through her belt. Then she was ready. Kicking the bucket onto its side, she hopped onto it and began rolling it forward with her feet, like a circus bear balancing on a ball. Rolling first this way, and then that, she zigzagged across the room to the other red circle.

Reynie and Sticky looked at each other in awe. Who *was* this girl?

Yet once again, as Kate reattached the bucket handle and emptied her pockets, Milligan entered the room. He returned her to the starting circle, this time taking away her bucket and tools, which she handed over with evident reluctance. She recovered quickly, however. Before Milligan had even closed the door behind him, Kate shrugged and cracked her knuckles, flattened her palms against the cement, and lifted her feet into the air above her. And this was how she crossed the room, walking on her hands, not once setting foot upon the floor.

"Never mind," said Milligan when she opened the door. He handed her bucket back. "You pass."

"What I don't understand," Sticky was saying to Reynie as they followed Milligan down a dark stairway, "is how you passed that test. I'm glad, of course, but I don't see how you did it. I crossed on my hands and knees so my feet didn't touch any blue or black squares, and Kate did her acrobat tricks, but you just walked right across the room. You were stepping on dark squares left and right!"

They had reached the bottom of the stairs now. Milligan ushered the children into a damp, dimly lit underground passage, where centipedes twisted away at their approach and other slithery creatures they heard but didn't see retreated into the shadows. By this gloomy route, he was leading them to what he had called their "final testing place," which struck Reynie as having a particularly ominous sound.

"Just walked right across?" said Kate. "Reynie, how did you get away with that?"

"It was another trick. Those weren't squares on the floor — they were *rectangles*. Their sides weren't all the same length."

"Gosh, that's true," Kate reflected.

Sticky slapped his forehead. "I got my pants dirty for nothing? I crawled across the floor like a baby for *nothing*? I'm so stupid! I can't believe they're letting me go on."

"You're hardly stupid," Reynie said. "You're here, aren't you?"

"Just where is here, anyway?" Kate asked. "Hey, Milligan, where are we?"

Without looking back or slowing down, Milligan said, "Right now we're passing under Fifth Street."

"I don't suppose we could walk above ground, could we?" Sticky asked. "Where there's sunlight and the path isn't wet? Where it doesn't smell like spoiled fish?"

"Where creepy things don't keep falling on our heads?" Reynie added with a shudder, brushing away a beetle that had tried to skitter under his shirt collar.

"Sunlight just ahead," Milligan replied. And sure enough, presently he led them up another set of stairs into an empty cellar, then through the cellar doors onto a quiet street lined with elm trees and old houses. The children couldn't see this right away — it took a moment for their eyes to adjust to the brilliant sunlight.

And in that moment, Milligan disappeared.

They had followed him out through the cellar doors, they knew that for certain, but whereas Milligan had been tall and straight in his battered hat and scuffed jacket, the children were now accompanied by a stooped little man with a big belly, wearing dark glasses and a bright yellow cap.

"Who are you?" Kate cried, crouching into a defensive stance. "Where's Milligan?"

"Right here," the man said wearily, lowering his sunglasses to reveal a pair of sad, ocean-blue eyes. "I'm in disguise."

The children regarded him closely. It was indeed Milligan. Somehow, without their noticing, he had stuffed his hat and jacket under his shirt to create the impression of a fat belly; had produced the cap and sunglasses (from where, they couldn't guess); and hunched his shoulders and bent forward to appear shorter than he was. It was a remarkable transformation.

"Are you a magician?" Sticky asked.

"I'm nobody," Milligan replied, and without further explanation, he pointed across the street to a three-story house with stone steps leading up to its front door. "Please go wait on those steps. Rhonda will be with you soon."

"Rhonda Kazembe?" Reynie asked. "The green-haired girl?"

But even as he spoke, the cellar doors slammed shut, and Milligan was gone.

"Do you suppose we're going to meet anybody *normal* today?" Kate asked.

"I'm beginning to doubt it," Reynie said.

The children went across the street and through the gate of the house Milligan had pointed out. It was a very old house, with gray stone walls, high arched windows, and a roof with red shingles that glowed like embers in the afternoon sun. Roses grew along the iron fence, and near the house towered a gigantic elm tree, perhaps older than the building itself, its green leaves tinged with the first yellows of autumn. Shaded by the elm's branches were an ivy-covered courtyard and the stone steps upon which they were to wait. The steps themselves were half-covered with ivy; they seemed an inviting place to rest. And indeed it was with some relief that the children, tired from the day's challenges, sat upon them now in the cool shade of the elm.

"Sticky," Reynie said when they had settled, "there's something I wanted to ask you about your parents. Did they know that —?"

"We already talked about this, remember?" Sticky said, interrupting him. Turning to Kate, he explained, "That yellow lady gave Reynie and me the runaround when we told her we had some phone calls to make. Reynie was afraid his tutor would be worried, and it was the same with me and my parents. Turns out she called them, but she was very odd about it. Very odd indeed. Did that happen to you?"

This was not what Reynie had been going to ask about. He had wanted to ask if Sticky's parents knew he'd spent "half the night" looking for the Monk Building. For some reason, Sticky was avoiding the subject.

"I didn't have anybody to call," said Kate with a shrug. "My mother died when I was a baby, and my father ran away and left me when I was two."

Sticky's face fell. "Oh. I'm . . . I'm so sorry."

"Don't worry," Kate said lightly. "I don't even remember them." She paused, reflecting. "Actually, I do have one memory of my father."

"That's one more than I have," said Reynie. "What is it?"

"Well, down the road from our house was an old mill pond, and my father took me there to swim once. I was only two, but a good swimmer. The water was cold, the day was warm, and I thought it all felt wonderful. I laughed and splashed until I was exhausted. Then my father — I can't picture his face, but I can still feel his strong arms lifting me out of the water — he carried me on his shoulders back to our house. I remember asking if we could swim there again, and he said, 'Of course we can, Katie-Cat.' I remember that very well. He called me 'Katie-Cat.'"

"You never went back to the mill pond, did you?" asked Sticky, looking even more regretful now that he'd heard Kate's story.

"No, the next thing I remember I was in an orphanage," said Kate.

Reynie shook his head. "It's strange, Kate. Your father sounds, well, he sounds —"

"Like a nice man?" finished Kate. "I know, I've often thought of that. I guess it shows that people aren't always what they seem. Or else he just changed. I suppose I'll never know."

"It's terrible," Sticky whispered, almost as if to himself.

"Hey, it's okay," Kate said cheerfully. "That was a long time ago. Anyway, I've had a fine life. The circus has been good to me."

Reynie widened his eyes and glanced at Sticky, but Sticky seemed too disturbed to have noticed what Kate said. Reynie looked back at Kate. "Did you just say the *circus* has been good to you?"

"Oh, yes," said Kate with a laugh. "When I was seven I ran

away from the orphanage to join the circus. They brought me back, but I just ran away again, and I kept running away every time they brought me back. Eventually it was agreed that I could join the circus and save everybody a lot of trouble. So that's what I've been doing the past few years. It's been great fun, too, but I was ready for something different. When I read about these tests, I said *adios* to my circus pals, and here I came."

"That's quite a life," Reynic said, more than a little amazed. "And has it — I mean, has circus life helped, then? You haven't ever missed your parents?" He was always curious about how other orphans felt. His own parents were never known to him, and so he didn't miss them in particular, but on rainy days, or days when other children taunted him, or nights when he awoke from a bad dream and could use a hug and perhaps a story to lull him back to sleep — at times like these he didn't *miss* his parents, exactly, but he did wish for them.

Kate, apparently, felt otherwise. "What's to miss?" she said breezily. "Like I said, I don't even remember my mother, and who wants a father who'll run away and leave his baby daughter all by herself? I'd much rather spend my time with elephants and clowns." She frowned. "Sticky, what's wrong with you?"

Throughout their conversation, Sticky's expression had grown more and more dejected, his big eyes sadder and sadder, so that at last his face had taken on the exact gloomy look of that miserable man Milligan.

Reynie put his hand on Sticky's shoulder. "Hey, are you all right?"

"Oh . . . yes," Sticky said, unconvincingly, "I was just, you know, feeling sorry for Kate. It must be terrible to think you weren't wanted."

Kate laughed (a bit stiffly, it seemed to Reynie) and said, "Weren't you listening, chum? I told you, I'm having a ball!" She went on to regale them with stories about circus life — hanging from trapezes, leaping through flaming hoops, getting shot from cannons — until gradually Sticky cheered up, and the matter of parents was dropped.

They had been waiting on the steps for perhaps an hour, and were beginning to grumble about how hungry they were, when the front door opened, and Rhonda Kazembe appeared. At least, they *thought* it was Rhonda Kazembe. She did have the same features and coal-black skin, and she was the same height as Rhonda, but gone were the puffy white dress and long green hair. Instead, her hair hung in lovely dark braids all about her face, and she wore a smart blue jumper and sandals. When she saw them on the steps, she laughed with pleasure.

"Hi, kids! Remember me?"

"Rhonda? Is it really you?" Sticky asked.

"I hope so," she replied. "Otherwise someone's played a very clever trick on me."

When Rhonda sat down with them and Reynie had a closer look at her, he realized something that he'd missed before. "You're not even a child!" he exclaimed. "You're a grown-up!"

"Well," said Rhonda, "a very small, very young grown-up, yes."

"I *knew* you were hiding something with that funny get-up, but I thought it had to do with the cheating."

"No," said Rhonda, laughing again. "It was just to call attention away from my age, and to distract you in general."

"I have an idea," said Kate, whose stomach was growling loudly. "Why don't you give us some food and tell us what this is all about?"

"Soon, Kate, very soon. There remains one more test, but after that, whether you pass or fail, I promise you all a good supper. Fair enough?"

"It's a deal," Kate said.

"Then let's begin. When I tell you to, each of you must go through this front door. At the very back of the house is a staircase. You're to reach the staircase as quickly as possible, hurry up the stairs, and ring the bronze bell that hangs at the top. Speed is important, so don't dawdle. Any questions?"

"Will this test be any harder than the last one?" Kate asked, with a show of bravado.

"Some find it quite difficult," said Rhonda. "But you should all be able to do it with your eyes closed."

"Will it be scary?" Sticky asked, almost in a whisper.

"Maybe, but it isn't really dangerous," Rhonda said, which did nothing for Sticky's confidence.

"Who goes first?" Reynie asked.

"That's an easy one," Rhonda answered. "You."

It had been a day full of challenges, all of which Reynie had met successfully, and when he stepped through the front door he was brimming with confidence. By this point he knew there would be some kind of trick involved; and knowing this, he felt sure he'd be ready for it.

He found himself in a brightly lit room with pitch black walls. The front door, which Rhonda had just closed behind him, had no knob on the inside and was likewise painted black, so that it blended into the wall. The room was rather cramped, perhaps six feet wide and six long (Kate would know for sure, he thought), and was entirely empty. Not counting the nearly invisible front door behind him, it had three exits: to the left, to the right, and immediately before him. These doorways had no doors in them, and the rooms beyond were unlit, so that Reynie couldn't see into them.

Are we expected to walk into dark rooms? he wondered. *This is going to make Sticky extremely unhappy.* But he was only thinking of Sticky to take his mind off himself, for the prospect of groping about in the darkness intimidated him more than he cared to admit.

"Well," he said aloud, to bolster his courage, "there's no time to waste, so here goes." He plunged through the doorway ahead of him (this ought to be the most direct path to the rear of the house) and, as if by magic, seemed to walk into the very room he had just left. It was cramped, brightly lit, painted black, and he could see a dark doorway in each wall.

"What in the world?" he said, turning to look behind him, then in confusion turning round again. At once he realized his mistake. If he hadn't turned around, he might have kept his bearings, but now he'd lost them. He was in a maze of identical rooms. Everything looked exactly the same in every direction.

His confidence was quickly draining away.

"Now, think," he told himself. "When you enter a room, its light must turn on automatically, and when you leave, it goes off. But there are light switches by each door. Perhaps if you throw a switch, the light stays on. It might be as simple as that."

With a quick inspection of the nearest doorway, however, this hope vanished. What Reynie had supposed were light switches were only decorative wooden panels. He was about to turn away and try to retrace his steps when it occurred to him the panels themselves might be important. He took a closer look at one. About the size of a playing card, the panel had four arrows etched into it, pointing in different directions and painted different colors. A blue arrow pointed to the right, a green one to the left, a wiggly-shaped yellow one straight ahead, and a purple one down.

Of course, Reynie thought, feeling foolish. The arrows weren't for decoration — they were meant to show the way. But which was he to believe? After going round to every panel he was no better off. Four doorways with four arrows each meant sixteen arrows to choose from, and there was no apparent pattern. Reynie racked his brain: Should he follow the green ones? Green arrows on a traffic signal mean "Go." But perhaps that was too obvious. Perhaps the red arrows were the ones to follow — perhaps that was the trick. Yet that hardly seemed fair. What if he'd been color-blind and couldn't even tell the difference?

No sooner had this occurred to him than he knew the secret.

Running his finger over the carved arrows in the panel before him, Reynie smiled. The only one you could know by touch would be the wiggly shaped one. What was it that Rhonda had said to Kate? "You should all be able to do it with your eyes closed." It had seemed she was offering encouragement.

Actually she was offering them a clue: Even in the dark, even with his eyes closed, Reynie could feel the panels with his fingers and find the wiggly shaped arrow.

Just to be certain, he hurried around the room, checking the panels. Sure enough, though the other arrows followed no particular pattern, the wiggly arrows all directed him toward the same door — the one whose wiggly arrow pointed straight ahead. Reynie took a deep breath, hoped for the best, and charged through. The next room looked exactly the same, but this time the wiggly arrows indicated the door on his right. He took it.

By the time he'd gone through ten rooms in this way, Reynie had no idea where in the house he was. He might have been at the front door again and would not have known it. Or he might be in the very middle of the maze. And with the walls painted black as they were, if all the lights went out he would be in utter darkness. Suddenly he wondered if they intended to turn the lights out on him as part of the test. The thought started an uncomfortable flutter in his belly. But just as he began to worry, he entered a room and stumbled smack into a staircase. With a shout of triumph he raced up the stairs onto a narrow landing, found the bronze bell Rhonda had told them about, and rang it.

There was a sound of quick footsteps coming down stairs. Then a door unlocked and out came the pencil woman with a stopwatch in hand. She examined it and said, "Six minutes fourteen seconds."

"Is that good?" Reynie asked.

Without answering, she said, "Please close your eyes and stand still."

Something about this made Reynie uneasy. Had he done

so badly? Was this meant to test his courage? He did as he was told, closing his eyes and bracing himself as best he could.

"Why are you flinching?" the pencil woman asked.

"I don't know. I thought maybe you were going to slap me."

"Don't be ridiculous. I could slap you perfectly well with your eyes open. I'm only going to blindfold you."

Having done so, she led Reynie down the stairs again. With her hand on his shoulder, the pencil woman guided him back through the maze into the first room, where she removed the blindfold. Starting the stopwatch, she said, "Please go ring the bell again."

This time it was easy. Reynie trotted through the rooms, glancing at the panels for guidance, and in a few short minutes had rung the bell again. The pencil woman came up behind him, reading her stopwatch. "Three minutes even," she said. She led him up more stairs into a sitting room and pointed him toward a sofa.

"Does this mean I pass?"

"We ask you to complete the maze a second time to see if you've actually solved it. We need to make sure you didn't just come upon the staircase by luck. If you've discovered the secret, you should be much faster the second time around. Which you were. Therefore you seem to have solved the maze. Therefore you pass. Therefore —" Interrupting herself, she took a cracker from her pocket and ate it very quickly, as if she hadn't eaten in days and couldn't wait another moment.

Reynie cocked his head curiously. "But why did you have me go through again when you could have just asked me? I could have *told* you the secret, you know."

"You'd be surprised how few children have pointed that out," said the pencil woman as she moved toward the door.

"You mean you wondered whether I'd notice that?"

The pencil woman winked. "And now we know, don't we?"

She hurried from the room, leaving Reynie alone on the sofa. He was getting used to her abrupt entrances and exits. Still, it was strange to find himself in an unknown house, sitting on this sofa by himself. He looked around the room. The walls were lined with books, many of them in languages he didn't recognize. In one corner stood an old piano; in another, a marvelous green globe. Reynie went to look at the globe. If the others took as long as he did to finish the maze, it would be some time before he had company. He might as well entertain himself.

But hardly had he given the globe a single spin — he hadn't even located Stonetown Harbor on it yet — when he heard the bell clanging outside on the stairway landing. It rang and rang, very loudly and with no sign of stopping, and from this he gathered it was Kate at the bell. Sure enough, within a few moments the ringing had ceased and the pencil woman had led Kate into the sitting room to join him. Kate was grinning ear to ear. The pencil woman had a hand to her forehead, as if perhaps all the bell ringing had given her a headache.

"She doesn't have to go through a second time?" Reynie asked, surprised.

"No point," said the pencil woman, and left them there alone.

"What do you mean, a second time?" Kate asked.

"I had to finish it twice to prove I'd solved it. But you got through so fast, I suppose it would be hard to do it any faster."

"Not as long as I have my bucket with me," Kate agreed.

After turning this over in his mind a few times, Reynie gave up and said, "Okay, what did your bucket have to do with getting through the maze?"

"Well, of course I saw right away that I was in a maze, and I knew that I had to get to the opposite side of the house. So I looked around for a heating vent —"

"A heating vent?"

"Sure. And there in the floor of the very first room I saw one, so I got out my army-knife screwdriver and removed the grate and squeezed down into the heating duct. It was a tight fit, I'll tell you — had to tie my bucket to my foot and pull it along behind me. Those old ducts run all over the house, but the central duct runs more or less in a straight line to the back, so with my flashlight in one hand and my army knife in the other, I just followed it all the way there, pried up the vent, and popped out by the staircase. I sort of had to bend the grate on that last one. I think maybe Old Yellow Suit's mad about that."

"I bet she'll forgive you."

"Don't you think? It's not like it'll be hard to fix. Only a little one-by-one grate. Hey, this is an impressive globe."

For a while the two of them entertained themselves finding places on the globe, but eventually they'd had enough of it, and Sticky Washington had yet to appear. Kate went over to the piano and tried to play it. The keys made no sound. Together they lifted the lid and looked inside. The piano strings had been removed, and in their place were more books.

"These people certainly have a lot of reading to do," Kate observed. "Oh well, no great loss. I only know 'Chopsticks,' anyway."

Almost twenty minutes had passed, and still no sign of Sticky. Kate began to sort through the items in her bucket, making sure each was in its proper place. She had found an arrangement that kept her things secure and within easy reach, and she was very particular about it. She was the sort of person who liked to be constantly busy, Reynie realized. She hadn't much use for idleness. Which reminded him of something he wanted to ask her. "You know, Kate, something's been nagging me. You told us you carry all these things around in your bucket because they're useful, right?"

"Absolutely," Kate replied.

"Then why the kaleidoscope? It's interesting to look through, maybe, but how is it useful?"

Kate stopped double-checking the things in her bucket and gave Reynie a searching look. At last she nodded. "You know, I think I can trust you, I can already tell. All right, here's the secret." She took out the kaleidoscope and popped off its colorful prismatic lens. Only then did Reynie see that the prismatic lens had been concealing a different lens beneath.

"The kaleidoscope is a spyglass in disguise," Kate explained. "It's a good spyglass and I wouldn't want anyone to steal it. The kaleidoscope, on the other hand, is rather a bad kaleidoscope. I don't think it would tempt anyone."

The very idea of disguising a good spyglass as a bad kaleidoscope made Reynie laugh with pleasure. "It's terrific!" he cried.

Kate wasn't sure what Reynie was laughing about, but she was eminently agreeable, and before long she was laughing with him. When Reynie had taken a good look at the spyglass, Kate tucked it away again and flopped onto the sofa. "Do you think Sticky's ever going to finish? I'm having a fine time and all, but I'm about to drop dead from hunger."

In answer to her question, the bell rang — only once, and almost imperceptibly, as if Sticky had just tapped it with his fingernails. Through the closed door they heard the pencil woman speaking in her brusque way, then an embarrassed murmur that must have been Sticky's response. After a moment all was silent again. Again they waited.

"Shouldn't be long now," Reynie said. "It's easy once you've figured out the secret. It only took me three minutes the second time through."

Three minutes soon passed, however. Then four, then five. Not until almost fifteen minutes had gone by did the bell ring again, just as softly as before. A moment later the door opened, and Sticky entered the room with the pencil woman behind him. He gave a great smile when he saw Reynie and Kate, not so much because he'd finished the test but because he was relieved to have company again.

"Congratulations," said the pencil woman. "You all pass."

The children cheered and clapped each other on the backs, and when they were done cheering and clapping, they realized that the pencil woman had left them yet again.

"She's awfully fond of leaving, isn't she?" asked Kate. "I never saw anybody who left so much. I suppose she expects us to wait again?"

"Maybe Rhonda's coming for us," Reynie said.

"I hope so. Otherwise I'm going to have to eat some of these books. Sticky, what on earth took you so long? Didn't you know how hungry I was?"

Sticky seemed about to cry. He was reaching for his spectacles when he saw Kate was only teasing him. Then he smiled and shrugged. "I had to go through twice."

"So did Reynie. But he said there's some kind of secret that gets you through faster. So why did it take you so long the second time?"

"It was a *little* faster," Sticky protested. "Now what's this secret you're talking about?"

"The secret to getting through the maze," Reynie said. "You know, the arrows."

"Arrows? You mean the ones on those panels?"

Reynie gave Kate a look of amazement, but Kate replied, "Don't look at me. I don't know anything about arrows, remember? I took a shortcut."

"That's true," he said. "Sticky, if you didn't use the arrows, how did you get through?"

Sticky shuffled his feet and said, "I just kept trying one door after the other, until finally I found the staircase. It was sheer luck."

"And you found it more quickly the second time? That's the *really* lucky part, I guess."

"Oh, no, that part was easy," Sticky said. "I just remembered how I got through the first time: First I took a right, then a left, then straight ahead, then right, then right again, then left, then left again, then right, then straight ahead, and so on, until I came to the staircase. I didn't have to waste time scratching my head over those panels, or worrying they were going to turn the lights off, or any of that stuff. I just hurried through exactly as I did before."

"Exactly as you —," Kate began, then just shook her head. "That's incredible."

Reynie laughed. "You did it the hard way, Sticky!"

"What's the easy way?"

"Follow the wiggly arrows."

"Oh," Sticky said thoughtfully. "That would have been useful to know."

the TROUBLE WITH CHILDREN

or, Why They Are Necessary

Rhonda · Mr. Benedict · Number Two · Milligan

Their supper was served in a cozy dining room with crowded bookshelves on every wall and a window overlooking the courtyard. Redbirds twittered in the elm tree outside the open window, a gentle breeze drifted into the room, and in general the children were in much better spirits, having passed the tests and at last having gotten some food in their bellies. Rhonda Kazembe had already brought them bowls of tomato soup and grilled cheese sandwiches, which they'd eagerly devoured; now she set out a great platter of fruit, and as the children reached happily for bananas and grapes and pears, she sat down and joined them.

"It's all part of the test, you know. Being hungry and irritable. It's important to see how you behave when other children are getting doughnuts and you're getting nothing, and how well your mind works despite being tired and thirsty. You all did brilliantly, I must say. Just brilliantly."

Sticky, who still felt sensitive about his performance in the maze, said, "I wouldn't say I did brilliantly. I didn't figure out the solution *or* find a shortcut, I just stumbled around like a twit."

"You mustn't belittle yourself," Rhonda said. "I daresay very few people could have done what you did the second time through, retracing your steps so exactly. You made over a hundred turns!"

"I doubt I could have done it," Reynie remarked.

"I *know* I couldn't have," said Kate through a mouthful of grapes.

Sticky ducked his head.

"Besides, you aren't the only child ever to have trouble with the maze," said Rhonda. "When I first went through it, I got terribly lost."

"You got lost in the maze?" Sticky said. The others' ears perked up.

"Oh, yes, several years ago, when I took these same tests. I thought I was very clever, because I knew right away that I was in a maze of identical rooms. I've often been able to sense such things. 'Well,' I thought to myself, 'if every room has three exits, and I always take the exit to the right, then I'll make my way around the house to the back in no time.' Of course, Mr. Benedict had thought of that."

"Who's Mr. Benedict?" Reynie asked.

"Mr. Benedict is the reason we're all here. You'll meet him after supper."

"What happened to you in the maze?" Kate asked.

"Well now, if you do what I did," Rhonda went on, "after about six rooms you come upon a dead end, and your clever little plan flies out the window. I was so frustrated, I didn't bother trying to solve the panels. Instead I just tried to follow the green arrows for a while — green so often means 'go' — and when that didn't work I tried the red ones. When the solution finally occurred to me, more than an hour had gone by."

"But you still passed?" Sticky asked, heartened to learn of someone else having difficulty with the maze.

"Of course she passed," said the pencil woman, entering the dining room. "Rhonda was the most gifted child ever to take the tests. She did so well on everything else, she would have passed no matter *what* happened in the maze."

"Don't be silly," Rhonda said. "If *you* aren't the most gifted person ever to have taken Mr. Benedict's tests, I'm the queen of England."

At this, the pencil woman's cheeks turned as red as her hair.

As he had already admitted, Sticky often got mixed up when he was excited, and in this frenzy of mysteries and revelations, he could hardly think straight. "What's that you said about being the queen of England?" he asked Rhonda. "Was it a riddle?"

Rhonda laughed. "That was only a joke, Sticky. I'm hardly a queen, you know, and I'm not from England. I was born in a country called Zambia and brought here to Stonetown when I was a child."

"Zambia? So did you speak Bembi, then, or one of the other Bantu languages?"

"Why, Bembi," Rhonda answered, taken aback. "And how on earth did you know that? Do you speak it?"

"Oh, no, I'm sure I couldn't. I can read most languages, but I have trouble speaking anything but English. Can't get my tongue to do what it's supposed to."

Rhonda smiled. "I can hardly speak it myself, these days — it's been so long." She gave him a significant look. "I rarely meet anyone who knows what the languages of Zambia are, much less who can read them."

"Sticky knows a good number of things," said Reynie.

"I wish he knew when we're supposed to meet this Mr. Benedict," Kate said. "It's been an awfully long day, and I'd like to learn what this is all about."

"As for that," said the pencil woman, "the reason I came in was to tell you that Mr. Benedict is ready to see you. He's waiting in his study."

"What about the other one?" asked Rhonda Kazembe.

"Apparently there's been some delay. Mr. Benedict said he will meet with these children now, and she can join them when she arrives."

The children wanted to know who this other girl was, but there was no time for questions, for Rhonda and the pencil woman ushered them out of the room and down a long hallway into the study of Mr. Benedict.

Like every other room in the old house, Mr. Benedict's study was crammed with books. Books on shelves that rose to the high ceiling, books in stacks on the floor, books holding up a potted violet in desperate need of water. On four chairs arranged before an oak desk rested still more books — which Rhonda and the pencil woman removed so the children could sit — and on the desk itself, piled in precarious, leaning towers, were even more. The children took their seats and looked about the study. Except for the books, the furniture, and the violet, it appeared to be empty.

"I thought you said he was waiting for us," Kate said.

"And indeed I have been," said a voice, and out from behind the desk where he'd been sitting, hidden by the piles of books, appeared a bespectacled, green-eyed man in a green plaid suit. His thick white hair was shaggy and mussed, his nose was rather large and lumpy like a vegetable, and although it was clear he had recently shaved, he appeared to have done so without benefit of a mirror, for here and there upon his neck and chin were nicks from a razor, and occasional white whiskers that he'd missed altogether. This was Mr. Benedict.

With a friendly smile, Mr. Benedict stepped round to introduce himself to the children, shaking hands and calling each by name. As he did so, Rhonda Kazembe and the pencil woman followed him, standing on either side as he moved from child to child. When he stepped back to lean against his desk, the two women again followed him and stood closely on either side, watching him with alert expressions, as if worried what he might do. It was very curious, and more than a little unsettling.

"First, children, I wish to congratulate you," said Mr. Benedict. "You have all done exceedingly well today. There is much to explain, of course, but I'm afraid the explanations must wait a bit longer, until we are joined by another." He took out a pocket watch, checked the time, and sighed. To the pencil woman he said, "Number Two, any word from Milligan about our missing young friend?"

"Not yet," said the pencil woman. "But he said it should be soon."

"Would you please go meet them? I want to be sure she's had a bite to eat."

The pencil woman gave him a doubtful look.

"I'll be fine," he assured her. "Rhonda is right here."

With an uncertain nod, the pencil woman took her leave.

"Did you just call her Number Two?" asked Kate.

"She prefers we use her code name," explained Rhonda. "She's shy about her real name. For no good reason, if you ask me. It's a perfectly fine name."

"For good reasons or not, we all have things we're shy about," said Mr. Benedict with a significant look at Sticky, who immediately took to polishing his glasses.

Kate and Reynie glanced at each other wonderingly.

"I know you have questions," Mr. Benedict said. "And I may be able to offer some answers now, though some must come later. What's on your mind?"

"I'd like to know who we're waiting for," said Kate.

"That I can answer. Her name is Constance Contraire, a test-taker like yourselves. I must say she's given us all quite a turn. A most amusing child. Rhonda, how many pencils did you say she brought with her this morning?"

"Thirty-seven," said Rhonda, with a shake of her head. "We tell her to bring one, and she brings thirty-seven."

"How do you know that?" Sticky asked.

Rhonda shrugged. "She told me so herself. Remember the storm drain? Constance stopped to help me, but instead of trying to get my pencil back, she simply opened her raincoat. She had pockets and pockets full of pencils. 'Thirty-seven,' she said. 'Just help yourself.'"

"Wasn't that cheating?" Kate asked. "Why wasn't she disqualified?"

"It was certainly taking a risk," said Mr. Benedict. "However, she refused the test answers Rhonda offered her, and the point of the test wasn't to see if you would bring only one pencil, you know. The pencil itself is inconsequential."

Reynie was curious about something else. "Why was she was wearing a raincoat? It was sunny outside today."

"You're an attentive listener," said Mr. Benedict. "That should serve you well — will serve us all well, I daresay. As for the raincoat, I believe she wore it to conceal the pencils."

"But *why* bring all those pencils?" Kate said, exasperated. "It's ridiculous!"

"If that amuses you, Kate," said Mr. Benedict, "you might also enjoy some of her test answers. Let me see, I believe I have them right here." He disappeared behind the desk, again followed closely by Rhonda, who stood watchfully as he shuffled among some papers. The children could see just the top of his rumpled head as he searched.

"Ah, here it is," he said, stepping back around the desk. As before, Rhonda positioned herself close to his side. He scanned the pages. "Oh, here's a clever one. Do you remember this question from the first test? It reads, 'What is wrong with this statement?' And do you know what Constance wrote in reply? She wrote, 'What is wrong with *you*?'" At this, Mr. Benedict burst into laughter — a squeaky, rapid, stuttering expulsion that sounded rather like a dolphin.

The children's faces wrinkled in confusion.

"Here's another," said Mr. Benedict. "Remember this one? It shows a picture of a chessboard with only a black pawn out of its original position, and it reads, 'According to the rules of chess, is this position possible?' Constance writes in response, 'Rules and schools are tools for fools — I don't give two mules for rules!'"

Again Mr. Benedict laughed his dolphin laugh. This time he couldn't stop, but laughed louder and louder, until tears entered his eyes. And then without warning, his eyes closed, his chin dropped to his chest, and he fell asleep.

Rhonda leaped forward to catch his glasses, which had slipped from his nose. Fortunately Mr. Benedict had been leaning against the desk — when he fell asleep, he only slumped forward a bit and didn't fall to the floor. Even so, Rhonda took him carefully about the waist and said, "Quick, one of you bring me a chair."

Kate jumped to her feet and slid her chair over. Rhonda lowered Mr. Benedict into it and eased his head into a comfortable position. His breathing deepened into a gentle snore, as if he'd been asleep for hours.

Recovering from his surprise, Reynie realized why Rhonda and Number Two stuck so close to Mr. Benedict when he walked around. If he often fell asleep like this, he must risk some nasty falls.

"Is he all right?" Sticky whispered.

"Oh, yes, he's fine," Rhonda said. "He'll be awake any moment. He seldom sleeps longer than a minute or two."

And indeed, even as she spoke, Mr. Benedict's eyelids fluttered open, and he rose abruptly from the chair and said, "Ah." Taking out his pocket watch, he squinted to read it, then touched the bridge of his nose as if searching for something. "I'm afraid I can't read without my glasses."

"Here," said Rhonda, handing them to him.

"Thank you." With his glasses on, Mr. Benedict checked the watch and gave a nod of satisfaction. "Only a few moments, then, that's good. I would hate to have left you waiting long." He gave a ferocious yawn and ran his fingers sleepily through his hair, as people often do when they first awake, which likely accounted for its disheveled state.

"This is another thing I need to explain to you," said Mr. Benedict. "I have a condition known as narcolepsy. Are you familiar with it?"

"Sure, it's a disorder characterized by sudden and uncontrollable attacks of deep sleep," said Sticky, then ducked his head shyly. "At least, that's what the dictionary says."

"The dictionary is correct. Although the condition takes different forms with different people, in my case an attack is usually triggered by strong emotion. For this reason I wear green plaid suits — I discovered years ago that green plaid has a soothing effect on me — and always try to remain calm. However, every now and then I must allow myself a hearty laugh, don't you agree? What is life without laughter?"

The children, uneasy, nodded politely.

"Now then, where did I leave off? Oh, yes, Constance. I take it you didn't find her answers as amusing as I do. I'm not sure, however — perhaps you laughed while I was sleeping?" He glanced at them hopefully, but was met with blank faces. "I see. Well, perhaps you'll find *this* amusing: Instead of answering the questions on the second test, she composed a long poem about the absurdity of the test and its rules, particularly about the missing fourth step — which apparently reminded her of doughnut holes, because these were the topic of a second poem. She is very irritated, it seems, that every doughnut contains a hole. She feels she is being robbed. I remember a particularly felicitous rhyme between 'flaky bereft' and 'bakery theft.' Let's see, where was it? I have it right here. . . ." He began flipping through the test pages.

"Excuse me," Sticky said. "Sir? How is it this girl passed the tests if she didn't answer any of the questions? I mean, if she didn't even try?"

"There are tests," said Mr. Benedict, "and then there are tests."

"I beg your pardon?"

"It will all come clear presently, Sticky. Ah, here they are at last."

The door was opening, and into the room now came Number Two, looking vexed, followed by Milligan, looking gloomy. And with them was Constance Contraire, looking very, very small.

It took a moment for the children to realize that Constance had arrived with the others. From Milligan's sad face, their eyes had to travel quite a distance downward before lighting upon the girl's. She was very little indeed, and very pudgy, too, which made her almost exactly the size and shape of a fire hydrant (a resemblance strengthened by her red raincoat and rosy red cheeks). Reynie's first impulse was to feel sorry for her — it must be difficult to be so much smaller than other children — but then Constance gave him a cross look, as if she positively disliked him, and Reynie's sympathy diminished.

Helping the girl into a chair (it wasn't a particularly large chair, but she still needed help getting up into it), Number Two said, "Rather than finish the maze, Constance chose a quiet corner and sat down to have a picnic. It took Milligan some time to find her."

"I'm not apologizing," Constance said.

"Nor were you asked to," replied Mr. Benedict. "I'm pleased to hear you've had supper. Did you enjoy your picnic, then? Have quite enough to eat?"

"Quite," said Constance.

"Very well. Thank you, Milligan."

With a nod, the unhappy man pulled his hat down over his eyes and withdrew from the study. Number Two, meanwhile, took up her position next to Mr. Benedict, who, after introducing Constance to the other children (she gave them all such crabby looks that no one offered to shake her hand), at last began to explain.

"My young friends," he said, his face growing solemn, "let me cut to the chase. I wish I could tell you that, having passed these tests, you are now to enter into a pleasant period of education. On the contrary, what I have to tell you is extremely *un*pleasant, extremely unpleasant indeed."

The children frowned in puzzlement. Was he joking? He certainly *seemed* serious. Perhaps this, too, was a test — a way of gauging their commitment.

"For years now," Mr. Benedict went on, "I have conducted these tests in hopes of forming a team of children to help me on an urgent project. You may be aware that some years ago Rhonda took the tests, as did Number Two. In fact a great many children have taken these tests, and yet I have been unable to form a team. Why is this? For one thing, very few children pass. For another, those who have passed have not done so at the same *time*, and this, you see, is crucial. I do not simply need a team; I need a team of *children*. Yet children do not remain children for long, and herein has lain the difficulty. Rhonda was a child only a few years ago, and Number Two a few years before that, but as you see they are now quite grown up. They have stayed on with me as assistants — and indeed their prodigious gifts have helped me tremendously — but like myself, they cannot form a part of the team."

So far, Mr. Benedict had said nothing that struck Reynie as particularly unpleasant. If anything, he had begun to feel even more proud of himself, and of his new friends, for having done something unusual. It was obvious that Mr. Benedict believed they had what it took to form this special team. But already he sensed that Mr. Benedict did not speak lightly — if he promised something unpleasant, Reynie was sure that something unpleasant would come. Next to him Sticky was squirming uncomfortably, apparently thinking the same thing. And Kate had just glanced in Reynie's direction, seen the uncertainty in his eye, and nodded her silent agreement: The bad news was coming.

"I see you are wondering where the unpleasantness comes in," said Mr. Benedict, "as well you might. Let me tell you, then: The project is dangerous. It is a mission — one that may put your lives at risk."

The children all straightened in their chairs.

"I want to make some things perfectly clear," said Mr. Benedict. "It is not my wish to put you in harm's way. Quite the opposite: I despise the notion. Children should spend their time learning and playing in absolute safety — that is my firm belief. Now then, assuming that I am telling the truth, can you guess why I would nonetheless involve you in something dangerous?"

"Why should we assume that you're telling the truth?" challenged Constance.

"For the sake of discussion," said Mr. Benedict, "let us assume that I am."

"If you're telling the truth," said Reynie, "then the only reason you would put us in danger is that you believe we'll fall into greater danger if you don't."

Mr. Benedict tapped his lumpy nose and pointed at Reynie. "Precisely. And I do believe this. I am certain, in fact, that you — and a great many other people — are in danger even as we speak, and that this danger shall only increase."

Sticky coughed and mumbled something about needing to use the bathroom.

Mr. Benedict smiled kindly down at him and said, "Sticky, never fear, you aren't compelled to join the team. I hope to explain a bit more about it, and then you'll be given the choice to stay or go. Fair enough?" After a moment's hesitation, Sticky nodded, and then Mr. Benedict added, "Now, do you truly need to use the bathroom, or can you wait a few minutes longer?"

Sticky truly did, but he said, "I can wait."

"Very well. Now, in the interest of further explanation, I'll ask you all another question. What is it the four of you have in common? Can you tell me?"

"We all passed your boring tests," said Constance.

"We're all gifted," said Kate.

"We're all children," said Sticky.

Mr. Benedict nodded at each response, then looked at Reynie, who said, "We're all alone."

Mr. Benedict raised his eyebrows. "What makes you think that?"

"For one thing," said Reynie, "the newspaper advertisement wasn't addressed to parents but to children, which makes me think you were looking for kids who might be alone. And then at that first test there were a lot of parents, but later in the Monk Building I saw only a handful of them waiting — and I know at least a few kids showed up all by themselves. And now here we are. I'm an orphan, and Kate's mother died when she was a baby and then her father left her, and I'm only guessing about Constance, but as for Sticky, well — I'm sorry, Sticky, but I think you've been hiding something. I think somehow you're alone, too."

"Before you say anything," said Mr. Benedict to Sticky, who was staring at Reynie with a shocked expression, "let me tell you this. I have always had a strict policy against taking on runaways. In light of the circumstances, however, I'm willing to make an exception. When it's time for you to decide about staying or leaving, please keep in mind it won't be necessary to make up stories. And if you decide to leave, Rhonda and Number Two will offer you assistance. I have no intention of letting you go out into the city again with no money, food, or shelter."

By this point Sticky had turned his shocked expression toward Mr. Benedict. He opened his mouth to speak, reconsidered, and finally stared down at his shoes.

Kate leaned over and put her hand on his shoulder. "A runaway, eh?" she whispered. "You've got more gumption than I realized, pal."

"All of you have answered correctly," said Mr. Benedict. "You're all gifted children who passed my 'boring' tests — in one way or another — and you've all shown yourselves to be unusually resourceful. For example, I happen to know that Constance has been living secretly in a public library in a city north of Stonetown, and that she managed to catch a bus, and then a subway, and finally a taxi to come here. And I know that Kate stole aboard a boxcar in Chicago, while Sticky stowed away on a river barge. You've all shown ingenuity in one form or another — and yes, in one form or another, you're all alone."

Again he paused, gazing at the children now with what appeared to be a mixture of great pride and great sympathy. Indeed, tears had welled up in his eyes, and the sincerity in his expression made Reynie — who was used to ignoring his loneliness — grow almost heartsick. He felt a keen desire to see Miss Perumal again. Had it only been this morning that she'd surprised him by crying when they parted? It already seemed so long ago.

"Oh dear," cried Rhonda just then, for Mr. Benedict, awash in strong emotion, had gone to sleep. With a sudden loud snore he toppled forward into the attentive arms of Rhonda and Number Two, who eased him to the floor.

"What's with him?" Constance asked.

"He has narcolepsy," said Kate.

"He steals a lot?"

"That's kleptomania," Sticky said. "Mr. Benedict *sleeps* a lot."

"Well, I don't like it," Constance said crossly.

"I assure you, Constance," said Number Two, looking vexed, "Mr. Benedict doesn't like it, either. None of us does. It simply can't be helped."

Before any more could be said, Mr. Benedict opened his

eyes, blinked a few times, and ran his fingers through his tousled white hair. Rhonda said gently, "Only a minute, Mr. Benedict. You were only out for a minute."

"Is that so? Very good, then, very good. Thank you, my friends, thank you as always." He patted Rhonda and Number Two on the arms, and they helped him to his feet.

"Usually happens when I'm laughing," he explained to the children, "but these days it's often something else. Now then, what was I —? Oh, yes. All alone. Let me tell you why that part matters. For one thing, children without guardians happen to be in a peculiar kind of danger that other children are not — this I shall explain later, to those of you who join my team. For another, it would be simply impossible for me to put at risk any child who *wasn't* alone. No matter how important the cause, parents are disinclined to send their children into danger, as well they should be. As it so happens, however, I now find myself in the presence of the best possible team of children I could ever hope for — indeed, have long hoped for — and with not a minute to lose. In other words, you are our last possible hope. You are our *only* hope."

The Tender
and the Messages

In the end, every child agreed to join the team, though the decision was more difficult for some than others. Kate took out a stick of gum and said, "I'm in," without even pausing to consider. Reynie, less fearless than Kate, had to give the matter some thought. If he didn't join the team, what would he do? Return to the orphanage? Seeing Miss Perumal again would be nice, but he would be in the same pickle as before: out of place among the other children, purposeless and lonely. Moreover, if Mr. Benedict was to be trusted (and for some reason Reynie did trust him) then feeling purposeless and lonely were the least of his problems. Something terrible was happening, and Mr. Benedict needed them to stop it. A strange sense of duty, not to mention a powerful curiosity, compelled him to join.

Constance was more skeptical. It was becoming clear that this was her natural approach to things. "So if I stick around, and you tell me this big secret, what's to stop me from going out and telling everyone?"

"Nothing will stop you," said Mr. Benedict. "You're free to leave at any time. However, if I hadn't determined I could trust you, you would never have been invited into this room. And for that matter, even if you were to tell, no one would believe you, for you are only a child. Is that not why you came to take these tests in the first place?"

Constance's face screwed up as if she might burst into tears — or, more likely, throw a screaming fit.

"I don't mean to attack you, child," Mr. Benedict said gently. "Let us strike a bargain. If you join the team, this shall be our understanding: You will follow my instructions, but only because you have agreed to do so, not because I told you to. No one is making you do anything. It is all of your own free will."

"Fine," said Constance at last. "Now where do we sleep?"

"I know you're tired, but first we must wait for Sticky to make up his mind."

Sticky had been shrinking in his chair. He had drawn his feet up beneath him, crossed his arms over his knees, and buried his face behind them. At Mr. Benedict's words, he looked up with an expression of something like panic, then quickly hid his face again. His voice muffled, his words mumbled, Sticky said, "May I make the decision tomorrow?"

"I'm afraid not, my friend. There's no time to waste. I hate to press you, but you must decide tonight."

"Do you think the team is good enough without me?" came the muffled voice.

"Frankly, no. I think the team needs you to succeed."

"Then how can I say no?"

Mr. Benedict spoke gently. "Sticky, it's quite reasonable for you to be afraid. It's a terrible thing for a child to be asked to join a dangerous mission. You have every reason to say no, and I will not blame you in the least."

"Come on, Sticky," said Kate, "it'll be fun!"

Sticky peeked out from behind his knees, first at Kate, who gave him a smile and a wink, then at Reynie, who said, "I'm with Mr. Benedict. I don't blame you if you don't join us. But I'd feel a whole lot better if you did."

"You would?"

Reynie nodded.

Sticky hid his face again. For a long time the room was silent, full of expectation. Although Constance yawned and scratched at an insect bite on her ankle, no one else moved or spoke a word. There was only the hushed sound of their breathing, and, from somewhere in the room, the ticking of a clock, which must have been hidden by books.

Finally Sticky looked up. "I'll do it. Now may I please use the bathroom?"

Much as the children longed for more answers, it had grown late, their eyes were heavy, and Mr. Benedict deemed they should rest tonight and leave further explanations for morning. In short order they were given toothbrushes, pajamas, and warm slippers — it was drafty in the old house at night — and shown to their rooms. The bedroom Reynie shared with Sticky was small but comfortable, with a worn rug on the wooden floor, bunk beds against the wall, and, of course, more bookshelves. When Reynie returned from brushing his teeth, he found Sticky already asleep on the lower bunk, the lamp still lit, spectacles still on his nose, and slippers still on his feet. On his chest, rising and falling with the deep, regular breaths of a solid sleeper, lay a thick book about tropical plant life that he'd taken from a shelf. It was open to the very middle. In only a few minutes, Sticky had read half the book.

Reynie marveled at this. He was a fast reader himself — faster than most adults — but compared to Sticky he must seem positively sluggish. Such an incredible gift, and yet here the boy lay, a runaway sleeping in a stranger's house. What had he run from? Standing there in the lamplit room, reflecting upon Sticky's life as he slept, Reynie experienced a curious mixture of admiration, affection, and sympathy — curious because although he'd known the boy for only a day, it seemed as if they'd been friends for ages. And Kate, too, he reflected. He was already quite fond of her. And Constance . . . well, with Constance he would have to wait and see.

Anyway, Reynie thought, *if nothing else comes of this, at least you're making friends. That's more than you had yesterday.* He eased Sticky's slippers from his feet and his glasses from his nose, setting them, along with the plant book, upon a bedside stand. Then he drew a cover over his friend, turned off the lamp, and crept from the room.

Down the dark, quiet hall — the girls must have been asleep, too — and down a flight of creaky stairs, Reynie made his way back to Mr. Benedict's study. He knocked softly on the door, and from within a voice called, "Please come in, Reynie."

Reynie entered to find Mr. Benedict alone in the room, seated on the floor with his back against the desk, surrounded by books, papers, and a variety of colored pens. He gestured toward a chair and said, "Have a seat, will you, while I clear some of this away?" He began sorting things into piles. "Awkward business, working on the floor, but that is my compromise with Rhonda and Number Two. They've grown overprotective, I'm afraid, and can hardly stand to leave me alone for a minute. Thus I promise them to remain seated as much as possible — and on the floor, when possible — and in turn they allow me some occasional privacy."

Mr. Benedict finished tidying his things and sat in a chair across from Reynie. "I've been expecting you. I imagine you wish to call Miss Perumal and apprise her of your situation."

Reynie nodded.

"You're very good to think of it. Number Two told me how you resisted her attempts to befuddle you on the same matter earlier today. I assume you realize her deceptions were another aspect of the testing?"

Again Reynie nodded. He hadn't known it at the time, but looking back on the encounter later he had suspected as much.

"You behaved admirably," Mr. Benedict said. "Polite but steadfast, and with appropriate consideration. Now, I'm afraid you can't make your telephone call this time, either, but it has nothing to do with being tested. As it happens, Miss Perumal phoned while you were being shown to your room. Her mother, it seems, has had an unfortunate reaction to her new medicine, and Miss Perumal found it necessary to take her to the hospital. She begs you not to worry, it's only a mild reaction and the doctors assure her that her mother will be spry as a robin come morning. But she wanted you to know how proud she is of you — proud but not surprised, she said — and sends you her best regards.

"And now," he continued, removing his spectacles and looking frankly at Reynie with his bright green eyes (they were made greener still by his green plaid suit), "I will anticipate your other questions. First, I've made all the necessary arrangements with Mr. Rutger at the orphanage: We have considerable skills and resources here and can do many things you might not expect. And second, on a more solemn note: No, you won't be able to contact Miss Perumal again. I'm afraid the urgency of our mission, and its necessary secrecy, forbids it. It is for Miss Perumal's protection as well as your own. But if all goes well — which is, of course, our most desperate hope — you will see her again. Indeed, if our mission is to succeed, it must do so very quickly, and so with luck your reunion will be sooner rather than later."

Reynie nodded again, though not quite as bravely as before, and glanced away to hide the tears in his eyes. He had thought this might be the case, but it still saddened him to think he might not ever again share a cup of tea with Miss Perumal or attempt to tell her, in his limited Tamil, about his adventures. He was sad at the thought of what lay ahead, yes, and more than a little afraid.

"I am sorry, Reynie," said Mr. Benedict with a quaver in his voice.

Reynie didn't look at him just yet. He kept his eyes averted until he had composed himself, which he did with a few deep breaths and a quick swipe at his tearful eyes. When he felt sufficiently recovered, he turned back to Mr. Benedict — who was sound asleep in his chair.

Before Reynie could rise and tiptoe from the room, however, Mr. Benedict's eyes popped open, and he laid a hand on Reynie's arm to stop him. "Forgive me," he said, clearing his throat and running his fingers through his unkempt hair. "Please stay just a moment longer. I wanted to ask you something. I wasn't asleep long, was I? I trust I haven't kept you up?"

"No, sir, only a minute or two."

"Ah, good. Usually it *is* only a minute or two, but occasionally it's longer. Now then, for my question."

"Yes, sir?"

"It regards the chess problem from the first test. You, Reynie, happen to be the only child ever to answer the question correctly, and I should like to hear your explanation for it. The board clearly shows that only the black pawn is out of its starting position, while all the other pieces and pawns rest on their original squares. Yet according to the rules of chess, the white player always moves first. Why, then, did you say the position was possible?"

"Because the white knight may have changed its mind."

"The white knight?"

"Oh, yes sir. The pawns can only move forward, never backward, so none of the white pawns could have moved yet. And the bigger pieces are trapped behind the pawns — because only knights can jump over things — so *they* couldn't have moved yet, either. But a white knight might have opened the game by jumping out in front. Then, after the black pawn was moved, the knight returned to its original square. So it looks like the white player never moved at all."

"Bravo, Reynie. You're quite correct. Now tell me, would you consider this a good move?"

"I'm no great chess player, but I would say not. By starting over, white loses the advantage of going first."

"Why, then, do you think the white player might have done it?"

Reynie considered. He imagined himself moving out his knight only to bring it right back to where it had started. Why would he ever do such a thing? At last he said, "Perhaps because he doubted himself."

"Indeed," said Mr. Benedict. "Perhaps he did. Thank you, Reynie, you've been very kind and very patient, and I'm sure you're ready for a night's sleep. I'll see you at breakfast, bright and early."

Reynie rose and went to the door, but there he hesitated. He looked back. Mr. Benedict had replaced his spectacles and lowered himself onto the floor again, was again leaning against the desk, and had taken up a book. His eyebrows rose expectantly when he noticed the boy lingering.

"Yes, Reynie?"

"Mr. Benedict, sir, have you read all the books in this house?"

Mr. Benedict smiled, glancing fondly about at the many books in his study before looking at Reynie again. "My dear boy," he said, "what do you think?"

Bright and early, Mr. Benedict had said, and indeed it was early, but it was far from bright. As the children rose and went down to the dining room (not knowing where else to meet), rain was slashing against the windows, wind groaned in the chimneys, and odd drafts sent papers flying from desktops and skittering across floors. The blackened sky outside seemed to creep gloomily into the house, dimming the lamps and lengthening their shadows; and along with the howling chimneys was heard the growling of thunder, low and menacing and close at hand, as if a tiger prowled the dark rooms beyond their walls. From time to time the lamps flickered with the thunder, and once — just as the children were taking seats at the table — they went out entirely. The room was dark only for a few moments, yet when the lamps came back to life, Milligan stood before the children with a pitcher of juice, having appeared out of nowhere.

Constance shrieked. The other children jumped.

Milligan sighed.

Filling their juice glasses, he said, "Rhonda's coming with toast and eggs. Number Two's stopping a leak in her bedroom wall, but she'll fetch Mr. Benedict when she's done."

"Milligan, may I have some milk, please?" Kate asked cheerily. She'd been awake longer than anyone, had already bathed and dressed in the fresh clothes Rhonda had given her, and — apparently unaffected by the storm — was in a much better mood than the others.

Without doubt she was in a better mood than Milligan, who nodded glumly and said, "Anything else?"

"You wouldn't have any tea, would you, Milligan?" asked Reynie. "And perhaps a little honey?"

"And candy?" asked Constance.

"No candy for breakfast," Milligan said, leaving the room.

Rhonda appeared with a tray of wheat toast, eggs, and fruit. "Good morning, everyone," she said. "Quite a bit of weather we're having, isn't it? On a day like this, you have to set something on every stray sheet of paper if you don't want a draft carrying it off. A map of Stonetown Harbor passed me in the hall just now, and on the stairs I found a grocery list I misplaced two weeks ago!"

"Leaks in the walls and drafts in every room," Constance grumbled. "You should have these things fixed."

"Leaks and drafts aren't priorities, I'm afraid," Rhonda said. "Our project — which is now *your* project, too — has required every spare moment, and all our resources have gone toward the research, the investigation, and the tests. Constance, will you pass the juice pitcher, please?"

"No," the girl replied, crossing her arms.

"Perhaps you'll be less cranky after you've eaten," Rhonda said, getting the pitcher herself. At this, Constance's pudgy, rosy cheeks grew redder still, so that her wispy blond hair seemed almost white in contrast, and her pale blue eyes shone bright as stars. Rhonda noticed this and said, "Constance, I had no idea how lovely your eyes were until just now. They're spectacular!"

This compliment, somehow upsetting to Constance, kept her quiet for some time.

Milligan returned with the milk, a pot of tea, and a jar of honey. Mumbling something to Rhonda about being on duty, he left without another word.

"What does he mean by that?" Sticky said. "'On duty'?"

"Milligan is our — well, for lack of a better word — our bodyguard. He has other tasks, but his first duty is to make sure we're safe. Of course, until now, we haven't been in direct danger, but now that you're here . . . I'm sorry, I don't mean to alarm you. The important thing is that he's here to protect you."

"Protect us from what?" Reynie asked.

"I'll let Mr. Benedict explain all that to you when he comes down. The main rule is this: You must never leave the house without Milligan's company. Inside the house, you're quite safe; we have defenses here. The maze, for example, wasn't just a test — it's the only entrance. And this reminds me: All the arrows in the maze point to the stairway, which isn't helpful if you're trying to *leave* the house. That's another reason you should never go without Milligan. We have a special way of opening the front door — you'll remember it has no inside knob — and Milligan knows the maze like the back of his hand."

"I've always thought that was a funny expression," Kate said. "Because how well do people really know the backs of their hands? Honestly, can anyone here tell me exactly what the back of your hand looks like?"

They were all contemplating the backs of their hands when Mr. Benedict came in, followed very closely and attentively by Number Two, who no longer wore her yellow suit but had changed into a comfortable pair of yellow coveralls, so that she still looked every bit the pencil. She stuck close to Mr. Benedict until he had greeted everyone and taken his chair, after which she swooped upon the platter of toast and eggs, accidentally jostling Rhonda in the process.

"Pardon me," she said, embarrassed.

"Not at all," said Rhonda. To the children she said, "Number Two is always hungry because she never sleeps. A person needs a great deal of energy to stay awake all the time, and thus a great deal of food."

"It also makes me somewhat nervous and irritable, I'm afraid," said Number Two. She proceeded to eat the crusts off her toast by turning it round and round and taking tiny, rapid bites.

"You *never* sleep?" Kate asked, after watching this curious procedure a moment.

Number Two swallowed. "Oh, yes, I do, but only a little."

"Don't we make a fine pair?" said Mr. Benedict, pouring himself a cup of tea. "I can't stay awake, and Number Two can't go to sleep." He started to laugh, then cut himself short, apparently not wanting to risk it. "By the way, Rhonda, have you seen my map of the harbor? It appears to have escaped the study."

"It drifted by me in the hallway," Rhonda said. "I placed it by the bell under the Swiss book on electron-positron accelerators."

"Thank you. Now, children, speaking of the bell, do you all remember where it is — on the second-floor landing? If you ever hear that bell ringing, I want you to gather on the landing immediately. It will only be rung in case of emergency, so don't delay. Drop what you're doing and go there at once. Understood?"

The children nodded uneasily. All this talk of danger and emergencies, without explanation, was beginning to wear on them.

"I'm sorry to put you ill at ease," Mr. Benedict said. "And I haven't much to say to comfort you. I *can* finally offer some answers to your questions, however. Who wishes to begin? Yes, Constance?"

To the great exasperation of the others, Constance demanded to know why they couldn't have candy for breakfast.

Mr. Benedict smiled. "A fine question. The short answer is that there is no candy presently in the house. Beyond that, the explanation involves a consideration of candy's excellent flavor but low nutritional value — that is to say, why it makes a wonderful treat but a poor meal — though I suspect you aren't interested in explanations but simply wished to express your frustration. Is that correct?"

"Maybe," Constance said with a shrug. But she seemed satisfied.

"Other questions?" said Mr. Benedict.

There were, of course, other questions, and all speaking at once, the children asked him to explain his "project" and why he needed children and what sort of danger they were in.

Mr. Benedict set down his teacup. "Very well. I shall explain everything, and you may listen as you eat your breakfast." (When he began, however, Constance was the only child who continued to eat. The others were unable to concentrate on anything besides his explanation.)

"Several years ago," Mr. Benedict said, "in the course of my research on the human brain, it came to my attention that messages were being delivered to people all across the world — delivered, I should say, quite without their knowledge. It is as if I secretly hid a letter in your pocket, and later you found and read it, not knowing where it came from. In this case, however, the messages were going directly into people's minds, which absorbed them not only without knowing where the messages came from, but without realizing they had received or read anything at all.

"The messages appear to be in a kind of code," Mr. Benedict continued. "They come across like poetic gibberish. But from early on I've had reason to believe they're having a powerful effect — a most *unfortunate* effect — on those who receive them, which is to say almost everyone. In fact, I believe these messages are the source of the phenomenon commonly known as the Emergency — though, I admit, I don't know to what end. And so I have devoted myself to discovering their ultimate purpose and who it is that sends them. Unfortunately, I've not entirely succeeded."

"But you've learned a great deal!" protested Number Two.

"Certainly I have. I know, for instance, how the messages are being delivered —"

"And where they're sent from!" Rhonda said impatiently.

"And what the Sender is capable of doing!" cried Number Two.

Obviously Rhonda and Number Two were worried the children might misjudge Mr. Benedict. Sensing this, he gave an appreciative smile. "Yes, my friends, it's true. We do know some things. For instance, we know the Sender uses children to deliver the hidden messages."

"Children?" Sticky said. "Why children?"

"And what exactly do the messages say?" Reynie asked.

"When you're quite finished with your breakfasts, I'll show you. In the meantime, let me tell you —"

"Please, can't breakfast wait?" Kate interrupted. "Let us see right now!"

"Well, if you all feel this way . . . ," said Mr. Benedict, noting their looks of impatience.

This time not even Constance resisted (perhaps because she was already full), and so the children were taken straightaway up to the third floor, down a long narrow hallway, and at last into a room packed with equipment. It was a terrific mess. On a table against the wall sat a television, a radio, and a computer, and upon every other available surface were scattered countless tools, wires, books and charts and notebooks, disconnected antennas, disassembled gadgets, and various other unrecognizable oddments. There was hardly anywhere to step as Mr. Benedict — closely attended by Rhonda and Number Two — led them over to the television.

"Listen carefully," Mr. Benedict said, turning on the television.

Instantly Reynie felt his skin crawl. It was a familiar feeling, he realized, but he had never paid it much attention before. Meanwhile, a news program had appeared on the screen. A red-haired reporter with shiny gold earrings stood outside the White House, where a crowd of people had gathered, as usual, to wave signs and demand something be done about the Emergency.

"They're calling for change," said the reporter, her features gathered in an expression of thoughtful seriousness, "and their cries are not falling on deaf ears. The President has repeated his agreement that something must be done, and soon. Meanwhile, in the halls of Congress —"

Constance gave a loud yawn. "I don't hear anything unusual."

The other children looked at Mr. Benedict. It was rude of Constance to say it that way, but she was right.

Mr. Benedict nodded. "Now pay attention, please. Number Two, engage the Receiver."

Number Two sat at the computer and with quick, agile fingers, typed a string of commands. The television screen flickered; its picture grew distorted. The children could still make out the wavery image of the news reporter gesturing toward the crowd behind her, but her voice faded away, replaced by that of a child.

"What in the world?" Kate said.

"Just listen," said Number Two.

The unseen child — it sounded like a girl about Kate's age — spoke in a plodding, whispery monotone, her voice half-drowned in static. At first only a few random words were clear enough to be understood: *"Market . . . too free to be . . . obfuscate . . ."* Number Two typed more commands into the computer; the interference lessened considerably, and the child's words came clearly now, slipping through the faint static in a slow drone:

> "THE MISSING AREN'T MISSING, THEY'RE ONLY DEPARTED.
> ALL MINDS KEEP ALL THOUGHTS — SO LIKE GOLD — CLOSELY GUARDED. . . ."

Again the words were overcome by static. Number Two muttered under her breath. Her fingers flew across the keyboard, and the child's slow, whispery voice returned:

> "GROW THE LAWN AND MOW THE LAWN.
> ALWAYS LEAVE THE TV ON.
> BRUSH YOUR TEETH AND KILL THE GERMS.
> POISON APPLES, POISON WORMS."

It went on like this. The child's voice never faltered, never ceased, but delivered the curious phrases in an eerie, chant-like progression. The news reporter, meanwhile, had vanished from the distorted picture, replaced by a cheerful-looking weather forecaster, but it continued to be the child's voice they heard. Mr. Benedict signaled Number Two, whose fingers flew over the computer keyboard. The child's voice faded. The weather forecaster was promising clear skies by afternoon.

Mr. Benedict switched off the television. On the blank television screen the children could suddenly see their reflections. Every one of them was frowning. When they realized this, their faces all adopted looks of surprise, then of intense curiosity.

"What does 'obfuscate' mean?" asked Constance.

Sticky, as if someone had pulled a string in his back, promptly answered, "To make so confused or opaque as to be difficult to perceive, or to otherwise render indistinct."

Constance looked frightened.

"It means to make things muddled," Reynie said.

"Thank you for the dictionary definition, Sticky," said Mr. Benedict, "and thank you, Reynie, for the translation." He crossed his arms and regarded the children. "This child's voice is currently being transmitted on every television, radio, and cell phone in the world. Which means, of course, it is being absorbed by millions of minds. And yet, although in an important part of every mind this child's messages are being heard, understood, and taken seriously, in another part — the part that is aware of itself — the messages remain undetected. But this Receiver I've invented is capable of detecting and translating them, much as Reynie translated Sticky's definition a moment ago."

"But how could people who speak different languages understand that kid?" Kate asked. "What about people in Spain?"

"The messages transmit in every language. I've tuned the Receiver to English only because that's what we all speak."

"This is too creepy," Sticky said, glancing nervously behind him. "It's like . . . like . . ."

"Like having a strange person whisper in your ear while you sleep?" Mr. Benedict suggested.

"Okay, that just made it creepier," Sticky said.

Reynie was shaking his head wonderingly. "How is this happening, Mr. Benedict? These messages — whatever they are — how are they being sent?"

"To put it simply," Mr. Benedict began, "they depend for their mobility upon external agents —"

"Mr. Benedict, that's hardly putting it simply," interrupted Rhonda with a significant look at Constance, whose face had darkened with frustration.

"Forgive me. You're quite right. *Simply* put, the messages ride piggyback on signals. Television, radio, cell phones — all these things make use of invisible signals, and the Sender has found a way to take advantage. The messages aren't picky; they will ride on any kind of signal. The Sender has discovered how to control the adhesive property of thoughts."

"The what?" asked the children all together.

"The adhesive property of thoughts. That is, the way thoughts are drawn to signals and then stick to them — much as little pieces of metal may be drawn to a magnet. They're attracted to all kinds of signals, even other thoughts."

"So the messages are just thoughts?" Kate said.

"Indeed," Mr. Benedict replied. "Although I wouldn't say '*just*.' Thoughts carry a great deal of freight."

"But why does the Sender use children to send them?" Reynie asked.

"A devilish trick," said Mr. Benedict, "and a necessary one.

You see, only a child's thoughts can be slipped into the mind so secretly. For some reason, they go unnoticed."

"No surprise there," Constance humphed. "I've never met a grown-up who believed me *capable* of thought."

"She's absolutely right," put in Number Two with a sharp edge in her voice. "People pay no attention to what children say, much less to what they think!"

Rhonda patted Number Two's shoulder. "Number Two is a bit testy about this. She was often ignored as a child."

"That doesn't change the truth!" Number Two snarled.

"Easy now," said Rhonda. "Only teasing."

"Sorry. Blood sugar's low," said Number Two, hastily unwrapping a granola bar.

"At any rate," Mr. Benedict continued, "I believe the Sender uses children as a sort of filter. After passing through the minds of children, the messages become virtually undetectable. Where adult thoughts would lumber into the mind like an elephant, children's creep in on cat feet and find a shadowy place to hide."

"Nobody notices them at all?" Sticky asked.

"Oh, some may be vaguely aware of mental activity," Mr. Benedict said, "but if so, they attribute the uneasy sensation to something else. They think, perhaps, they've had an original idea, or have drunk too much coffee."

"I don't recall ever having felt that way," said Constance. "Like something's happening but I don't know what."

The others shook their heads, indicating they hadn't either.

"That is because you love the truth," said Mr. Benedict. "You see —"

Number Two interrupted him. "Mr. Benedict, before you

go on, won't you take a seat? Makes me so nervous, you standing there like that. Too many hard things about. Just look at this chair, and the desk, and the television cabinet, and all these tools —" Turning this way and that, Number Two was pointing at almost everything she saw.

"Fine, fine, Number Two, we'll all sit," said Mr. Benedict, settling into a cross-legged position on the floor. He gestured for the others to join him. Shoving aside books, papers, and odd pieces of machinery, the children made room to sit. Number Two took a deep breath to calm herself.

"You see," Mr. Benedict began again, "although most people care about the truth, they can nonetheless — under certain circumstances, and given proper persuasion — be diverted from it. Some, however, possess an unusually powerful love of truth, and you children are among the few. Your minds have been resisting the hidden messages."

"Is that why your test asked whether we liked television and radio?" asked Reynie.

Mr. Benedict tapped his nose. "Exactly. Of course, it's possible you enjoy watching an occasional TV show, or listening to the radio every now and then, but in general you find you don't like it. This is because your minds, so unwilling to be deceived, are avoiding exposure to the messages."

"I don't see what's dangerous about all this," Constance said with a sour expression. "So people are receiving some kids' thoughts and don't realize it. That hardly seems reason to panic."

"We haven't yet come to the panic part," replied Mr. Benedict gravely.

"Oh," said Constance.

"Great," said Sticky.

"Something is approaching," Mr. Benedict said. "Something dreadful. These messages are connected to it, but they are only the beginning. What's coming is worse, far worse — a looming darkness, like storm clouds sweeping in to cover the sky."

"Wh-what," Sticky stammered, "wh-what *is* it?"

Mr. Benedict scratched his rumpled head. "I'm afraid I don't know."

The children blinked. Was he joking? He didn't *know*?

"Ah, I sense your confusion," said Mr. Benedict. "I should have said I don't *exactly* know."

Rhonda spoke up. "We have good reason to believe in this coming threat, children. It's just that —"

"But if you have good reason," Constance interrupted, "why are you just sitting around? Call the government! Alert the authorities!"

"An excellent point, Constance," said Mr. Benedict (who, it seemed to Reynie, was surprisingly tolerant of the girl's rudeness). "In fact I was once a trusted advisor to certain high officials, many of whom presided over government agencies. But things have changed. Not only have those agencies been dismantled — and a number of good men and women gone missing — but officials formerly attentive to my remarks have grown skeptical of them. They have come to look upon me as a friendly kook, and some even regard me with suspicion. Everything I do now, I do in secret."

"Did you just say 'good men and women gone missing'?" asked Reynie, hoping he had misunderstood.

"Vanished," said Mr. Benedict grimly. "Years ago, when it first came to my attention that some operatives had disappeared, I naturally inquired about them. But my questions, no matter to whom I put them — and I put them to many people — were met with an astonishing lack of regard. It was perfectly silly, I was told, to be asking such questions. Somehow it was believed that these missing agents *chose* to go away — were given plum assignments in sunny climates, perhaps, or else had gone into early retirement — although there was no evidence of any such thing. No one seemed to care where the agents had gone. But everyone knew, so I was told again and again, *everyone* knew the agents hadn't gone *missing*. No, no, the very idea was preposterous."

The children were dumbstruck. Government agents had disappeared and nobody cared? Nobody even believed it?

Reynie found his voice first. "So that's how you know these strange messages are having an effect on people."

Mr. Benedict nodded. "Quite right, Reynie. At least, it's one example."

"Wait a minute," Kate said. "How do you know the messages have anything to do with that?"

"Because of that phrase we heard on the Receiver," said Reynie. "'The missing aren't missing, they're only departed.' Don't you think there's a connection?"

"Hey, you're right!" said Kate, who had already forgotten that phrase.

Constance seemed exasperated. "Okay, so the authorities are being snookered by these hidden messages. But how could they resist the facts? Show them your Receiver gizmo, Mr. Benedict. They'll *have* to believe you."

"I'm afraid they won't," said Mr. Benedict. "The Receiver would be considered insufficient evidence. For all they know, the messages might be my own invention, generated by the

Receiver itself. I am no longer considered a trustworthy source of information."

Reynie was puzzled. "But Mr. Benedict, if you explained how it worked — scientifically, I mean — how could they not believe you? Surely you can demonstrate the principles involved!"

Mr. Benedict hesitated. "A reasonable suggestion, Reynie. A very . . . Now let me see. How to put it? I can't exactly . . . Well . . ."

Number Two interrupted him. "What Mr. Benedict is too embarrassed to say, children, is that even if he did explain it, no one would believe him because no one would *understand* him. That's the downside to being a genius — just because *you* understand something doesn't mean anyone *else* will. Mr. Benedict is too modest. He can never bring himself to say it."

"He's tried to explain it to any number of people," Rhonda put in. "But not only are they skeptical to begin with, Number Two and I — and a few of the other assistants — are the only people who have understood him."

Mr. Benedict's cheeks and forehead had gone pink with embarrassment. He coughed. "As usual, my friends, you overstate my accomplishment. Nevertheless, the essence of what you say is true. Among the authorities these days it is difficult to find a sympathetic listener."

"In other words, compared to you, they're all dummies," Kate said with a laugh.

"That is perhaps not the most polite way to put it, Kate," said Mr. Benedict.

Unlike Kate, the others were in no mood to laugh. Hidden messages being broadcast to the world, good men and

women gone missing, the authorities beyond convincing —
and the children were somehow going to be involved in all
this? The prospect had caused a deep, indefinable dread to
settle upon them like a cold mist.

Constance's reaction, by now a predictable one, was to express irritation. "Fine, I get it. A lot of people have vanished
without a trace, and someone's sending out secret messages,
and nobody will believe you about it. But *we* aren't really
in danger, are we?" (Though her tone was scoffing and irritable, it was evident from her eyes — which darted back
and forth — that Constance was growing afraid.) "You said
we were all in danger . . . but that was just an exaggeration,
wasn't it?"

"I am sorry to say it, Constance," Mr. Benedict said
somberly, "but I did not exaggerate in the least. You are all in
danger even as we speak."

And indeed, even as they spoke, the bell on the landing
began a furious clanging.

The Men in the Maze

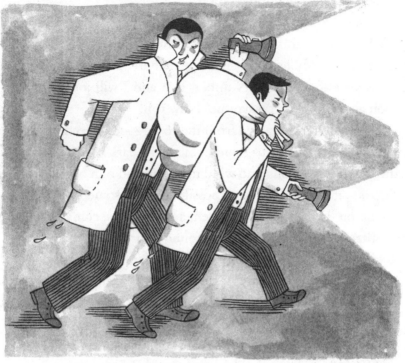

A great deal happened in a very short time: Mr. Benedict fell asleep, having been startled by the emergency bell, and toppled sideways into the ready arms of Number Two. The children hadn't even time to trade looks of alarm before the bell stopped ringing, the lights went out, and Constance screamed. And then, after much jostling and elbow-bumping and fumbling in the dark, Kate found her flashlight and switched it on, and Constance was gone.

"Where'd she go?" Reynie cried.

"Maybe she went down to the landing like we're supposed to," said Sticky.

"Somehow I doubt it," said Kate.

"Okay, all of you," said Rhonda urgently as Number Two tried to shake Mr. Benedict awake, "hurry down to the landing at once. Milligan will meet you there, and he can find Constance if necessary. Number Two and I will join you as soon as Mr. Benedict wakes up. Now run!"

The children stumbled from the room — Kate leading the way with her flashlight — and out into the dark hallway. With the thunder rumbling and wind moaning and rain beating on the roof, it would be quite impossible to hear someone sneaking up on them, and the children, aware of this, clung to one another in the darkness as they found their way to the stairs. Trembling at each fresh burst of thunder, they made their way down to the landing. Kate's flashlight beam passed over the bell, hanging silent and still, then fell upon a very sad face.

"Where's Constance?" Milligan said.

"What did I tell you?" Kate said to the boys.

"We were hoping she'd be here," said Reynie.

Milligan looked grim, even more so than usual. "She may have slipped past me in the dark. This complicates things. No time to take you to a safe place — if she's in the maze we might lose her any second. But I can't leave you here alone. You'll have to come down with me."

"Into the maze?" Sticky asked. "In the dark?"

"There's no help for it. Now grab onto my jacket, Sticky, and you others grab onto him. Whatever you do, stay with me. And Kate, turn off your flashlight. It will only help them find you."

"Them?"

"Yes," Milligan said. "They've come for you. Now don't speak."

None of the children spoke (though two of them gulped), and down into the maze they went. The lights were out here too — they no longer came on when you entered a room. It was perfectly black, and in this perfect blackness they moved, stalking from room to room, until Milligan suddenly froze. The children caught their breath. At first Reynie saw nothing. Then, looking behind him, he glimpsed two flashlight beams passing through one of the other rooms. He squeezed Sticky's arm. Sticky squeezed back even harder.

From the direction of the flashlights came a sudden cry of pain — it was Constance's voice — followed by a thudding sound, as of someone falling to the floor. A man's voice hissed, "I have her!"

"Come," Milligan whispered, hurrying toward the lights. The children followed, holding fast to one another. It was awkward walking so quickly together in the dark, and though Kate moved with the grace of a cat, the boys stumbled trying to keep up. Perhaps they slowed Milligan's progress too much, for when they entered the room a few moments later, the flashlights were gone. The room lay black and still. It seemed quite empty except for a sharp, spicy fragrance that lingered in the air.

"I smell your cologne," Milligan said, speaking into the darkness.

"I hope you like it," said a man's voice. The flashlights snapped on behind them, casting their shadows onto the wall. "Now, please turn around. Turn around very slowly. Let's all stay nice and calm."

Milligan started to turn, but the terrified children, realizing they'd been tricked and not wanting to believe it, clutched at one another and did not move.

"That's a little *too* slow," said the voice. "Come on now. Let's have a look at you. Don't worry, we won't shine the lights in your eyes. I know that's uncomfortable."

Milligan pressed the children's shoulders and slowly turned them toward the voice. The man had spoken the truth — the flashlights were pointed downward — and in the glow cast by their beams Reynie could just make out who carried them. He didn't know what he had expected to see, but it wasn't this: two handsome men, one of them impressively tall, staring back at him with pleasant, welcoming expressions. The men wore tailored suits and large, expensive-looking silver watches, and over their suits they wore fine long raincoats that dripped water onto the floor. Both smiled in an unexpectedly friendly way. In fact, their bright smiles — along with their elegant appearance — were for an instant so surprising and disarming that Reynie almost relaxed. Almost. But then his eyes fell on a lumpy canvas bag in the shadows behind them. Out of the bag poked one of Constance's tiny feet.

"Did you really think we couldn't hear you coming?" asked the tall man. He spoke cheerfully, as if he and the children were sharing a joke. "Why, you're a herd of buffalo! Now raise your hands above your heads, please."

Reynie was frightened, but he couldn't see why they should obey. The men seemed to carry no weapons. But Milligan did as the man said — obviously he knew something Reynie didn't — and so with hearts galloping, Reynie and Kate let go of each other and raised their hands, too. Sticky, however, had grown confused in his fright and would not let go of Milligan's jacket.

"Please tell the bald boy to raise his hands," insisted the tall man.

"It's all right, Sticky," said Milligan. "Do as he says, child. Come now, let go."

At last Sticky managed to release his grip. The moment he did so — and to the great surprise of everyone present — Milligan leaped toward an open doorway and vanished from the room. He had moved so quickly, and so unexpectedly, that no one had a moment to react before he was gone. The men looked at each other and burst out laughing.

Reynie felt his mouth go dry. Sticky let out a whimper.

"Some protector!" laughed the shorter man. "I must say, he did a fine job protecting *himself*. I've never seen anyone move so fast."

The tall man chuckled. "Did he seem familiar to you at all?"

"Now that you mention it, he did," said the other, scratching his head. "Though I can't place how. Anyway, let's get this over with."

"What are you going to do with us?" Kate demanded. Though her legs trembled, her voice was defiant.

The tall man tucked his flashlight under his arm and held out both hands, palms forward, in what was meant to be a comforting gesture. "Now just stay calm," he soothed. Meanwhile the shorter man was doing exactly the same thing — tucking away his flashlight and holding out his hands. It was then that Reynie noticed that the men's huge silver watches were identical, and that for some reason they each wore *two* — one watch on each wrist.

"If you children stay nice and still," said the tall man, flashing a sympathetic smile, "I promise this won't hurt a bit."

"Oh, come on, let's tell the truth for once," said the other. "Just for kicks."

The tall man rolled his eyes. "All right, the truth is that this will hurt. A *lot*. But if you hold still," he said, shaking his arms to clear the watches from his suit cuffs, "I promise it won't hurt *long*."

Reynie felt Kate and Sticky stiffen beside him. They didn't know what was coming, but they knew it was going to be awful. The men started laughing again. Reynie heard an electrical hum. . . .

Abruptly, the laughter ceased. It was interrupted by two odd whistling sounds — *swit, swit* — upon which the tall man closed his eyes, dropped his flashlight with a clatter, and sank to the floor. The other did exactly the same, slumping unconscious on top of his partner. The flashlights, rolling free, sent their bright beams willy-nilly about the room.

One of the beams settled on the doorway behind the fallen men, where Milligan now stood holding a tranquilizer gun. He stepped over to pluck two tiny feathered darts from the men's shoulders, saying as he did so, "Remember, children. For every exit, there is also an entrance."

The dining room seemed an altogether different place now. The rain had let up, the drafts were gone, and bright sunlight streamed through the window. Yet the mood in the room was dark. On the table the children's breakfast lay just as they had left it — only an hour had passed since Reynie asked Milligan for tea and honey — but the teapot and honey jar might well have been props in a play, so unreal and insignificant did they seem now.

Everyone sat at the table except Constance, who was sitting on the floor. The men in the maze had given Constance quite a shock (an actual shock, delivered by way of wires that flicked like snakes' tongues from their watches, she'd said), and she remained somewhat addled. Her wispy blond hair stuck out in all directions like a small child's drawing of a sun, and her eyes seemed to roam about independently of each other. Moments before, she had walked in a circle around her chair — attempting without success to sit in it — then dropped to her bottom on the floor, where she said she believed she would sit for the time being.

Mr. Benedict was watching her with concern. "Are you sure she's all right, Rhonda? You examined her carefully?"

Rhonda nodded. "She'll feel better soon."

"Okay, who were those men?" Kate blurted out.

"Professional kidnappers," Mr. Benedict said. "Crafty fellows who work for the Sender. You'll recall he uses children to send his messages."

"So he *captures* them?" Kate said.

"He has subtler methods, too. But some children, yes, he captures. His scouts have an uncanny nose for vulnerable children. Don't worry, they've been deposited far from here and will be unconscious for quite some time, thanks to Milligan."

Number Two clucked her tongue. "If only Constance hadn't gone into the maze. Constance, why on earth did you decide to go down there, anyway?"

"I didn't *decide* to," Constance snapped. "I was trying to go down to the landing like Mr. Benedict told us to" — the boys looked at Kate, who acknowledged with a shrug that she'd been wrong — "but I tiptoed down one flight of steps too many. Then I heard someone behind me, so I went deeper into the maze to get away. But they found me," she said with a shiver. "They definitely found me."

Number Two patted her shoulder. "Don't worry, Connie, you're safe now."

"Don't call me Connie," she said crossly. She rose unsteadily from the floor and made another attempt at the chair. This time she managed to climb into it.

"I'm glad you're feeling better, Constance," said Mr. Benedict.

"But won't those men come back?" Reynie asked.

"It's possible," Mr. Benedict said. "Which is why we must work quickly. As it is, I'm hoping we can avoid detection long enough to launch our investigation."

"And if we can't?" said Constance, as if she rather expected failure.

"If we can't, child, all is lost!" Mr. Benedict cried. Instantly he looked regretful. In a softer tone he said, "I'm sorry to raise my voice. Failure in this instance is an upsetting prospect. Now, please, let me explain. These men intended to take you to a school called the Learning Institute for the Very Enlightened."

"I've heard of that place," Reynie said. "Some kids from the orphanage wanted to go there, but Mr. Rutger said it was against policy and wouldn't allow it."

"Doubtless it was, at least against *his* policy. Aside from being the orphanage director, Mr. Rutger is headmaster of your academy, is he not? I believe he gets paid per student."

"Even those with special tutors?" asked Reynie.

Mr. Benedict gave him a significant look.

Reynie was indignant. "So that's why he wouldn't send me

to an advanced school! He wanted me on the academy's rolls — just out of greed!"

"It's possible he thought it was in your best interest," Mr. Benedict said. "Greed often helps people think of reasons they might not discover on their own. At any rate, it *was* in your best interest not to go. The Institute will admit any child, but it is particularly fond of orphans and runaways. In fact, as you can see, such children are sometimes taken to the Institute whether they wish to go or not."

"The hidden messages are coming from the Institute, aren't they?" Reynie said.

"I believe the school was created for that very purpose," said Mr. Benedict. "Every so often the Sender must have new children, and the Institute receives a steady stream."

"I can't believe the Sender gets away with it," Sticky said.

"He's very cunning, Sticky. The Institute is a highly secretive, well-guarded facility — not the usual thing for a school, you know — yet it enjoys a wonderful reputation. The hidden messages have convinced everyone of the Institute's great virtue."

"There's an often-repeated phrase in the hidden messages," Rhonda explained. "*Dare not defy the Institute.* Obviously it's a kind of defense mechanism."

"Thus the Institute has completely escaped regulation," Mr. Benedict said. "It operates according to its own rules, without any interference."

"That's outrageous!" Kate exclaimed. "I can't believe no one goes looking for those kids!"

"I'm afraid runaways and orphans vanish even more easily than government agents do," said Mr. Benedict. "Lest you forget, 'The missing aren't missing, they're only departed.'"

The children looked at one another, appalled.

"I'm glad Milligan was here to protect us," Sticky said with a shudder. "The Institute is the last place I'd want to be."

At this, Mr. Benedict looked somewhat uncomfortable. He cleared his throat. "Yes, well, the scouts won't carry you to the Institute against your will, it's true. But to the Institute you must certainly go. You are to be my secret agents."

Codes and Histories

It took Kate Wetherall about three seconds to embrace her new role as a secret agent. While the other children gaped, blinked, and pinched themselves to be sure they weren't dreaming (actually, Constance pinched Sticky, who yelped and pinched her back) — in short, while the other children were adjusting to the news, Kate was peppering Mr. Benedict with questions: What was their mission to be? Would they need code names? Was it possible to use a somewhat *longish* code name?

Mr. Benedict waited until they'd all calmed down. Then

he explained their mission: how they were to be admitted to the Institute the following day, how he would draw up all the necessary papers, and how (much to Kate's disappointment) they would *not* be required to use code names. They must be themselves, Mr. Benedict said. They would have secrets enough to keep.

"What are we to do, exactly?" Sticky asked.

"Exactly what they want you to do," said Mr. Benedict. "Learn. You must be excellent students. One of the few things we know about the Institute is that certain privileges are granted only to top students. No doubt it is these children the Sender uses to send his hidden messages."

"So you're hoping we'll gain some secret knowledge," Reynie said.

"Indeed. How the Sender's messages accomplish such profound effects, what the particulars of his plan are — anything you uncover may help us find a way to defeat him."

"So that's it?" Sticky said. "You just want us to be students?"

"Much more than that," Mr. Benedict said. "For not only must you learn what they teach, you must also try to learn what they do *not* teach. Every odd detail, every suspicious aspect of the Institute — any unusual elements at all, you must report to me. You never know what curious tidbit might hold the key to the Sender's entire plan. Anything you notice may be of use."

Kate was rubbing her hands together. "So you want us to sneak around, maybe break into some offices, and —"

Mr. Benedict shook his head. "Absolutely not."

Kate stopped rubbing her hands. "No?"

"You must find out all you can," said Mr. Benedict sternly,

"and you must report it to me, but you must take no unneces-sary risks. Your mission is dangerous enough as it is."

Kate looked crestfallen. The other children looked re-lieved.

"Now then," Mr. Benedict went on, "we must communi-cate often — and in secret. For this we'll use Morse code."

"Morse code!" Reynie cried, amazed.

"*Nobody* uses Morse code anymore," said Kate.

"Precisely why it is useful to us," said Mr. Benedict. "As you may know, the Institute is located on Nomansan Island, which lies in Stonetown Harbor a half mile out. From a hid-den position on the mainland shore, we shall constantly watch the island. Every day and every night, at every moment, your signals will be watched for. It will be up to you to choose the safest time. We'll be ready for it."

"But we leave tomorrow, and we don't even *know* Morse code!" Constance complained.

"Actually, I do," said Sticky. "I can teach you, if you like."

Constance stuck her tongue out at him.

"You're all quick learners," said Mr. Benedict. "I have no worries about that. And Constance," he said, raising an eye-brow, "I advise you to take Sticky up on his offer. For this is an important point I wished to discuss: You are a team now. Whether you always agree is inconsequential, but you must take care of one another, must rely upon one another in all things. I don't exaggerate when I say that every one of you is essential to the success of the team, and indeed, to the fate of us all. You must remember that."

Constance rolled her eyes. "Okay, fine, George Washing-ton, you can teach me that stinky Morse code."

"Call me Sticky, please. Just plain Sticky is fine. You don't even have to use my last name."

"When do we begin, George Washington?"

Sticky scowled. "Don't *call* me that!"

Kate leaned over to Reynie and whispered, "I think we may have more trouble than Mr. Benedict expects."

It was suggested the children study Morse code in the dining room, but the afternoon was so beautiful, and the shady courtyard so inviting, they begged to pack lunches and study outside. Mr. Benedict agreed on the condition that no one venture beyond the gate, and that Milligan accompany them. So out they went into the courtyard, where Sticky and Constance now sat on a stone bench under the elm tree, while Kate and Reynie sprawled on the ivy-covered earth nearby. Milligan, disguised as a gray-haired gardener in a straw hat, puttered gloomily about the iron fence, tending to the rose bushes.

"It's a simple code," Sticky was explaining. "It uses dots and dashes — short signals and long signals — to stand for letters and numbers. The letter *A*, for example, is made with one short signal and one long signal, or a dot and a dash. Here, I'll show you." Borrowing Kate's flashlight (Kate had her bucket with her as always), Sticky turned it on and off again very quickly. "That was the short signal — the dot," he said. Then he turned it on for a full second. "And that's the long signal — the dash. Together they make an *A*, and the other letters are much the same. *B* is a dash and three dots, *C* is dash, dot, dash, dot, and so on. It's all written out right here," he said, pointing to the charts Mr. Benedict had given them.

"Let's practice," Sticky said. "Constance, you use the flashlight and the chart to spell out a message, and we'll figure out what you're saying."

Constance's hands were so small that she needed both of them to hold the flashlight, so Sticky held the chart up for her. Squinting at the paper in concentration, she flashed the light once very quickly, followed this with two longer flashes, then paused.

"Dot, dash, dash," Sticky said.

Kate referred to her chart and said, "That's a *W*, isn't it?"

Constance nodded and flashed the light again: four quick signals.

"Four dots," said Reynie. "That's an *H*."

Again Constance nodded, and in this way they proceeded through the rest of her message. As Mr. Benedict had remarked, they were all quick learners, but even so it took them some minutes, for everyone but Sticky had to keep checking the charts. Finally, though, Constance flashed the code for her last letter (dash, dot — an *N*), then looked expectantly at Sticky, who immediately began to fidget. The message had been: *Why did you run?*

"Hey, that's a good question," Kate said. "Why *did* you run away, Sticky?"

"It would take too long to answer in code," Sticky said. "Let's just practice with a different message, something short."

"Skip the code and tell us," Kate insisted. "If we're going to be a team, we should get to know each other better, don't you think, Reynie?"

"She's right," Reynie said. "It's best that we all know."

"I suppose so," Sticky said miserably. "But it isn't a very pleasant story to tell."

Nor was it a pleasant story to hear, and as Sticky told it, the children's faces grew long, so that they resembled miniature versions of Milligan (who had, in his silent way, drawn close to listen). It turned out that Sticky had once been quite content with his life — the agreeable child of agreeable parents — but the situation changed once his gifts became known.

This happened one April day when his mother (whose knees were arthritic, and whose wheelchair needed extra oiling in damp weather) wondered aloud, in a rare fit of irritation, why it had to rain so much. As Sticky helped his mother into her chair, he launched into a detailed explanation of weather systems and local geography. He'd always been a shy, silent child — this was the first time he'd given any hint of his considerable knowledge. His mother checked him for a fever.

That evening she told his father, who asked Sticky to repeat what he'd said before. Sticky did, word for word. His father had to sit down. Then he rose again, went into the den, and returned carrying several volumes of an outdated encyclopedia. Questioning Sticky together, the Washingtons discovered that their son, who was only seven at the time, carried more information inside his head than a college professor, perhaps *two* professors, with an engineer thrown in to boot. Astonished and proud, they could hardly have been more excited if they'd found buried treasure.

And in a way they had, for right away they began entering him in quiz competitions, which Sticky won easily. He took home substantial prizes: a new encyclopedia to replace the outdated one, a new writing desk, a cash prize, a savings bond. The more Sticky won, the more excited his parents grew. They encouraged him to study constantly, to read through their meals together, to stay up late reading, to stop wasting time with his friends. The pressure to win began to distract him. His parents grew angry when he missed questions — which he began to do more and more, as he tended to get mixed up when nervous — and scolded him for not caring about them. If Sticky cared, they said, he would try harder to win, since only by winning would he bring wealth and happiness to the family.

This came as a surprise to Sticky, who knew they'd never been wealthy but hadn't realized they were unhappy. And for him it was different — the more he won, the unhappier he became. But though he sometimes missed questions whose answers he knew, he still won the contests easily, gaining admission to bigger contests with bigger prizes, until at last his parents were perfectly dazzled by the prospect of fortune, and Sticky was perfectly exhausted. Despite complaining and even begging, however, he couldn't persuade them to let him stop. If he wanted to be rich and famous, they said, he must keep winning. When he replied that he didn't care to be rich and famous, they didn't believe him and said he was only being lazy.

Finally Sticky decided to make a point by pretending to run away. He left a note, then hid for several days in a cellar closet his parents thought was boarded up, but which Sticky had found a way to enter. From there he was able to venture forth to sneak food, use the bathroom, and do a little spying on his parents. At first he was pleased by what he saw: The Washingtons, extremely distressed, had raised an outcry about their lost son, seeking help from all quarters. But then something unfortunate happened. A rich man, himself a former quiz champion, heard of the case and gave a large sum of money to the Washingtons to aid their search. Word of his generosity quickly got around, which inspired other philanthropists — unwilling to be outdone — to send even *more* money; and before long people everywhere were sending gifts to the Washingtons, who were growing rich. To his great astonishment and mortification, Sticky saw his parents begin trying less and less to find him, instead devoting their time and energy toward the proper disposal of their newfound riches. At last, one day, when he managed to overhear his father saying something about being "better off now" — better off with him *gone*, Sticky realized — he could no longer bear their betrayal. He ran away for good.

"I'd been on my own for weeks," he concluded, removing his glasses to wipe away a tear, "when I saw Mr. Benedict's advertisement in the paper. That's my story. You all know the rest. Now can we get on with the practice?"

After a short, unhappy silence, the others agreed, and Constance took up the flashlight. Her message went more quickly this time; it was a single word: *sorry*. The others were taken aback. Even Milligan, who had retreated to his roses and seemed not to be paying attention, raised his eyebrows.

"That's okay," Sticky said.

"Aren't we a depressing bunch?" said Kate. "If we continue like this, we'll have to start calling it *remorse* code."

"What's remorse?" asked Constance.

"Feeling sad about something you did," said Reynie.

"Oh, do you feel sad, George Washington?" asked Constance.

Sticky twitched with irritation. "She was talking about *you*. And please don't call me that."

"I didn't call you 'that.' I called you George Washington.

Ask the others. They heard me. I definitely did not call you 'that,' George Washington."

Kate sighed and muttered, "So much for remorse."

"And what about Milligan?" Constance said. "Why is *he* so sad?"

All eyes went to their bodyguard, who had left off tending the roses and was oiling the gate hinges. He looked as if he could use an oiling himself — he moved quite creakily, and with a pronounced stoop, so that he truly seemed as old as he appeared in his disguise. He cast not a glance in their direction. Either he hadn't heard the question or else was pretending he hadn't. But Constance wouldn't let this pass.

"Milligan! Come tell us why you're so dreadfully glum!"

"Good grief," said Sticky, "do you have to drag out everybody's sad tales? Why don't you leave him in peace?"

She wouldn't listen, however, and after a few more stubborn requests, Milligan at last set down his oil can and shuffled over to them. "All right," he said in a resigned tone. "I'll tell you."

The children all sat up straight.

"Several years ago," Milligan began, "I awoke, blindfolded, in a hard metal chair. My hands and feet were cuffed together, a metal restraint held my head in place, and as I came awake, a man's voice said, 'This nut is a hard one to crack.' Indeed I felt I *had* been cracked — I had a ferocious headache, I was hungry and exhausted, and for some reason my fingers and toes were stinging. Worse: When I tried to recall where I was, and how I had come there, I found I couldn't."

"Amnesia?" Reynie said.

Milligan nodded. "Apparently I'd received a serious blow to the head. I could recall nothing at all — not my past, not my purpose, not even my name. To this day I have no memory of who I am."

"Then why did you say your name was Milligan?" Constance asked, almost accusingly, as if he'd lied to them.

"When I regained consciousness, it was the first name that flew into my mind. Perhaps it was in fact my name, but it didn't *feel* like my name, if you understand me. It seemed to apply to me somehow, and to be important, and so perhaps it is my name, but I'm afraid I'll never know."

"What happened next?" asked Kate.

"Well, next I heard the same voice say, 'Let's rouse him again. I grow weary of this one.' Then, shaking my arm, he said, in a very different, gentle tone, 'Wake up, my friend, wake up,' unaware I'd been awake long enough to have heard him discussing me like a cut of meat.

"Pretending to come awake, I said, 'What? Have I been asleep? Where am I?' To which he replied, 'You're safe; that's the important thing. We've rescued you from certain death and are here to help you. Now, is it true you remember nothing?'

"I didn't, of course, as I've told you. And apparently I had told the man this too. But as he now seemed to expect that answer and seemed intent on taking advantage of it somehow, I said, 'On the contrary. I remember everything perfectly.'

"The man cried, 'What? You're lying!'

"'Hardly,' I said. 'I'm sorry you find it so distressing.'

"Then the voice grew cunning and said, 'If you remember so clearly, tell me why you are here.'

"'I believe I'll leave the telling to you,' I replied.

"'The sneak! You're lying to us, you dirty —' the man

shouted, and then, strangely, all was silent, as if someone had clapped a hand over his mouth.

"After a while I said, 'Dirty *what*? Please tell me — the suspense is killing me.'

"The voice returned, much calmer now. 'It won't be suspense that does it,' he said. 'If you don't crack tomorrow, we'll toss you into the harbor.'

"'Well, I'm sure I would infinitely prefer that fate to the smell of your breath,' I replied, upon which he struck me hard across the face and ordered me taken from the room.

"As it happened, that blow did me a good turn, for it loosened the blindfold. I had only just left the room when the blindfold began to slip, and though my captors didn't realize it, I could soon see fairly well. Two men in suits were leading me along a stone passage. They moved slowly to accommodate my pace, which was hampered by my chain-cuffed ankles. As we walked, I studied my hands, still cuffed in front of me, and became aware that one was clutching something. Wonderingly I opened my fist, noticing as I did so that my fingernails had been bitten beyond the quick, so that my fingertips were raw. (This explained why they stung, and judging from the pain in my toes, my toenails had been bitten off as well.) In my hand I discovered a tiny device, rather like a twisted hairpin. To my great surprise I realized it had been fashioned from my fingernails and toenails. All this I must have done myself, but I had no memory of it.

"Imagine then how amazed I was to discover that I knew what the little device was for. I slipped it into the lock of my handcuffs (my fingers seemed to know what they were doing, though I did not), and just as we came to a stairway, I heard the lock spring — I'd picked it in less than a minute. Before they knew I was free, I had knelt down and cuffed the men's ankles together. Then I hopped out of reach, and my captors, trying to pursue, fell on their faces. Before they could regain their feet, I had picked the locks on the ankle cuffs, snapped them onto the men's wrists, and bounded down the stairs.

"After that, my getaway was fairly simple. I broke out into the darkness of a rainy night. I was pursued, of course, but I made my way through a hilly terrain until I came to a cliff overlooking the harbor. The water looked shallow and lay about a hundred feet below me, but as I had no other choice, I dove straightaway. There followed some troublesome business of swimming to the mainland while pursuers in boats tried to capture me with nets and hooks, that sort of thing. But I proved a good swimmer, and the rocks in the channel are terrible for boats. In the end I escaped."

All of this had been spoken softly, without the least trace of excitement or drama in Milligan's voice. But the children, listening, could hardly contain themselves, and when he'd finished, they burst forth with questions: How had he come here? What was he doing on Nomansan Island in the first place? It *was* Nomansan Island, wasn't it? And those men in suits . . .

"Yes, it was the same men, the ones you saw in the maze. They weren't sure where they know me from, but I certainly remember them. And yes, it was Nomansan Island — it was the Institute — that I escaped from. Why I was there I can't say, but Mr. Benedict is convinced I was a secret agent, an employee of a government agency long since dismantled. I have no way of telling."

"Maybe Mr. Benedict can find out," Reynie said.

"It was that hope that led me to him," Milligan admitted.

"I'd spent months seeking information about my past, but no one believed my story, and no one had any answers. Finally I learned about a man worth meeting — not a government agent himself, but a brilliant man of mysterious purposes who always seemed to know more about everything than anyone else did. This, of course, was Mr. Benedict. But though he's helped me make sense of what's happened, and has earned my loyalty, the entire business is so extraordinarily secretive and complicated that I've long been convinced I will never learn anything about my past."

"How awful," said Reynie.

"Yes, it's too bad," said Sticky, though not quite convincingly, for at the moment he rather wished he couldn't remember his own past, given the grief it brought him.

"Hey, does your amnesia have something to do with your silly disguises?" Constance asked.

Milligan clamped his straw hat more tightly on his head. "My 'silly' disguises are useful for other reasons, but yes, Constance, it would be unfortunate if some enemy from my past recognized me, but I couldn't recognize him. It's better never to be recognized at all."

"So there's really no hope your memory will return?" Kate asked.

"Oh, I suppose there's some *slight* hope. Mr. Benedict has tried hypnosis and other treatments on me, all without luck. Still, he says it's possible some significant event, or the appearance of an important object or person from my past, or some other unknown thing, might break down the door and let my memories out. I'm afraid, however, that I'm not much given to hope anymore."

"If not for hope, what keeps you going?" asked Reynie,

who had an ugly suspicion that there might come a time, and not so far away, when things would seem hopeless to *him*, too.

"Duty," said Milligan. "Nothing else, only a sense of duty. I know the Sender is out to do harm. I feel obliged to stop him. Or at the very least, to try."

"And do you think we can?" Reynie asked. "Do you think he can be stopped?"

In response Milligan only went back to his oil can. He did not look at the children again.

When the children had studied Morse code until dots and dashes swam in their heads even with their eyes closed, Rhonda called them inside. It was early evening now, the light in the dining room window was a soft amber color, and all through the house the wooden floors, curiously enough, groaned and creaked like a ship at sea.

"That happens sometimes after a morning rain," said Rhonda as the children took seats at the table. "Don't worry, it's a sound old house — we won't sink." She set several pages of notes before each of them. "Now that you understand your mission and have a good start on your Morse code, Mr. Benedict would like for you to understand better what we're up against."

The children's ears perked up. There was more? Reynie began to flip through his papers, some of which bore faint smears of peanut butter.

"Number Two has summarized everything in these notes," Rhonda said. "If you read quickly, you should be able to finish before supper. Mr. Benedict will come by in a little while to answer any questions."

"He wants us to read *all* of this?" Constance said, as if she couldn't believe Mr. Benedict's nerve.

Rhonda only smiled and went out.

The children — all except Constance, who was too busy humphing — set to their notes. Sticky read so quickly that he seemed hardly to have started before he'd finished. He sat quietly, deep in thought, waiting for the others. Ten minutes later, Reynie had finished, too, and Kate, noting this, set aside her last few pages and asked the boys to fill her in.

What the children learned from the notes was this: The Institute on Nomansan Island generated all its own electricity using the power of the tides — an endless source of energy. The Institute's tidal turbines were considered the best in the entire world; they were also capable of producing enough energy to power a *hundred* Institutes, let alone one.

These turbines had been invented by a man named Ledroptha Curtain, who, as a young scientist, had published impressive papers on a wide variety of topics — everything from tidal energy to mapping the brain — until abruptly the papers stopped. No one heard from him for many years.

Then one day he reappeared and founded the Institute, apparently having turned his genius to matters of education.

There was no doubt: Ledroptha Curtain was the Sender. And yet about certain things there was quite a lot of doubt indeed. For instance, the hidden messages being sent from the Institute were broadcast only a few times each day, and on a very weak signal. But the tidal turbines should be able to produce an enormous amount of energy, much more than necessary to power the Institute — and certainly enough to transmit the Sender's messages on a high-powered signal rather than a weak one. Why, then, had Curtain made his turbines so extravagant if he didn't intend to use that extra power? And why did he send out his messages intermittently when he could be broadcasting around the clock?

"He's been saving it up," Reynie said, narrowing his eyes. "It's what Mr. Benedict was trying to explain this morning. There's something bad approaching. Some *new* thing —"

"The thing to come," said Mr. Benedict, who had appeared in the doorway. With a nod of approval he joined them at the table, accompanied by Number Two. "It sounds as if you've finished the notes. I know they're complicated — do you have questions about them?"

"I think I understand them pretty well," said Constance. (The others looked at one another in disbelief.) "Right now, the hidden messages are sent at low power, several times a day, by the Sender — a man named Ledroptha Curtain. But his tidal turbines are extremely powerful, so it sounds like at some point he's going to start boosting the strength of his messages."

"Bravo, Constance!" Mr. Benedict said. "Well done!"

The other children scowled.

"Well done, *all* of you," Mr. Benedict added, with a wink that made them feel a bit better. "Now, then, do you have other questions?"

"I do," said Kate. "What happens when the Sender boosts the power?"

"We know only one thing for certain," said Mr. Benedict. "With just a very slight increase, the Sender will eliminate the need for televisions or radios to transmit his messages — he'll be able to broadcast his messages straight into everyone's minds. Even those of us with an uncommon love of truth will no longer be able to avoid the broadcasts."

Sticky looked horrified. "How . . . how will that *feel*?"

"Don't tell me we'll hear those kids' voices in our heads," Kate said, a disgusted look on her face.

"In rare cases, perhaps," said Mr. Benedict, "with exceptionally sensitive minds. But most of us will simply feel irritable and confused — essentially the way we feel now whenever the television is on and the messages are being broadcast."

"You said 'with a very slight increase,'" said Reynie. "What happens when the power gets boosted all the way — when the messages are sent at full strength?"

Mr. Benedict tapped his nose. "*That* is when we'll hear voices in our heads. I can't imagine it will be pleasant."

"It sounds awful," Kate said, her lip curling at the very thought. "So why does he want us all to think we're crazy?"

A shadow had crossed Reynie's face. "That's *not* what he wants, is it, Mr. Benedict? At least not the main thing. Otherwise what's the point of waiting?"

"Okay, now I'm confused," said Kate, and the other children signaled their agreement.

"I believe Reynie is wondering," said Mr. Benedict, "why the Sender would wait all this time to boost the power if he could have done so years ago. Am I right?"

Reynie nodded.

"I agree," Mr. Benedict said. "The voices aren't the point. They are the side effect, the unintended consequence of a dark and ambitious undertaking. The Sender has spent all these years preparing people for something — preparing them for the thing to come."

"But what *is* the thing to come?" said Constance.

"That is precisely what we must find out," said Mr. Benedict, "before it is too late."

"And if we *are* too late?" asked Sticky nervously. "Will it really be that bad?"

Mr. Benedict grew solemn. "For us, and for all the people like us — all those whose minds cleave so strongly to the truth — I am convinced it will be . . . most disagreeable. You must understand that the Sender has not gone to such enormous trouble — for so many years, and at such extravagant expense — to allow any interference with his plans. He has already shown himself to be quite ruthless. No, children, I believe that by virtue of our minds' resistance, we shall — how to put it? — I believe we shall receive special attention."

At these words a black cloud of possibility bloomed in the children's minds, a darkness in which scary thoughts flickered like bolts of lightning.

Special attention.

Their mouths went dry as bones.

Reynie's mind was awhirl. Part of him wanted *not* to believe Mr. Benedict. Could he really be trusted? He was an odd man, and the things he told them were odder still. It would be such a relief to think his predictions about the thing to come were nothing more than wild speculation. And yet Reynie did trust Mr. Benedict, had trusted him almost immediately. What troubled Reynie was that he so badly *wanted* to trust Mr. Benedict — wanted to believe in this man who had shown faith in him, wanted to stay with these children who seemed to like and respect Reynie as much as he did them.

And so the question was not whether Reynie could trust Mr. Benedict, but whether he could trust himself. Who in his right mind would actually want to be put in danger just because that let him be a part of something?

Reynie didn't know. He only knew he didn't want to go back.

the NAMING of the CREW

Kate Wetherall

Reynie Muldoon

Sticky Washington

Constance Contraire

In preparation for the children's departure, Mr. Benedict told them, there was much necessary information to be gathered, and paperwork to be completed, and signatures to be forged, and orders to be given, and fees to be paid, and phone calls to be made. Except for their brief meeting with the children, Number Two had not left her computer, nor Mr. Benedict his desk, for hours. And since Milligan was standing guard, and Rhonda herself was too busy to do more than bring their supper and excuse herself, the children dined alone.

Afterward Reynie and Kate went into the sitting room to practice their Morse code. Despite their urging, however, Constance crabbily refused to join them. Instead, while Sticky helped them practice, she composed a poem about a bunch of bossy gargoyles who liked to eat cat food and pick their ears. It was an unpleasant poem, and the gargoyles' names, not very cleverly disguised, were Kateena, Reynardo, and Georgette. After reciting this to the others, Constance went straight to bed without brushing her teeth or saying good night.

In truth this came as a relief to the other children, who were already more than tired of Constance's ways, and who gathered in the boys' room to discuss this very concern. She had tried their patience all evening — indeed, ever since they'd met her — and the prospect of her joining them on a dangerous mission had them worried.

"We simply can't do it," Kate said for the tenth time. She was hanging upside down from the top bunk to see if her hair would touch the floor, but her golden-blond locks came three inches shy, as she had suspected. "She's nothing but a burden. She's cranky, she's not especially bright as far as I can see, and she's probably the clumsiest kid I've ever met — she's always dropping things, and she walks like a landlubber on a ship. How are we supposed to succeed with someone like that on our team?"

"Kate's right," said Sticky, looking up from a geology book. "Constance will only make things harder."

"I feel the same way," Reynie admitted. "But doesn't it seem strange that Mr. Benedict would let her join us if she wasn't important?"

"He may be a genius, but even geniuses make mistakes," said Kate, whose face had gone red as a tomato. She dropped backward off the bunk, flipping in the air to land on her feet, and casually pulled her hair back into a ponytail. "Maybe he feels sorry for her."

"Maybe he does," Reynie said, "but surely he wouldn't let his feelings spoil the mission. He must have good reasons for including her."

"There's only one way to find out," Kate said. "You have to go talk to him."

"I do? Why me?"

"Because you're the only one who can do it. If Sticky goes, he'll just mumble and wipe his glasses. If I go, I'll end up complaining about her, as I've been doing for the last half-hour. For instance, did you see the way she sneaked a bite of my pie at dinner? And it was the only dessert we had all day!"

"It's true," Sticky said, finishing his book and thumping it closed. "I'll get tongue-tied, and Kate will get steamed. It has to be you, Reynie."

And so, a few minutes later, it was Reynie who knocked on the study door.

"Come in, Reynie," said Mr. Benedict. As before, Reynie found him on the floor, this time with a half-eaten biscuit in one hand, a graph of some kind in the other, and biscuit crumbs on his green suit jacket. "I was just taking a late supper. Would you care for a biscuit? There's another on my desk, though I'm afraid it's cold — I was so intent upon my work I forgot to eat until now."

"No, thank you," Reynie said. Even if he'd been hungry he couldn't have eaten a bite — he felt very ill at ease. It didn't seem quite decent to complain about Constance, nor did he like the thought of expressing doubt in Mr. Benedict, whom he liked very much. But it must be done, and he was preparing himself to begin when Mr. Benedict said, "I assume you've come about Constance."

Reynie swallowed and nodded.

"And that you speak not only for yourself, but for Sticky and Kate as well?"

Perhaps some day, Reynie thought, he would get used to Mr. Benedict's always knowing what was on his mind.

"I understand completely," said Mr. Benedict. "And if we had time, I should be happy to explain my choices to you in great detail. But as we do not, allow me to assure you that Constance is far more gifted than she seems, and that it is not from pity, blindness, or rash hopefulness that I include her in this mission. On the contrary, I believe she may be the very key to our success."

"If that's true, then I suppose she's worth the trouble."

"Sometimes, Reynie, trouble itself is the key."

"Sir?"

"I daresay you'll understand me in time. Now, listen, it's true I have a certain sympathy for Constance. Like her, and like yourself, I grew up an orphan, and I know what it is to feel miserable and alone. However —"

"You're an orphan?"

"Certainly. My parents were Dutch scientists, killed in a laboratory accident when I was a baby. I was sent to this country to live with my aunt, but she, too, died, and so into an orphanage I went. However, what I intended to say was that while I sympathize with Constance, it is not from sympathy I include her, no more than it is from sympathy I include you or anyone else. Fair enough?"

"I believe so."

"Very well, then, will you do me a great favor? Will you tell your friends what I've said and return to give me their verdict? If anyone should choose not to go on, I had better know at once."

The sense of urgency was apparent in Mr. Benedict's tone, and Reynie lost no time hurrying back to relate his answer to Sticky and Kate, who sat cross-legged on the floor, thumb-wrestling to pass the time. They weren't happy about the news, but neither were they inclined to quit, so Reynie left them to their thumb-wrestling and hurried back to Mr. Benedict's study. He was about to knock on the door when he heard voices inside. He hesitated, not wanting to interrupt.

"I can't stand it!" Mr. Benedict was saying. "I can't *stand* putting them in danger! It goes against everything I believe in."

"I know," came the reply, and Reynie recognized the voice of Number Two. "I know, Mr. Benedict, we all feel that way. But if they don't go, then it's over — the curtain falls. You said so yourself. We have no choice. Now please calm yourself before —"

Mr. Benedict said something Reynie could not make out, but it was clearly an expression of anguish, or perhaps fury, and then Number Two was saying, "Oh dear. And with a mouthful of biscuit, too. Wake up, dear Benedict" — there was a patting sound — "wake up, or I fear you may choke."

After a moment came a snorting noise, then a cough, and then Mr. Benedict said, "Ah. Was I very long gone?"

"Only a moment," said Number Two gently.

"Good, good. Thank you for your commiserations, my friend, and now you'd best be off, back to your confounded computer. I'm sorry to work you so."

"I know as well as you that it must be done. Just let me water this violet, for the sake of my conscience, and then I'm off. Poor thing, it's on the edge of death."

"I know, I've neglected it shamefully, I've hardly had a moment. Thank you, Number Two. Now go on and take that biscuit — no use protesting, I saw you staring at it — and if you pass our young hero in the hall, please tell him to walk straight in."

Reynie's heart fluttered. Hero? Was Mr. Benedict referring to *him*?

"He's an extraordinary child, isn't he?" said Number Two, her speech somewhat hindered by a mouthful of biscuit.

"Indeed he is. They all are, which is why I so despise the thought — however, I won't go on and on. Mustn't drop off to sleep again; it will take us all night as it is. Shall we meet at midnight to see how things stand?"

"Midnight it is. I'll tell Rhonda," said Number Two, flinging open the door. "Why, Reynie! Speak of the devil, Mr. Benedict, here he is. Go on in, child, I must rush off."

Reynie stepped inside. "Everybody chooses to continue, Mr. Benedict. We'll do our best to get along with Constance."

"I'm glad to hear it, and I have no doubt you will, Reynie," said Mr. Benedict, his eyes already returning to the graph in his hand. "Thank you, indeed. Now you'd best get some sleep. Difficult day ahead of you tomorrow."

Reynie hesitated. "Sir, if I can't sleep, may I come back here? I promise I won't bother you. I'll be very quiet. It's just that my nerves are all jumping."

"Say no more, Reynie," said Mr. Benedict, who had begun calculating a figure on the graph with one hand and taking notes in a tablet with the other, as if neither required more concentration than pulling on socks. "My study is your study. Come in whenever you wish."

Reynie nodded, put his hand on the doorknob, and again hesitated. "Mr. Benedict?"

"Hmm? What is it, Reynie?"

"I wanted to say thank you, sir."

Mr. Benedict looked up. "*Thank* me? Whatever for?"

"Just — just thank you, sir. That's all."

Mr. Benedict gave him a long, puzzled stare. Finally, with a shrug, a shake of his head, and an affectionate smile, he said, "Reynie, my good young friend, you are most entirely welcome."

Early in the morning, before the sun had thrown its first ray or the redbirds chirped their first note, all four children were gathered in the boys' bedroom. Too anxious to sleep, they had risen almost magically at the same time and sought each other out. Now they sat cross-legged or sprawled on the floor, speaking in hushed voices. The house was quiet, but they weren't the only ones awake. Beyond their own voices they could hear, drifting down the drafty halls, a frenetic, muted tapping — the sleepless Number Two on her computer keyboard — and from somewhere above them the occasional creak of a floorboard.

The children were engaged in a whispered debate. It had been decided they should have a name. This had been Kate Wetherall's idea, of course, but everyone agreed, even Constance. If they were to go on a secret mission to a place where they would be entirely alone among strangers, if they must absolutely depend upon one another as fellow agents and friends — if, in short, they were to be a *team* — they must certainly have a name. And so they had set about choosing what to call themselves.

"I was thinking something like 'The Great Kate Weather Machine and her Stormy Companions,'" said Kate. "It kind of plays on a weather theme."

Her suggestion was greeted by general silence and, from Constance, a stormy look indeed. After a pause Kate said, "Well, does anyone *else* have an idea?"

"How about 'The Four Kids Gang'?" offered Sticky. "Or 'The Secret Agent Children Group'?"

Constance's storm-cloud scowl, if possible, grew even darker; Reynie cleared his throat; and Kate said, "Um, Sticky? Those have to be the most absolutely *yawn*-causing names I've ever heard."

"But they're accurate," argued Sticky, looking hopefully at Reynie, but Reynie only shook his head.

"If we're just trying to be accurate, then how about 'The Doomed to Fail Bunch'?" said Constance. "Honestly! We can't even *name* ourselves."

"Listen," said Reynie, ignoring her. "What is it that drew us all together? Maybe we should start there."

"Mr. Benedict," said Kate and Sticky at the same time.

"All right, how about something with his name in it, to remind us of our mission?"

"'Mr. Benedict's Very Secret Team'?" said Sticky.

Everyone groaned.

Kate said, "How about 'Mr. Benedict and the Great Kate Weath —'"

"Don't even finish that," said Reynie.

"The Mysterious Benedict Society," Constance said, rising as she spoke. Then she left the room, apparently convinced that no more discussion was necessary.

And, as it turned out, she was right.

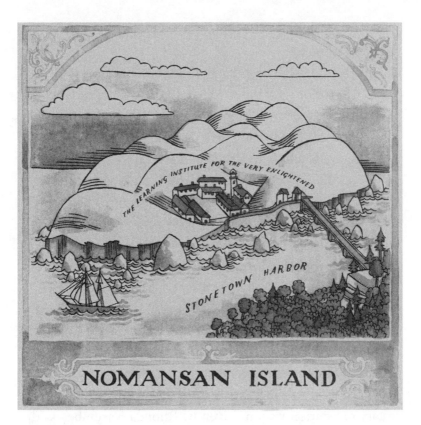

NOMANSAN ISLAND

Stonetown Harbor had always been a busy port: ships steaming in and weighing anchor at all hours, countless stevedores and sailors as busy as ants, and the docks piled high with cargo. All of this activity occurred in the shadow of Stonetown itself, a city that existed for the sake of its port, and which had grown so large and busy because of it. Near the harbor's southern slope, however, lay a channel of treacherous shoals, studded here and there with great boulders that still bore the scars of ancient shipwrecks, and as a consequence this southern part of the harbor was always quite still.

It was here, among these ship-scarred rocks, that Nomansan Island was found.

The island's shore was jagged rock itself, with only the occasional spot of sand upon which a boat might land; yet the captain of any craft attempting to land there must be very brave or foolish, for the currents in the surrounding water were unpredictable, and the shallows famously difficult to navigate. The only practical approach to Nomansan Island was by the long, narrow bridge that ran from its bank to the mainland's wooded shore a half mile away. The city had not developed along this part of the shore, but had grown northward along the inland river, leaving a few acres of woods untouched. (One day, no doubt, the woods would be noticed — like a nagging itch — and quickly chopped down, but for now they remained.) It was through these woods, and toward this bridge, that the members of the newly formed Mysterious Benedict Society were headed.

They were moving swiftly upon a seldom-used road, in a weary old station wagon driven by Rhonda Kazembe. As the car passed beneath the trees, Reynie noticed the first colors of autumn in their overhanging branches. The outer leaves were going red, yellow, and orange, while the inner ones still held the deep green of summer, so that the trees appeared candy-coated. A lovely sight, but Reynie was unable to enjoy it. His companions felt much the same. Within minutes they would be admitted to the Learning Institute for the Very Enlightened, and they were apprehensive. The closer they came to the island, the more real the danger felt.

Rhonda was pointing through the trees toward the mainland shore. "Our telescopes will be hidden there in the brush," she said. "We'll be setting them up right after I drop you off, and from then on we'll attend them at all times. If you stand anywhere on this side of the island, we should be able to see you through the telescopes as if you were two feet away. Whenever you have something to report, we'll be ready for it. And if *we* have anything to tell *you*, we'll send a message in return. It's up to you to find the safest time to communicate. Most likely it will be after dark, when the others are asleep.

"Even then," Rhonda added, "there's always the slight chance our messages to you will be observed from the island. For this reason they must necessarily be cryptic —"

"What's cryptic?" cried a shrill voice from the backseat.

"I'm sorry, Constance. By cryptic I mean vague or mysterious. We won't ever use names, and will never give obvious directions except in case of emergency. In most cases we'll rely on your ability to figure out what we mean. It's more difficult this way, but we must take precautions for your safety. Even with precautions, your situation will be extremely dangerous."

With the words "extremely dangerous" fresh in the children's ears, the car rattled out of the woods into plain view of Nomansan Island. And there, on the island's near side, was the Institute: an arrangement of massive gray buildings, a broad plaza, and a slender tower that resembled a lighthouse, all of which appeared to be built entirely of island stone. From this distance the Institute blended so thoroughly into Nomansan's stony crags it seemed a part of the island itself. Behind it and on either side rose up steep hills, and beyond the hills could be seen the peaks of still more hills, and beyond those still more. A flagpole jutted from the side of the Institute's tower, supporting a long red banner that rippled in the breeze. Printed upon the banner, in letters large enough to be read from the mainland, was the word LIVE —

an acronym, obviously, for the Learning Institute for the Very Enlightened.

"At least it doesn't say *die*," Kate mused.

"Oh, yes, very encouraging," said Sticky, whose forehead had begun to sweat.

Reynie stared out the window at the approaching bridge. To cross it, they had to first check in at a guard house, and Reynie was nervous despite Mr. Benedict's assurances. New students were admitted all the time, and Mr. Benedict had made every arrangement, had followed every proper procedure, but still. . . . It was normal to feel nervous, Mr. Benedict had said. All children get nervous on their first day at a new school, and all secret agents get nervous on the first day of a mission. Combine the two and your chances of nervousness are greatly increased.

At the bridge entrance two people stepped out of a guard house and waved the car to a stop.

"Steady now," said Rhonda in an undertone. "Nothing to worry about yet."

The guards were a young man and woman wearing sunglasses, smiles, and expensive suits, with well-polished shoes that gleamed in the morning sun. As the woman motioned for Rhonda to roll down the window, no one could help but notice the huge silver watches on her wrists. Reynie squeezed the armrest.

"May I help you?" asked the woman, peering in. A sweet, citrusy perfume drifted through the window. The woman was all smiles, the picture of friendliness. The other guard also smiled, but Reynie could tell he was studying them with great attention.

"These are your new students," Rhonda said. "Three

transferring from Binnud Academy and one from Stonetown Orphanage."

"Wait here, please." The woman stepped back into the guard house. The other guard stayed put. He cocked his head to hear something the woman was telling him, but he kept his eyes on the car.

"Steady," Rhonda intoned again, just loud enough for the children to hear. But Reynie noticed that — ever so subtly — she had shifted the car into reverse. Just in case.

Reynie took a deep breath and held it. He hoped his friends remembered their stories. His own was easy enough, since it was the truth: Mr. Rutger, properly persuaded, had made a special exception in his case. The others, though, were from a special temporary school for orphans called Binnud Academy. That morning, as they'd said their good-byes over breakfast, Mr. Benedict had pointed out that if they said "Binnud Academy" aloud, it would remind them his thoughts were with them always.

"As are mine," Number Two had said. Distracted by emotion, she was drying her eyes with a slice of bread. "My thoughts and all my prayers."

All of the adults had seemed especially bleary, exhausted, and sad — except Milligan, who always looked that way — yet even so, there was a flicker of excitement, indeed of hope, in every eye.

"Go now, children," Mr. Benedict had said, "go and show them what you're made of."

At this moment Reynie felt sure they were made of jitterbugs. His knees trembled, and he could barely keep his teeth from chattering. Sticky was scrubbing his glasses so hard they squeaked, and Constance had her eyes squeezed tightly shut, unconvincingly feigning sleep. Even Kate squirmed a little. The guard seemed to be taking an awfully long time.

When she finally came out, her smile hadn't faded in the least. Reynie just had time to wonder whether this meant she did or did *not* have something to hide . . . and then she was at the car, saying, "Welcome, kids! You're all clear and right on time. Please drive across to the island gate. I'll radio for them to let you in."

As Rhonda rolled the window up and put the gear in forward again, all four children released deep breaths. Then they passed over the long bridge toward their fate.

After their suitcases had been unloaded from the station wagon, and Rhonda had signed a form and bidden them farewell, the children were left to wait in a loading area by the bridge gate. Their escorts would collect them shortly, the gate guards said. In the meantime they were to step aside, please, as this was a busy area and not the sort of place for children to be underfoot. Workers in white uniforms were hauling crates from a nearby storage shed and loading them into a big truck. And they did indeed seem very busy, tirelessly loading and stacking until it made your back hurt just to watch them.

The children moved off to the side of the loading area, dragging their suitcases behind them. (Rhonda had packed changes of clothes for each of them, including outfits she had sewn overnight to fit Constance's diminutive size.) They hadn't much to do or look at to occupy themselves, even though they very much wanted to be occupied to take their minds off their nervousness. There was only the guard house, the storage shed, and the loading area — all of which were apparently off limits — and a stone wall that blocked their view of the harbor. After twiddling their thumbs a few minutes, the children stacked their suitcases and took turns standing on them to peek over the wall. (Constance required all four suitcases; the others managed with two.)

They were interested to discover some activity beneath the bridge — more workers in white uniforms, navigating a boat among the pilings. The workers carried oversized wrenches, cranks, and other tools, and were using them to make adjustments on some unseen apparatus beneath the water's surface. Like the workers loading the crates into the truck, those in the boats seemed earnestly intent upon their work. They spoke but rarely, and then in quiet tones, as if they held some great reverence for the task set before them.

Must be the turbines, Reynie thought, climbing down from the suitcases. Sticky and Kate had come to the same conclusion, but Constance wondered aloud what in the world those people could possibly be doing down there. Were they trying to fix the *water*?

Reynie wasn't sure whether or not Constance was joking. He had started to answer, regardless, when his voice was drowned out by the rumbling of an engine. The workers had finished loading the big truck. Two men in suits had climbed into the front, and as the gate opened for them, they waved cheerfully to the children and drove away over the bridge.

"Did you see that?" Constance cried. "They're wearing those shock-watches! The bridge guards, too. Have you noticed?"

"Lower your voice," Kate hissed. "Are you crazy? Of course we've noticed."

Constance was indignant, but there was no time for a

full-blown argument to develop, for just then the children's escorts arrived.

The escorts were dressed identically in blue pants, snappy white tunics, and blue sashes, but they could never be mistaken for each other. One was a stocky, red-haired young man with icy blue eyes and a nose so skinny and sharp it resembled a knife. The other was a powerfully built young woman with a greasy brown ponytail and small, piggish eyes of an indeterminate color. They introduced themselves as Jackson and Jillson.

Reynie extended his hand. "My name's —"

"There'll be time for that," Jillson said, turning away. "Let's get moving. We'll take you to your rooms first so you can dump your luggage."

Surprised, Reynie lowered his hand. He knew it was Jillson who had been rude (she and Jackson hadn't offered to help with their suitcases, either), but he still felt foolish.

"*She's* a nice one, isn't she?" Kate whispered.

The children were led up a long gravel path toward the Institute buildings. They crossed the broad stone plaza, then a modest rock garden, then waited as Constance shook the gravel from her shoes. At last they were taken into the student dormitory, where, since the girls' room lay at one end of a long stone corridor and the boys' at the other, they were forced to separate.

Reynie and Sticky's room, aside from being very clean and tidy, was rather what they would have expected: bunk beds, two desks and chairs (but no bookshelves), a wardrobe, a radiator, a large television cabinet (well, *that* was unexpected), and a window overlooking the plaza. Reynie went to the window. Beyond the plaza lay the glittering channel, brilliant in the sunlight and choppy with white-capped waves, and beyond that the wooded shore, where Mr. Benedict's telescopes were going to be hidden. The children could send their Morse code messages from this very window. Reynie's stomach fluttered. His mind might understand he was a secret agent now, but his body still had a hard time believing it.

Jackson leaned against the doorjamb. "If you need anything, ask an Executive. You can always tell an Executive by the uniform — blue pants, white tunic, blue sash. The Executives run the show here. A lot of us are former students who did so well as Messengers that Mr. Curtain hired us on. Don't get us confused with Messengers, though. Messengers wear tunics and a sash, too, but their pants are striped. They're just students like yourselves, only they're top of the class and have special privileges. *Secret* privileges, I might add. Anyway, you'll learn all about this soon enough. Right now just get yourselves unpacked, watch some TV if you want." He switched the television on for them. "You'll have your orientation tour in an hour. Then you'll meet Mr. Curtain."

"Who's Mr. Curtain?" said Reynie, who thought it best to give the impression of knowing as little as possible. The less you knew, the less people suspected of you — and perhaps the more they told you.

Jackson sneered, then forced the sneer into a smile. He looked like a red-headed crocodile. "I keep forgetting how ignorant you kids are when you get here. Mr. Curtain's my boss. He's the founder of the Institute, the reason we're all here. Got it?" It was clear Jackson was the sort of young man who considers himself rather smarter than he is, and who is naturally cruel but thinks himself a decent fellow. When the smaller boys didn't answer him quickly enough, he snapped, "Do you understand me or don't you? You speak English, right?"

The boys nodded.

"Good. I'll see you in an hour."

When Jackson had gone, Sticky switched off the television. "Did you hear that? *Messengers*. We know what that means, don't we?"

"We'd better find the girls," Reynie said.

"We're right here," said a muffled voice from above them. A ceiling panel slid aside, and Kate Wetherall's head appeared through the gap. "There aren't any support beams over your bunk bed, so one of you move that chair over, will you? I'm going to lower Constance down. What are you *doing*, anyway?"

The boys had been on edge already, but at the sound of an unexpected voice directly overhead, Reynie had thrown up his hands as if to ward off a blow, and Sticky had tried, unsuccessfully, to hide behind his suitcase. With a sheepish grin Reynie slid a chair under the gap. A moment later Constance's tiny feet appeared, then the rest of her body, as Kate, hanging by her legs from a beam, lowered her carefully to the chair. The boys helped her to the floor while Kate secured her rope to the beam and climbed down to join them.

"Don't bother thanking me," she said to Constance, who was scowling and brushing insulation from her clothes.

"Why should I thank you? You drag me up into the ceiling, through a heating vent, crawling through spider webs in the dark, across all these hard boards saying, 'Don't put your knee there! You'll fall through and break your neck!' and 'Don't breathe so loudly! Someone will hear you!' until my heart's in my throat and my knees are killing me, and you expect me to thank you?"

"Not at all," said Kate. "I was happy to do it."

Constance's eyes seemed ready to pop from her head.

"Did you ever consider just walking down the corridor?" Sticky asked.

"I figured we'd better have a hidden entrance," she replied, "in case we want to meet secretly. I'll bet those Executives are always patroling the place. I don't like them a bit. Jillson made fun of my bucket, and she kept calling us 'little squirts' and bossing us around. I thought Constance was going to bite her leg off."

"I considered it," Constance said.

"She's a tough-looking one, though," Kate reflected. "Six feet tall, arms like a gorilla, and ties her ponytail with *wire*. Probably uses it to strangle kids who cross her."

"Let's be sure not to cross her, then," Reynie said, then told them what Jackson had said about Messengers.

"Jillson told us the same stuff," said Kate. "So the voice we heard on the television must be some Messenger kid, right?"

"It must be. And it sounds like the other students don't know much about what the Messengers do — they don't get these 'secret privileges' until they become top students. That means we've got to rise to the top, and fast, so we can become Messengers and figure things out as soon as possible."

"Why don't we poke around and figure some things out for ourselves right now?" said Kate, who had a passion for poking around.

The others agreed, and so Kate fetched her rope and replaced the ceiling panel, and they set out down the corridor.

Hurrying to keep up with Kate, who always moved in high gear, Reynie was almost to the dormitory exit before he noticed Constance wasn't with them. They all went back. Constance stood just outside the boys' room, pointing at a patch of mildew on the ceiling and wrinkling her nose. "That's disgusting! I mean, that's nasty! I *hate* mildew!"

"Um, Constance," Reynie said. "We're in a hurry, remember?"

They set out again, this time keeping an eye on Constance. But aside from being easily distracted, Constance was an intolerably slow walker. When they urged her to hurry, she obstinately refused. When they let her fall behind, she was irritated they didn't wait up.

"It's not my fault my legs are shorter than yours," she complained. "I can't be expected to walk so quickly."

"How about if one of us lets you ride piggyback?" Reynie suggested.

"That's stupid," Constance said. But in the end she let Kate hoist her up, and in this way, at last, they made it out of the dormitory and into sunlight.

The children decided to follow a narrow, well-kept track of crushed stone that zigzagged up a tall hill by the dormitory. In a few minutes they had reached the hilltop, where they were presented with an excellent view of the island. Its entire terrain was one series of hills after another, some of them gentle rises, some looming peaks.

The children gazed down upon their new school. The Institute's gray stone buildings were so similar to one another and so closely packed it was difficult to judge precisely where one ended and another began. They were arranged in a rough U shape around the broad stone plaza and were connected by stone walkways and stone steps. Seen from this perspective, with the stone tower rising up just beyond the dormitory, the buildings gave the impression of a fortress rather than a school.

And yet, in the bright sun of morning, the Institute didn't seem such a forbidding place, not as menacing as they'd imagined; in fact the whole island was rather lovely. The hillsides were a patchwork of sand, green vegetation, and clusters of boulders stitched together by crisscrossing gravel paths. And here and there along the paths, flowering cactuses had been planted in great stone pots. An energetic brook ran down from a nearby hill, following its course over and around the stones, sometimes spilling in miniature waterfalls as it made its way to the island shore, which lay but a short distance downhill from the Institute. Aside from the splash and murmur of water and the distant calls of cliff swallows, the island was remarkably silent, with no children in sight and only an occasional, white-uniformed worker sweeping a walkway or hastening off to some unknown duty.

"I guess everyone's in class," said Sticky. He gave Kate a quizzical look. "Why are you getting out your kaleidoscope?"

"It's a spyglass in disguise," Reynie said as Kate removed the kaleidoscope lens.

Kate trained her spyglass on the stone tower.

"Look, there's a window just above the Institute flag. I'll bet something important's up there. It's the highest window on the island. There's always something important behind the highest window." She handed Constance the spyglass.

"It's probably just so they can reach the flag," said Sticky. "There has to be a way to bring it in and clean it, you know."

"Maybe," said Kate. "It would be simple enough to sneak in and find out. The window's not as high as it seems — not if you were on that hill. First you'd need to get over that rock wall" — she pointed near the top of the hill — "then hop the brook and climb the rest of the way up. The tower's built right into the hillside, see? With a decent stretch of rope you could lasso the flagpole, then climb up and stand on the pole while you got the window open."

"You call that simple?" Reynie said.

Kate shrugged. "Simple *enough*."

"Anyway," Reynie said, "it's in plain sight and you'd surely be spotted. I don't think that's what Mr. Benedict had in mind when he told us not to take unnecessary risks."

Kate sighed. "I suppose that's true."

Constance, in the meantime, was looking disgusted. "This is a terrible spyglass, Kate. It makes everything look far away."

Kate turned the spyglass around and handed it back to her.

The children lingered on the hilltop for some time. It was pleasant up there, with the grand view and the breeze, and though none of them said it, they were reluctant to go back down and meet the Executives again. Kate was more reluctant than any of them, not because she feared being caught as a spy (though, like the others, she was nervous about that), but because she hated to stop exploring. Exploring was what she did best, and Kate liked always to be doing what she did best. Not that she was a bad sport; in fact, she was a very good one, and she rarely complained. But Kate had spent all her life — ever since her father abandoned her, which affected her more than she cared to admit — trying to prove she didn't need anyone's help, and this was easiest to believe when she was doing what she was good at.

So when Sticky anxiously suggested they head back, Kate couldn't help heaving another sigh. Everyone else felt like sighing, too, however, so no one asked Kate what hers was for.

Reynie helped Constance climb onto Kate's back, and the children began making their way down to the dormitory. Kate kept a hopeful eye out for anything unusual, but unfortunately there was nothing to see except boulders and sand and swaths of green vegetation.

Halfway down the hill, Sticky stopped. "*That's* odd."

Kate's eyes lit up. She glanced all around. "Something's odd? What's odd?"

Sticky pointed several yards off the path toward a lush green bed of ivy — or something like ivy — covering the ground near a cluster of boulders. "See that ground vine with the tiny leaves? It's a rare plant called drapeweed that flourishes in thin soil."

"Oh boy," said Constance. "A rare plant."

Kate's face fell.

"What I was going to say," Sticky persisted, "is that some of it was planted more recently than the rest. Mature drapeweed develops a woody brown stem, but young drapeweed has tender green shoots. Otherwise they look the same."

The others peered at the drapeweed, trying to make out the shoots and stems beneath the dark green leaves. It was true: A large patch in the middle was different from the rest, although the difference was so subtle only a botanist — or Sticky — would have noticed it.

"What do you think?" said Constance. "Maybe something's been buried there?"

"Or some*body*," suggested Kate. She looked at Reynie. "Shouldn't we check it out?"

Reynie was pleasantly surprised. He still wasn't used to other children wanting his opinion. "I think so," he said after a moment. "But let's be careful."

"Careful about what?" Kate said. "It's a plant."

"I don't know. It makes me uneasy somehow."

"It's probably nothing," said Sticky, who began to think he shouldn't have said anything. He followed the others off the path. "Maybe some of the vine developed fungus and died, and a gardener just filled in the bare spot. Drapeweed *is* prone to fungus. . . ."

The others stopped at the edge of the drapeweed bed. It was about twice the size of a living room rug and — to Kate, at least — about half as interesting. "Looks like a patch of ivy," she said, hitching Constance higher on her back. "Does it give you a rash?"

"No, it's perfectly harmless," Sticky said, walking toward the middle of the bed. Kate and Constance moved to follow him. "I'll pluck a younger shoot and show you the —"

In the next moment, the drapeweed seemed to swallow him.

TRAPS & NONSENSE

Kate and Constance were two steps behind Sticky when he fell through the drapeweed. If he'd been the least bit farther away, there would have been no saving him. Nor would Sticky have stood a chance had it been any other child lunging to grab him. As it was, with a desperate dive onto her belly, Kate barely managed to snatch Sticky's hand before it disappeared.

Their troubles were far from over. Kate's dive to the ground had sent Constance tumbling over her shoulders. In a flash she caught the girl's ankle before she, too, disappeared — but then the weight of her two catches began to drag Kate forward into the hole.

"Um, Reynie?" Kate called through gritted teeth. "A little help?"

Reynie rushed over and grabbed Kate's legs.

Hauling Sticky and Constance to safety was an arduous, tricky business (and an unpleasant one, too, as Constance complained the whole time of Sticky's elbow in her ribs). But eventually Reynie and Kate had dragged them back up onto solid ground, where all four now lay on their backs, looking up at the sky and panting from the exertion.

"Apparently drapeweed isn't 'perfectly harmless' after all," Constance said.

Sticky looked at her. He wanted to be irritated, but found that he was so relieved to be alive he could only smile.

"In fact it appears to be carnivorous," Kate said.

Before long they were all chuckling. The danger was past, and somehow the excitement had helped them shed a little of their anxiety. Glancing at one another with satisfied smiles (as if to say, "We did it, didn't we? Together we did it!") they rose and dusted themselves off. They gathered near the hole in the drapeweed — though not *too* near — and tried to peer in. All they could see was darkness and trailing tendrils, and even these were slowly being covered up. The flexible stems and shoots thrust aside by Sticky's fall were stiffening and spreading back into place. Like a footprint in springy grass, the hole would soon disappear entirely.

Kate crawled to the edge of the hole, pushed aside some tendrils and shone her flashlight down into the darkness. "It's a pit. Twenty feet deep." She glanced back at Sticky. "Deep enough to break your legs."

Sticky wiped his forehead. "Thanks for the grab, Kate. I do like my legs."

"I would thank you, too," said Constance, "except I wouldn't have fallen into the hole if you hadn't dived, so my thank you and your apology cancel out."

Kate laughed. "Whatever, Constance. As long as I don't have to apologize, I suppose."

The children stood by the drapeweed for some time, pondering their discovery. No one could think of any good reason for it to be there. Why had someone gone to the trouble of covering that dangerous hole?

"There's only one answer I can think of," Reynie said at last.

"A trap?" Kate said.

Reynie nodded.

"Oh, goody," Constance said. "Now there're traps, too."

"But why is it here?" Sticky wondered. "What is it for?"

Kate snorted. "Really, Sticky, you amaze me! A trap is for catching things — or people."

Sticky didn't answer. He was tip-toeing back to the path, careful of every step.

The children made it to their rooms almost exactly when the Executives were supposed to come for them. It was probably a bad idea to keep Executives waiting, Sticky had said. But it was they, not the Executives, who waited. When half an hour had passed with no sign of Jillson, Constance suddenly sang out:

"Now we have waited for thirty consecutive
Minutes to see some old dirty Executive.
Thirty long minutes I could have been sleeping.
But *she* doesn't find her appointments worth keeping."

Kate was startled. "What are you, a cuckoo-clock poet?
Cut it out, she might be right outside the door!"

Jillson was, in fact, right outside the door, but to Kate's relief she entered with no more than her previous bossiness —
no hint of indignation. The walls and doors must be very solid,
Kate reflected; it would be difficult to eavesdrop through
them. This would be to the children's advantage when they
had secret discussions, but it would also make spying on others more difficult — a fact that irritated Kate, though not
nearly as much as when Jillson said, "Hurry up now, squirts. I
can't wait on you all day."

Kate bit her tongue. "We're ready."

"You'd better be," said Jillson. Then her face clouded.
"Hey, why isn't your television on? Is it broken?"

"We, uh, we just turned it off, just now," Kate lied.

"Why would you do that?"

Kate blinked. "Because we were leaving the room?"

"Oh," Jillson said again, considering. Finally she grunted.
"Well. Whatever floats your boat."

They joined Jackson and the boys in the corridor. The Executives had a sheet of paper with them now that listed the
children's names, and after checking to be sure each child
was accounted for (they still didn't bother with handshakes),
they began the Institute tour. After a quick pass through the
dormitory — nothing but student quarters and bathrooms —
they walked outside, where Jillson told them they were free to

roam anywhere they wished, so long as they kept to the paths. "Too dangerous off the paths," she said. "The island's covered with abandoned mine shafts."

The children exchanged glances.

"They're from the early days, when Mr. Curtain built the Institute," Jillson explained. "Before Mr. Curtain bought the island, people said there was nothing here but rocks. What they didn't know was what *kind* of rocks. Turns out the whole island was rich in precious minerals. Mr. Curtain knew this. He built the bridge, brought in mining equipment and workers — a whole *colony* of workers. Their dormitory was the first building constructed. It's now the student dormitory." Like a proper tour guide, Jillson pointed to the student dormitory right in front of them, even though they knew what it was.

Dutifully the children looked and nodded.

"Mr. Curtain became one of the richest men in the world," Jillson went on with a proud smile. "And can you guess how he used his wealth?"

"Doubtful," Jackson murmured.

"He built the Institute?" Reynie offered.

Jackson looked surprised.

"Exactly," said Jillson. "A free school, as you know. Doesn't cost a dime to come here. All thanks to Mr. Curtain's generosity. He asks nothing in return, mind you — not even attention. Mr. Curtain is every bit as reclusive as he is generous. Never leaves the Institute, never takes a vacation. Too much important work to do, he says, broadening the minds of the next generation."

The Executives led them across the rock garden onto the large central plaza, which lay fronted and flanked by the

Institute's massive stone buildings. As they walked, Jackson identified the buildings in turn: "Starting from the right you see your dorm, of course — you remember your dorm, don't you? — and just to the left of it, that one with the tower is the Institute Control Building. It houses Mr. Curtain's office, the guard and Recruiter quarters, and the Executive suites. You'll never have reason to go there unless Mr. Curtain calls you to his office. Or unless you become Executives yourselves some-day." Jackson looked the children over and shook his head, as if he rather doubted that possibility.

"Anyway," he went on, "next to the Institute Control Building you see the cafeteria — right in front of us here — and then the classroom building. That building set off to the side there is the Best of Health Center, which is what we call the infirmary, and the building way on up that path is the gym. The gym is always open, except when it's closed. And there you have it. Those are all the Institute buildings."

"What about that one?" Reynie asked, pointing to a rooftop just visible over the classroom building.

Jackson scowled. "I was *getting* to that, Reynard. That's the Helpers' barracks. You know what barracks are, right? It's where the Helpers live."

"Helpers?"

"Do you not have eyes?" Jackson scoffed. "Haven't you seen the grown-ups in white uniforms scuttling about, sweeping walkways and picking up trash and whatnot?"

Reynie nodded. He couldn't have known they were called Helpers, of course, but he chose not to point this out.

"The Helpers do the maintenance," Jillson explained, "and the cleaning, the laundry, the cooking — all the unimportant tasks, you know. Now come along, squirts, and don't drag your feet. There's still a lot to see inside."

The Executives bustled them into the classroom building, which had seemed large enough from the outside but was perfectly enormous within. Brightly lit corridors branched out from the entrance in all directions. With Constance struggling to keep up (and looking very unhappy about it), the children were led down corridor after corridor. At last they stopped in one that was lined on both sides with classroom doors.

"Now, there are an awful lot of corridors in this building —," said Jillson.

"And not just this building," Jackson put in. "Some connect to the Helpers' barracks and the cafeteria, which have their *own* corridors, obviously."

"Obviously," Jillson said. "So the next thing you shrubs need to know is how to find your way around. Now don't fret. It seems confusing, but it *isn't* confusing. Which happens to be an important principle you'll learn here at the Institute."

"It isn't confusing?" said Constance, who was turning round and round, clearly confused.

"Look beneath your feet," Jackson said. "See that stripe of yellow tiles? Just keep to the corridors with yellow tiles on the floor and you can't get lost."

Obediently the children looked at the floor. Reynie had noticed the yellow tiles but hadn't thought anything of them — he'd assumed they were decorative. He must remember not to assume *anything* about this place.

Jillson put a finger to her lips and drew the children over to peek through the window of one of the doors. A gangly

Executive stood in front of about thirty attentive young students, leading them in a memorization exercise:

"THE FREE MARKET MUST ALWAYS BE COMPLETELY FREE.

THE FREE MARKET MUST BE CONTROLLED IN CERTAIN

CASES.

THE FREE MARKET MUST BE FREE ENOUGH TO CONTROL ITS

FREEDOM IN CERTAIN CASES.

THE FREE MARKET MUST HAVE ENOUGH CONTROL TO FREE

ITSELF IN CERTAIN CASES.

THE FREE MARKET . . ."

"What on earth are they talking about?" Sticky asked.

"Oh, that's just the Free Market Drill," said Jackson. "Very basic stuff. You'll pick it up in no time."

"Sounds like nonsense to me," said Constance.

"On a certain level *everything* sounds like nonsense, doesn't it?" Jillson said as they continued their tour. "Precisely the kind of lesson you'll learn at the Institute. Take the word 'food,' for example. Ask yourself, 'Why do we call it that?' It's an odd-sounding word, isn't it? 'Food.' It could easily be considered nonsense. But in fact it's extremely important. It's the essential stuff of life!"

"It still sounds like nonsense," Constance muttered, "and now I'm hungry."

It wasn't just this talk of food that made Constance's mouth water — and the other children's, too, for that matter — but the *smell* of food as well. They were being led into the cafeteria now, a huge bright room crowded with tables, much like any other cafeteria except for the smells. Drifting in the air were what seemed to be a thousand delectable scents: grilled hot dogs, hamburgers, and vegetables; melted cheese; tomato sauce; garlic; sausage; fried fish; baked pies; cinnamon and sugar; apple tarts; and on and on. Beyond the empty tables, on the other side of a counter, they saw Helpers scurrying about in the kitchen, half-hidden behind clouds of steam and grill smoke.

Kate had her nose in the air like a bloodhound. "It smells like a bakery, a pizzeria, and a cookout all at once."

"That's another great thing about the Institute," said Jackson. "The Helpers prepare wonderful meals. You can eat anything you want, and as much as you want, too. Just go up and tell them what you'd like. Don't be offended if they don't say anything. Helpers aren't supposed to talk to you unless you ask them a question. Pretty soon you don't even notice them. I remember when I was a student, I liked to play tricks on them — nothing they could do about it, you see, because no rule said I couldn't. But now I hardly pay attention to them, except to keep them in line."

"It sounds like there are no rules here at all," Sticky said.

"That's true, George," said Jillson. "Virtually none, in fact. You can wear whatever you want, just so long as you have on trousers, shoes, and a shirt. You can bathe as often as you like or not at all, provided you're clean every day in class. You can eat whatever and whenever you want, so long as it's during meal hours in the cafeteria. You're allowed to keep the lights on in your rooms as late as you wish until ten o'clock each night. And you can go wherever you want around the Institute, so long as you keep to the paths and the yellow-tiled corridors."

"Actually," Reynie observed, "those all sound like rules."

Jackson rolled his icy blue eyes. "This is your first day, so I don't expect you to know much, Reynard. But this is one of the rules of life you'll learn at the Institute: Many things that sound like rules aren't actually rules, and it always sounds as if there are more rules than there really are."

"That sounds like *two* rules I'll learn," Reynie said.

"My point exactly. Now come along, everybody. We need to hurry — you're to join the other new arrivals for Mr. Curtain's welcome speech. Constance, stop dawdling. You, too, George, hustle it up."

"Would you mind calling me Sticky?" the boy asked, hustling it up.

"Is Sticky your real name?" asked Jackson.

"It's what everybody calls me," Sticky replied.

"But is it official? Is there an official document somewhere that declares 'Sticky' to be your official name?"

"Um, no, but —"

"Well, if it isn't *official*, then it can't be *real*, now can it?"

Sticky just stared.

"Good boy, George," said Jackson, leading them back toward the classrooms.

BEWARE THE GEMINI

The children were shown into an ordinary classroom, where sunlight streamed through the windows, the desks sat empty, and an Executive waited to speak with Jackson and Jillson. As the children chose their seats, the Executives held a private discussion. Then Jillson and the other Executive hurried out.

"Shouldn't be long," Jackson told the children. "The other group's finishing their tour, and apparently our Recruiters have brought in some unexpected new arrivals. They're being admitted right now, so we'll start a few minutes late. Okay?" He stepped out of the room; then he stepped back in. *"Okay?"*

"Okay," the children replied.

Jackson shook his head scornfully and withdrew.

"He's a sweetheart," Kate said.

"I don't know how you can joke," said Sticky. "My stomach's all in knots."

Reynie's stomach felt much the same. "Did you hear what Jillson said about mine shafts?"

"You bet I did," Kate said. "It makes no sense. Why set traps and then warn us about them?"

"They don't want us to leave the paths," Reynie speculated. "And if we do, they want to know it — they want to catch us at it."

Kate's blue eyes shone with excitement. "If that's true, there might be traps *everywhere*."

"You two aren't helping my stomach," Sticky said.

Soon the door swung open and a dozen other new arrivals entered, escorted by several Executives and a pair of men wearing fine suits and two watches apiece. There followed a flurry of introductions, desk-choosing, and general mayhem, during which the Executives watched the children very intently, as if they didn't quite trust them not to bolt from the room or start a brawl. Reynie was painfully aware of their eyes upon him — he already felt conspicuous. But new kids *always* felt conspicuous, he reminded himself. And so he smiled and nodded, trying hard to seem as happy and eager as the other newcomers.

His fellow members of the Mysterious Benedict Society were making the same attempt, some with less success than others. Kate smiled charmingly. Sticky managed a grimace that resembled a smile, though it also resembled the expression you might wear in a sandstorm. Constance nodded a few times in a friendly way — until the nodding grew sleepy and her eyelids drooped. Reynie nudged her. Constance jerked her head upright and blinked in surprise, as if she didn't quite know where she was.

As it happened, this was exactly how a couple of the other newcomers looked — a hefty, bell-shaped girl and a wiry boy sitting near the front. Both wore dazed expressions and ill-fitting clothes (hers were too small, his too large), and both had wet hair from recent baths. Except for Constance, they were the only children who didn't seem happy and excited. Perhaps they were just sleepy, though you would have thought fresh baths and the dread of a new school would have gotten them wide awake.

Reynie saw one of the men in suits glance at the dazed-looking children — giving them a little wink and a friendly smile — and suddenly it hit him. *Recruiters*, Jackson had said. That must be what the Institute scouts were called. Which probably meant that the "unexpected new arrivals" Jackson had mentioned were . . . Could it be? Could these kids really have been kidnapped? And they just sat there looking *sleepy*? That seemed unlikely, Reynie thought. He must be missing something. And yet . . .

Reynie's attention was drawn away. The commotion was dying down. Jillson had taken her place at the front, apparently waiting for a cue from Jackson, who stood in the doorway. Jackson nodded, and Jillson raised her hands for silence. A hush fell over the room. Then, in a booming voice, Jillson announced, "And now, everyone, it is our great pleasure to introduce to you the esteemed founder, president, and principal of our beloved Institute: Mr. Ledroptha Curtain!"

Everyone watched the door with anxious eyes. For a long,

expectant pause, they heard nothing except a sort of distant whine, but the whine grew louder by the moment, giving way to a tremendous grind and screech — as of a car changing gears and spinning its tires — and into the room shot a man in a motorized wheelchair, moving so quickly and with such apparent recklessness that every child in the room scooted backward in fear of being struck. Mr. Curtain had perfect control of his chair, however, and as he raced down the rows he expertly dodged the children's feet and the sharp corners of their desks, smiling as he went.

The wheelchair was unlike any they'd ever seen: It had four evenly spaced wheels, like a cart, with button controls on the armrests and pedal controls beneath each foot. Mr. Curtain was snugged into the padded chair with a seat belt across his chest and lap, and the chair rolled so quickly that his thick white hair flew back from his head. He wore large round glasses with silver reflective lenses, so that his eyes couldn't be seen; his cheeks and chin were reddened by a recent shave; and his nose was large and lumpy, like a vegetable.

His entrance would have been a shocking sight for any child, but it was far worse for those of the Mysterious Benedict Society. That nose (so much like a vegetable) and that hair (so thick and white) would have been enough to give them a start, but that suit he wore — that *green plaid* suit — was the clincher. With faces aghast, the four children gaped at the man, and then at one another, for they saw at once that Mr. Curtain was Mr. Benedict himself.

Reynie's mind was racing, searching for an explanation. Had Mr. Benedict been kidnapped? Was he being forced somehow to pretend he was Mr. Curtain? But why? And how could he have done it so quickly? They'd seen Mr. Benedict just that morning. Perhaps Mr. Benedict had a split personality, like Dr. Jekyll and Mr. Hyde? That seemed unlikely, too. But *everything* was unlikely these days, and Reynie preferred almost any explanation to the one that seemed most plausible: For some awful, unknown reason, Mr. Benedict had tricked them.

Even as Reynie thought this, the man introduced as Mr. Curtain brought his chair to a screeching stop, whirled it about, and shot forward to sit right beside him. He positioned his chair so perfectly that his face was mere inches from Reynie's — so close that Reynie could see his own alarmed and searching face reflected in those shiny silver lenses; so close that he smelled the man's pungent breath. And then Mr. Benedict — that is, Mr. Curtain — leaned closer still. Any closer and that lumpy nose would poke Reynie in the eye. "What is it, young man? Why are you looking at me that way?"

Reynie thought fast. Either Mr. Benedict — Mr. Curtain — somehow didn't recognize him, or else he was pretending not to. "It's . . . your nose! It looks like a pink cucumber!"

His friends stared at Reynie in amazement, but several children burst into giggles. Mr. Curtain frowned, his fists clenched, his face darkened — and yet for a long time he did not speak. His fury seemed to be building up to an explosion. Reynie waited in mounting dread. But then the color drained from Mr. Curtain's face, his frown changed into a satisfied expression . . . and he even smiled.

"You children," he said. "I always forget. Children are capable of such open rudeness. That's all right, young man, I won't hold it against you. We need students who aren't afraid to speak the truth. What is your name?"

"Reynard Muldoon, sir. But everyone calls me Reynie."

"Welcome, Reynard," said Mr. Curtain, and with this he turned and rocketed to the front of the room, where he spun once more to face the students, throwing his arms wide. "Welcome, Reynard Muldoon, and welcome, all of you! Welcome to the Learning Institute for the Very Enlightened!"

There was a burst of applause, and Reynie and his friends again glanced at one another — more secretly this time — with looks of unhappy bewilderment. *Everything's backward,* Reynie was thinking, trying desperately to make sense of it all. *Mr. Benedict puts you at ease, but Mr. Curtain terrifies you. Mr. Benedict admires children, but Mr. Curtain looks down on them. And Mr. Benedict seems to know everything about you, but Mr. Curtain seems to know nothing . . . at least not yet.*

Meanwhile Mr. Curtain had begun his welcoming speech: "At other academies," he declared, "children are only taught how to survive. Reading skills, mathematics, art and music lessons — such a waste of a student's time! Here at the Learning Institute for the Very Enlightened," Mr. Curtain boomed, writing the name out on a chalkboard and circling all the capital letters, "we show our students how to L.I.V.E.!"

There followed another great round of applause, but Reynie was still thinking, *Everything's backward.* And gazing at the circled letters on the chalkboard, he felt a sudden, terrible chill. For *LIVE,* spelled backward, is *EVIL.*

As Jillson had explained, the children were free to leave their lights and televisions on "all night long," if they chose, provided their rooms were dark by ten o'clock. When that hour struck, Reynie was peering through a crack in the open door. Sure enough — just as Kate had predicted — an Executive was on patrol. This one, a gangly teenager with gigantic feet, had just turned off the corridor light, and in the relative darkness was checking to see if any light escaped from beneath the students' doors. Reynie switched off their own light and quietly closed the door.

"Who's out there?" Sticky asked.

"S.Q. Pedalian. Remember him? Kate joked that 'S.Q.' must be short for 'Sasquatch.'"

A knock sounded on their door. When Reynie opened it, S.Q. Pedalian stood in the doorway with his arms crossed. His good-natured face, high above them, was just visible in the moonlight coming in through their window. "You fellows need to keep it down," he said, though not unkindly. "You're new, so I thought perhaps you wouldn't understand the rules, or lack of them. And sure enough, when I put my ear to your door and listened, I could hear a sort of murmur, which means you were talking, and that won't do. You're free to talk, of course, but only if you don't make any sound."

"Okay," the boys mouthed soundlessly.

"Okay, just so you know. Have a good night now," he said, pulling the door closed and crying out in pain. The door opened quickly, S.Q. withdrew the tip of his foot, and the door closed again.

"That must happen to him a lot," Reynie whispered.

From above them came the rustling sound of a ceiling panel being slid aside, and in the glow of a flashlight beam they saw Constance's dusty, cobweb-covered, exasperated face. Sticky fetched a chair, and soon Constance and Kate had come down to join them. Kate turned off her flashlight just as a cloud passed over the moon outside. Instantly the room was shrouded in gloom.

"What can it possibly mean?" Kate whispered.

"It's a nasty trick," Constance said.

"I think he's crazy," said Sticky. "What do you think, Reynie?"

Reynie had pondered this all day. "I think we should send a message to the shore. If we *haven't* been tricked — if Mr. Benedict is being forced to act against his will, or if there's some other explanation — the reply may give us some idea what to do."

The others agreed, and Sticky was elected to send the message, he being the quickest with Morse code. Climbing onto the television cabinet, which stood beneath the window, Sticky peered out over the plaza below. At the edge of it he saw a familiar figure facing away from the Institute, gazing down toward the bridge. "We'll have to wait. I can see Mr. Benedict — I guess I mean Mr. Curtain."

"What's he doing?" Constance asked.

"Just sitting in his chair doing nothing."

"Maybe he's contemplating what a terrific madman he is," Kate said.

"Hold on," Sticky said. "A couple of Executives have gone out — and now they're all leaving together. Boy, he sure can move fast in that thing. They're puffing to keep up." Sticky looked in all directions. The plaza was empty, and he saw no lookouts on the paths, no boats on the water, no one on the distant bridge. "Okay, the coast is clear."

Kate handed him her flashlight, and in Morse code Sticky flashed their message: *We see Mr. B when we see Mr. C. How can this be?*

They had decided to be as brief and cryptic as possible, in case an unseen Executive spied the signals. Now, as they waited minute after long minute for a response, they began to worry the message hadn't been understood. Or worse: that it hadn't been seen at all.

"There's no one there," Constance said loudly. The other three shushed her. She stuck out her tongue but continued in a whisper: "This proves it was a trick. The others are all in on it. They wanted to get us on this island, and now we'll never get off again."

"Let's be patient," Reynie said. "If they don't respond soon, we'll send the message again. If they don't reply to that, then I'll have to agree with Constance: We've been tricked, or else something has gone terribly wrong, and we'd better start thinking about how to get away."

"Hold on!" said Sticky. "I see a light in the trees! They're flashing a response."

The others held their breaths for what seemed a terribly long time. Then Sticky whispered, "Boy, when Rhonda said they were going to be cryptic, she meant it."

"So what's the message?" Kate asked.

"It's some kind of riddle," Sticky said. He recited it for them:

> **"When looking in my looking glass**
> **I spied a trusted face. Alas,**
> **Not to be taken for him am I.**
> **Beware, therefore, the Gemini."**

"Oh, *that* certainly clears things up," said Constance, rolling her eyes.

"Sounds like he looked in the mirror and saw himself, then decided he was *not* himself," said Kate. "I'm afraid that does clear things up — Mr. Benedict really is crazy."

Sticky shook his head. "It's not Mr. Benedict who sent the message, remember? I just saw him down on the plaza."

"Oh, yeah," said Kate. "It must be one of the others, then. But what are they trying to tell us?"

Reynie was chewing his lip thoughtfully. "Let's hear the message again, Sticky."

Sticky repeated it.

"What's a Gemini, anyway?" asked Constance.

"A constellation, a sign of the zodiac, or a person born under that sign," said Sticky.

"You're not very helpful, George Washington," said Constance. "Who are the zodiacs, and why are they so keen on making signs?"

"The zodiac is more like a diagram that has to do with stars and planets and whatnot," said Reynie, trying to make it simple. "Your zodiac *sign* has to do with when you're born. If you're born in late April, for example, you're a Taurus, the sign of the bull. You can also be a Pisces, the sign of the fish, or a Capricorn, the, uh —"

"Sign of the goat," said Sticky.

"Right, sign of the goat, and so on — you get the idea. Your sign depends on your birthday."

"So now we're supposed to find out when somebody was born? Who? This is ridiculous!" Constance declared.

"I think I know what the message means," Kate said in a suddenly uncomfortable tone. "It's saying some people aren't who they seem, that we can't trust the people we thought we could. In other words, Constance is right — we've been tricked. Whoever sent us the message must have been duped as well. It's Rhonda or Number Two trying to warn us."

"It's a little late to warn us, isn't it?" Reynie pointed out. "And what's this about a Gemini?"

Kate looked very uncomfortable indeed. "She must think one of us took part in the deception. Someone had a secret pact with Mr. Benedict to help get the others on the island."

"You're saying one of *us* is the Gemini?" said Sticky, appalled.

"I'm sorry," said Kate. "It's the only thing I can think of."

At this suggestion everyone grew quiet, looking at one another with unpleasant feelings of suspicion.

"Well, there's no point in putting it off," Kate said. "If I'm right, we can figure this out pretty quickly. Let's tell each other our birthdays."

Everybody but Constance gave their birth dates at once — not a Gemini among them. But Constance refused. "This is nonsense. Even if I *were* a Gemini, which I'm not, we don't know for sure that's what the message means."

"If you're not a Gemini," Sticky said, "why don't you prove it?"

"You prove it yourself," Constance snapped. "How do we know you didn't lie? Can you prove when you were born, Mr. Capricorn?"

"Uh . . . ," Sticky began, for of course he could not.

Constance turned to Kate. "What about you, Miss Taurus? Can you prove that you're *for* us?"

Kate hesitated, trying to think of an indignant response that rhymed. Unfortunately, nothing seemed to rhyme with "Constance."

"Can *anybody* here prove it?" Constance challenged.

"She's right," Reynie said, with a feeling of great relief.

"There's no way to prove it." (Even in the dim moonlight he noted Constance's look of gratitude — she'd been very worried about being considered a traitor.) "That's actually good news," Reynie went on, "because I'm convinced Mr. Benedict wouldn't send a message that made us turn against one another — not if there wasn't some way of proving the truth. The message must mean something else."

"You keep forgetting," Sticky said. "Mr. Benedict is here on the island. He's not sending us any messages. He can't be both places at once."

"That's it!" Reynie cried. The others shushed him.

"That's it," he repeated, this time in an excited whisper. "Both places at once! Sticky, what's the sign for a Gemini?"

"Sign of the twin," Sticky said offhandedly. His eyes widened. "Wait a minute!"

"That's right," said Reynie. "I think Mr. Benedict has a long lost brother."

As is always the case with a society, some arguing remained to be done. Kate wanted to know why Mr. Benedict hadn't told them he had a twin on the island, to which Reynie replied that he probably hadn't known himself. But if he hadn't known it *then*, Kate persisted, how did he know it *now*?

"The looking glass," Reynie said with a grin. "Remember? *'When looking in my looking glass I spied a trusted face.'* Mr. Benedict wasn't referring to his mirror — he meant his telescope! They just set them up today, remember?"

"So he saw Mr. Curtain for the first time today," said Sticky, "when looking through his telescope."

"I'll bet it was quite a shock," Reynie said.

"But how could Mr. Benedict not know he had a twin?" Kate asked. "They were *born* together."

"They must have been separated as babies," Reynie said. "Mr. Benedict told me he was an orphan. When his parents died, he was sent here from Holland to live with his aunt. Mr. Curtain must have been sent somewhere else."

"But they're both geniuses, and they've always been interested in the same things," Kate said, her imagination catching on, "and so at last they've been drawn together!"

"Wow," said Sticky.

"Uh-huh. I'm sleepy," said Constance, who chose not to be impressed.

Reynie ignored her. "It's strange news but good news. At least now we know we haven't been tricked. Sticky, better send them a message that says we understand."

Sticky did so, and at once the light in the woods began flashing a response. Sticky watched closely, relating the words as they came: *Good job. Good night. Good lu . . .*

"They stopped signaling," Sticky whispered, frowning. In a moment he saw the reason. "Executives! A pair of them have gone out onto the plaza. They're just standing around talking. Now they're sitting on a bench. Looks like they're going to stay awhile."

"The message was almost finished, anyway," Kate said with a terrific yawn, "and frankly, I'm toasted. Can't we call it a night?"

Reynie and Sticky agreed, but Constance was incredulous. "How can we call it a night? We don't even know what they were going to say!"

Kate laughed. "Good grief, Constance! Are you joking?"

Constance was indignant. "Are *you*? It couldn't possibly have been 'good grief'! The second word started with 'lu.'"

Startled, Kate opened her mouth to reply, but Reynie cut her off. "It's a good point, Constance. In fact I'm pretty sure they were going to say 'Good luck.' Don't you think?"

Constance seemed skeptical about this. After all, she said, they couldn't be *sure* that's what the word was going to be. But as she was sleepier than any of them — she'd been rubbing her eyes for an hour — she consented to adjourn the meeting.

"Meeting adjourned," the others said.

Lessons Learned

The Learning Institute for the Very Enlightened was unlike other schools. For one thing, the cafeteria food smelled good and tasted even better. Beyond that, there were no textbooks, no field trips, no report cards, no roll call (if you were missing, an Executive came to find you), no rickety film projectors, no lockers, no team sports, no library, and, weirdly enough, no mirrors to be found anywhere. Nor was there any separation between beginning and advanced students: Class groups were assigned at random, regardless of age or accomplishment, and everyone in that group sat in the same classrooms together, learning the same lessons. The lessons had been designed by Mr. Curtain himself, and when all of them had been gotten through, they were repeated from the beginning. Thus all the lessons were eventually reviewed many times — and the students who learned them best became Messengers.

None of this was familiar to the members of the Mysterious Benedict Society. And yet, in certain ways, the Institute did remind them of other schools: Rote memorization of lessons was discouraged but required; class participation was encouraged but rarely permitted; and although quizzes were given *every day*, in *every class*, there was always at least one student who groaned, another who acted surprised, and another who begged the teacher, in vain, not to give it.

"Time's up!" S.Q. Pedalian called out during the morning class one day. "Pass me your quizzes, everyone — and no dallying, please. A stitch in time saves time, you know."

"Nine," corrected a Messenger in the middle row. Reynie recognized her from his other classes. A tall, athletic teenager with piercing eyes and raven-black hair, she was much older — and bolder — than most of the students, and had a reputation as the leader among Messengers. Her name was Martina Crowe.

"Nine stitches?" S.Q. said. "No, Martina, I'm certain it's just one stitch."

"No, a stitch in time saves *nine*," Martina scoffed.

"Exactly," S.Q. replied.

With the quizzes all collected, the room fell silent as S.Q. went through the pages, marking grades in his book. It was the hourly ritual. In every class, an Executive first presented the day's material, then the material was reviewed — and sometimes the *review* was reviewed — and then the students were given a quiz over the previous day's lesson. If the material weren't so strange, no doubt it would have been easily mastered.

Today, the Mysterious Benedict Society's third full day of classes, S.Q.'s lesson had been called "Personal Hygiene: Unavoidable Dangers and What Must Be Done to Avoid Them." Like all the lessons at the Institute, this one was a barrage of details — pages and pages worth — but the gist was that sickness, like a hungry predator, lurked in every nook and cranny. Every touchable surface was a disease waiting to happen, every speck of dust an allergen poised to swell your nose and clog your ducts, every toothbrush bristle a bacterial playground. On and on it went, and all of it was greatly exaggerated, Reynie thought, though not entirely untrue. What made the lesson so confusing was the "logical conclusion" S.Q. said must be drawn: Because it was impossible, in the end, to protect yourself from *anything* — no matter how hard you tried — it was important to try as hard as you could to protect yourself from *everything*.

There was some kind of truth hidden in there, Reynie thought, but it was camouflaged with nonsense. No wonder it gave students trouble. Luckily, he and Sticky had been making perfect scores. To confirm this, Reynie glanced over at his friend, who gave a small nod and a thumbs-up. Probably wasn't even difficult for him — Sticky remembered everything he laid eyes on. So far, so good. Reynie twisted in his seat to look at Kate. She puffed her cheeks, crossed her eyes, and put her hands to her head as if she thought it might pop. *Not* good. Reynie decided not to look at Constance; his optimism had been spoiled enough.

The other students sat mostly in stupors, worn out from

the class, or else were scouring their notes in hopes of discovering they'd done better than they thought. The Messengers, though — there were four in the class, wearing their snappy white tunics and blue sashes — were indulging in a peculiar habit Reynie had noticed. Every few moments one of them would glance at the door, eyes focused with keen expectation. Martina Crowe was especially fixated.

They were waiting to be called out by an Executive — called away for their "secret privileges." And whenever an Executive *did* appear in the doorway — as Jackson did now — every Messenger in the room stiffened with anticipation.

"S.Q.," Jackson announced. "I need Corliss Danton and Sylvie Biggs."

The Messengers in question leaped from their desks, hastily gathering their things. With beaming faces and nary a backward glance, they followed Jackson out. Martina Crowe stared hungrily after them.

"For the newcomers among us," S.Q. said, "let me remind you that you, too, could be privy to the special privileges enjoyed by our Messengers. Study hard! Especially you brand-new recruits — who are doing very well, by the way. Rosie Gardener, Eustace Crust . . . *very* well done. You each got several answers correct. Keep up the good work." He smiled encouragingly toward the back of the room and returned to his grading.

Reynie turned in his seat to see whom S.Q. was speaking to — and then he could hardly stop staring. *New recruits*, S.Q. had called them, and indeed, these were the two whose dazed expressions had caught Reynie's attention the first day — the bell-shaped girl and the wiry boy he'd suspected of being kidnapped. They scarcely seemed the same children now. Their looks of sleepy confusion had disappeared, replaced by a look of purpose, even of pleasure, in their eyes. These were not the expressions of children who had been kidnapped and secreted away against their will. But then why had they been escorted by Recruiters? And why else would they be called "recruits"?

Reynie suspected himself of leaping to conclusions. He used to think he was good at understanding people — Miss Perumal had told him so more than once — but these kids were a mystery to him. Somehow he was getting it all wrong; he had to be. And speaking of getting it wrong, Reynie's eyes now fell on Constance, sound asleep with her face on her desk. Reynie felt suddenly depressed. He needed to stop turning around.

S.Q. finished grading the quizzes and stacked the papers on the edge of his desk. "Okay, everyone, class dismissed. You may check your quizzes as you leave. And someone had better wake Miss Contraire. I'm fairly certain she's alive — I saw her twitch. Reynard Muldoon and George Washington, please stay after class. I need to speak with you."

Reynie's throat tightened, and he glanced at Sticky, who looked as if he'd been stung by a hornet. Were they suspected of something? As the others filed out of the classroom, Kate gave the boys a meaningful look. *Good luck*, her eyes said. Constance stumbled blearily past without looking at them, and then the two boys started up to S.Q.'s desk.

Their path was suddenly cut off by Martina Crowe, who fixed them with a stare of barely contained fury. Startled, the boys stepped back, as if they'd come upon a rattlesnake.

"That's right," Martina hissed. "Step. Back." She glared at

them, radiating menace. Reynie wondered what to do. Should he ask what was wrong? Would this encourage her to attack?

"Martina?" S.Q. said from his desk. "Do you need something?"

"I know why you want to speak with them," Martina said, not taking her eyes from the boys' alarmed faces.

"Good for you. Now, I *do* need to speak with them, so please excuse us."

"I'll go," Martina said. "But not far." She leaned toward the boys and whispered, "Do you hear me? Not far!"

Certainly not far *enough*, Reynie thought as she stalked from the room. Why was she so angry? Did she suspect them of something, too? Trembling now, the boys approached the desk.

S.Q. looked grave. "I'm afraid you two are in hot water."

"But why?" asked Reynie. Sticky wobbled as if he might fall down.

"You have Martina on edge, that's why. Frankly, fellows, I'm simply astoundished. Or rather, I should say, *astonded*. No, that's not, not quite —"

"Astonished?" Reynie prompted. "Astounded?"

S.Q. nodded. "Those, too. Furthermore, I'm amazed. How are you boys doing so well on your quizzes? You're making perfect scores! I think Martina overheard me talking about it with another Executive, by the way, which is why she dislikes you now."

Sticky regained his balance. Reynie's breathing slowed. They weren't in trouble, after all. Except, for some reason, with Martina Crowe.

S.Q. gave them an appraising look. "How do you explain your grades? It's unlikely anyone is helping you. You're brand new, and other students naturally shun new kids, so *they* wouldn't be helping you."

"I remember things," said Sticky simply.

"I try hard," said Reynie.

S.Q. looked as if this was just what he'd suspected. "Rememberingness and effortfulness, both fine qualities. It seems you two have an abundant supply. I just wanted to congratulate you and tell you to keep it up."

"Like Eustace and Rosie?" Reynie asked.

"Oh, those two? They're a different case, boys. They're special recruits. Special recruits get extra attention in the early days, by order of Mr. Curtain. They're a little slow to come round, and they need encouragement. But you watch, one day they'll be top students. Special recruits often end up as Messengers, and many become Executives. Take Jackson and Jillson, for example — they were special recruits themselves."

"What makes special recruits so special?" Sticky asked. He almost sounded jealous.

S.Q. seemed troubled by this question. "Well, as for that, I can't really say, uh, here nor there. All you need to know is — well, you don't need to know anything. Except for the material, that is. Obviously you must know that. And how to . . . actually, I suppose there are many things you *should* know, but —" He checked himself, cleared his throat, and said, "Just work hard, boys, and you'll have nothing to worry about."

"Except Martina," said Reynie. "She looked like she wanted to throttle us."

S.Q. laughed. "She probably does! You're showing her up. Perfect quiz scores are extremely rare. If you boys continue like this, you'll be Messengers in no time — and so naturally the Messengers hate you. There's a limited number of Messengers, you see, and no guarantee that any will *stay* a Messenger. Have a bad week on your quizzes and another student might take your spot."

"Does that happen often?" Reynie asked.

"Hardly ever," S.Q. said. "Messengers can't bear to lose their special privileges. I remember how awful I felt whenever I had to turn in *my* sash and tunic. Happened to me several times. But eventually I got all the lessons down like butter — like a pat of butter — got them *down pat* — and never lost my position again. Until I was made Executive, that is. Anyway, I suppose to Martina you seem like a threat. I understand her feeling, though of course there's no call for her to be so cranky about it."

Cranky was hardly the word, Reynie thought. *Venomous* was more like it. They would have to watch out for Martina Crowe.

People and Places To Be Avoided

Reynie and Sticky spent the rest of the morning looking nervously over their shoulders. Between classes they hurried through the corridors, not wanting to be ambushed by Martina, and when at lunchtime they spotted Martina lingering near the cafeteria counter, they put off getting their lunches despite the insistent growling in their bellies. Instead they found a table and waited for Kate and Constance. When the girls returned from the counter, Reynie and Sticky quickly related what S.Q. had told them about Messengers, and also what had happened with Martina. The cafeteria was so absurdly loud they could speak in normal voices and not be overhead, but it was all Kate could do to keep her voice below an outraged shout.

"Where is Martina now?" she said, glancing left and right.

"I'm trying *not* to see her," Sticky said.

"Easy, Kate," Reynie said. He nodded discreetly toward a distant table. "She just sat down at one of the Messenger tables. Every now and then she shoots darts with her eyes. But let's not worry about it. We'll need to avoid her, that's all."

Constance wiped her mouth with her sleeve. "Hey, when you boys get your lunch trays, bring me back some ice cream."

"Whatever happened to asking?" Sticky said. "Whatever happened to *please*?"

Reynie looked at Constance, who by way of answering Sticky was poking her tongue out. She did have terrible manners, it was true: She spilled food with abandon, chewed with her mouth open as often as not, and held her utensils like shovels. But Reynie found her behavior more sad than irritating. He knew she must never have had anyone to teach her better manners. He had no idea what her life had been like before — Constance hated being asked questions and generally ignored them, or else responded by making rude sounds — but it was obvious she'd had little guidance.

Constance noticed Reynie looking at her. She bugged her eyes and opened her mouth to show him her chewed-up food. She didn't like being looked at any more than she liked being asked questions.

Reynie and Sticky went up to the counter to order their lunches. The Helpers were stirring soups and tossing pizza dough and otherwise attending to a huge array of dishes, all of which smelled heavenly, and the boys' mouths were watering like sprinkler systems. Reynie finally settled on lasagna and chocolate milk — and ice cream, since Sticky refused to do Constance's bidding. Reynie just didn't feel like dealing with a whining session.

The Helper who took his order nodded silently, averting her eyes, and set about preparing the tray. Reynie watched her uneasily. Only a few Helpers had ever spoken to him, and not one had made eye contact. Apparently Mr. Curtain had laid down strict rules about this. It was a strange requirement of the workers' jobs, this constant show of deference, but the Helpers met it admirably. In fact they were so silent and shy of eye contact that Reynie tried not to greet them or even look at them much. To him this felt profoundly rude, but doing otherwise always seemed to make the Helpers uncomfortable.

Sticky must have been thinking about the same thing, because when they had rejoined the girls at the table, he said, "Can you imagine a worse job than being a Helper?"

"Aren't they a sad lot?" said Kate. "No talking, no eye contact. No way I could work a job like that — I'd have to be sedated."

"Hey, maybe they *are* being sedated," Sticky suggested. "Maybe there's something in their food!"

Kate shook her head. "I've seen them eating the same food they serve us, and we're just fine, aren't we?"

They all looked uncomfortably at Constance, who had finished gulping her ice cream and let her sticky chin drop to her chest. Her eyelids were fluttering, and her breathing had deepened into a snore.

"Well, but she was that way before we got here," said Reynie.

⌁⁖⁓

It was a long and wearisome day. The afternoon classes went much the same as the morning ones: First Reynie would feel heartened by how well he and Sticky had done on the quiz, then dismayed by the hateful looks their successes brought them — from other students and Messengers in general, but especially from Martina. And if Kate and Constance were drawing no such unpleasant attention themselves, it was only because they were having a terrible time with the quizzes, which was even more discouraging.

When the last class was dismissed, the four of them went out onto the plaza and sat on a stone bench. (All but Kate, who bounced in place, burning off energy.) Most of the Institute students spent the hour before supper playing in the gym, or else watching television in their rooms, but the Mysterious Benedict Society had wanted a little time to themselves. As it turned out, they spent their whole time on the plaza undisturbed by Martina or anyone at all, and yet they spoke hardly a word. The reason was that they could not stop staring — with a curious mixture of fascination, fear, and uneasiness — at Mr. Curtain in his green-plaid suit, silvery glasses, and demonic wheelchair.

The plaza was a favorite spot of his. The children had seen him there the day before, too, and also at night. It was well known that Mr. Curtain often sat there for an hour or so in the afternoons, during which time no one ever disturbed him but Executives — and *they* came to him only with urgent matters. This afternoon was no different. Everyone who crossed the plaza gave Mr. Curtain a wide berth, and no one ever passed in front of him, as he seemed to delight in gazing off toward the bridge in the distance, and no one wished to disrupt his view.

Gazing aside, Mr. Curtain was hardly idle. He had a stack of newspapers with him and was going through them meticulously, occasionally marking things, and smiling mysteriously. From time to time he opened a large book, which he carried in his lap, and made a note inside it. Then he would gaze off into the distance again. Eventually Mr. Curtain spun around and shot across the plaza, disappearing inside the Institute Control Building and snapping the children out of their trance.

Having spent so much time staring, and since at supper they were unable to get a table to themselves, the children would have to wait until after lights out for any secret discussions, for the evenings were devoted to studytime. It was essential that Reynie and Sticky continue to do well on their quizzes — especially if Kate and Constance didn't *start* doing well. And, at any rate, one of the few rules the Executives seemed willing to admit to was that students were not allowed in one another's rooms. Private meetings among regular students were the sort of thing strictly frowned upon at the Institute, where all secrets were reserved for Messengers and Executives.

There was no prohibition regarding the dormitory corridors during studytime, however, and before the children holed up in their rooms to labor over their notes, they lingered a few minutes outside the door to Reynie and Sticky's room. If they didn't talk to each other now, it was only because they were eavesdropping. They had discovered that, at this time of day, there was a considerable amount of activity and conversation in the corridor, which always provided an opportunity to learn something. Here and there along the corridor, little clusters of students stood talking, reluctant to knuckle down and study yet, and a steady stream of children toting toothbrushes and toiletries passed in and out of the bathrooms.

This evening the most obvious eavesdroppees were Reynie and Sticky's neighbors, a couple of thick-headed, thick-middled older boys who had made a point of never speaking to Reynie and Sticky. The boys stood in their doorway playing a game that involved kicking each other in the shins without crying out, and as they kicked and grimaced back and forth, they speculated endlessly about the Messengers' secret privileges. This was a favorite conversation among non-Messengers, but never a productive one, and it was no different with these boys. It soon became clear neither had any idea what the privileges were, only that they were much to be coveted.

The boys' talk quickly wore thin, and Reynie was just about to give up and go study when Jackson's voice boomed down the corridor: "Corliss Danton! There you are!"

A few doors down, Corliss Danton jumped. (Everyone jumped, but Corliss jumped the highest.) He turned to look with strangely guilty eyes at Jackson, who came marching toward him through the little clusters of students, all of whom flattened themselves against the walls to let him pass. The corridor, just moments ago all gossip and hubbub, fell silent as a graveyard. Corliss straightened his Messenger sash as Jackson came up. "What — what's the matter, Jackson?"

"You know what the matter is, Corliss," said Jackson. "Mr. Curtain needs to speak with you. I've come to show you to the Waiting Room."

At the mention of the Waiting Room, Corliss — who was fair-skinned to begin with — turned positively white. The boys from the neighboring room flinched and took a quick step backward, trying to disassociate themselves. A murmur spread down the corridor.

"But . . . but . . ." Corliss cleared his throat. He tugged at the bottom of his tunic. "But come on, Jackson. Why would I be punished? What —?"

"You aren't being punished. Mr. Curtain only wants to speak with you. But he's busy at the moment, so you'll have to wait. Come with me right now."

Corliss shook his head and stepped back. "I . . . you know what? I don't think so. I think I'll just . . . just . . ." He glanced left and right, contemplating the corridor exits.

Jackson's tone was casual but firm. "I understand you don't like to wait, Corliss. Nobody likes waiting. But if you don't want to go to the Waiting Room *and* lose your special privileges, then you'd better come along right now."

Corliss cringed. "N-no, that won't . . . won't be necessary. I'll go with you, Jackson. I suppose one way or another I'm going to have to wait, is that right?"

"One way or another."

Corliss took a deep breath to steady himself. "Okay, you bet. Whatever Mr. Curtain wants. You'll get no complaints from me."

Jackson winked. "That a boy. Let's get moving." He put his hand on Corliss's shoulder and walked him out the far exit.

The moment Corliss had gone, the corridor erupted into a cacophony of excited conversation. One girl even burst into tears; she'd once been to the Waiting Room herself, apparently, and was distraught at the mere mention of the place. As the girl's friends tried to console her, Reynie and Sticky's thick-headed neighbors were still staring at the exit through which Jackson had led Corliss as if to his doom.

"The Waiting Room," one boy said. "I didn't know *Messengers* ever got sent to the Waiting Room."

"Let's not talk about it," said the other, shaking his head. "I think it's bad luck to talk about it. I don't need that kind of luck." The boys went into the room and closed the door behind them.

Reynie and the others looked anxiously at one another.

"I think perhaps we ought to avoid being sent to the Waiting Room," said Constance.

"You think?" said Kate.

Sticky took out his polishing cloth.

LOGICAL CONCLUSIONS AND MISCALCULATIONS

When the ceiling panel slid aside that night, Kate's was the only face that appeared.

"Where's Constance?" Reynie whispered.

"Down for the count," Kate replied. "Drowsiest kid I've ever met. Fell sound asleep at her desk. I couldn't wake her."

"I guess you can fill her in later," Reynie said doubtfully, and Sticky shook his head with a look of disapproval.

"I'm so glad to see you boys," Kate said, sitting on the floor. She crossed her legs in an elaborate, pretzel-like formation the boys would have thought impossible. "I'm sick of studying.

I must have gone over my notes a hundred times, but none of it sticks in my head. It makes no sense! 'You must work longer hours to have more time to relax'? 'You must have war to have peace'? How are these 'logical conclusions'? Please tell me!"

Reynie gave a weary laugh. "What about 'It's important to protect yourself because it's impossible to protect yourself'?"

"Oh, yes, the hygiene lesson," Kate said disgustedly. "That one's the best. I would never have thought brushing my teeth could make me feel so hopeless."

Reynie cocked his head. Something about what Kate said seemed familiar. But what was it?

"The stuff doesn't make a bit of sense to me, either," said Sticky, "but I don't have trouble remembering it. I can help you study, Kate."

"When?" Kate said, exasperated. "There's never any time! No, I need to just do it myself."

"Oh . . . oh, okay," said Sticky meekly, his feelings obviously hurt.

Kate was too preoccupied to notice. She was absently braiding her hair into complicated knots, then unbraiding it again. "I really don't get it, boys. What's the point of learning this mush?"

It suddenly occurred to Reynie what had struck him as familiar. "I think it's connected to the hidden messages! Remember that phrase we heard on the Receiver? 'Brush your teeth and kill the germs'? That has to be related to the hygiene lesson, don't you think?"

"Hey, you're right!" Kate said, brightening.

"And now that I think of it, on our first day here we overheard the kids in S.Q.'s class going on and on about the market this, the market that —"

"The Free Market Drill," said Sticky.

"Exactly! And 'market' was the very first word we heard come through Mr. Benedict's Receiver, remember?"

Sticky nodded — of course he remembered — but Kate only shrugged.

"I'll have to take your word for it," she said. "Anyway, the classes are obviously linked to the hidden messages. So the question is how it all fits together."

"The sooner we become Messengers, the sooner we find out!" said Reynie excitedly.

"We aren't Messengers yet, so hold your horses," said Sticky, who was still trying to recover from his wounded feelings and felt a bit testy. "We've only been here a few days."

"It's true," Reynie sighed. "All right, let's report this to Mr. Benedict."

They prepared to send a report to the mainland, only to be thwarted by the presence of Mr. Curtain on the plaza. And then, just as Mr. Curtain was finally going inside, a couple of Executives came out for a leisurely stroll over the Institute grounds. They seemed intent on strolling every walkway and path in sight. The night was growing late, and the children, exhausted, decided to adjourn. They couldn't very well succeed in their classes if they couldn't stay awake in them.

"The report will keep," Kate said with a yawn, "and in the meantime we'll sleep. You boys have a good night."

She scurried up her rope, drew it into the ceiling after her, and disappeared. With a mixture of amusement and admiration, Reynie and Sticky watched her go. Kate's method of coming and going still took some getting used to.

"What must it be like, getting around the way she does?" Sticky wondered.

Reynie shrugged. "Dusty, I imagine."

Long after Kate had gone her dusty way and the boys had gone to bed, Reynie lay awake, calming his nerves by composing a mental letter to Miss Perumal. He could never actually *write* the letter, of course — he could never send it — but it soothed Reynie to think of Miss Perumal, in a setting far from this responsibility and danger, sipping her tea and correcting his Tamil grammar. He reflected upon the pleasant afternoons they'd spent walking in Oldwood Park, discussing this thing or that — her mother, or the aged trees in the park, or baseball, or dogs. And the times, too, when he'd told her about some savage teasing he'd got from other children, upon which Miss Perumal never offered advice — which would have been useless — but only nodded and clucked her tongue, smiling sadly at Reynie as if his memory were her memory, too, as if they shared it. Well, he supposed they *did* share it, now that he'd told her of it. And somehow this had always lightened its effect on him — even, on occasion, cheered him right up.

Reynie had just ended the letter when he heard Sticky rise and move about the room, and then, after a pause, whisper, "Reynie, are you awake?"

It would have been a nice way to go to sleep; Reynie was feeling calm for the first time all day. But he couldn't very well thank Miss Perumal in his letter for always being there to listen, then turn around and not be there for Sticky. "Yes, I'm awake," he replied.

"The coast is clear now."

Reynie looked down from his bunk.

Sticky had put on his spectacles and was peering out the window. "If Kate hadn't taken her flashlight, we could send the report. We should remember that next time. We might as well get *something* out of a bad night's sleep."

"We could flip the light switch," Reynie suggested.

"I suppose so," Sticky said doubtfully, with a twinge of worry in his voice, "but what if there's someone outside? I can't keep an eye out from over by the light switch."

"There are two of us, remember. I'll watch out the window."

Sticky was casting about for his polishing cloth. "Makes me nervous," he said, finding the cloth on his desk and giving his glasses a brisk rub. "I keep thinking about that Messenger's face when Jackson told him about the Waiting Room. The last thing we want is to be suspected of something." He put his glasses on and sighed. "Now I wish I hadn't mentioned it. But I suppose we ought to?"

"We'll do it quickly and get it over with," Reynie said.

The light switch, unfortunately, made a sharp clicking sound when it was thrown. Sticky cringed with every click, as if he were being shocked, and by the end of the message his trembling, sweaty fingers were slipping off the switch. At last the message was sent, however, and no one had discovered them.

Peering toward the mainland shore, Reynie chuckled. "They want to know what we're still doing up."

Sticky felt too anxious to smile. "Anything else?"

"We're doing excellent work, we must continue to be careful, and now we should really get some sleep."

"They said all that?"

Reynie climbed down from the television. "Well, they said, 'Excellent. Careful. Sleep.'"

"They don't have to tell me twice," Sticky said, slipping

into bed. "Especially not the careful part. My stomach's all in knots, Reynie. It feels that way all the time."

"I know," Reynie said, climbing up to his bunk. "Same with me. But at least we know Mr. Benedict and his crew are out there watching. We're not alone, right?"

"I suppose that should be encouraging," Sticky said uncertainly.

"I take it you don't find it very encouraging."

"No," Sticky replied, pulling his sheet up tightly under his chin. "No, ever since I first saw him, I keep imagining Mr. Curtain chasing me down, getting closer and closer. He seems a lot closer than Mr. Benedict and the others do, way off on that shore."

This time Reynie said nothing. He understood too well how Sticky felt. If only he knew of something comforting to say, something to ease Sticky's anxiety — and, yes, something to ease his own. He thought and thought. He lay awake a long while, thinking. Surely there was *something*.

But if there was, he could not think of it.

Sticky's anxiety took its toll on him; he slept quite poorly, and all the next morning he had trouble staying awake. By the time Jackson's class started, his eyelids felt heavy as anvils. It required a heroic effort — including a lot of painful pinches on the leg — to keep his eyes open and pay attention to Jackson's long, droning lecture. At last Jackson finished, however, and despite his drowsiness, Sticky had managed to lock all the information securely in his head. The end-of-lecture review would not require his attention, which meant it would require willpower instead — it would be all he could do to stay awake. He needed to occupy his mind with something.

And so Sticky focused on Corliss Danton, who was back in class this morning, looking no worse for wear. On the contrary, he seemed the exemplary student: He sat ramrod straight in his desk, listening with attention, and his Messenger uniform was impeccable. In fact his entire person fairly shone. From finger to foot, his fair skin was rosy from scrubbing; even his fingernails seemed meticulously groomed. He looked as though he would smell like a bar of soap. Corliss obviously meant to make a good impression, Sticky thought. He wanted to appear cleansed of any past wrongdoings.

Only after Corliss had glanced past him toward the door a few times did Sticky realize he was not entirely recovered from his visit to the Waiting Room. His face was weary, even dazed, as if he hadn't slept a wink, and an unmistakeable remnant of misery showed in his eyes. Not for the first time, Sticky found himself wondering what sort of ordeal Corliss had gone through. Then he found that he didn't want to think about it, as it made his stomach hurt. And then he found that he was asleep.

Sticky wouldn't have *known* he was asleep, though, had Martina Crowe not hissed, "You! Skinny bald-headed four-eyes! What are you doing sleeping? Aren't you supposed to be the *super* student?"

Sticky's eyes snapped open. On all sides of him students were tittering, and the Messengers (including Corliss) were sneering disdainfully. In a flush of embarrassment, Sticky reached for his spectacles.

"Watch him go to polishing his glasses now!" said Martina. "What a weirdo!"

"Silence!" shouted Jackson from the front of the room. His icy sharp gaze fell on Sticky. "You can say whatever you like when you have permission," Jackson said, adding: "Right now no one has permission."

Paralyzed, Sticky couldn't even manage to nod.

Kate, however, was too outraged to hold her tongue. "But it wasn't Sticky who spoke!"

Martina, who happened to be sitting right in front of Kate, whirled about with a look of shock. Kate met her gaze defiantly, which surprised Martina even more. Before they could exchange words, though, Jackson had come charging down the aisle to stand over Kate. "Did you raise your hand to ask permission to speak?"

Kate shook her head, and then, with a bright look, raised her hand.

"No," Jackson said. "You don't have permission to raise your hand. And let me just warn you and your friend," he said with a glance at Sticky, "it won't benefit you to challenge a Messenger."

Martina ran a hand through her raven-colored hair and nodded with remarkable smugness. Kate's face burned bright red — she fairly radiated fury — but she held her tongue. Jackson returned to the front of the room, and the students returned to their busy note-taking.

All except Sticky, who was too upset to concentrate. Instead he stared miserably at Jackson, and then at his other tormentor, Martina, who seemed exceedingly pleased with herself. His gaze was distracted by a movement below Martina's desk. Kate was slipping her feet back into her shoes. But why had she taken her shoes off? It was too cool for bare feet. Just then Martina shot a glance toward Sticky. Sticky averted his eyes and didn't look that direction again. He could feel the malice even without looking.

And so it was that when Jackson dismissed class and Martina leaped from her seat, Sticky heard, but did not see, Martina crashing face-first onto the floor. He glanced over in surprise. Notebooks, papers, and pencils had spilled everywhere, and Martina was raising herself slowly to her hands and knees, spluttering and shaking her head as she tried to get her bearings. Messenger or no, her fumblings prompted a burst of laughter from the other students — except for Kate, who pretended not to notice as she grabbed Sticky's arm, dragging him toward the door.

"I tied her shoelaces to the desk," she whispered. "With my toes."

"Great," Constance said at lunch. "Not only do we have a dangerous secret mission, but now we have enemies, too. Nice work, Kate."

Kate laughed. "She was already the *boys'* enemy. I just added myself to the list. What did you expect me to do, let her get away with it? She called him bald-headed, for Pete's sake."

"I *am* bald," Sticky said, running a hand over his scalp. "It's my own fault. I used hair remover when I ran away, to disguise myself."

"*That* explains it," said Reynie. "I'd wondered but was afraid to ask."

"Isn't hair remover supposed to sting like the dickens?" Kate asked.

"I'd heard that, so I invented my own mixture, adding other ingredients to keep it from stinging."

"Did that work?" Constance asked, plainly hoping it didn't.

"No," Sticky admitted. "It felt like my head was on fire, and now it's taking forever for my hair to grow back! It hasn't even *started*!"

The others smiled. Then grinned. Then giggled. And finally — unable to help themselves — they burst out laughing. Sticky groaned and ducked his head, but at last even *he* had to smile. For a while their laughter wiped away the troubles at hand, and they were reluctant to give it up.

But eventually — too soon — their laughter fell away. And unlike Sticky's hair, the troubles at hand did not hesitate to come back.

POISON APPLES, POISON WORMS

That afternoon in class, Jillson lectured on the national economy. She also spoke about education, crime, the environment, war, taxes, insurance, health and medicine, the justice system . . . and *fruit*.

"You see," Jillson said near the end of the lesson, "all these terrible problems are the result of one thing: bad government! Don't get me wrong, government is a good thing. Without government you can solve none of the world's horrible problems — unless you have a *bad* government, in which case the problems only get more horrible. Sadly, all the world's governments are bad ones. Like a poison apple" — here Reynie's ears perked up — "our governments look beautiful, shiny, and wholesome from a distance, but once you've partaken of them, they prove quite deadly. What's more, they shelter more than one wicked official — like poison worms in that poison apple."

Poison apples, poison worms, Reynie thought. That was another hidden-message phrase they'd heard through Mr. Benedict's Receiver. He wasn't surprised — he knew the classes were connected to the hidden messages — but he did wonder exactly how it all fit together. He felt sure he could figure it out if only —

Without warning, Reynie's mood shifted. His optimism drained away, and he was suddenly angry with Jillson — stupid, lecturesome Jillson! — and not just Jillson, either, but . . . really, he was angry with just about everybody he could think of. It was an unusual feeling for Reynie, and very distressing. He felt as though the walls were pressing in on him, as though he wanted to get up and run from the room. He felt like yelling and kicking things — preferably Jillson.

What was going on? Was the pressure finally getting to him? Completely frazzled, Reynie laid down his pencil and glanced over at Sticky — who was glaring at his quiz as if he wanted to tear it up and toss it into a fire. *Oh, no*, Reynie thought, *he's bungled it somehow*. For a moment he felt mad at Sticky, too. But then Sticky, catching his eye, nodded as usual and gave a feeble thumbs-up. It wasn't the quiz, then. And now Sticky was staring at Reynie with a concerned expression — which was how Reynie realized he was scowling himself. He looked over at Kate and Constance. Both had their heads in their hands and looked ready to scream. And yet none of the other students seemed affected in the least. So why would only the four of them . . . ?

Martina's poisoned us! Reynie thought. He was immediately convinced of it. Martina had slipped something into their lunches — perhaps she'd ordered the Helpers to do it. All his anger now flowed in Martina's direction.

When class was finally over, it took Reynie several seconds to realize why the other students were getting up and leaving. Jillson was staring at him and his friends as if they were a bunch of lunatics. "I said go!" she barked. "Or do you want to stay here all day?"

The four of them bolted from their desks. They needed an emergency meeting.

Most students were headed to the gym to play games before supper, and Mr. Curtain was not in his favorite spot. The plaza was deserted. The children crossed to the farthest corner, made sure no one was in earshot, and all began talking at once.

"Are you feeling what I'm feeling?" Reynie asked.

"What's *this* all about?" Kate said.

"So you feel it, too? I think my head's going to split open!" Sticky said.

"My first thought was that Martina poisoned us," Reynie said, "but —"

"Poison?" Kate said. "No, I don't think so. This is all in my head."

Reynie and Sticky agreed. It wasn't a physical problem,

exactly; it was something else. But then what *was* it? The three of them began comparing their symptoms.

Only Constance said nothing. She listened as the others talked about how irritable and angry they felt, as if they were engaged in a furious argument, and as they spoke, she seemed to be shrinking. It was Reynie who noticed this — that Constance, with a look of anxious bafflement, had begun to crouch down as if to protect herself from an attack.

"Constance, what is it?" Reynie asked, his brow wrinkling with concern. "What's wrong?"

"That's . . . that's all?" Constance asked in a weak voice. "You just feel kind of annoyed?"

"*Extremely* annoyed," Kate said. "Really, I've never felt so cranky in my life."

"So you don't . . . you don't hear . . . ?" Constance trailed off.

She didn't have to finish. Reynie couldn't believe they hadn't thought of it right away. The experience must have rattled every bit of sense out of all their heads. Hadn't Mr. Benedict specifically predicted this? *Most of us will simply feel irritable and confused*, Mr. Benedict had said, *essentially the way we feel now whenever the television is on and the messages are being broadcast*.

"Mr. Curtain's boosting the power," Reynie said gravely, and when Kate and Sticky looked at him, still not comprehending, he said, "It's the hidden messages. Our minds are reacting to them."

Sticky gasped. Kate slapped her forehead. Of course! The hidden messages had begun to transmit directly into their minds — no more need for television, radios, or anything else. All the other students were undisturbed because, just as

Mr. Benedict had said, only minds with an unusually powerful love of truth noticed anything was happening.

"So we can't avoid them anymore?" Kate said. "Well, *that's* depressing."

"I think there's more," Reynie said. He knelt beside Constance and put his hand on her shoulder — and Constance, for once, didn't complain. "There *is* more, isn't there, Constance?"

Kate and Sticky looked from Reynie to Constance, who was nodding and hiding her face behind her hands. She actually seemed to be fighting back tears. All of their minds were resisting the hidden messages, but Constance — and only Constance — could hear the Messenger's *voice*.

In rare cases, with exceptionally sensitive minds, Mr. Benedict had said. And here was such a case, such a mind: Constance Contraire. The development shocked them all, especially Constance, who was so disturbed by it she spent the evening with her head under her pillow. She was no better by the time Kate smuggled her into the boys' room for their meeting.

"It might be useful, you know," Sticky whispered, trying to cheer her up. "A way to gauge Mr. Curtain's progress. On a really, really awful day, one of *us* might not be able to tell the difference between a normal bad mood and a hidden-message mood. But if you can hear the actual *voices* — well, then, you're like our canary in the coal mine!"

"A canary in a coal mine?" Constance mumbled without looking up.

Sticky failed to notice Reynie's warning look. "Oh, yes — miners used to bring canaries with them to gauge oxygen levels in the mine. If the canary died, they knew the oxygen was running out and they'd better get out of there."

"If the canary *died*?" Constance repeated.

Sticky looked suddenly regretful.

"That was perhaps an unfortunate comparison," Reynie said.

"The point is you're important," Kate said. "Okay?"

"I already knew that," Constance snapped. "I didn't need all this mumbo-jumbo in my head to tell me. And I definitely didn't need Martina Crowe in there whispering it — she was the one doing the last message, in case you're wondering. I dislike her enough *outside* my head, much less *inside* it. In fact, I think I'll write an insulting poem about her . . . although, come to think of it, 'Martina' makes for a tricky rhyme."

Reynie, Kate, and Sticky glanced at one another with cautious optimism. Constance seemed to be feeling a little better. They all were, actually. They had spent the evening adjusting to the hidden-message broadcasts (there had been three more since Jillson's class) — trying not to snarl at one another, or smash their fists on desktops, or slam drawers. Studying had been positively excruciating, like trying to read while someone bangs out an annoying tune on a piano — and with fingers on the wrong keys, at that. But an hour had passed since the last broadcast, and the children's moods had improved. Which helped them focus on the fact that their situation, unfortunately, had *not*.

The thing to come was getting closer. Mr. Curtain was not broadcasting his messages at full-power yet — otherwise all four of them would hear voices, not just Constance. But matters had obviously worsened, and the children had only just arrived on the island. Were they already too late? What should they do?

"Coast is clear," Sticky said when he'd climbed onto the television and looked out the window. He took the flashlight from Kate. "What should I say?"

"Mr. Benedict will already know the messages are stronger," Reynie reflected. "He and the others are surely feeling it, too. Just tell him that Constance is hearing voices. He hadn't expected that."

"Got it," Sticky said, turning to the window. " 'Constance hearing voices.' Here goes."

"But don't use her real name!" Reynie warned.

"Oh, right," Sticky said sheepishly. "Of course not."

"Are you just *trying* to get me caught, George Washington?" Constance grumped.

"Sorry," Sticky said, gritting his teeth as he always did when Constance used his full name. "I'll just say, um . . ." He looked to the others for help.

Reynie glanced at Constance, who was scowling impressively, ready to complain about whatever they suggested. Resisting the first thing that came to mind, Reynie suggested they refer to her as "the smallest one."

Constance grudgingly accepted this, and soon Sticky had sent the message. A few minutes later, he received a response from the mainland:

> **Time is shorter than we thought.**
> **Thus to get what must be got**
> **You must become what you are not.**

"It sounds like he wants us to put a rush on things," said Sticky, climbing down from the television.

"Fine by me," said Kate. "But how, exactly? What does he mean, 'what must be got'?"

"Whatever it is, we have to become something different to get it," Reynie said.

"But what could that be?" Constance said.

They all looked at one another. None of them had any idea. They didn't even know where to start.

The message broadcasts were hard on all of them. They felt another one during lunch the next day (it was Corliss Danton, according to Constance), which had them gritting their teeth, growling at each other, and fighting the urge to throw silverware. And another came during the evening, so that they were compelled to study with their nerves being plucked like banjo strings. The last broadcast finally relented just as Reynie was closing his notebook. He laid his head on his desk in relief.

"I am *so* glad that's over," said Sticky, who had spent study-time lying on his bed grimacing. "You finished?"

With an effort, Reynie nodded.

They heard Jackson's booming voice in the hallway announcing lights-out.

"I'll get the light," Kate said, dropping to the floor behind Reynie.

Reynie gasped and fell out of his chair. Sticky banged his head on the top bunk. Kate switched off the light and climbed onto a chair to help Constance down from the ceiling.

"Maybe you should start knocking," Sticky grumbled, rubbing his head.

"And spoil the surprise?" Kate asked.

"Listen," Reynie said, scrambling back up. "I've been going over Mr. Benedict's message in my head all day, and I think I'm starting to figure it out. What is it Mr. Benedict sent us here to get?"

"Information," Sticky said. "You think that's what he meant by 'what can be got'? Just information?"

"*Secret* information," Reynie said. "Which is why we need to become Messengers as soon as possible. We must become what we are not."

Constance rolled her eyes. "But that's obvious! We already know that."

"You're right," Reynie admitted. "That's why I said I'm *starting* to figure the message out — I think there must be more to it. I'm just not sure what, except that we need to hurry up."

"We're going as fast as we can, though," Kate said. "You boys are making perfect scores on the quizzes, and Constance and I — well, we're doing our best, aren't we?" She glanced doubtfully at Constance. "At least I know I am."

"What's that supposed to mean?" Constance said, frowning.

"I just don't want to speak for you," said Kate evasively.

"My point," Reynie interjected, "was that we have to find a way for you and Constance to do better on the quizzes."

"Ugh," Kate said, heaving a dramatic sigh. She collapsed onto the floor, throwing out her arms as if she'd been knocked flat. "To tell the truth, I think I'm beyond help. My brain simply won't absorb that nonsense, no matter how hard I try."

"Same here," said Constance. "No way can I improve on those quizzes. I'm too tired to study any more than I already do."

"Which is hardly any," Kate muttered.

Constance flared. "Let's see *you* study with voices spouting gibberish in your head!"

"At least I've been trying!"

"Hold on, hold on," Reynie said. "Let's go back to Mr. Benedict's message. What can we think of that we all are not?"

"Grown-ups?" Sticky suggested.

"True," Reynie said gently. "But I don't think we can hurry up and get *older*, can we?"

Constance pointed out that none of them were antelopes eating canteloupes, or textbooks with hexed looks, or cattle from Seattle.

"You're just trying to annoy us, aren't you?" Kate said.

Constance grinned.

"The fact is," Sticky said in a defeated tone, "there are an infinite number of things that we aren't."

"Yes, but Mr. Benedict expects us to figure this out," said Reynie, "so we should be able to narrow it down. Let's consider what he knows about us — something we all have in common, something that could be changed."

"He only just met us," Kate pointed out. "He can't know that much about us, can he?"

"Well, he knows we're orphans and runaways," Sticky offered, then quickly added, "I know, I know. We can't all suddenly have families. So what else?"

"We're all gifted," said Constance. "We all passed his silly tests."

"And none of us watches television or listens to the radio," said Kate, "because of our minds' unusually powerful love of truth, right?"

Sticky scratched his head. "I don't see how watching television is going to make us Messengers any faster."

"Wait a minute!" Reynie said, leaping to his feet. "Our love of truth!"

The others fell silent and looked at him. Reynie had begun to pace and whisper to himself. "Become what we're not . . . to become Messengers faster . . . and Mr. Benedict *knows* that we're not, because . . . yes, I think I have it!"

Kate shone her flashlight at Reynie, who stopped in his tracks. His exultant expression shifted into one of doubt, and he squinted uncomfortably in the flashlight beam. He cleared his throat, hesitated, and cleared his throat again.

"Well?" Constance demanded. "What's the big idea?"

At last Reynie managed to come out with it. And it was no wonder the others hadn't thought of it themselves, for what Reynie suggested was something that would never have occurred to them, something quite foreign to their natures, something none of them had ever attempted.

They must learn how to cheat.

"It only makes sense," Reynie quickly explained, when he saw his friends' horrified expressions. "None of us accepted

Rhonda's offer to cheat, remember? That was part of the test. Mr. Benedict is saying we must become what we are not — *cheaters* — so we all can become Messengers more quickly!"

"You've got to be kidding!" Kate cried. "That can't be what Mr. Benedict means!"

Sticky was shaking his head. "Didn't he choose us because we *didn't* cheat?"

"Well, I'm all for it," Constance said with a snort. "Let's cheat like the wind!"

Kate was appalled. "I can't believe you two! Where's this powerful love of truth Mr. Benedict talked about?"

Reynie wasn't surprised by his friends' responses. He too had been wary of the notion when it occurred to him. But were they not secret agents? Was not their very presence on the island a deception? Kate and Sticky's reaction was just an instinctive response, he thought; they would come around in a minute.

Still, Reynie was troubled by Kate's question. Where *was* his powerful love of truth? His mind resisted the hidden messages . . . but maybe not as much as his friends' did. How could he know? Hadn't he been sorely tempted to cheat on Mr. Benedict's tests, when Rhonda made the offer? Was he perhaps not quite the truth-loving brave soul Mr. Benedict and everyone else thought him to be?

"Get real," Constance was saying. "Mr. Curtain is the big deceiver, remember? We can beat him at his own game!"

Kate and Sticky had their doubts, but they were less adamant now. Sticky was polishing his glasses, saying he supposed it *might* be all right, and Kate had begun to pace, saying, "It's just that I never imagined myself . . . I don't know, it's just hard for me to think that way. Reynie, do you really think that's what Mr. Benedict is suggesting?"

"There's one way to find out," said Reynie, who really hoped he was right — not because he wanted to cheat, but because if cheating was Mr. Benedict's idea rather than his own, Reynie would feel better about himself.

Sticky sent their query at once: *Please advise about cheating.*

A few minutes later a light began flashing in the woods. Sticky relayed the message as it came: *Do Not*

"I guess that settles it," Kate said.

"There's more," said Sticky.

The rest of the message was this: *Get Caught.*

"I guess *that* settles it," said Constance.

"Cheating practice" occupied the Mysterious Benedict Society for two full hours that night. The moment the children received permission, they applied themselves to finding the best strategies for "earning without learning," as Constance called it. None of them had ever tried it before, and at first they made a very poor showing indeed. But they were nothing if not quick learners, and by the time they called it a night, they all felt reasonably confident they could cheat a cheater out of cheating lessons, nine times out of ten.

Their hard work paid off the next morning. The girls' quiz scores finally began to improve. Given her height and sharp eyesight, it was simple enough for Kate to sit behind Reynie and copy over his shoulder, while Reynie kept his paper at a helpful angle. Their greatest difficulty lay in watching out for witnesses, but Kate and Reynie were good at this, and their teamwork produced excellent results. In fact, they were so heartened by their success that not even the morning's hidden-message broadcasts dimmed their optimism.

Sticky and Constance's cheating strategy was more complicated. Constance was too short to copy over a shoulder, and note passing was much too risky, so at last Reynie had suggested Morse code. Notoriously fidgety, Sticky signaled the answers by tugging his ear or tapping his temple — motions he disguised with head scratches, collar-straightening, and spectacle-polishing — and Constance sat in the back row, where none of the other students would notice her watching him.

The strategy worked, but not without problems. In the corridor between classes Constance complained under her breath, "Every time you have a *real* itch, I get the wrong answer."

"Sorry," Sticky said sheepishly. "I get itchy when I'm nervous. I'll try to do better."

"Don't just *try*," Constance said. "*Actually* do better."

"Hey, my fidgeting isn't the only problem, you know!" Sticky hissed. "It would help if you had practiced your Morse code at *all*!"

Constance's face turned so red, her pale blue eyes glistened so brightly behind angry tears, and her wispy blond hair was in such a state of dishevelment that she looked more like a small child's painting of a person than an actual person herself. A fierce display of vivid colors in odd proportions, she seemed to have stepped right out of a canvas for the sole purpose of throwing a fit.

"Now, children," Kate said in a motherly tone, stepping between them. "Let's not quibble about who's to blame. Blaming is *wrong*. The important thing is to get along with one another, so that we may have better success *cheating*."

"Not funny," said Constance, but the joke did take the edge off her fury, and she said no more.

Nor did Sticky, who regretted his outburst, not least

because it was imprudent to discuss cheating in the corridor, and even worse to mention Morse code. Was he crazy? What if he'd been overheard? The very prospect of the Waiting Room made him woozy.

And so the morning passed: struggling to ignore hidden-message broadcasts, concentrating on the lessons, cheating on every quiz. The four had a bit more to think about than the other students. Yet the boys continued making perfect scores, the girls were coming along nicely, the broadcasts eventually let up, and by lunchtime everyone was in an upbeat mood.

At the same time, they were on high alert for clues. Between classes they'd heard the rumor that Charlie Peters, one of the oldest Messengers at the Institute, was graduating. He hadn't been in class all day, and some Executives had been seen with him in the dormitory that morning. This was the usual thing, someone said. Graduates never spoke to a soul when they left — apparently they were too high and mighty even to say good-bye to old friends. They had no *choice*, said another student; the Executives never allowed it.

"I wonder what that's all about," Reynie said as they made their way to the cafeteria for lunch.

"Good question," Kate said. "And here's our chance for some answers." She pointed down an adjoining corridor, where S.Q. Pedalian had just appeared, escorting Charlie toward a distant exit. "Quick, you try to talk to him while I distract S.Q."

"How do you propose to do that?" Constance asked. But Kate had already dashed off down the corridor, and Reynie and Sticky were hurrying after her.

"S.Q.! Hey, S.Q.!" Kate called out. "I wanted to ask you a question about your lecture this morning."

S.Q. turned to see Kate barreling toward him. "I'm afraid I can't talk right now, K —"

Before S.Q. could finish, Kate took a spectacular fall. Her feet shot out from under her; her arms and legs flew in every direction; her bucket clanged and scraped against the stone floor, sending up sparks; and at last — with her feet first in front of her and then somehow behind her — Kate tumbled and slid to a stop a few yards away from S.Q., where she did a very convincing job of rolling her eyes back into her head.

"Kate!" S.Q. cried, hurrying to check on her as the boys came running up. "Step back!" he ordered. "Give her room to breathe!"

As Kate made a great production of fluttering her eyelashes and rolling her eyes loopily about, Reynie and Sticky edged past S.Q. to talk to Charlie Peters, who stood a little distance away, gazing impassively down the corridor, apparently not the least interested in Kate's fate. A terribly pale boy, with pale eyes, pale hair, and pale skin, Charlie looked like a figure made of wax. When the boys approached, he didn't even acknowledge them. He wore a faintly confused expression, as if he couldn't see why he had to leave the Institute, why he couldn't just keep on being a Messenger forever.

"She'll be fine," Reynie said, jerking a thumb toward Kate as if Charlie might actually care. "Falls down a lot, but she always recovers."

"What?" Charlie said, looking at the boys for the first time.

Reynie's face took on a sympathetic expression. "Oh, I guess your mind's on other things, since you're graduating.

No one could blame you for that. I'll bet you're sad to go, aren't you? You'll miss all those special privileges."

"What special privileges?" Charlie said warily. "I don't remember any special privileges. Being a Messenger is a responsibility, a matter of leadership. When you're a Messenger, you're so busy helping Mr. Curtain that you hardly have time to think. In fact," Charlie said, looking disappointed now, "in fact, it seems like only yesterday I was made Messenger, and now I'm going home already. I've been so busy that everything in between seems like a blur."

"Busy doing what?" Sticky asked.

Behind them, S.Q. was struggling to help Kate back to her feet. Kate was making it difficult by slipping on things that had spilled from her bucket.

Charlie grew agitated. He glanced left and right, then fixed them with a decidedly suspicious look. "I can't say."

"But why not?" Reynie urged. "Did they threaten you? Can you tell us *anything*?"

Charlie shook his head doubtfully. He seemed to be considering, though, and the boys felt their hopes rise. Then he shook his head again, more vigorously this time. He seemed extremely distressed by their questioning. "I can't say," he repeated. "I really can't."

"— lucky to be alive," S.Q. was saying to Kate behind them. Then his voice sharpened. "Hey! You boys get away from Charlie!"

"Okay, bye, Charlie," Reynie said quickly, and Sticky gave a playful salute, but Charlie only stared at them with a distraught expression, as if they'd done him some grievous wrong. Casting the boys a disapproving look, S.Q. took Charlie's arm and led him away toward the exit.

"Any luck?" asked Constance, who had finally come down the corridor and was standing there, conspicuously unhelpful, as Kate gathered her things.

Reynie picked up Kate's slingshot and handed it to her. "He isn't talking. He wouldn't say why."

"I did all that for nothing?" cried Kate, dismayed.

"I'm not sure," Reynie said. "There's something curious about what Charlie said. Something . . ." He frowned. "I'm going to have to think about it."

"Anyway, Kate, don't tell us you didn't enjoy doing that," Sticky said.

"That's true, I did," Kate admitted, with an impish grin. "How did it look?"

"Like you fell out of an airplane," Reynie said as they started toward the cafeteria again.

"Really?" Kate gazed at him with shining eyes. She was deeply touched.

Tests and Invitations

During the last class of the day, near the end of the lecture review, the classroom door flew open and Jackson came in. "Don't mind me," he said to the Executive he'd interrupted, though from the way Jackson strutted, it was clear he enjoyed the attention. "Just posting the new Messenger list."

Every student in class sat up straighter. The new Messenger list! It was well known that the list hadn't changed in over a month. Now Charlie Peters's departure had left an open slot. Who had filled it? As Jackson hung the paper at the front of

the room, everyone strained their eyes to make out the names.
Kate was the only one sharp-eyed enough to succeed. "No
luck yet," she whispered to Reynie. "Your name's not on it."

The moment class was dismissed, the students swarmed
toward the list. Martina Crowe, the first in line by virtue of
her sharp elbows, announced that Bonnie Hedrickson was
the new Messenger. This prompted a collective moan of disappointment. Still, no one stepped out of line. Everybody
wanted to see for themselves, perhaps hoping Martina was
playing a joke, or that Bonnie's name would magically disappear, replaced by their own.

The Mysterious Benedict Society had gathered near the
back. "Let's get out of here," Kate said. "It's Bonnie, all right.
I saw her name."

"You three go on," said Reynie, who felt strangely compelled to see the list up close. "I'll meet you on the plaza."
And so the others left, and Reynie got in line, wondering why
he felt drawn to look. Perhaps he was not so different from
the other students after all. Perhaps he, too, hoped for something impossible.

"The secret privileges!" said a girl wistfully.

"And those tunics!" said a boy. "I'll get on that list if it
kills me!"

Reynie leaned sideways to see who was at the front of
the line. Rosie Gardener and Eustace Crust, the two special
recruits. Despite their confusing behavior, Reynie still suspected them of having been kidnapped, and he found himself
wondering yet again how they had come to be so pleased with
their fates. Those initial dazed expressions long since evapo-
rated, the special recruits were all eagerness now, and both
had greedy glints in their eyes. Reynie watched them leave

the room with an unexpected pang of sympathy. Who had they been before? Had they, like Sticky, run away from home? Had they ever known parents at all? What kind of miserable life had they had, that the Institute seemed so wonderful to them now?

As the line moved forward, Reynie had a flash of insight. He imagined the special recruits' futures as they themselves must imagine them: With nowhere else to turn, no parents or grandparents begging for their returns, they would devote themselves entirely to the Institute. They would rise through the ranks of Messenger, wear their fancy tunics and sashes, and one day, when the time came, they would turn their backs on the outside world to become Executives. It wouldn't matter how they had come here, or what had come before. That part was already forgotten, or else *would* be forgotten in the pleasurable rush of being important. Of being a part of something.

Standing before the list now, Reynie didn't even look at it. His sympathy, he realized, had shifted into something else, a different feeling altogether. What was it? It certainly wasn't pleasant. Then with surprise he recognized it: *jealousy.*

"How strange," Reynie said to himself.

"What is strange?" said a man's voice.

Reynie whirled to find himself face-to-face with Mr. Curtain, who stared keenly at him from behind his silver lenses. Lost in thought, Reynie had lingered after all the others had filed out, and now he found himself alone with the Sender himself.

"I — I beg your pardon, sir?"

"You said something was strange," said Mr. Curtain, drumming his fingers upon a great, thick book in his lap. "I daresay you were referring to the Messenger list."

"Oh, yes, sir," Reynie said, then lied: "I expected to find my name on it. I've been making perfect scores."

"That is what I thought," said Mr. Curtain. "The minds of children are easily read, even gifted children like yourself, Reynard."

"I'm glad you think I'm gifted," said Reynie, sensing an opportunity. "I want to become a Messenger more than anything."

"Of course you do," said Mr. Curtain. "All the Executives have reported how well you're doing. Both you and your friend George Washington have far exceeded expectations. In fact, in the history of the Institute, no one has ever mastered so much material so quickly."

Mr. Curtain's chair had been rolling closer, slowly, almost imperceptibly, so that now their faces were very near to each other. "It is a strange coincidence, is it not, that two such gifted children should be admitted to the Institute at the very same time, and that they should be such close friends?"

Hidden behind those reflective lenses, Mr. Curtain's expression was difficult to read. Was he suspicious? Reynie's heart, already beating double-time, kicked into a higher gear. "As for being admitted at the same time," he said, "that *is* a coincidence. But it's no surprise that two good students should become good friends, especially if they're roommates."

"True," said Mr. Curtain with an approving crook of one eyebrow. "You are a bright child, a *very* bright child, Reynard, and I believe you would make a fine Messenger. Do you believe that yourself?"

"Oh, yes, sir, very much!" cried Reynie with as much enthusiasm as he could muster.

"Good. But you must remember, Reynard, that you are new. Your time has not yet come. Not yet. It will come soon, however, if only you are patient. I trust you are capable of patience?"

"I'll do my best, Mr. Curtain."

"That is all we ask, my boy. I must confess I am not a patient man myself." Here Mr. Curtain's voice changed. Where it had been briefly paternal and encouraging, it now turned searching. "Take, for example, your female friend, the diminutive Miss Contraire. I am losing patience with her. My Executives have just reported that although her quiz scores are improving, she remains quite unruly — sleeping during lessons, refusing to speak when questioned, making sour faces at the Executives, that sort of thing."

Inwardly, Reynie groaned.

"She doesn't seem dedicated," Mr. Curtain went on. "Her insolent behavior contradicts her quiz scores. I don't understand her motivations, and when I don't understand something, Reynard, it is natural that I don't trust it."

"Perfectly natural, sir," Reynie agreed. "But you know what they say about people you don't trust."

"No," said Mr. Curtain, lifting one eyebrow. "What do they say?"

"If you don't trust them, keep them close."

Mr. Curtain burst out with a screechy laugh that made Reynie jump. "Keep them close. Very good. There is even more to you than I'd thought, Reynard Muldoon. Very well, I'll keep her close, as you do, and perhaps one day she will prove useful."

"Perhaps so," Reynie said. He had the distinct feeling that

something between them had changed — as if he had passed a test. *A test I didn't know I was taking,* he thought with a curious sense of déjà vu.

"Yes, keep them close," said Mr. Curtain, stroking his chin. He seemed to be considering something. "Yes, that is the best way to control the problem. And control is the key, my boy. Never forget that. Control is always the key."

"No, sir," said Reynie. "I won't forget."

Mr. Curtain smiled. "Very well, Reynard, I have decided something. I should like to speak with you further. Come with me to my office, won't you? Step along quickly now. I hate to waste time getting from one place to the next." And spinning his chair about, Mr. Curtain rocketed from the room.

Reynie hesitated only long enough to take a deep, deep breath, then hurried after him.

Mr. Curtain did hate to waste time. Reynie had to run to keep up with him. Through the empty corridors and across the cafeteria, where the Helpers were busy preparing supper, Mr. Curtain never slowed — not even when he approached the door onto the plaza. Slamming it open with the front of his chair (and scattering frightened students left and right), he zoomed across the plaza and the rock garden, his wheels spitting up bits of gravel that stung Reynie's arms. Racing along behind, Reynie saw his friends across the plaza, staring after him in wonder and not a little apprehension. He waved to reassure them, though at this moment he could have used some reassurance himself.

As Mr. Curtain banged through the door to the Institute Control Building, it occurred to Reynie that every door in the

Institute must have been designed to be opened in this violent manner. Mr. Curtain clearly would not bear having to wait for a door to open. Nor to wait for any lagging students, and so Reynie hurried on. They passed down a number of door-lined corridors, which must be the Recruiter quarters and Executive suites. At last they came to a plain metal door, whereupon Mr. Curtain stopped so abruptly that Reynie — who had expected him to smash it open without slowing — almost ran up against the back of his wheelchair. Now he saw the numeric keypad beside the door. Mr. Curtain kept his office locked. Directing Reynie to look away, Mr. Curtain punched in the number code, the door slid swiftly open, and Mr. Curtain shot into the office. Reynie had to leap forward before the door closed again.

Mr. Curtain's office was an oblong, white-stoned room with no windows. It seemed bony and cold, like an empty skull. The bare stone floor had not even a rug, and there was a drain in it, perhaps for the sake of cleaning. High on the wall behind Mr. Curtain's desk, in a heavy silver frame, hung an old map of Holland (Mr. Curtain's place of birth, Reynie remembered) along with several sketches of Stonetown Harbor and Nomansan Island. Beneath the sketches stood a row of locked cabinets — bookshelves, Reynie realized, but locked so no one could get at the books. Mr. Curtain's desk, a dull-polished, Spartan metal affair, was carefully organized with file boxes and short stacks of paper. On one corner of the desk sat an artificial violet in a pot. The flower looked perfectly real, was in excellent condition, and unlike Mr. Benedict's *live* violet, required no care. How strangely similar the two men were, Reynie thought, and yet how utterly different.

Mr. Curtain motioned for Reynie to sit across the desk

from him, then set his large black book upon the desk. It was clearly an old book, with a binding that had been mended more than once and with several pages dog-eared throughout. The book fell open to a place Mr. Curtain had marked with a paper clip, and Reynie saw that the pages were covered with handwriting. It was a journal!

Mr. Curtain was drumming his fingers on the desk and regarding Reynie in silence. It suddenly occurred to Reynie that perhaps *he* was expected to speak. "Did — did you want to show me something in that book?"

Mr. Curtain frowned. "*This* book? Certainly not." He reached forward and snapped the journal closed. "I was only collecting my thoughts, Reynard. Tell me, what do you think of my map? I saw you looking at it as we entered."

"Your map of Holland, sir? It's quite lovely."

"Isn't it, though?" Mr. Curtain said, his tone shifting to fondness. "I was born in Holland, you see — an orphan like yourself. I spent my childhood there, too, and a terrible childhood it was. Taunted and bullied, ridiculed and abused by other children. I don't miss my childhood, but I do, on occasion, miss Holland, a country with an admirable tradition."

"If you don't mind my asking, sir, why did the other children torment you?"

"I *do* mind your asking," Mr. Curtain said coldly, but then he collected himself and said in a friendlier tone, "We both know you've had similar experiences, do we not, Reynard? For being different?"

Reynie hesitated, then nodded.

"People are capable of great wickedness, Reynard. They cause each other such misery. This is why I'm particularly proud of my work. Despite having been persecuted myself, my chief goal in life is to bring happiness to all." He smiled a tight smile, a smile that gave Reynie the feeling Mr. Curtain half-believed what he said, but also that something else, something much larger and darker, lay beneath.

"Now, Reynard, to the point," said Mr. Curtain. "I don't believe there's ever been such a clever student at my Institute as you. You have a shrewd, strong mind. I saw this at once. And you are a natural leader."

"I don't know about that, sir. I —"

"Don't argue with me, Reynard," said Mr. Curtain. "I dislike contradiction."

"Sorry, sir."

Mr. Curtain's tone softened. "A natural leader, I say. Oh, you may not see it yourself, but I daresay I can see a bit more than you. The way your friends gather about you, the way your enemies wish to destroy you — don't think I haven't noticed these things. It is familiar to me, you see. You remind me of myself at your age."

"I'm . . . flattered, sir. I'm sure you were a brilliant student."

"No doubt," said Mr. Curtain with a smile. "And I had my share of enemies, too. Children despise superior minds, you know, especially in leaders, who must often make unpopular decisions."

Reynie thought suddenly of Kate and Sticky, who had been so shocked at his suggestion to cheat on the quizzes. But they didn't *despise* him, he knew that. . . .

"One problem with being a leader," Mr. Curtain was saying, "is that even among your friends you are alone, for it is you — and you alone — to whom the others look for final guidance." (Reynie felt a pang. That was true, he thought. He did feel that way sometimes.) "I'm not saying this is your experience *now*," Mr. Curtain went on, "for you are only a boy. But in your future you may wish to choose carefully with whom you associate. No point in being a regular sort of person, Reynard. You have a greater calling, a duty to yourself, and you must pursue it with all your heart and mind."

"And . . . how should I do that?" Reynie asked.

"This is what I'm arriving at," said Mr. Curtain. "When you are a little older and more experienced, I have you in mind as an Executive."

"An Executive!"

"I see you are amazed. You should not be. No, the question is not whether you have the ability to be an Executive — you have that in abundance — but whether you have the inclination. You are an orphan, I know. No doubt you have little to miss in your old life. And so I urge you strongly to consider what might constitute a *new* life — a life as an Executive."

"Well, from what I've seen —," Reynie began.

Mr. Curtain screeched — that is, laughed — and cut Reynie short. "Ah, yes, what you've *seen*. There is more to being an Executive than what you've *seen*, Reynard. There soon will be, at any rate. See here, I am about to tell you something only my Executives and a handful of Messengers know. You're to hold this information in utmost secrecy. If it comes back to me, I will know it was you who told it, do you understand?"

Reynie could not imagine what he was about to be told. His heart and stomach seemed to be switching places inside him, then changing their minds and switching again. "I understand, sir."

"Very well," said Mr. Curtain. "Here is the secret: Things

are going to change, Reynard. They are going to *improve*. I will not say precisely how. That will come later, after you have proven yourself. Suffice it to say that the Institute as you know it is destined to change. Grand things lie in store. The Improvement is quite near, and after it has occurred there will be no such thing as Messengers anymore. Much to the heartbreak of my students, I know, but it is for the better."

Reynie almost started in his seat. No more Messengers? Why not?

"Even so," Mr. Curtain was saying, "I shall still need Executives, and I intend to keep on a few of the best Messengers to groom for higher service when they come of age. Obviously I am thinking of you . . . and perhaps your friend George Washington, too, though about him I am less certain. He possesses enormous talent, but I fear the fidgeting belies an underlying weakness. However, I am loath to dismiss him out of hand. I have an open mind, you see. In fact," he added with one of his short, screeching laughs, "*open* minds are what I prize most!"

Mr. Curtain pressed a button on his chair, and the office door slid open. Reynie was being dismissed.

"Thank you, sir," Reynie said, stepping out into the corridor, where Jackson stood waiting for him.

"Don't thank me," Mr. Curtain called as the door slid closed. "Impress me!"

When at last the lights were out, the girls had descended from the ceiling, and Reynie had told his friends everything that had happened, the first thing Constance could think to say was, "You don't trust me?"

"Come on, Constance," Sticky said. "That's just what he wanted Mr. Curtain to think. It's better than having him suspicious of Reynie, too, you know."

Kate pretzeled up her legs and thrust her chin into her hands. "The Improvement," she said. "So that's what Mr. Curtain calls the thing to come. And he said he won't need Messengers anymore?"

"That's what he said," said Reynie. "But I knew better than to ask why. I still need to prove myself to him."

"Well, we'd better pass all this on to Mr. Benedict," Sticky said, climbing up onto the television. As soon as the coast was clear, he sent their report, outlining all they'd learned: Mr. Curtain called the thing to come the Improvement, it was coming very soon, and Messengers wouldn't be needed. A few minutes later a response began flashing among the mainland trees.

"Here it comes," Sticky said.

Do not worry, the message said.

And then, after a short pause: **But do hurry.**

Everything As It Should Be

Before supper the next day, the Mysterious Benedict Society, hopeful for clues, climbed the hill beyond the gym to take a look around. It was quite a high hill, but if you moved at a quick pace — and Kate *always* moved at a quick pace, even with Constance riding piggyback — you could follow the winding path to the summit in a matter of minutes. This Kate did, with Reynie and Sticky panting along behind her at some distance. By the time the boys reached the top, she was already surveying the area with her spyglass.

Reynie mopped his brow. "See anything?"

Kate shrugged. "Grass and rocks, bushes and rocks, vines and rocks, sand and rocks. Lots of rocks," she said, lowering the spyglass. Then, ever so casually, she added, "I also found another trap."

"A trap?" Sticky said, glancing all around, as if the trap might sneak up and grab him.

"Don't worry, it's way down there, in a little grassy area behind the Institute Control Building. You can't see it from anywhere else, but if you aim the spyglass over the roof of the classroom building, you can just see it." She offered the spyglass to Sticky, who declined. He didn't care to see any more traps. Reynie took a look, though, and sure enough, from this spot you could just make out the telltale drapeweed and boulders behind the building.

Reynie returned the spyglass to her. "I wonder why both traps are right next to a group of boulders."

"Don't you think it's to make them harder to see?" Kate said. "By moonlight or sunlight, the drapeweed would almost always be in shadow."

"Crafty," said Constance.

"Drapeweed was a perfect choice, then," said Sticky. "It's a shade-loving plant."

"Put away the spyglass," Reynie murmured. "We have company."

Two Helpers had appeared on the path below them, each lugging two buckets full of gardening tools. They were making their slow way up the hill, clearing weeds and debris from the paths. As they drew near, they moved wordlessly to the edge of the path, so as not to disturb the children.

"Good afternoon," Reynie said, forgetting that he usually

avoiding greeting Helpers. He was nervous about the spyglass and had wanted to seem casual.

The Helpers, a man and a woman, glanced at Reynie with fearful suspicion. To ease their worries he smiled good-naturedly and gave a little wave — then immediately regretted it. The Helpers, feeling compelled to reciprocate, stopped walking and set down their buckets so they could wave back.

"Nice buckets," Kate said.

"Thank you, miss. They do the job," said one of the Helpers, a short rotund man who looked rather like a bullfrog and sounded even more like one.

At the sound of his voice, Reynie started. He knew this man! He took a step closer and peered at the man's face. The Helper took a step backward and averted his eyes.

"Mr. Bloomburg?" Reynie said. "I almost didn't recognize you!"

Greatly discomfited, the Helper turned to his partner, a wisp of a woman who seemed to be trying to hide behind her hair. "Is he speaking to you?"

"Have you gone mad?" the woman hissed, first rolling her eyes at her partner, then flashing a miserable, conciliatory smile at the children. She made an effort to speak calmly: "He said *Mister*. Didn't you, young man? Anyway, my name's not Bloomburg."

"Well, neither is mine," said the man, and, looking at the ground near Reynie's feet, he said, "Please don't take offense, but my name is Harry Harrison."

"You aren't Mr. Bloomburg?"

"I don't mean to be contrary," said Harry Harrison (the other Helper signaled her vigorous agreement), "and I hope you won't be displeased. But no."

The other children were staring at Reynie, who seemed dreadfully confused. "But . . . but . . . how long have you worked here?"

The Helper glanced at his partner. "A long time, wouldn't you say, Mary?"

"I know *I've* been here a long time," the woman said, looking at the ground, "and you've been here for most of that, so yes."

"I hope that's okay," said Harry.

"But how long, exactly?" Reynie pressed.

"I'm sorry," Harry said, and he did indeed seem very sorry. "I don't believe I remember the exact date. Do you, Mary?"

"The exact date, no. But certainly a long time."

Reynie put his hands on his head. "You've never visited Stonetown Orphanage?"

"You seem agitated," said Mary in a worried tone. "I'm sorry if we've upset you. Aren't we sorry, Harry?"

"Very sorry indeed," said Harry, miserably. "We didn't mean to bother you."

"You haven't upset me," said Reynie, sounding very upset. "But are you not troubled that you can't remember exactly when you came here?"

At this, both Helpers shook their heads and said, "Everything is just as it should be."

The children's eyes widened, but the Helpers seemed unaware of the oddity of their response. They were only waiting to be dismissed, hoping the children would not abuse them or get them into trouble.

"I'm glad to hear that," Reynie said at last. He seemed finally to be recovering. He even managed to chuckle and say, "I'm sorry, I'm really a dunce. You just look so much like him . . . this person I used to know. Obviously I've made a mistake. Nice talking to you, though."

The Helpers were relieved. "Oh, indeed . . . very nice . . . a great pleasure . . . ," they said, taking up their buckets and hurrying down the other side of the hill.

"Okay, what was *that* all about?" asked Kate when they were out of earshot.

Reynie's brows were knitted with concentration. "That was Mr. Bloomburg, no doubt about it. His face, his shape, that froggy voice — there's no question it was him. And yet he pretended not to know me — pretended not to be *himself*. Now why would he do that?"

"Maybe he's a secret agent," Constance said. "You know, like Milligan was. And you were blowing his cover."

"Mr. Bloomburg?" Reynie said. "I doubt it."

"He did kind of remind me of Milligan, though," Sticky said. "Did anyone else notice how sad he seemed? How sad they *both* seemed? In their eyes, I mean. I'd never gotten a good look at a Helper's eyes before — they're always looking away. But with these two I could plainly see it."

"That's true," Kate reflected. "I don't think I've ever seen anyone so sad as Milligan, but these two came awfully close. Reynie, do you think — *Reynie*, what's wrong?"

The color had drained from Reynie's face. He stood staring off into the distance, at nothing in particular, and indeed he looked as if nothingness were exactly what he wished to see.

"Are you okay?" Sticky said.

Reynie didn't answer. He had finally come to understand something that would have seemed obvious had it not seemed impossible: Milligan, the missing agents, Mr. Bloomburg — they had all had their memories stolen.

Once this had occurred to him, a great many puzzle pieces suddenly fit together. When Milligan was captured, he'd thought Mr. Curtain *discovered* his amnesia, when in fact Mr. Curtain had *caused* it. That was why Mr. Curtain got so angry when Milligan said his memory was fine. Mr. Curtain had wanted to steal his memory, or wipe it away — or whatever it was that might be done to memories — and then retrain him as a Helper. Just like the other agents. Mr. Curtain had transformed all those meddlesome people into his own private workforce, and they didn't even realize it.

The Helpers had been programmed to believe that "everything is as it should be." But you could see it in their eyes. Their lost lives, their lost families — something inside them missed those things terribly.

"Reynie, you're worrying us," said Kate. "What's the matter? Reynie!"

At last Reynie's eyes focused, and he turned to his friends and told them what he'd just realized.

Kate, Sticky, and Constance stood dumbfounded — struggling, just as Reynie had, to accept that such a thing was possible. And yet, once you believed it was possible, so many things could be explained. It finally made sense how the special recruits, if they'd been kidnapped, could seem so untroubled: They had been kidnapped, all right; they just didn't *remember* it. And Charlie Peters! He had seemed so dazed — just like the special recruits on their first day — and then so disturbed when the boys asked him about special privileges. "I can't say," he'd told them. He was disturbed because he really *couldn't* say — he couldn't remember!

"This is crazy, but it all seems to fit," Kate said, pacing on the path. "Except why aren't the special recruits as sad as the Helpers? They seem pretty happy to be here."

"Charlie didn't seem that sad, either," Sticky reflected. "He got upset, but he wasn't really sad. It must be different with lacunar amnesia. Maybe —"

"Wait a minute," Constance demanded. "Back up and say that again in human words."

"Lacunar amnesia? It means you can't remember a specific event."

"That explains it," Reynie said. "You only get sad if you can't remember all the things that are dear to you. If you only lose a *little* of your memory, you just get confused for a while — confused but not sad."

"That's exactly how I feel right now," said Kate. "Who *is* Mr. Bloomburg, Reynie? Why is he here?"

"He was a school facilities inspector. He'd come around the orphanage every six months or so. Mr. Rutger was afraid of him — afraid he'd find something wrong and the orphanage would have to pay for repairs — but Mr. Bloomburg was a good man. Always laughing, always talking. He chatted constantly with anyone who'd listen. And afterward he'd give the kids ginger snaps. A very friendly, very kind man . . ."

Reynie trailed off. He gazed across the harbor channel toward the mainland, as if by gazing he might somehow get back there, and not just to the land, but to a time when he didn't know all the things he knew now.

"What was he talking about all the time?" Kate asked.

"His children," Reynie said.

"Oh," said Kate soberly.

"He loved them dearly," said Reynie. "And now look at

him, afraid of every child he sees. It's not even a year since I saw him last."

Kate was putting it together. "So Mr. Bloomburg came to the Institute to make an inspection, which was never supposed to happen, and he didn't like what he found —"

"And Mr. Curtain made sure that he never went back," Reynie finished.

"But how could Mr. Bloomburg forget his *children*?" Sticky protested. "It doesn't seem possible. Can it really be possible? Can *any* of this be possible?"

Reynie made no reply.

"I just can't believe it," Sticky said, wishing he really couldn't.

OF FAMILIES

LOST AND FOUND

The mood in their meeting that night was subdued: no bickering, no laughter, only a general feeling of grim resolve. Now that the children finally knew some things, they all rather missed *not* knowing them.

If only they had proof of what they knew! But all they had was their word, and the word of children, they knew, amounted to nothing. If the authorities wouldn't listen to Mr. Benedict, they certainly wouldn't listen to children. Reynie and the others could argue all day that Mr. Curtain was erasing people's memories, that dozens of government agents were being held captive on Nomansan Island — but they couldn't begin to explain *why* it was all happening, and without proof, no one would help them try to find out.

"If we could lay our hands on that journal," Kate had said, "do you think that would be proof enough?"

"Fat chance," said Sticky. "Mr. Curtain always has it with him."

"Anyway, even if we stole it and convinced people to read it," said Reynie, "they'd think it was a hoax. Mr. Curtain's messages have made sure of that."

"At least *we* could read it," Kate said. "You know it's chock full of information, and some of it might be exactly what Mr. Benedict needs. . . ." She sighed. "But you're right, swiping it would be too risky. I wish we could do *something*, though."

"We're doing all we can, aren't we?" Sticky said. "We're telling Mr. Benedict everything we know."

"Speaking of that," said Reynie, "we should send our report. There's a lot to tell."

So much to tell, in fact, that Sticky was complaining of a blister on his finger by the time he'd finished the report. A few minutes later a reply flashed from the mainland trees:

What has been lost may yet be found. Have hope.

"Is he saying *he* has hope," said Constance irritably, "or is he telling *us* to have hope?"

"Either way," Reynie said, "I think he believes those people might be able to get their memories back. Maybe he thinks he can find a way to do it. That's a pretty hopeful thing, isn't it?"

"Assuming we can stop whatever Mr. Curtain's up to," Sticky said.

Constance stood up. "You're not helping my hopefulness,

George Washington. I'm going to bed." She frowned at the ceiling, then looked at Kate. "I'll need a ride."

After the meeting was adjourned and the girls had gone, Sticky and Reynie climbed into their bunks. Reynie hardly felt like sleeping, but he did need to calm down and clear his thoughts, and so lying in his bunk he turned to his usual method. He wrote a mental letter:

> *Dear Miss Perumal,*
>
> *Every time I think of poor Mr. Bloomburg and his family, my mind returns to you. How would your mother — whom I know you love so much — feel if you just suddenly vanished from her life? It is an awful thing to consider. She loves and depends upon you, and I know you depend upon her, too. I never think of you without remembering your mother, too.*
>
> *With these thoughts on my mind, I had a strange feeling earlier tonight. Looking around at Sticky, Kate, and Constance, I wondered how I'd feel if one of them disappeared. Sometimes Constance drives me crazy, but now I can't imagine being here without her. I can't say for sure, because I have no experience, but — well, is this what family is like? The feeling that everyone's connected, that with one piece missing the whole thing's broken?*

Reynie paused in his letter to consider. Of the four of them, Sticky was the only one to have a memory of family life. Was it worse for him, Reynie wondered, to have felt loved and then rejected? Or was it worse to have always felt alone? Kate said she had no memory of her dead mother, nor of her father who abandoned her. And Constance — well, they knew almost nothing of Constance, but Reynie had the feeling that she, too, had never known a family.

Reynie's mind went back to his last night at Mr. Benedict's house. It seemed so long ago now, yet he remembered it with absolute clarity. Much like tonight, he had felt too worked up to sleep, and despite the late hour he had slipped quietly out of bed and crept down to Mr. Benedict's study. Mr. Benedict had welcomed Reynie to sit up with him if he had trouble sleeping; and obviously he'd quite expected Reynie to do so, for when Reynie arrived, a cup of hot tea was waiting for him on Mr. Benedict's desk. There was even a little jar of honey (and judging from the way Mr. Benedict's papers stuck to his fingers as he worked, he had already been into it himself).

"You have a question for me?" Mr. Benedict said, as Reynie sat down.

Reynie laughed. "How do you always know?"

"I'm not sure," Mr. Benedict admitted. "Perhaps it's a matter of empathy. I know that if I were you I'd have questions." He scratched the top of his head with one of his pencils. "Though come to think of it, perhaps it's a matter of odds. You seem the type always to have questions. Thus at any given moment, it's a safe bet for me to assume you have one."

"I was wondering if you ever wish you had a family," Reynie sputtered. He hadn't meant to speak so directly, but once he'd begun to ask it, the words just tumbled out.

Mr. Benedict nodded. "Certainly when I was your age I did. But not anymore."

Reynie wasn't sure whether to be comforted or depressed by this revelation. He'd been wondering how it would feel for him to grow up without relatives. "You . . . you grew out of it, then? You stopped wanting it?"

"Oh, no, Reynie, you don't grow out of it. It's just that once you acquire a family, you no longer need to wish for one."

Reynie was caught off guard. "You *have* a family?"

"Absolutely," Mr. Benedict replied. "You must remember, family is often born of blood, but it doesn't *depend* on blood. Nor is it exclusive of friendship. Family members can be your best friends, you know. And best friends, whether or not they are related to you, can be your family."

Reynie had drunk up those words like life-saving medicine. Even though the next morning he would leave on a dangerous mission, even though he knew something terrible was coming down the pike, those words of Mr. Benedict's had made all good things seem possible. Reynie had gone to bed thinking of the people he might one day — if everything turned out all right — consider a part of *his* family.

And now, lying in his dark room at the Institute in an altogether different mood, Reynie finished the letter he had begun to one of those very people.

At least I had you, Miss Perumal, if only for a while. Maybe you weren't my family, but you were the closest thing I had — maybe that I'll ever have. And now things are awful and seem likely to get worse, and I worry that I'll never have the chance to tell you what it meant to me. . . .

"Reynie?" whispered Sticky from the bunk below.

Reynie cleared his throat. "Yes?"

"Were you having a bad dream? It sounded like you were crying."

Reynie wiped his eyes. "I just . . . just can't get over what he's done to those poor people."

"I know," Sticky said. "It's maddening to think what might be in that journal of his — to think there might be something we could use to stop him . . . but I know there's no way we can lay hands on it."

Reynie sat bolt upright. "Sticky!"

Sticky nearly fell out of bed. "What? What is it?"

"Maybe we're looking at this the wrong way," Reynie said. "Maybe we don't *have* to lay hands on it!"

The last class was dismissed into a perfect fall afternoon. Blue skies, cool temperatures, the subtlest of breezes. The sun seemed to rest upon a distant hilltop like a giant orange on a giant table.

On the plaza, Mr. Curtain sat in his favorite spot, gazing off toward the bridge, reading a newspaper with a look of satisfaction, occasionally making a note in his journal. A few students had gathered at the edges of the plaza and in the rock garden, passing the time before supper. As always, they gave Mr. Curtain plenty of room. No one dared go near him while he was working — which is why so many jaws dropped when Reynard Muldoon was spotted walking toward him. Did the new kid not know any better? Was he just dying for a visit to the Waiting Room? No student had ever approached Mr. Curtain on the plaza before.

Reynie guessed this, which is why his breath came so short. But keeping his shoulders squared and one hand behind his back, he did what no other student dared to do. He approached from the front, knowing he would have only one shot at this; his plan would be spoiled if Mr. Curtain turned his chair. "Mr. Curtain, sir?"

Mr. Curtain glanced up, his lenses gleaming like polished chrome in the sun.

"Sorry to bother you," Reynie said quickly. "But I couldn't help noticing that your book has a lot of dog-eared pages. I must say I was surprised."

Mr. Curtain seemed unsure whether to be angry or incredulous. "You're surprised I have pages to which I often refer?"

"Oh, no, sir! I'm surprised nobody has ever given you a suitable present." Reynie showed Mr. Curtain what he'd been holding behind his back — a fistful of thin blue ribbons. "Book markers! I thought they should be special, so I asked a laundry Helper for some sash material — I'm sure you recognize that shade of blue — which she cut into ribbons and sewed up nicely along the edges." Reynie held out the ribbons, which were indeed elegantly stitched. "I hope you like them."

Mr. Curtain was taken aback. He was flattered, it was true, yet his expression clearly showed that he agreed with Reynie, that he rather thought someone *should* have given him such a present before now. It was a proper attention that had been lacking. "Thank you, Reynard," he said with a tight nod. "An appropriate gift indeed, from one young scholar to his superior. I shall put them to good use." Mr. Curtain returned to his newspaper.

"Sir?" Reynie said. "Aren't you going to put them in?"

Mr. Curtain grunted impatiently, his expression darkening. The boy was a nuisance. And yet the nuisance *had* flattered him, and the ribbons *would* be useful. His expression softened a little. Finally he sighed and set aside his newspaper. Flipping his journal back to the first dog-eared page, he slipped a ribbon inside. He was beginning to turn the page when Reynie said, "What exactly *is* that book, sir?"

Mr. Curtain paused. "It's a journal, Reynard. Every great thinker keeps a journal, you know." He returned to his bookmarking.

"I must say, it's an awfully big journal."

"What better place to record 'awfully big' ideas, eh?" said Mr. Curtain, which was just what Reynie had thought he would say. "Now, Reynard, no more interruptions. I have a great deal of work to do." Mr. Curtain flipped to the next dog-eared page.

"Sir? One last question?"

"A *very* last question, Reynard," Mr. Curtain said, looking up. "Go ahead."

"Why are you always gazing off toward the bridge?"

"Ah, I suppose it does appear that I'm looking at the bridge," Mr. Curtain said with a smile. "In fact I'm gazing fondly toward one of my greatest accomplishments — the tidal turbines. I trust you know about the turbines?" Reynie nodded. "I thought so; they're quite famous. They are an extraordinary invention, you see, and part of the great tradition."

"The tradition, sir?"

"Do you not recall my mentioning my homeland's admirable tradition? I was referring to the great conquest — the conquest of the sea. Holland claimed much of its land from the sea, you know. Dikes and polders, my boy! Nothing in the world less controllable than the sea, and yet the Dutch found a way to control it. And now, in my own way, I have done the very same thing. My turbines capture the ocean's infinite energy, which I use for my own purposes. Is it not remarkable?"

"It's the most remarkable thing I've ever heard," Reynie said, equally impressed by Mr. Curtain's remarkable vanity.

"No doubt," said Mr. Curtain. He clapped his hands together. "But enough delay. Even greater things lie ahead, Reynard, much greater things, and we must waste no time achieving them." He began paging through the rest of his journal, inserting the ribbons.

Mr. Curtain was turning the pages with disheartening speed, but Reynie dared not interrupt again. Instead he allowed himself one glance — and a brief one, at that — behind Mr. Curtain, toward the hill path leading up beyond the dormitory. A short distance from the bottom, the path curved around a large potted cactus. Nothing unusual about this — there were many such cactuses set along the Institute paths — but this particular cactus seemed to have several *arms*. A cactupus, Reynie thought with an inward smile.

"There," said Mr. Curtain, holding up the journal, with the ends of ribbons sticking out here and there. "Satisfied?"

"Oh, yes, sir," said Reynie, though in truth he was disappointed. He could see many dog-eared pages remaining. (He would have liked to bring more ribbons, but the timid Helper had given him all the sash material she could spare. She'd been afraid to disappoint him but terrified to give him more.)

"You're quite welcome," Mr. Curtain replied, as if it were Reynie who'd been given the present and not himself. "And now you may leave."

This time Reynie needed no urging. He hurried off the plaza and across the rock garden, where several students gaped at him, surprised to see him still alive. He even seemed to be *happy*. Then Reynie reached the path and hurried uphill toward the cactupus.

Constance stood high above on the hilltop, keeping a lookout — actually doing what she'd been asked to do, which was promising. Behind the cactus, Kate was on her hands and knees, and Sticky stood precariously on her back. He was peering through Kate's spyglass, which he had steadied atop a high cactus branch.

"Did he get anything?" Reynie whispered to Kate, so as not to disturb Sticky.

"You don't have to whisper," Sticky said. "I did get a little, and I'll get more if he'll just write anything. He's on a fresh page, but now he's gazing away again."

"Only a little?" Reynie said.

"He was turning the pages pretty fast. . . ."

"Sorry, I tried to stall him as best I could."

"And I could only see a small part of each page," Sticky said. He glanced down at Reynie with an impish smile. "But I do remember what I saw."

"Is it any good?" Reynie asked.

"Beats me. I haven't had time to think about it. There's a difference between remembering and thinking, at least for me." He returned to the spyglass. "Could you see us at all?"

"Kate's forearms and your elbows, but you're pretty well hidden," Reynie said. "Anyway, from below it's impossible to see what you're doing."

"What about from above?" Sticky asked. "Are we still clear in that direction?"

Reynie turned to check on Constance. It was good that he did. Constance was hurrying down the path toward them. For Constance, though, "hurrying" meant running a few steps and tripping, running a few steps more and stumbling. . . .

And walking about twenty yards behind her was Jackson.

"Jackson's coming!" Reynie hissed.

He was immediately knocked to the ground. Sticky, in his fright, had fallen off Kate's back and crashed onto Reynie. The spyglass flew out of Sticky's hand and onto the gravel path . . . and before the boys could gather themselves, Jackson had brushed past Constance — knocking her roughly to her knees — and was upon them. "What's going on here?"

"We were . . . trying to make a human pyramid," Reynie said.

"A human pyramid? With three kids?" Jackson said with a sneer. "That's pathetic. And what's this?" He had seen the spyglass and was bending to pick it up.

Kate sprang forward and snatched it away. "It's mine, that's what it is!"

Jackson stared at Kate, amazed a student had spoken to him that way. Then his amazement gave way to anger. "You'll show it to me *here*," he said in a threatening voice, "or else in the Waiting Room. It's your choice, Wetherall."

Kate stared back at him, defiant. The others held their breath.

"Fine," Jackson said with a smile. He was beginning to enjoy himself. "Let me just tell you how this works. I'm about to grab your arm — and I intend to squeeze so hard it hurts — and escort you to the Waiting Room. If you try to run away or fight me, I'll personally see to it that you get kicked out of the Institute . . . *after* you go to the Waiting Room. How does that sound?"

Kate had no choice. Reluctantly she held out the spyglass. As Jackson snatched it from her grasp, Sticky turned away, his face hidden in his hands. He couldn't bear to look.

Jackson burst into laughter. "A kaleidoscope? You risked going to the Waiting Room for a *kaleidoscope?*" He put his eye to the lens.

"Yes, but it's *my* kaleidoscope," Kate said.

"Well, you can keep it," Jackson said in disgust. He handed Kate her spyglass back. "This is the sorriest kaleidoscope I've ever seen."

Reynie grimaced his way through studytime, trying to ignore a broadcast that went on for two hours. After it ended, Reynie noticed Sticky was still grimacing. Sticky had spent all of studytime reproducing what he'd seen in Mr. Curtain's journal and was still at his desk. "What's the matter?" Reynie asked him. "Forget something?"

Sticky groaned. "Forgetting isn't the problem. Art is the problem." He threw down his pencil. "There was a diagram in there, but I can't draw worth a flip. Words and numbers, yes. Pictures? Hopeless."

"You can always try again," Reynie said, looking over Sticky's shoulder at the drawing. It seemed to depict a mound of spaghetti with numbered meatballs. "We have a minute before lights out. It'll be easier if you don't have to use the flashlight."

"Flashlight or floodlight, it won't matter. I'd do just as well in the dark. This was my fourth try. It was supposed to be a diagram of Mr. Curtain's brain, with lots of numbers on every region."

Reynie stared doubtfully at the picture. "Are you sure it was Mr. Curtain's brain?"

"It said 'MY BRAIN' at the top of the page."

"Oh. Well, I don't suppose there was a key to those numbers, was there? Or an explanation of the diagram?"

Sticky shook his head. "Not on that page."

Reynie patted him on the back. "Then don't worry about it. We don't need a diagram to know what a brain looks like."

Sticky's face shone with relief. "Really? Oh, I hoped you would say that!" He tore the page into tiny bits. Reynie helped him shred the other attempted drawings, too, most of which resembled misshapen balls of yarn with numbered threads. They finished just as the girls made their appearance in the ceiling.

Everyone was eager to begin. In no time the lights were off and they were all seated in a circle on the floor.

"Okay, I have all the entries written down," said Sticky, showing them a thin stack of papers. "They cover a lot of time — the first is from years ago, and the last was written to-day. Shall I read them aloud?"

The others agreed, and so, starting with the first entry, Sticky read:

*No one seems to realize how much we are driven by
FEAR, the essential component of human personality. Everything else — from ambition to love to
despair — derives in some way from this single
powerful emotion. Must find the best way to make
use of this.*

"Well, *that's* cheery," Kate said.

"I'll bet Mr. Curtain's just a big scaredy cat," Constance
said. "So he thinks everyone else is, too."

Sticky, who happened to consider *himself* a prime speci-
men of scaredy cat, moved on without comment. The next
entry, he said, was dated a year later:

*Much to my disappointment, I have concluded there
is no such thing as perfect control. I have come to
understand, however, that the illusion of perfect
control can amount to the same thing.*

"He's all about illusions," Reynie reflected. "The Institute's 'lack of rules' is an illusion, not to mention its excellent
reputation. And the Emergency, too — the hidden messages
make everything seem more hopeless and out of control than
it really is. But then where is this illusion of *control*?"

"I didn't see anything about that," Sticky replied. He
glanced at his papers. "The next few entries are all about
using children as filters to keep the messages hidden. It's
nothing we don't know. I'll skip them for now. I'm afraid the
next part is a bit technical. Ready?"

The others said they were (though Constance squeezed
her eyes shut as if expecting it to hurt), and Sticky continued:

> *Brainsweeping a success! High-power, close-contact transmission works perfectly well as a forcible procedure! Retraining should also succeed: 'Contentment' messages will 1) counteract a brainswept individual's tendency to question, and 2) lessen the chronic mournfulness effect.*
>
> *Predicted side effects of retraining: timidity, anxiety, self-doubt.*
>
> *Conclusion: satisfactory.*

Constance put her hands on her head. "Umm . . ."

"Brainsweeping must be Mr. Curtain's term for destroying people's memories," Reynie said. "If they're in his machine — I think that's what he means by 'close-contact transmission' — then he can brainsweep them against their will, which is what he means by 'forcible.' That must be what happened to Milligan, except Milligan got away before Mr. Curtain could 'retrain' him."

"But the other agents weren't so lucky," Sticky said. "Mr. Curtain retrained them with 'contentment' messages that tell them not to question anything!"

"And to feel less sad," Kate said. "But that part must not have worked so well. They all still suffer from that pesky 'chronic mournfulness effect.'"

"There's more about it in the next entry," Sticky said.

> *Long-term brainsweeping and retraining results mixed: Helpers manageable but still dispirited. Worse, too-frequent relapse of memory, often in association with trigger object. Typical episode begins*

with the last important thing remembered: names of significant persons, unfulfilled obligations, etc. Most irritating. Note: Two of last four episodes occurred near mirrors. Reflection must be promoting self-identification. Solution: Remove mirrors.

Kate rubbed her hands together. "Now I'm *really* starting to feel like a secret agent. We're figuring things out! What's next, Sticky?"

Sticky checked his papers. "We're almost finished. The next entry explains why the special recruits aren't so sad. It's more or less what we thought."

"Can you just give it in a nutshell?" Constance asked, then added: "Please?"

The others resisted looking at one another, and no one spoke. It was perhaps the first time Constance had ever used that word, and though she'd quite possibly said it by accident, no one wished to spoil the moment. If they mentioned it aloud, she might retract it. And so Sticky only nodded and gave the next entry in a nutshell.

"Remember when we talked about lacunar amnesia, or forgetting particular events? Apparently Mr. Curtain can use his machine to wipe out *specific* memories without taking away everything — without doing a complete brainsweep. It makes people dazed for a while, but then they get better, and the memories rarely come back."

"So if those Recruiters had managed to kidnap us," Kate said, "Mr. Curtain would have made sure we didn't remember it. That's why special recruits aren't scared."

"But because they weren't *completely* brainswept," Reynie

said, "they aren't *sad*, either. Which makes them better Executive material. I'll bet most of the Executives used to be special recruits. Maybe even all of them. After all, they had no families to return to on the mainland."

"I suppose that should make it harder for me to dislike them," Kate observed. "Since they were kidnapped orphans and all."

Everyone considered this for a minute. Then they looked at one another and shook their heads. They couldn't help it. They still disliked the Executives.

"But that doesn't mean we shouldn't try to help them," Reynie pointed out. "If Mr. Benedict can figure out how to bring their memories back, maybe they can start over — maybe they'll learn how not to be so nasty."

"I'm not holding my breath," Kate said.

Sticky flipped a page. "Guess what? The date of this next entry is the day we arrived on the island."

At last — all facilities now complete! Proper officials in proper places. Public mood at proper levels. The Improvement is very close at hand. Everything is ready except final modifications and the final few shipments, one of which is being loaded even as I write. Farewell! I've dispatched a Helper crew to adjust turbine output — shall require a great deal more from them in coming days.

"We saw that!" Kate said. "We saw them working on the turbines! And we saw that truck the Helpers were loading!"

"Those crates," Reynie said. He slapped his forehead. "I'm so stupid! It should have occurred to me. . . ." He looked at the others, feeling completely foolish. "I'm sure you already know what I'm talking about."

The others stared back at him, having no idea.

"I liked that part about your being stupid, though," said Constance.

"*Recruiters* were driving that truck, remember?" Reynie said. "So it must have had something valuable in it — something Mr. Curtain wanted to protect. Why else would he need such security?"

"Oh, yeah, I was just going to think of that," Kate said with a laugh. "You're too hard on yourself, Reynie."

"But if I'd thought of it sooner," Reynie argued, "Mr. Benedict might have been able to investigate! For all we know, the rest of the shipments have been sent out by now. We may never know what was in those crates."

"Maybe not," said Kate, "but we can still report it, *and* we can keep an eye out ourselves. Right?"

"True," Reynie admitted. He still felt like a dolt, but he preferred not to dwell on the feeling. "Sticky, how many more entries do you have to read?"

"Two," Sticky said. The next one was this:

Success! As of this morning, the messages are transmitting directly. To my great satisfaction, the Whisperer is now capable of

"That's it?" Kate asked.

"Sorry," Sticky said. "His hand was covering the rest."

"The Whisperer," Constance said. "So that's what he calls his dumb machine."

Reynie said nothing. He was wondering what new thing

the Whisperer was capable of now. He knew one thing for sure: If Mr. Curtain was happy about it, then it spelled bad news.

Sticky was preparing to read the last journal entry. "This is where he seems to go completely bonkers. I can't make heads or tails of it."

It's Curtain for You! Trust Ledroptha Curtain. Curtain makes things better. Feel certain about Curtain. No, Feel certain with Curtain. Curtain Has Control.

"Bizarre!" said Kate.

"Is he talking to himself?" asked Constance.

"Sounds like he's trying to convince somebody of something," Reynie said. "But who would that be?"

"It just supports my personal opinion that he's a wacko," Kate said with a shrug. "But wacko or not, he's awfully careful about keeping his secrets — which is why this has been so extremely, marvelously, wonderfully satisfying!"

Unable to sit still any longer, Kate leaped to her feet, pumped her arms in the air, and in a barely restrained whisper said, "Can you believe we actually spied in Mr. Curtain's journal and got *away* with it? The Sender himself! I say three cheers for us! Three cheers for the Mysterious Benedict Society!"

Reynie and Sticky whispered three cheers, but Constance rolled her eyes and said cheering was for babies.

"I see you're back to being yourself," Kate said with a chuckle. "But I'm not going to let it bother me." Constance scowled and started to reply, but Kate went right on talking.

"We're on a roll, everyone. We're really getting somewhere! I say we report all this to Mr. B, then tomorrow we take a peek at the loading area with my spyglass. Let's try to figure out what's in those crates!"

The others agreed; they sent their report, and two hours later Reynie was drifting away to sleep, having finished an upbeat mental letter to Miss Perumal and feeling hopeful for the first time in ages. Maybe, he thought, Mr. Benedict really *could* do something to stop Mr. Curtain. And then maybe he could help Mr. Bloomsburg and Milligan and everyone else get their memories back. It was possible, wasn't it?

Reynie breathed deeply, stretched out, and let sleep overcome him. As dark as things seemed, at least they didn't seem entirely hopeless. The children were finally making some progress. Who knew what would happen tomorrow?

Of course, Reynie could not know what would happen, and this was fortunate. For if he had known, he would never have slept so easily.

Caught in the Act

The very next day Sticky was caught cheating. In a display
of triumphant fury, Jillson marched to the rear of the room,
snatched Sticky's hand — with which he'd been tugging his
ear lobe — and demanded, "What's this?"

Terrified, Sticky mumbled, "My . . . my hand."

"Yes, but what were you *doing* with your hand?"

"Scratching my ear?"

"I'm not as stupid as I look, you know!" Jillson roared,
then hesitated, realizing what she'd said, before scowling and

saying, "That's it, Washington, you're going to the Waiting Room! Stand up!"

Jillson glanced at Reynie and Kate, and at Constance in the back, obviously suspecting one of them as a cheating partner. But the fidgety bald boy was the only one she felt confident about. "Stand *up*," she repeated, yanking Sticky to his feet as if he weighed no more than a bird. "The rest of you sit tight. I'll send another Executive to monitor your quiz — which, thanks to this cheater, you'll all have to start over from the beginning."

Boos and jeers erupted as Sticky was dragged from the room, casting one last frightened glance back at Reynie before disappearing. With an awful, helpless feeling, Reynie watched him go. He looked back at Kate, who shook her head grimly. Sticky was in deep trouble. They were *all* in deep trouble.

"Too bad, so sad," said Martina.

"What exactly *is* the Waiting Room?" asked Eustace Crust, one of the special recruits.

"Ask Corliss Danton," said Martina smugly. "Tell them, Corliss."

Corliss, who at the mention of the Waiting Room had buried his face in his hands, was silently wiping tears from his eyes. "It's . . . just a place you go when you're waiting to meet with Mr. Curtain. An . . . unpleasant place."

Reynie looked at Constance, whose face was even more sullen than usual, and fearful as well. He wanted to give her a comforting look, but she wouldn't even glance in his direction. Anyway, what good would a look do? He was no more confident than Constance that the end wasn't hurtling toward them.

It was bad enough that Sticky's worst fear had come true, but if Sticky told Mr. Curtain everything — and who could blame him if he cracked under such pressure? — it would mean the end of their mission . . . and the beginning of something *else*. What would Mr. Curtain do if he found out? Would he take away everything? A complete brainsweep? And not just for Sticky but for all of them?

Maybe they weren't even worth the trouble, Reynie thought grimly. They were orphans, after all — or in Sticky's case, believed to be. Might they not just . . . go missing? *Departed*, Mr. Curtain would call it. *Really* departed. Reynie had a panicky feeling in his belly, the kind he always got when he dreamed he'd fallen from a precipice. Only with dreams he always woke up.

After their last class of the day, the Mysterious Benedict Society — minus one member — gathered in the rock garden.

"I hope Sticky isn't suffering terribly," Kate said. "He dreaded the Waiting Room more than anything. If it had to happen to one of us, it should have been me."

"Don't worry," Constance said glumly. "You may still get your chance."

Reynie didn't point out that the Waiting Room might be the least of their worries. "Look, until Sticky comes back, I think we need to keep to our plan. Let's go check out the loading area."

The others agreed, and, with Constance riding piggyback, they left the rock garden and walked across the empty plaza. It was a bleak day, and no one, not even Mr. Curtain, was out to enjoy it. There were a few students on the path that led to the gym, however, and Reynie and the others passed them without a word. Kate had decided the hill beyond the gym would offer the best view of the loading area, so this was where they were headed now.

As the children mounted the hill, an early evening mist began to settle, and through its haze the lights of distant harbor traffic shone in blurred colors. Far to the north a foghorn groaned, reaching them less as a sound than as a trembling in their bellies, as if their bodies were pipes in a somber old organ. It was a somber evening all around.

Reaching the summit did nothing to improve their mood. Far below them, down by the bridge gate, the loading area was completely deserted. No trucks, no Helpers, no crates in sight, no point even in getting out the spyglass. The gate guards were huddled in their guardhouse, keeping warm and dry. Reynie gazed over the water toward the mainland shore. It seemed no more than a shadow in the mist, as impossible to determine as their fate.

Reynie's gaze drifted back toward the Institute. The usual crowd of students had gathered at the gym, waiting for the doors to open. From this height they looked like insects, eagerly massed at the entrance of a bug trap. In theory the gym was open all day long, and students were encouraged to use it "any time at all," but of course classes, meals, and studytime took up most of the day. In the remaining free minutes, hopeful students often took turns tugging at the door, which remained stubbornly closed. Just before supper, however, Jackson and many of the other Executives would appear from inside the gym and let the students in. If anyone had the gall to ask why the door had been locked, Jackson would respond that it *hadn't* been locked; the students had simply been unable to open it.

Constance, too, was looking down at the little crowd of students milling outside the locked doors. "The gym's always open, except when it isn't," she said, mimicking Jackson. She mopped her damp face with her damp sleeve. "What do the Executives *do* in there, anyway?"

Constance had only meant to express her annoyance (in fact she was composing an insulting poem in which Executives licked the gym floor clean), but Reynie looked at her as if she'd turned to gold.

"That's a good question! I always assumed they were exercising — just keeping the gym to themselves. But what if they're up to something else?"

Kate brought out the spyglass. "Guess what? There's a window in the back. I could take a peek. I'd need to find a way to reach it, though — it's a good ten feet off the ground. What do you think, Reynie?"

Several things raced through Reynie's mind at once. It would mean going off the path, which meant risking traps, not to mention serious trouble. But maybe they were *already* in serious trouble and didn't know it yet, and what they found out might be extremely important! Reynie frowned. He wished he had more time to deliberate, but there *was* no more time — the gym door would be unlocked any minute.

"I'll go with you," he said. "I can stand on your shoulders."

Kate grinned. "Okay! Here's the plan: We'll drop behind this hill to be out of sight of the gym, then circle around those smaller hills and sneak up from the back."

"Aren't you forgetting someone?" said Constance.

"We need a lookout. From up here you can see every-thing, and we'll be able to see you. If anyone heads around the building, jump up and down and wave your arms."

"Oh, goody," said Constance. "I get to stand here by my-self and be misted on."

But Reynie and Kate had already hurried off. They moved quickly downhill, running over damp sand and scrub brush and narrow swaths of grass, steering clear of boulders, keep-ing an eye out for drapeweed. Finally they came up to a low rise at the rear of the gym. Here they were hidden from view, and as Kate waited for Reynie to catch his breath, she jerked her thumb behind them, where the land erupted into a jum-bled labyrinth of dunes and rocky hills. "Our escape route," she whispered, "if we need one."

Reynie squinted up to the high hilltop where they'd left Constance. He could just make out her small red figure against the backdrop of gray sky. He thought she might be moving, though only slightly. "Is Constance waving? Can you tell?"

Kate peered through her spyglass. "Just picking her nose. Let's move."

Quickly they climbed over the rise and scrambled down behind the gym, where the ground gave over entirely to crumbled gray stone, as if the building had shed pieces of it-self onto the land around it. Good, Reynie thought. No foot-prints. He was worried, though, by the discovery of a back door that Kate hadn't seen or thought to mention. Reynie pointed and frowned. They didn't want surprise visitors. Kate was already working on it — she pointed to a large petrified tree limb lying among the stony rubble nearby. Together she and Reynie dragged it over and braced it against the bottom of the door.

Kate gave a satisfied nod and knelt down. Reynie climbed onto her shoulders. He steadied himself with his hands against the stone wall and got his feet set on her shoulders. Slowly, smoothly, Kate straightened up. Reynie's chin came to the bottom of the window. He could just see inside . . . and what he saw was the most curious thing.

Two lines of Recruiters — there were dozens of them — stood back to back down the length of the gym floor, as if preparing for a dance. Each of them faced some kind of cut-out figure, but Reynie wasn't sure what they were. At the far end of the lines stood Jackson, S.Q., and a great many other Executives. Jackson was shouting something Reynie couldn't make out. Again as if in a dance, the Recruiters adopted different poses. Some spread their arms as if welcoming an embrace. Others reached out as if to shake hands in greeting. And still others raised their hands, palms forward, in a calming gesture that Reynie recognized too well. All of them were smiling, smiling. Jackson shouted again.

Reynie could see the figures more plainly now. The figures came in all sizes, from small children to full-grown adults. He shuddered.

This was no dance. The Recruiters were preparing for something. But what? Hadn't Mr. Curtain's journal said new children were no longer necessary? And this many Recruiters certainly weren't required to guard the bridge gates. No, they were preparing for something else. The Improvement. The thing to come.

"All right, everyone!" Jackson shouted. "That's it for today!"

The Executives started making their way down the lines, collecting the paper figures. The practice was over, and it suddenly occurred to Reynie that he'd never seen Recruiters leaving the gym — which must mean they used the *back* door. His stomach did a flip. He and Kate needed to get out of here. "Kate," Reynie whispered, glancing down. "We need —"

He didn't finish, for just then he glanced back through the window and saw S.Q. staring up at him.

Fear shot through Reynie like a dose of hot poison. His nerves tingled all over his body, and in his panic to get down, he toppled from Kate's shoulders.

"Are you all right?" Kate whispered.

"Run!" Reynie cried, regaining his feet. "Run, run, run!"

Reynie was halfway up the rise when Kate overtook him and caught his arm in an iron grip. "Come on!"

The back door gave an ominous *thump*, then another, followed by the sound of angry curses. The tree limb had bought them a few extra seconds. Together they dashed up the rise, with Reynie half running and half being dragged behind Kate, feeling as if he'd been tied to a galloping horse. He cast one glance up at Constance — a red smudge on the hilltop, jumping up and down and waving furiously — and then he and Kate flung themselves down the other side of the rise, out of sight.

"Tell me they didn't recognize you," Kate said, pulling him to his feet.

"I don't know," said Reynie.

"Then let's head for the hills and hope for the best."

And so they fled: away from the gym, away from the paths, away from the Institute — into the tangled rock-jungle of sand dunes, ridges, and crags that made up the island's interior. Weaving among the hills, keeping low, constantly changing directions, they ran as if their lives depended upon it —

which indeed they might have. In his mind's eye Reynie kept seeing S.Q.'s disapproving, accusing eyes. Had he been recognized? *Had* he been?

When Kate thought they'd put enough distance between themselves and the gym, and was convinced they hadn't been followed, the two children hunkered beneath a scraggly copse of stunted cedar trees to rest. It was just in time — another step and Reynie might have collapsed into a useless heap. Between ragged breaths he told Kate what he'd seen, right up to the part when he'd seen S.Q. frowning at him from across the gym.

Unbelievably, or *almost* unbelievably, Kate made a joke of it. "Well, if he recognized you, he's probably wondering how you got to be so tall." She chuckled. "The poor guy, he's not the brightest —"

Reynie groaned. He'd just realized something. Having only just sat down, he struggled to his feet again. "We need to split up."

"Why? I thought we'd just circle back up to Constance —"

"Listen, Kate, they'll know it took two people. The window's too high for one person to have looked through without help, remember? You go back for Constance. If S.Q. recognized me, at least you can claim you were miles away when it happened."

"Gosh, you're right," Kate said, adjusting her bucket on her belt. "You head that way, then, and I'll fetch Constance. If we're lucky we'll be laughing about this over supper."

"If we're lucky," said Reynie, who was not feeling lucky at all. In fact he had the awful feeling he wouldn't see Kate again. If Mr. Curtain knew the truth, by tomorrow Reynie might become someone else entirely — a mixture of mysterious pain and forgotten purposes, forgotten dreams. His friends' faces would blur, like photographs somehow being *un*developed, then disappear entirely. The mission would fail. All would be lost.

Suddenly, Reynie felt compelled to grab Kate's hand. "Thanks for helping me get up that hill back there. I never could have made it in time by myself."

Kate waved him off. "Oh, good grief. Just do me a favor. If you get sent to the Waiting Room, tell Sticky I said hello."

Reynie's face fell. "It's not funny, Kate."

For a moment — a fleeting moment — Kate looked desperately sad. "Well, of course it's not funny, Reynie Muldoon. But what do you want me to do? Cry? Now get going, will you? And make sure I see you at supper!" She turned and hurried into the gloom.

And so, in the darkness and mist, Reynie picked his way alone through the forbidding hills. In half an hour he arrived, weary and wet, at a path on the far side of the Institute. Nobody accosted him in the student dormitory, where he slipped into his room and changed. And no one looked askance at him as he crossed the plaza. He had yet to meet an Executive, though. Reynie hesitated a long time at the cafeteria door. Then telling himself he must at least *pretend* to be brave, he went inside.

He saw the girls right away. They sat in damp clothes at a table to themselves. Constance resembled a wet hen — same shape, same dour crankiness, and only slightly larger — but Kate smiled when he came in, and the sight of her sunny face gave Reynie a pinprick of hope. He reminded himself Kate was capable of smiling in dire circumstances. He shouldn't assume good news. Still, nobody seemed to be paying him any attention, and the Executive on duty only gave him a bored look and turned away. So perhaps Kate really did know something.

Kate really did. The moment Reynie sat down, she told him he was safe.

Reynie thought he would die of relief.

"They were questioning students when Constance and I came down the hill," Kate said. "Nobody saw you. Jackson asked us and we told the same story. He was yelling at S.Q.: 'Is that really the best you can say? An average-looking boy? An awful lot of boys are average-looking, S.Q.!' And poor S.Q., he just kept arguing that *this* boy was *especially* average-looking. Jackson seemed ready to strangle him."

Reynie couldn't believe what he was hearing. He was safe! Really safe! And then, just as suddenly as the weight had lifted from his shoulders, it returned. For now that one worry had passed, others quickly crowded in to take its place. Sticky was still in danger. And if Sticky was, they all were.

"Are you okay?" Kate asked. "You look terrible."

"At least he's dry," said Constance, who was blotting her hair with a napkin.

"You haven't seen Sticky, have you? Or heard anything?"

The girls shook their heads. They all grew very solemn, then, and finished their meal in silence.

THE WAITING ROOM

Reynie sat alone in his room. It was after nine o'clock, and Sticky had still not shown up. A message broadcast had just ended, and Reynie, worn out, was making himself go over the day's notes one last time. For once he was glad to be studying his lessons — studying helped take his mind off worse things. He'd even been grateful for the message broadcast, which was so irritating and made it so difficult to concentrate that he'd had no space left over in his brain to worry about Sticky. Even so, Reynie felt awful, and now to make matters worse, he *smelled* something awful, too. His nose wrinkled with disgust.

What was that? Had something crawled under the floor and died?

Then the door opened. It was Sticky.

He was covered in slimy, black stinking mud, and he walked into the room like a zombie. From his red, hugely swollen eyes it was obvious he'd been crying for hours. But it wasn't the eyes themselves that caught Reynie's heart — it was their look of total despair.

Reynie leaped up and threw his arms around Sticky. "You're out!"

Sticky pulled away without speaking. He removed his spectacles, studied their mud-spotted lenses, and set them on the desk without bothering to clean them. Then, still not saying a word, he went out of the room. Reynie grabbed some of Sticky's things and ran out after him. In the corridor he squeezed past two Helpers already mopping up Sticky's muddy footprints in weird silence. A couple of boys were leaving the bathroom, holding their noses and trying not to step in the muddy spots on the floor. Reynie ran into the bathroom.

Sticky had stepped into a shower stall without undressing and was trying to grip the faucet handle, but his slimy hand kept slipping off. Finally he grabbed it with both hands and wrenched on the hot water. He flinched when the spray struck his face, then stood impassively, eyes closed, as black water swirled at his feet.

Reynie watched him anxiously. "I've brought you some soap, Sticky. And a towel and clean clothes."

Sticky made no reply.

"Hey, get undressed and use this soap, all right?" After

Reynie had repeated this several times, Sticky gave a dull nod and reached for the soap.

Reynie washed up at the sinks — he was filthy and rank from hugging Sticky — then went to their room, changed clothes, and waited. He stared at the door, afraid of what was coming. Afraid to have his suspicions confirmed. He'd been doing his best to remain calm, but he was trembling all over. He felt sure Sticky had been brainswept. And Mr. Curtain wouldn't erase Sticky's memories just for cheating, would he? If not, then why had this happened? What crime would call for such terrible action? There seemed to be only one answer: Sticky had told Mr. Curtain everything.

When Sticky finally returned, he dumped his wet clothes in the corner, put on his muddy glasses without cleaning them, and then, without once looking at Reynie, he pulled his suitcase from beneath the bed.

"Sticky, what's happened?"

No reply.

"You have to talk to me, Sticky! I'm afraid something terrible has happened to you. Not just the Waiting Room, I mean, but something even worse."

In a dull tone just tinged with anger, Sticky said, "I don't suppose there's anything worse than that place. What would *you* know about it?"

Reynie caught his breath. Sticky remembered the Waiting Room — and come to think of it, he remembered where his suitcase was. There was still hope! "You're right, Sticky. I don't know anything that's happened. Can you tell me?"

"I don't want to talk about it," Sticky said, opening the wardrobe with trembling fingers. "And I don't intend to go back there. I'm running away. They told me Mr. Curtain couldn't see me today, that S.Q. will come for me again in the morning. I'm to meet with Mr. Curtain 'if he's available.' So either I'll have to go back to that . . . that *nightmare*, or else I'll have to face Mr. Curtain, where I'm certain to go to pieces, Reynie, where I'm certain to lose control and tell on you and everyone else —"

The more Sticky spoke, the more emotion crept into his voice, until at last, shaking, he covered his eyes and dropped to his knees. "I can't do it, Reynie. I can't go back there, and I can't face Mr. Curtain without failing you. I just can't. I have to leave. I have no choice."

Reynie's eyes suddenly filled with tears. "Listen to me, Sticky. I'm so sorry for what you've been through. Really I am. But I can't tell you how glad I am you're still in there. I thought they'd taken your memory! But it's still *you* in there, Sticky — still my good friend!"

"Not for much longer," Sticky said miserably. "I'm going to crack, Reynie. You know how badly I handle pressure. I'll flub it tomorrow, and you'll all be caught. What kind of friend will I be then?"

Reynie closed the suitcase. "You're not going to flub anything."

"How can you know?"

"I can see it in you," Reynie said with perfect conviction. "You'd hold fast tomorrow even if I didn't have a plan — which I do. When your friends really need you, they can count on you. I just *know* it. And I do need you, Sticky. I need you here as a friend."

Sticky's eyes flickered like a candle on the verge of guttering. "It's . . . nice of you to say," he said doubtfully. Then he shuddered. "But Reynie, it'll kill me if I have to go back to that place. All those hours, with every second crawling by — and *other* things crawling by, things you can't see — constantly sinking into that goop, the smell so horrible, like something dead, like maybe it's *yourself* that's dead —"

"You won't have to spend another day in there," Reynie said. "I swear it."

"You bet your boots you won't," said Kate, whose head appeared in the ceiling above them. She lowered Constance into the room. "If they send you back there, we'll find a way to get you out, no matter what. Okay, chum?"

Shakily Sticky rose to his feet.

"It's going to be all right," Reynie said. "I'm sure you'll see Mr. Curtain first thing in the morning."

"But that's no good, either! It's terrible! How can I keep from giving you all away? He knows we're friends, he knows I was cheating, and he'll just put two and two together. . . ." Sticky caught his breath, held it a moment, and started over. "Okay, you mentioned a plan, didn't you? Do you really have one?"

"I'll tell you about it," Reynie said, handing him a roll, "but first you should eat. I smuggled some food for you."

For the first time, Sticky's eyes brightened and stayed bright. "I *am* awfully hungry."

"Ten o'clock!" roared Jackson from just outside the door. Everyone jumped. No one had heard him creeping down the hallway. "Lights out!"

As he hurried to the light switch, Reynie gave Kate a questioning look.

"We turned ours off before we left," she said a little too loudly.

Immediately Jackson rapped at the door. "Do you boys have someone in there with you? You know that's against the rule. No room visits, period! And even *more* no room visits during lights out!"

"It's just the two of us," Reynie replied.

This was just what Jackson had hoped Reynie would say. If he caught the boys with visitors now, they were not only breaking one of the Institute's very few rules, but lying about it as well. He flung open the door and switched on the light. "Aha! There you —" but he cut himself short, for he saw only the two boys, sitting on the floor.

"Isn't the light supposed to be off?" Reynie asked him.

With a scowl Jackson reached to turn off the light, then thought better of it. "Not just yet," he said, strolling over to the wardrobe. "First I'd like to see who you have in *here*." He threw open the wardrobe doors.

Nothing but clothes inside.

"If you don't mind, we'd like to get some sleep. Sticky's had a long day."

"And whose fault is that?" Jackson said, kneeling to look beneath the bottom bunk. Only the boys' suitcases. He rose and stared at Reynie, who smiled pleasantly, and then at Sticky, who only shrugged. Jackson sneered. "How *did* you like the Waiting Room, George?"

Reynie suddenly boiled over with anger. He had spent the evening in such a state of emotion, he couldn't seem to stop himself. "How can you do that to people, Jackson? Send them to a place like that, and then tease them about it?"

Jackson feigned puzzlement. "What do you mean, 'a place like that'? The Waiting Room isn't such a bad place. And it's perfectly safe. A little mud never hurt anyone. Washes right off, doesn't it? It may have a bit of an odor, but an odor can't hurt you any more than mud can — or darkness, for that matter. Darkness is good for you. Rests the eyes. Prevents sunburn . . ."

Livid though he was, Reynie fought to regain control of himself. He should never have said anything in the first place. It did no good to argue with an Executive.

Jackson was still lecturing with obvious pleasure. "And yes, I suppose there are a great many flies and beetles and crawling things — but they didn't bite or sting, did they? You aren't afraid of a fly, are you, George?"

"No," Sticky replied in an even tone. But he was glaring at Jackson. It was such an angry look — so full of defiant outrage — that Reynie actually felt encouraged. There was strength in Sticky. It was just easy to miss. Easiest of all for Sticky himself.

Jackson missed it, too. "Of course you aren't. So let's hear no more nonsense," he said, screwing up his face as if talking to a pitiful baby, "about the Waiting Woom being such a nasty wittle pwace." Then he grinned wickedly, shut off the light, and left the room. His boots thumped away down the corridor.

Constance's stifled voice called out, "Good grief! Do you intend to keep me in here forever?"

"Quiet," Reynie whispered, peeking out the door. The corridor was empty. He nodded at Sticky, who dragged his suitcase from beneath the bed.

"It's a good thing you're so small," Sticky whispered as Constance climbed out.

"Oh, yes, lucky me! So small you can pack me in the luggage. Why don't *you* try curling up in a suitcase?" Constance said, forgetting that Sticky had spent his entire day standing in filth, darkness, and bug swarms.

The ceiling panel slid aside and Kate dropped down into the room again. "Now what's this about a plan?" she said, as if they'd never been interrupted.

PUNISHMENTS & PROMOTIONS

Both boys were awake before dawn. And they had stayed up late the night before, going over the plan. But Sticky wasn't at all sleepy. Fear was keeping his eyes wide open. As he got dressed in the dark, he whispered up to the top bunk, "Reynie, they didn't happen to blindfold you when you went to Mr. Curtain's office, did they?"

"A blindfold? No."

"Then I guess I'll know right away if I'm going to the Waiting Room. That's something, I suppose."

Reynie rolled over and looked down from his bunk. "They blindfolded you? Why?"

"Didn't say. Jillson just dragged me onto the plaza, put the blindfold on, and spun me around until I threw up. I mean I literally threw up. Then she laughed and led me inside and down some stairs to the Waiting Room. I had to wear it when I left, too."

Reynie furrowed his brow. Why would they blindfold Sticky like that?

Just then someone banged on the door. Sticky stared at the door a long moment before opening it. S.Q. Pedalian stood in the dusky corridor, eating a cinnamon roll. His mouth stuffed full, he beckoned for Sticky to follow him. The time had come.

Sticky took a deep breath. "Wish me luck, Reynie."

Reynie nodded. "Don't worry, you'll do great."

Sticky followed S.Q. down the corridor. The dormitory was perfectly silent, save for the echo of their footsteps and the occasional gulping sound from S.Q., who was munching his cinnamon roll with gusto. Then they were outside in the chill morning air, where S.Q. stopped, licked his fingers, and — to Sticky's horror — reached into his pocket.

"S.Q.?" Sticky asked in a strained voice. "Am I . . . am I to *wait* a little longer, or —?"

"Oh, no, Mr. Curtain can meet with you," said S.Q. casually, pulling out a banana, not a blindfold. "Now, Sticky" — S.Q. was the only Executive who ever called Sticky by his nickname, though only by accident — "that is, *George*, allow me to give you some advice. I'm an Executive, you know, and I understand the way things work around here." Glancing left and right, S.Q. lowered his voice. "I like you, George, you're a nice kid, and very bright. And you're an orphan, which makes you a good candidate for Executive someday if you'll just straighten right up and fly . . . if you fly straight and right . . ."

"Straighten up and fly right?"

"Yes, all of those," S.Q. said, relieved. "My point is, don't blow your chances right off the bat. Whatever you do, do *not* admit to Mr. Curtain that you cheated. If you did cheat, I mean. I'm not saying you should lie. That's even worse. Don't admit to cheating, and don't lie."

"You're saying my best course of action right now is not to have cheated in the past."

"Exactly," S.Q. said.

"That's helpful."

S.Q. grinned. "Thought it would be. Mr. Curtain hates a cheater more than anything. Otherwise he's a genial fellow. So just keep that in mind during your meeting — the most important thing is not to admit you cheated."

"Thanks," Sticky said in a weak voice. His head had begun to ache. S.Q.'s advice was exactly the opposite of Reynie's.

He would have liked some time to consider his new dilemma, but in less than a minute he was standing outside the metal door to Mr. Curtain's office. Beads of sweat appeared on his smooth scalp. What should he do? If anybody should know this sort of thing, it would be an Executive. Yet S.Q. was not the brightest bulb in the Executive chandelier. Reynie, on the other hand, was very shrewd about people. . . . And now S.Q. was knocking on the door. Sticky rubbed his throbbing temples. He felt on the verge, once again, of growing paralyzed. Or worse: flub-mouthed.

The door slid open. S.Q. motioned for Sticky to enter. Whatever course he chose, he had to choose it now.

Mr. Curtain sat in the middle of the cold stone room, his fingers laced together, his chin lifted expectantly. The gigantic silver-eyed spider, waiting for the fly.

"I'm sorry I cheated, sir!" Sticky declared as he went in.

The door slid closed behind him, but not before he heard a shocked S.Q. mumbling something about the poor kid cracking under pressure.

Mr. Curtain drummed his fingers on the journal in his lap, regarding Sticky with those unseen eyes. Sticky was hard-pressed not to fidget. A bead of sweat trickled down the curve of his bald head, made its way to his earlobe, and hung there, trembling. It tickled Sticky maddeningly, but he held still. Suddenly Mr. Curtain shot forward in his chair — Sticky nearly jumped out of his shoes — and screeched to a stop with his face inches away.

"Do you care to explain yourself?" Mr. Curtain said coolly.

Sticky had memorized the speech. (If he hadn't, he might never have gotten a word out.) He stammered, swallowed, then began: "I'm very sorry, sir. I didn't want to do anything wrong. But she put so much pressure on me —"

"You mean Constance Contraire, I assume," interrupted Mr. Curtain with a look of satisfaction.

"Constance? Oh, no, sir. She's too stubborn even to let me help her with homework. I'm sure you've noticed how stubborn she is. You notice everything about everybody, if you don't mind my saying so, sir."

"Hm," said Mr. Curtain. "I *have* noticed that, it's true. But if not Constance Contraire, then of whom are you speaking?"

"Well, as I was saying, sir, she put so much pressure on me, and I wasn't sure what to make of it, she being a Messenger and all —"

"WHAT?" Mr. Curtain bellowed, his face instantly purple. "A *Messenger*? Snakes and dogs, I'll —" He cut himself off, and for a few moments went absolutely silent, as if trying to decide just what horrible thing to do to Sticky. Send him back to the Waiting Room? Fling him into a patch of drapeweed? Crush him beneath the wheels of his chair?

Sticky closed his eyes.

When several moments had passed, however, without his being sent, flung, or crushed, Sticky opened one eye. The color had faded from Mr. Curtain's face so that it no longer looked like an eggplant with glasses; only the tip of his lumpy nose retained a crimson hue. And he had begun drumming his fingers again. "George," Mr. Curtain said, more calmly now, "why are you looking at me with one eye?"

Sticky quickly opened his other eye. "I . . . I . . ."

"Never mind," said Mr. Curtain. "Now explain yourself. Are you telling me a Messenger made you cheat?"

"I'm sorry to say so, sir. It made her furious that Reynie and I were doing so well. She couldn't believe we already knew more than she did. She humiliated me in class, and later she told me she'd keep doing it — or even worse — unless I agreed to help her. The quizzes were so much easier if I just gave her the answers, she said. And if I did, she would make it easier for *me* — by not tormenting me."

"You are speaking of Martina Crowe," Mr. Curtain said.

Sticky nodded.

"Hmm. I shall have to look into this. Your cheating doesn't trouble me much, I must say, so long as I understand the situation. The secret is control, do you see? I simply wish to know the circumstances so that I can manipulate — that is, so that I can *manage* them. No matter what the circumstances, George, so long as they are controlled, we may have harmony. Do you understand?"

"I believe so, sir."

"Very well. I'm sorry you had to wait to speak with me on this matter. I understand it is an unpleasant thing to wait. Unfortunately there's no help for it sometimes — I'm quite busy. The good news is that you will not be punished."

"Thank you, sir," Sticky said humbly.

"And George?"

"Yes, sir?"

"You *are* doing rather well, aren't you?"

"Apparently, sir."

Mr. Curtain was looking Sticky up and down and nodding to himself, as if appraising a fine new piece of machinery that would come in handy.

"Nice work," said Constance. "You're a natural liar."

It was less diplomatic congratulations than he'd received from Reynie and Kate — who had cheered and clapped him on the back — but Sticky was too relieved to quibble.

They were on their way to lunch, trailing well behind the rest of the students so that they could speak privately in the corridors. They were all pretty pleased with themselves — not least because Martina Crowe was in hot water. And now, as they approached the end of the corridor, they overheard Jackson and Jillson talking in an empty classroom.

Looking at one another in silent agreement, they stopped walking to listen.

"— finally caught who was spying in the gym," Jackson was saying. "A waste, though. He was a good Messenger. And a special recruit, you know. Mr. Curtain would probably have kept him on, trained him into an Executive one day. I guess now he'll be retrained as a Helper."

"Too bad," Jillson said. "Shouldn't have been so average-looking."

"What he shouldn't have been was so *curious*," said Jackson. "The nerve of that kid! Always asking questions — it's what got him sent to the Waiting Room last time, you know. I thought he'd learned his lesson."

"Apparently not," said Jillson. "Any word on the accomplice?"

"His partner in crime? Not yet. Personally I can't see what there is to worry about, but you know Mr. Curtain. Can't be too careful, he says. We're supposed to be extra vigilant, keep an eye out." Jackson grunted. "And I guess you heard he's changing the door codes."

"No! Again? I *hate* learning new codes!"

"Tell me about it," Jackson said. "Would have saved us some trouble if the kid had ratted on his partner, but he denied everything to the end. Like I said, it's a shame. Probably would have made a good Executive."

"Quiet," Jillson said. "Did you just hear something?"

In the corridor, the children's eyes widened. They held their breath.

"Only my stomach growling," Jackson said. "Get your stuff together, won't you? Let's go eat."

That was the children's cue to move. With relieved expressions, Sticky, Kate, and Constance hurried quietly on down the corridor. Reynie followed behind, trying to calm himself. Jackson's news had quite upset him.

After they'd safely rounded the corner, Kate said, "Can you believe it? That's two narrow escapes now! First Sticky got off the hook for cheating, and now you're off the hook for spying, Reynie!"

"Yeah," said Reynie, his face flushed with guilt. "It's . . . it's great news."

"And now Martina's *on* the hook," Constance said. "This might actually be a good day."

By supper the rumors were flying. Martina Crowe had not been in any of her classes. Some said she was enjoying a long session of her special privileges — whatever those were. Others argued that the secret privileges never lasted this long. More likely, someone said, she'd been sent to the Waiting Room — a student had seen Jackson and Jillson escorting her across the plaza. Martina Crowe? Going to the Waiting Room? *Who* had seen that? For this no one had an answer, so maybe it was just a rumor.

Reynie had begun to feel rather ill. It was starting to seem everything he did got someone hurt. First he'd suggested they cheat, which landed Sticky in the Waiting Room. Then he'd spied through the gym window, for which some poor, average-looking kid was paying the price. Now there was this plan he'd put into effect — the plan to get Martina bumped from the Messenger list. It had seemed clever at the time, but was he sure about that? For all his caution and wits, he was turning out to be a dangerous person to be close to. He looked at his untouched meal with distaste. He shoved it away and put his face in his hands.

"Reynie?" Kate said. "What's the matter?"

"It was my plan," Reynie mumbled.

"Hey, if anybody deserves the Waiting Room, it's Martina."

"If anyone deserves it . . . ," mumbled Sticky, who felt every bit as bad as Reynie. He *knew* how terrible the Waiting Room was — at the very mention of it he had broken into a cold sweat — and he had been the one to condemn Martina with a lie. It didn't matter how cruel she was. *No* one deserved the Waiting Room, not even Martina.

To make matters worse, at that very moment a hidden message broadcast began.

"It's that boy Harold Rockwell," Constance grumbled to herself. "Shut *up*, Harold."

Reynie gave Constance a bleak look. It had occurred to him to wonder what would happen to her when Mr. Curtain boosted the signal power all the way. If Constance could hear voices *now*, what would it be like for her *then*? What would it do to her? Had she thought to wonder about this herself? For her sake, Reynie hoped not. If he were in her shoes he'd be terrified.

This day had gone from good to bad to worse. And from there to *worse* than worse.

"Watch your toes, everyone," Kate murmured.

S.Q. Pedalian was squeezing between two nearby tables, where students were wincing and crying out as he passed. Reynie tucked his feet safely out of reach. S.Q. came up and looked appraisingly at them. "Why the long faces, kids? Everything all right?"

The children tried to appear cheerful so he would leave them alone, but for once S.Q. judged correctly. "You can't fool me. I know downtrodden faces when I see them. I'm surprised at you! Here Stick — I mean, here young George has got off clean and easy, you're doing great on your quizzes, and yet the whole lot of you sits around like the cat got your pudding. Er, the pudding . . . no, got your tail. . . ."

No one felt like helping him, and after a moment S.Q. gave up. He adopted a shrewd expression, which, on S.Q., looked rather as if he had severe indigestion. "Now don't tell me you're fretting about not making the Messenger list yet! Is that it? Listen here," he said confidentially, leaning in close to them, "I'll tell you a secret, because you're good eggs. You're closer than you think!"

Reynie nodded glumly. "Is it because Martina's not a Messenger anymore?"

S.Q. cocked his head. "How could you possibly know that?"

"*Everybody* knows," said Kate.

This surprised both S.Q. and Reynie, who said together, "They do? How?"

Kate pointed across the cafeteria, where Martina had just come in, escorted by Jillson and Jackson. She wore her tunic and sash as always, but not the typical striped pants of a Messenger. No, her pants were solid blue, and as the other Messengers cheered and clapped, her face shone simultaneously with malevolence and triumph.

Martina had been made an Executive.

Half a Riddle

That evening, at precisely 10:01, S.Q. Pedalian knocked on the boys' door. He knocked first with his feet, by accident, and then with his knuckles. Getting no response, he opened the door and peered in. In the dim room he saw the boys lying on their bunks in their pajamas. Something caught his eye, however, and he looked upward. Only shadows on the ceiling.

"S.Q.? Is that you?" Reynie asked in a sleepy voice.

"Sorry, boys," S.Q. said, snapping on the light. "I didn't think you'd be asleep so early — it's only just now lights-out. Mr. Curtain wants to see you. Hop up now, both of you, and get dressed. You know, I could have sworn I saw one of your ceiling tiles move."

"Probably just a shadow," Reynie suggested, fumbling with his trousers and shoes.

"Or a mouse," said Sticky in a cracked voice. His mouth had gone very dry.

S.Q. scratched his head. "A mouse, hm? That's probably it. A lot of students have complained about mice in their ceiling lately. I suppose we'll have to put out some traps." As Reynie made a mental note to tell Kate to look out for mousetraps, S.Q. ushered them from their room.

Both boys were in a state of high alarm. Obviously Martina had convinced Mr. Curtain she hadn't cheated, for how else would she have been made an Executive? Thus Mr. Curtain must know that Sticky lied, and no doubt Reynie had been implicated as his accomplice. Which was as it should be, Reynie thought miserably. It was his plan that got Sticky into this mess — twice.

At the entrance to the Institute Control Building, S.Q. stopped. With a sympathetic expression, he knelt down and put a hand on each of their shoulders. "I imagine you two are wondering what Mr. Curtain wants to speak with you about."

"Oh, yes!" cried the boys together, and Reynie's heart leaped. If he had a moment to *prepare*, maybe he could think of something to say, something that . . .

"I wish I knew," S.Q. said, shaking his head. "I hope it's nothing bad."

Sixty seconds later the boys were alone with Mr. Curtain in his office. Trying to breathe evenly (and mostly failing), they waited for him to speak. Mr. Curtain had put down his journal and rolled out from behind his desk. But instead of his usual zooming about, he was inching toward them, very, very slowly, contemplating the boys in a way that gave them the impression of a predator — a wolf spider came to mind — seeking just the moment to pounce upon its prey. They had to fight the urge to recoil.

"No doubt," said Mr. Curtain as he drew near, "you are wondering why Martina Crowe was made Executive. After all, according to you, George, she was a bully and a cheat. Isn't that right?"

Sticky reached for his spectacles, checked himself, and thrust his hands into his pockets to still them. "Yes, sir."

"It's true, Mr. Curtain," said Reynie. "We *were* wondering that."

"Yes. I know. And now I shall tell you why. Do you remember what you said to me the other day, Reynard, when we discussed Miss Contraire? You said the best way of dealing with those you don't trust is to keep them close. I agreed with you then, and I agree with you now. Of course, had Martina Crowe not been such an excellent candidate for Executive, I would have sent her packing at once. But she has always been useful, and as I told George, the cheating itself doesn't trouble me, so long as I understand the situation. At any rate, the situation has been rectified. Miss Crowe and I had a brief discussion of the matter (she denied the cheating, I might add), and ultimately she was promoted. Everything is settled.

"Everything, that is, except for *your* situation," Mr. Curtain went on. "Which is why I have sent for you."

"Our . . . situation?" said Reynie. He could hear Sticky trying to swallow.

"Indeed," said Mr. Curtain. "For as of this moment, you are both made Messengers!"

The boys were stunned. Here they'd been afraid something terrible was in store for them — instead, their mission had leaped forward! Messengers at last! Their faces broke into huge grins.

"Oh, thank you!" Sticky cried, hoping he sounded more grateful than relieved.

"We won't disappoint you," said Reynie.

"I should hope not," said Mr. Curtain. "I have two new Messenger slots to fill, and as a matter of urgency I am promoting you a day earlier than planned. Here are your new uniforms."

Returning to his desk, Mr. Curtain produced two white tunics, two pale blue sashes, and two pairs of striped trousers. "Wear them with pride. And then . . . who knows? One day you may forego those striped pants for solid blue ones, just as Martina Crowe did today!"

When S.Q. had finally left off slapping the boys on the backs in painful congratulation and lumbered away down the corridor, Reynie and Sticky exchanged relieved glances and closed their bedroom door behind them. The door's closing revealed the silhouette of Kate Wetherall pressed flat against the wall behind it. She switched on her flashlight and whispered in an exasperated tone, "You didn't even knock!"

"It's our own room!" Sticky replied.

"I'm surprised you didn't hear us in the corridor," Reynie said. "S.Q. was patting us on the backs so hard my teeth were clacking together."

"To tell the truth," Kate said sheepishly, "I was asleep until I heard the doorknob turn. I only had to time to leap across the room and hide." She jerked her thumb toward the lower bunk, where Sticky's covers and pillows were in lumpy disarray. "And first I had to throw the covers over Constance. You were gone so long, she fell asleep on Sticky's bed. I meant to keep guard, but I guess I nodded off."

"Some guard," said a groggy voice from beneath the covers.

"Anyway," Sticky said, "we're glad you're here. We have some news."

He and Reynie held up their new uniforms.

"Messengers!" Kate exclaimed. "I can't believe it! And here we were worried you'd gotten in big trouble!"

Constance sat up, rubbed her eyes, and squinted at the uniforms.

"Oh, yes," Reynie said with a laugh. "So worried that you both fell asleep."

Kate gave him a disapproving look. "We *were* worried," she insisted. "And I'm sure Mr. Benedict is, too. We told him you'd been called to see Mr. Curtain. We should let him know the good news right away."

"You sent a report?" Sticky asked, surprised.

"Took us forever," Constance said, stretching. "Morse code's a little rusty."

Rusty was not exactly the word for Constance's Morse code, but the boys resisted comment. They were both glad to hear a report had been sent. They'd been unable to send one the night before — a night crew of Helpers had been working on the plaza, filling cracks and replacing broken stones.

Sticky climbed onto the television, made sure the coast was clear, and began flashing a message.

"Our 'special privileges' begin tomorrow," Reynie told the girls. "That's all he told us."

"Nervous?" Kate asked.

"What do you think?" Reynie said. "I feel like I swallowed a beehive."

"Here comes a response," Sticky said from the window. "*Glad . . . proud . . . now pay attention.*"

"Sounds like he's about to tell us something important," Reynie said. He went over and peered out the window with Sticky. Sure enough, the light in the woods continued flashing its coded message:

**With open eyes now you may find
A place you must exit to enter.
Where one —**

"Where one what?" Sticky said, when the message broke off and didn't resume. "Why did they stop?"

Reynie groaned. "It's Mr. Curtain," he said, pointing. "He's going out onto the plaza."

"*Now?*" Sticky hissed, watching the familiar figure rolling into view below. "In the middle of the message? He couldn't have waited twenty more seconds?"

"At least we have a start," Reynie said.

But a start was all they had, for even after a long discussion, the children were left stymied. The last, unfinished line gave no clue at all, and the first seemed pointless, as it hardly seemed necessary to tell them they needed to keep their eyes open. Which left only the middle line, and that one utterly baffled them. How on earth could you enter a place by exiting it?

"We'll have to try again tomorrow," Kate said finally, stifling a yawn. "I can't think straight anymore tonight. At least you boys made Messenger. That's an encouraging development."

The others agreed, the meeting adjourned, and in a few minutes the girls had disappeared into the ceiling and the boys had gone to bed. Reynie had just begun to compose a mental letter to Miss Perumal when Sticky whispered into the darkness.

"Reynie, you awake?"

"Wide awake," Reynie replied.

"I wanted to ask you . . . does this 'encouraging development' scare the wits out of you as much as it does me?"

Reynie laughed. "It may be the worst encouraging development I've ever experienced."

In the bunk below, Sticky laughed, too. Their laughter relaxed them the tiniest bit — and that was all it took. In moments their exhaustion overcame them, and both boys fell asleep.

THE WHISPERER

When the knock sounded on his door, Reynie was in the midst of a terrible dream. He had written down his letters to Miss Perumal, and Jackson, having found the letters on the desk, was pounding them with his fist. *Bang! Bang! Bang!* "We've got you!" he cried with a wicked laugh. "Don't worry, you won't be punished! It's the Waiting Room for you — what *fun* you'll have there! And when you've disappeared beneath the stinking mud for good, we'll get your beloved Miss Perumal, too!"

"No!"

"What do you mean, 'No'?" said Jackson. "Isn't this what you've been working for?"

This was an unexpected response, and Reynie, startled, opened his eyes. Jackson stood in the doorway, staring at Reynie with an expression of wild impatience.

"I'm sorry," Reynie said, coming fully awake. "I was dreaming. What did you say?"

"I said hurry up and get your tunic on. I'm to take you to Mr. Curtain immediately. Today's your big day! Special privileges, Reynard! Now wake up your skinny bald friend and hustle, will you? I want to get a muffin on the way." Jackson stepped out of the room to wait.

When, after considerable shaking, Reynie had roused Sticky, the two of them threw on their Messenger uniforms.

"This is it," Reynie whispered. "We have to be on our toes."

Sticky nodded. "Good luck."

They shook hands resolutely.

"It's about time," Jackson muttered when they came out. "Now follow me." He set off in double-time for the cafeteria. It was just before dawn, with no one astir but a few silent Helpers mopping floors, sweeping walkways, or scaling ladders to scrub mildew from ceilings. In the cafeteria, too, the Helpers were already hard at work. Jackson helped himself to a freshly baked blueberry muffin and a glass of cold milk. "Better choke something down quick," he said to the boys. "You don't want to be in the Whisperer with an empty stomach. It's very draining. You need all the energy you can get."

At this, the first open mention of the Whisperer, goose bumps rose on the boys' arms. Their stomachs flipped, too, but dutifully they reached for muffins and milk and, just as Jackson said, choked them down. Sticky, already losing his nerve, couldn't help trying to stall. "What about classes?"

"What do you think all those classes are *for*, George? I don't see how you've ever made Messenger if that's how dimwitted you are. You'll have plenty of time for classes after your session. The Whisperer is what's important, boys. It's the whole reason we're here."

After all the secrecy that had come before, it was very strange indeed — in fact it was thrilling — to be spoken to with such candor and trust. They really were Messengers at last! Reynie almost had to remind himself that his new position wasn't an honor to be prized.

"All right, then, swallow and follow," said Jackson, turning on his heel. The boys gulped their milk and hurried after him. Out on the plaza, in the gray light of dawn, Jackson ordered them to stand still. "If you ever become Executives," he said, tying cloths over their eyes, "then you'll be allowed to learn the route to the Whispering Gallery. Until then, it's blindfolds and no talking. Understand? Now, then, round and round you go." He grabbed their shoulders and spun them about until they were so dizzy they stumbled and bumped into each other. Jackson allowed himself a moment to laugh. Then he took them by the elbows and set off.

They were marched across the plaza, down a walkway, and finally over a patch of grass. Then came a sort of scuffing, thumping noise — it sounded like Jackson kicking something out of the way with his boot — and the boys were led inside. They went down a short passage, then up some winding stone steps. And then more winding steps. Steps after steps after steps. They must be heading up to the top of the flag tower, Reynie thought. No other place in the Institute could have so many steps.

With their leg muscles burning and chests heaving, the boys finally reached the top. Jackson gave them a few good spins — perhaps just for the fun of it — and removed their blindfolds. They stood in a bright, narrow stone passage. Before them loomed a great metal door.

Jackson pressed a speaker button on the wall. "Your new Messengers are here, sir."

"Very well," said Mr. Curtain's voice through the speaker. The door slid heavily open.

"What are you waiting for?" Jackson said. He gestured impatiently, mumbling something about numbskulls not taking hints, and the boys stepped through the open doorway. The door slid closed behind them.

"Welcome to the Whispering Gallery!" said Mr. Curtain, spinning his wheelchair away from the desk at which he'd been working. He beckoned them forward with a crook of his finger. "Come in, boys, and take a look around!"

The Whispering Gallery, though quite large, was furnished only with a single desk, two cushions in the corner, and, in the center of the room, a strange contraption resembling an old-fashioned beauty-salon hair dryer. So this was the Whisperer: an oversized metal armchair with a blue helmet bolted to the seatback, and another helmet (this one red) protruding into empty air behind it. It looked surprisingly simple — no running lights, computer screens, or whirring gizmos — and indeed, considering its purpose, the entire room seemed simple. Smooth, uniform stone walls, a lack of furniture or decoration, and only a single window.

Kate was right, Reynie thought. There *is* something important behind the highest window.

"If you're wondering why the Whispering Gallery is so austere," said Mr. Curtain, "the answer is security. You will find no heavy metal objects or sharp devices lying about, nothing with which my Whisperer might be damaged, nothing to be used as a weapon. The Whisperer's computer system and power supply are safely protected by two feet of metal and stone. The walls are solid stone as well. The door through which you entered is the only door, and I am the only one who can open it. Control, boys! Control is key. The Whispering Gallery is perfectly controlled.

"I say all this to impress upon you the importance of our project," Mr. Curtain continued. He gestured for them to sit on the cushions. "Why else would such security be necessary? It is a great honor to be made Messenger, and I hope you will not squander it."

"No, sir," the boys said together.

"Here, at last, is your special privilege," said Mr. Curtain. "Only Messengers are allowed to help me with my project, and you may be assured it is a *marvelous* project. Now, I'm sure you're wondering what the Whisperer is — am I right?"

The boys nodded.

"Of course I am. My machine cannot help but provoke curiosity. It looks simple, does it not? Only a chair with a helmet? Don't be fooled! The Whisperer is a miraculous invention — *my* miraculous invention — and is sophisticated beyond reckoning. Have you ever heard of a machine capable of transmitting thoughts? Of course not! Would you even have thought it possible? Never! And yet it *is* possible. My Whisperer makes it possible."

Mr. Curtain waved elegantly at the contraption behind him, rather like a game show hostess displaying fabulous prizes. "It has been fashioned with the human brain as a model — *my* human brain, in fact, which as you might suspect is quite an excellent one. And it is my brain that controls it! No need for keyboards and computer screens, knobs and dials, bells and whistles. The Whisperer *listens* to me. For not only is it capable of transmitting thought, but also — to a certain extent — of *perceiving* thought. And although currently its proper function depends upon my being present and connected —"

"You mean you have to be hooked up for it to work?" Sticky blurted.

Mr. Curtain's wheelchair rolled forward until the front wheels pressed the edge of Sticky's cushion. Mr. Curtain's reflective glasses and protuberant nose eased toward Sticky's face like a snake testing the air. "You are only a child, George, so I do not expect much of you," Mr. Curtain said coolly, "but if you are to be a Messenger you must be made aware of something. I do not take kindly to interruption."

"Sorry," Sticky mumbled, looking down.

"Good," said Mr. Curtain. "And yes, I must be 'hooked up' for it to work — for now. It is undergoing modification, you see. For years I have employed the Whisperer as an . . . educational tool. But greater things are in store. Once my modifications are complete, the Whisperer will become a wondrous *healing* device, boys — a device capable of curing maladies of the mind. No, it's perfectly true! I see the surprise on your faces. But I assure you, my invention is destined to bring peace to thousands — perhaps even millions — of troubled souls. And you boys will have played a part. Is it not exciting?"

As if to demonstrate his excitement, Mr. Curtain shot backward in his wheelchair at breakneck speed, screeching to a stop beside his desk. (*His entire life must feel like an amusement-park ride*, Reynie thought.) A moment later he had shotback over to the boys with a brown package in his hands.

"What you are wondering *now*," Mr. Curtain said, "is how Messengers play a part. The answer is this: The Whisperer requires the assistance of unsophisticated minds. *Children's* minds. You see, though my machine is stunningly complex, its mental processes still pale in comparison to my own. For the Whisperer to do, well, certain things I *wish* it todo — I will not waste time explaining details you cannot comprehend — my thoughts must first pass through a less sophisticated mind. This is where my Messengers come in.

"Now, do not be daunted," Mr. Curtain went on. "It's an easy matter. When you occupy the seat, the Whisperer directs you to think certain phrases — it whispers to you, do you see? — and when you think these phrases, the Whisperer's transmitters do the rest. Your function is that of a filter: my thoughts, once they pass through your minds, are more easily processed. Do you understand what I mean by this?"

"They go down easier," Reynie said. "Like candy rather than medicine."

"Precisely!" said Mr. Curtain, seeming pleased. "But the thoughts *will* be medicine, make no doubt of that — one day soon they will be medicine for countless minds. For now, our project consists of inputting data. Which is to say, we are filling the Whisperer's computer bank with necessary information."

So *this* was the explanation Mr. Curtain gave his Messengers: "inputting data." They weren't even told they were actually sending messages — that they themselves were whispering to others!

Mr. Curtain had laced his fingers together atop the brown package in his lap and was looking at the boys expectantly. With a hint of impatience, he said, "And now for your questions." The boys got the distinct feeling that if they *didn't* have questions, he would be most displeased.

Sticky, trying to do his part, cleared his throat and squeaked, "What . . . what is that package for?"

"Excellent question, George!" cried Mr. Curtain, which clearly meant it was the question he had wanted to be asked. "The package is for demonstration purposes." He held up the box. "Tell me, how many things do I hold in my hand?"

"One?" Sticky replied.

Mr. Curtain looked at Reynie. "Is that your answer, too, Reynard? I hold one thing in my hand?"

There must be something inside the box, Reynie thought. But he sensed this was not a time Mr. Curtain wished to be impressed. Rather, Mr. Curtain wanted to surprise the boys for "demonstration purposes," and so Reynie replied, "It certainly *looks* like one thing."

"Ha!" Mr. Curtain cried, seeming quite pleased indeed. "And yet observe." He turned the package upside down, and out of it spilled hundreds of little pieces of paper. "One package, yes, but one package may contain many things, do you see? Now clean up these paper scraps — I despise a messy floor."

As the boys scrambled to pick up the paper, Mr. Curtain continued, "What do I do if I wish to transmit an enormous amount of information in a short space of time, hmm? Do you think I can sit in my Whisperer every minute, every hour of the day, dictating to my Messengers? Hardly! There is work to be done, modifications to be made, an Institute to be run, plans to be implemented! And so how do I accomplish the inputting of all this data? *Packaging*, boys. I transmit packages, and every package contains an incredible amount of information."

Reynie and Sticky finished cleaning up and sank onto the cushions again.

"I am going to say something to you now," said Mr. Curtain. "One phrase only. But I want you to pay attention to what happens in your minds when I say it. Are you ready?"

The boys nodded.

"Poison apples, poison worms."

The boys blinked, startled, for in a single moment an entire lesson — an entire class period of listening to Jillson drone on and on about bad government — had blossomed in their heads.

Mr. Curtain was smiling. "One package, many thoughts. If you have mastered the material, then the proper phrase will conjure it — like the magic words that coax a genie from a bottle. Do you see?"

In fact the boys understood much more than Mr. Curtain realized. Finally it all made sense! Mr. Benedict had wondered how the hidden messages could be so simple and yet have such profound effects. It was one of the things he'd hoped they might find out. Now they knew: Mr. Benedict's Receiver was able to detect the "package" phrases, but not the information *contained* in them. He could hear the magic words, but he couldn't see the genie!

"Very well," said Mr. Curtain, when he saw that the boys understood, "you have been sufficiently briefed. And now the moment of truth. Reynard, have a seat in the Whisperer. George, you may observe from your cushion. If all goes well, the session should last about half an hour. Then you shall have your turn."

Reynie rose and approached the machine. His mouth went pasty and bitter-tasting as he recalled Mr. Curtain's saying that the Whisperer could perceive thoughts. "To a certain extent," he'd said — but to *what* extent? How much could it see? Would the Whisperer reveal him as a spy? Reynie stopped and stared at the metal chair and the blue helmet, racked with indecision. Should he try to resist somehow? Try to mask his thoughts? Was it even possible? He had no way of knowing, and no time to consider.

"Reynard?"

"Sorry, sir. Just . . . just savoring the moment."

With clammy hands Reynie took his seat in the chair. Mr. Curtain, meanwhile, zipped around to the rear of the Whisperer, reversing himself so that his back was to Reynie's as he fitted the red helmet over his own head. "Ledroptha Curtain!" he barked. Instantly the blue helmet lowered itself onto Reynie's head, contracting to fit snugly against his temples. At the same time, metal cuffs popped out of the armrests and closed over his wrists.

"Never fear," said Mr. Curtain. "The cuffs are only to keep you secure. Please relax."

Reynie took a deep breath and tried in vain to stop trembling. After a moment he realized it was his *seat* that trembled — the Whisperer was pulsing with energy. He closed his eyes.

Good, said a voice in his head. It wasn't his own voice, nor was it Mr. Curtain's. It was the Whisperer's. Not unkind, but not friendly, either. Impossible to describe, it was simply . . . there. *Good*, it repeated. *What is your name?*

Reynie still wasn't sure if he ought to resist a little. How much could the Whisperer detect? If he gave an inch, would it take a mile? He was trying to decide how to proceed when the Whisperer's voice in his head said, *Welcome, Reynard Muldoon.*

But he hadn't answered! Opening his eyes in surprise, he saw Sticky on his cushion watching with intense concern. Reynie tried to concentrate. Of course — this wasn't like talking. He hadn't *realized* he'd thought his name, but once you were asked to think of your name, you couldn't *not* think of it, no matter how you tried. Like the Whisperer's voice, the answer was simply there.

Reynard Muldoon, what do you fear most?

Spiders, Reynie lied, trying to regain some control. Spiders made Reynie nervous, but he wasn't afraid of them. Certainly they were not what he feared most. That was something he didn't want the Whisperer to know.

But responding to Reynie's involuntary answer, the Whisperer said, *Don't worry, you are not alone.*

At once Reynie was filled with an astonishing sense of well-being. He felt so good, so at peace, he could hardly hold his thoughts together. So *this* was why those other Messengers looked so happy, why they craved their sessions so intensely! When you did what it wanted, the Whisperer rewarded you by soothing your fears. Reynie would never have guessed it could feel so wonderful.

Reynie had another problem now. A very troubling problem. Having been made to feel so wonderful — and so easily, so unexpectedly — Reynie found he *wanted* to give in to the

Whisperer. Wanted it desperately. This was a disturbing development, and while he still had some trace of determination left — before he lost himself entirely — Reynie decided he must learn something if he could.

Mr. Curtain? he thought. *Can you hear me?*

Let us begin, said the Whisperer.

Mr. Curtain, can you hear my thoughts?

Let us begin.

Mr. Curtain didn't seem to be hearing him. So maybe the Whisperer could only seek out certain things and was incapable of detecting anything else. Reynie had to hope so.

Let us begin, the Whisperer repeated with an unmistakable hint of impatience.

He could not put it off any longer.

Okay, Reynie thought, bracing himself. *Okay, I'm ready.*

When Reynie opened his eyes again, Sticky stood over him, staring at him as if he might be dead. Reynie blinked and stretched. (He saw relief in Sticky's eyes.) He was fatigued, but pleasantly so, as if he had worked hard at some extremely enjoyable task. The cuffs had retracted into the armrest, the blue helmet had been lifted from his head, and Mr. Curtain was at his desk, making a note in his journal and speaking quietly into his unseen intercom.

"Are you okay?" Sticky whispered. "You were in that thing for two hours."

"Two hours!" Reynie repeated, amazed. It had seemed like only a few minutes. He remembered the first stream of words entering his mind, remembered dutifully repeating them, his mind relaxing into a feeling of marvelous happiness. There was nothing at all to fear, nothing at all to worry about. In fact, now that Reynie thought about it, he was a little cranky. He wanted to slip back into that feeling. He was struck with a pang of bitter jealousy that Sticky was about to take his place in the Whisperer.

"Does it hurt?" Sticky asked. "Are you all right?"

Sticky's worried expression brought Reynie to his senses. "No . . . no, don't worry. Just relax. I think . . . I think we're safe for now. We can talk later."

"No whispering, boys!" Mr. Curtain called, wheeling over to them. "I dislike all secrets save my own."

"Sorry, sir," said Reynie. "I was only telling him not to worry, that it doesn't hurt."

Mr. Curtain laughed his screechy laugh. "Of course it doesn't hurt. It wouldn't be useful if it did. To function properly, my Whisperer has always needed children, and children are averse to pain — I've found that out through experience. No, it doesn't hurt, George. Quite the opposite. I daresay Reynard can assure you the session was perfectly wonderful. And unusual, I might add — two hours was far, far longer than I expected. As I have said before, Reynard, you have a strong mind. New Messengers rarely make it half an hour before their concentration flies apart and they slip into a daze. Even my seasoned Messengers never last more than an hour."

Mr. Curtain seemed tired himself. Perspiration glistened on his forehead, and his lumpy nose was splotched with red. Tired but happy, just like Reynie. "I am very pleased, Reynard. Very pleased, indeed. I believe we have more to discuss now. And if George's session goes even half so well, our discussion will include him, too. Wouldn't you like that, George? Of course you would. Meanwhile, I've sent for some juice. Using the Whisperer calls for frequent refreshment."

Reynie rose shakily from the seat. His mind kept returning to the phrases he'd been compelled to think: ". . . *Brush your teeth and kill the germs. Poison apples, poison worms. The missing aren't missing, they're only departed. . . .*" And with each phrase came the memory of the pleasure he'd been given by thinking it. He wanted to sit back down, go straight into another session. . . .

Reynie shook his head. He couldn't believe how strongly the Whisperer took hold of you. Also how much it took *out* of you — he felt so weak he stumbled over to a cushion and collapsed upon it. Sticky followed and hovered over him, wanting to help somehow, not knowing what to do.

Mr. Curtain, meanwhile, had pressed a button on his chair, and the Whispering Gallery's metal door was sliding open. Jillson the Executive entered with a plastic jug and paper cups.

"Anything else, sir?" Jillson eyed the boys with grudging approval. She held an esteem for Messengers she didn't have for other students.

"That will be all, Jillson," Mr. Curtain replied.

Jillson went out, and Mr. Curtain poured the juice. Plastic jug and paper cups. No glass. Mr. Curtain was indeed careful. But even if they'd had a heavy glass bottle, something hard to conk him over the head with, what then? The Whisperer's computer circuitry was safely hidden beneath the stone floor, its chair and helmets made of strong metal. How could they possibly do anything about it?

"Ready, George?" said Mr. Curtain. It was more of a command than a question. Sticky gulped and took his place in the machine. Once again Mr. Curtain fitted the red helmet over his head and growled, "Ledroptha Curtain!"

The blue helmet lowered, the cuffs appeared, and Sticky squeezed his eyes shut. His hands strained unconsciously against the cuffs, wanting to get at his spectacles. He was obviously frightened.

Reynie watched from the cushion. Poor Sticky. In a moment his fear would dissolve, replaced by something wonderful — which was far more troubling than the fear, for how could they work to defeat Mr. Curtain if they found his invention irresistible? Even now, free of the Whisperer's metallic grip, Reynie found himself longing for that sensation of perfect security, of not being alone. . . .

His thoughts were interrupted by Sticky's nervous voice crying out: "Sticky Washington!"

A pause.

Then more quietly: "Fine. *George* Washington."

The Whisperer had asked his name, and Sticky, without realizing, had answered aloud. Apparently it preferred Sticky's given name.

Reynie watched his friend anxiously clutch the armrests. He wished he could help him, but there was nothing to be done. Next the Whisperer would ask what his greatest fear was, and poor Sticky would be powerless to hide it. He must face the worst, and indeed it was with a distinctly quavering voice that Sticky spoke his reply to the Whisperer's unspoken question.

"Not being wanted," Sticky said. "Not being wanted at all."

At lunchtime Kate was tossing grapes into the air — so high they almost struck the cafeteria ceiling — then catching them in her mouth, where they made a satisfying *plock*! She did this without thinking, as it was an old habit with her always to toss grapes when she ate them. And so, although she might seem distracted, Kate was actually listening carefully as the boys told of their experience in the Whispering Gallery. This was proven when Reynie said the Institute was going to close, and Kate — glancing down in disbelief — received a *tunk*! (forehead) instead of a *plock*!

"It's true," Sticky said. "Mr. Curtain foresees a 'call to greater duty' in the near future. He warned us to keep it quiet. He'd already told us that one word about the Whisperer gets your Messenger status revoked — and believe me, no Messenger wants to chance that. I suppose if he knew we were telling you *this* . . ."

"He'd toss you out of the tower," Kate said, wiping grape juice from her forehead.

"He told us all this," Reynie said, "because he's considering keeping us around after the change — the Improvement, as he calls it — to be trained up as Executives. He said we'd get to use the Whisperer once a week as a reward for our service."

"Is it really as great as all that?" Constance said. "Sitting in a stupid chair doing nothing?"

Reynie and Sticky glanced at each other and quickly glanced away. Neither wished to admit how overcome he'd been by the Whisperer. In fact, Reynie had struggled not to sound excited — even fond — when he described it to the girls. Did he really want to say aloud that Mr. Curtain's machine had made him feel . . . well . . . *happy?*

Instead, Reynie changed the subject. "It's exhausting, is what it is. That's why Mr. Curtain needs so many Messengers. He alternates them to keep their minds fresh. Given the number of Messengers, our turn should come again in about a week, assuming — oh, for crying out loud, there goes another one!"

The children scowled and clutched at their heads. Constance, though, looked not just annoyed but perplexed — as if this were her first hidden message broadcast instead of her thirtieth.

"Constance?" Reynie said. "Are you —?"

"Quiet," Kate hissed. "Here comes a sash."

"Hello, George, hello, Reynard," the Messenger said, ignoring the girls. He was a stout boy with braces so heavily rubber-banded that his mouth looked like a cat's cradle. "On behalf of the other Messengers I want to congratulate you, and to invite you to join us at one of the Messenger tables for meals. You know — to mess with the Messengers, ha ha!"

"Ha ha," said Reynie, as politely as possible. It wouldn't exactly help their mission to offend the other Messengers, but neither did he wish to be split up from Kate and Constance. He glanced at Sticky, who had a curious, expectant look on his face, as if he really were considering joining the Messengers. What was he thinking?

"Thanks so much," Reynie said quickly. "But do you have any concerns about stomach viruses? It may be a day or two until Sticky and I get over ours."

"Stomach viruses?" said the boy.

"Stoma —? Oh, yes," said Sticky, catching on. "We spent most of last night throwing up. It was bad, too — I felt like I was being turned inside out. But Reynie's too cautious. We're probably not contagious. We should go ahead and join you." He grabbed his tray and made as if to rise.

"Uh, no . . . no, I think Reynard's probably right," said the boy, backing away. He covered his mouth and spoke from behind his hand. "You can never be too careful with these things. Why don't you fellows give it a few days, and when you feel absolutely better, I mean one hundred percent, then come on over and join us."

"That's awfully nice of you," Reynie said as the Messenger hurried away.

"Quick thinking," Kate said. "And you, too, Sticky — pretty bold work. But what happened to the Sticky Washington I know? You know, the shy and timid one?"

"Give me a break," Sticky said, ducking his head.

"Ah, there he is!"

Sticky tried to smile, but in truth he was decidedly troubled. If Reynie hadn't spoken up just then, he wasn't at all sure what he would have done. He had actually *wanted* to join the Messengers! Was that all it took to sway him — being asked? Did he want so much to be wanted that he would do, well, *anything*? It was as if the Whisperer had opened a door, and now Sticky couldn't close it again. He was so ashamed he could hardly look up.

Reynie, meanwhile, felt deeply disturbed. The more he thought about his response to the Whisperer, the more convinced he was that becoming a Messenger had been a bad development, a blow to their mission rather than a boon — because he was too weak to handle it. He needed to get through the mission and off this island before he faced the Whisperer again. His next turn probably wouldn't come for several days, and yet already he found himself glancing at doors.

Reynie cleared his throat. "I think we need to —"

"Please!" Constance snapped, covering her ears. "Reynie! Will you please . . . stop . . . *talking*!"

Taken aback, Reynie closed his mouth and stared at her in surprise.

"What is your *problem*?" Sticky said sharply.

Constance lowered her hands and looked at Reynie with a mixture of ruefulness and irritation. "Sorry about that," she said tersely. "It's just that you've been on this whole time, and it's already getting old. One of you, maybe. But two of you is too much."

"On?" Reynie repeated. "Two of me?"

"You know," Constance said, tapping her head. "You're *on*. The broadcast — it's you talking."

The others looked at one another in amazement.

Reynie was flabbergasted. "Are you . . . are you sure, Constance? I mean I'm — I'm right here!"

Constance thumped the side of her head, as if trying to clear water from her ears. "It's like you're in stereo."

"Wow," Kate said, impressed. "This must be really weird for both of you."

"You know what this means?" Sticky said. "Mr. Curtain is recording the Whisperer sessions! He can record thoughts!"

"But if he can do that," said Kate, "then why does he need fresh Messengers all the time? Why not just play his recordings?"

"I think I know," said Reynie, finally recovering from his astonishment. "He hasn't always been able to do it. Remember the 'modifications' he wrote about in his journal? He said it this morning, too — he said his Whisperer was 'undergoing modification.'"

"That explains why he's not going to need Messengers after the Improvement," Sticky said. "Once he's finished recording all his messages, he'll have no use for Messengers anymore."

"And he'll be able to broadcast his recordings around the clock," said Constance. She sighed miserably and closed her eyes. "That's just peachy."

That wasn't all, Reynie thought. He had a strong suspicion that as soon as Mr. Curtain had recorded his messages, he would boost them to full-strength. It was all going to be part of the Improvement. But for Constance's sake, Reynie decided not to mention this aloud. She was already frightened, no doubt. Sitting there, eyes tightly shut, anxiously wondering what lay in store for her. . . .

Reynie felt an itch in the back of his mind. He had recently felt the very same way himself. But his eyes hadn't been closed, exactly. . . .

"We're almost out of time, aren't we?" Sticky was saying. "I never thought we'd still be on the island when all the bad stuff happened. Of course, I hoped it never *would* happen."

"I wish we could be doing something!" Kate said. "If we could just figure out what Mr. Benedict . . ." She paused. "Reynie, why are you looking at Constance like that?"

Constance opened her eyes to find Reynie staring at her.

"Mr. Benedict said with open eyes *now*," Reynie muttered, almost to himself. "Meaning *before* they were *closed* — or blindfolded!" Abruptly he stood up. "Quick, everyone, we still have time before class."

Kate leaped to her feet. Her blue eyes twinkled with excitement. "Where are we going?"

"To find a place you must exit to enter."

Moments later the Mysterious Benedict Society stood on the plaza, exactly where the boys had stood that morning when Jackson blindfolded them. A few students milled about in the rock garden, but there were no Executives in sight.

"This is the spot, isn't it?" Reynie asked.

"I'm pretty sure," said Sticky, who still wasn't sure what

Reynie was up to. Reynie had been in too much of a hurry to explain.

"And how many steps did we take before we went inside?"

Sticky told him, and Reynie looked at Kate. "Which door would that take us to?"

Kate asked Sticky to take a few steps while she watched. Then, one by one, she studied the Institute buildings. Finally she shook her head. "Based upon the length of your stride, that many steps wouldn't take you to any door of any building in the whole Institute, front or back."

"Oh," Sticky said, certain he had disappointed Reynie somehow. "I'm sorry. I was so nervous, you know. I guess I've misremembered."

"I don't think so," said Reynie, who, far from looking disappointed, was growing more and more excited. "We left the plaza, remember? Went down a walkway — and then across *grass*."

"Grass?" Sticky said. "Hey, that's right! I was so anxious I didn't even think about that. And you know what? It was the same when Jillson took me to the Waiting Room."

Reynie nodded. "When Mr. Benedict said we must exit to enter, he meant we must exit the *buildings* to enter someplace *else* — a place we can't get to from inside!"

Kate's face broke into a grin. "It's the traps, isn't it? The number of steps you took would bring you almost exactly to the one behind the Institute Control Building."

"But why would we want to enter the traps?" Constance asked doubtfully.

"Not the traps themselves," Reynie said. "Remember how we thought the boulders were to help hide them? I think it's the other way around. The traps are there to keep us away from the *boulders* — because the boulders are hiding secret entrances!"

"Secret entrances!" Constance said, trying hard not to look impressed. "How did you think of that?"

"Actually I should have thought of it sooner," Reynie said. "Sticky had already told me Jillson took him outside and blindfolded him. Obviously the Executives wanted to keep something hidden — something other than the Waiting Room, I mean, because no sane person would ever want to find *that* place. I'll bet you anything the next line of Mr. Benedict's message was going to be something like 'Where one of you has been before.'"

Sticky was mystified. "But how would Mr. Benedict know?"

"They're watching the Institute through their telescopes, remember? And the plaza's in plain sight of the mainland. They must have seen Jillson blindfold you and take you behind the Institute Control Building. That's how Mr. Benedict knew about it."

"So you mean something *good* came out of that?" Sticky asked, his eyes suddenly shining with tears. "I didn't go to the Waiting Room for nothing?"

"You aren't going to start crying on us, are you?" asked Constance rudely.

"Not now," Sticky growled, removing his spectacles and swiping at his eyes. "I believe you've cleared me right up."

"Anyway," Reynie said, "the passages that lead to the Waiting Room and the Whispering Gallery may also lead somewhere else. Somewhere important. We need to get inside them and find out."

"So what's next?" Kate asked. "Sneak around to the boulders behind the building? We still have a few minutes before class."

Reynie considered. "I think the ones up behind the dormitory would be safer. There's too much activity down here."

"Safer is good," Sticky said.

Kate was bouncing on the balls of her feet. "So what are we waiting for?"

"The right moment," Reynie replied.

As it happened, Reynie had a particular "right moment" in mind — the moment the day's classes had ended, when all the Recruiters and most of the Executives would be in the gym, marking the steps of their eerie dance. There would be far less of a chance of bumping into someone in the secret passages, he pointed out. But they would only have a few minutes. They needed to hurry.

Luckily hurrying was something at which Kate excelled. By the time the others had made it halfway up the hill to the stretch of path nearest the drapeweed patch, Kate had already reached the hilltop well above them. A quick check to make sure no one was coming up the other side of the hill; a quick scan of the plaza to see if anyone was looking this way; then Kate gave the "all clear" sign, and the others ran over to hide behind the boulders. A minute later she joined them.

"We've found the entrance," Sticky told her, pointing to a barely detectable outline in the stone. "The question is how to open it. We've already tried pushing it, sliding it, and begging it. No luck."

"Open Sesame!" Constance cried, then scowled at the unmoving boulders as if she hated them.

At the moment Reynie wasn't particularly fond of them, either. He hadn't considered that it might be difficult getting *into* the secret entrances once you'd found them. Now here they stood, thwarted, while precious seconds ticked away.

Kate glanced around to be sure they couldn't be seen, but Mr. Curtain had placed the entrance very carefully. The back of the boulders couldn't be seen from anywhere below — not from any window or door in the Institute. The same was true for the boulders behind the Institute Control Building. If students stayed on the paths and walkways as they were supposed to, they would never spot an Executive using a secret entrance.

Reynie, meanwhile, was casting about for a hidden lever or knob — anything that might open the door. Finding nothing, he growled, "Come *on*! We don't have time for this!" He gave the door a frustrated kick.

To the amazement of all, the stone door immediately swung up and away, revealing an open archway.

"You kick it?" Sticky cried incredulously.

Reynie nodded, finally understanding. "Mr. Curtain likes to ram through doors," he said. "Have you noticed?"

The children hurried through the archway into a small, empty foyer. The wall swung closed behind them, and immediately a light came on overhead. It was so bright they almost had to squint. Before them an equally bright passageway curved away in a steep descent. Reynie had thought to post Constance near the entrance as a lookout, but he saw now that a lookout was pointless. After the passage curved away from the foyer, it descended for quite some distance uninterrupted by other doorways or passages. If someone came in through the foyer, there would be no place for a lookout to hide. The children had no choice but to keep together and hope for the best.

Quickly, quietly, they moved down the passage. Constance was riding piggyback, Kate and Reynie were tiptoeing, and Sticky, who was bad at tiptoeing (he brought his knees rather too high, so that he looked and sounded like a prancing horse), carried his shoes and walked silently in his socks. In the bright light, with no nooks or crannies to duck into, they all felt quite vulnerable.

Near the bottom of the hill they came upon another passage that branched off to their right and slanted steeply downward. They wouldn't need to investigate it, though; they knew at once where it led. A remarkable foul odor hung in the air, and the passage descended to a lonely black door with an iron padlock. Near the door the stone floor was slick with black mud, and from beyond it came a high-pitched humming noise, punctuated with little clicks and scratches. Reynie turned. Sticky stood a few paces behind them, trembling and closing his eyes.

"Let's move on," Reynie said quickly. He and Kate took Sticky by the arms just as his knees appeared ready to buckle. He leaned on them gratefully as they hurried on.

A dozen paces more and the children had come to another passage that branched off to the left. This one led to a simple metal door.

Regaining his composure, Sticky quit leaning on Kate and Reynie and set his shoulders. Whatever the door concealed, he wanted to confront it bravely — or at least more bravely than he'd handled the Waiting Room. And so, while Kate and

Constance looked questioningly at Reynie (who seemed hesitant to be the one to open it), Sticky took the opportunity to press forward and give the door a sharp kick. This produced a sound very much like that of a hammer coming down upon a finger — a sort of dull *donk* — and Sticky fell to the floor, clutching his foot.

Reynie pointed to a numeric keypad beside the door. "It's not like the outside doors," he whispered. "It's locked."

Sticky winced and put his shoes back on. So much for regaining composure.

"What's that?" Kate said, pointing to a piece of paper stuck to the wall above the door. "It looks like a note. Here, Constance, let me lift you up." In a moment Constance had the note. Printed in distinctive, awkward handwriting, it read: *LOSE the new code? Turn OVER for new code!*

At the bottom of the paper an arrow pointed down.

The children sucked in their breath. Could it be as simple as this? Could they be so lucky? Eagerly Reynie flipped the paper over. On the back was another note, this one in different handwriting: *Attention all Executives: You cannot leave notes like this. S.Q., this had better be gone by tonight. Stop trying to be clever. — Jackson*

"I knew it was too good to be true," said Constance.

"I don't get it," Sticky said. "Why would S.Q. say 'turn over for code' if he wasn't going to write the code on the back?"

"It's S.Q., remember," said Kate. "Maybe he forgot to write it. My question is why Jackson didn't just take the note down himself."

"And miss a chance to scold S.Q. in front of the other Executives?" Constance said.

"Good point," Kate said.

Reynie was studying the note. "There's something . . ." The others looked at him expectantly. He rubbed his chin. "Well . . . why did Jackson tell him not to try to be clever?"

"Because Jackson knows it's pointless for S.Q. to try?" said Constance.

"But he *did* try — that's what Jackson's saying. So the question is, what did S.Q. do that he thought was so clever? Surely it wasn't just leaving the note so high up. It was hard to reach, maybe, but not hard to spot."

Kate read the note again. "Okay, why does he capitalize LOSE and OVER? It's not just for emphasis, is it?"

"I think it's to call attention to them," Reynie said. "There's something special about them. . . ." He trailed off, considering.

"Well . . . both words have four letters," Sticky offered, hoping somehow this was a helpful thing to point out.

"Maybe the code's in invisible ink," Constance suggested.

"With invisible ink he could have just written the code on the front," Reynie said. "What would be the point in turning the note over?"

"You think everything S.Q. does has a point?" Sticky said.

Suddenly Reynie stifled a laugh. "Wait a minute! I have it! Turning the note over *is* the point! S.Q., you devil!"

"Um, Reynie?" said Kate. "We did turn it over, remember? There's nothing there."

"We turned to the back of the paper," Reynie said. "S.Q. didn't mean that. He meant to turn the note *upside down.*"

"I still don't get it," Sticky said.

"Think of it this way. What if the note read: '*Is* LOSE

341

the new code?' The answer is 'Yes, but you have to turn it OVER!'" Reynie turned the note upside down and pointed to the word LOSE. The letters were now numbers: 3507.

"Hey, that *is* clever," said Sticky. "For S.Q., I mean."

"We're just lucky he's not clever enough to remember the code without leaving notes," Reynie said.

The note was returned to its proper place, and the children prepared themselves. Now that they'd had a moment's pause, their minds had filled up with questions: What would they find behind this door? What if it was terrifying? Or what if it was exactly what Mr. Benedict needed? Or what if — this had suddenly occurred to Reynie — what if S.Q.'s note had been left *on purpose*, to trick sneaking children like themselves?

Reynie saw a troubled look cross Kate's face. Had it occurred to her, too? Mr. Curtain suspected another snoop on the island — that was why he'd changed the door codes, after all. So what if . . . ?

"We need to think about this," Reynie whispered.

But Kate was already reaching for the keypad. "No time for thinking. He's coming!"

"H-he?" Sticky repeated.

That was why Kate's expression had changed. She'd heard something, and now Reynie and the others heard it, too — down in the main passage, growing louder by the second, an electric whine, a shifting of gears. . . .

It was Mr. Curtain.

They had no choice but to go through this door, even though Reynie had no answer to his last burning question: What if it was a trap?

PRACTICE MAKES PERFECT

The door slid open. The children dashed through. They found themselves in a warm, bright room that smelled heavily of newsprint and ink. It seemed to be some kind of press office. Two tables stacked with printed material stretched across the middle of the room, and in the far corner an oversized printer was spitting out page after page. A television stood near the printer — its screen flashing but the volume turned down — and on top of it sat a glass of juice. The room appeared to be in the process of being disassembled: Two long tables had been folded up and leaned vertically against one wall; several empty wooden crates were stacked against the other. This was clearly a busy place, and only temporarily empty.

Mr. Curtain rolled into the room twenty seconds later carrying a tall stack of newspapers in his lap. *Empty* was how the room appeared to him, too. Humming a chipper tune, Mr. Curtain shot over to the printer and began sorting through the printouts.

Meanwhile, the entire membership of the Mysterious Benedict Society, crammed inside an empty crate like a bunch of discarded dolls, peered out through the spaces between the crate's wooden slats. Reynie, because of the unfortunate angle of his neck and the weight of Constance upon it, was only able to see a bit of floor. Constance's view of the ceiling was little better. Sticky, however, was in the perfect position to see the evidence of the unfortunate thing that had just happened; and by pinching Kate's ankle to get her attention, then repeatedly blinking and rolling his eyes, he tried to explain it to her. His eyes, wide as saucers, seemed to Kate more anxious and panicky than usual. This was understandable, she thought, given their predicament. Although, wasn't something missing? Something about his eyes? And was he trying to point something out to her? Kate swiveled her own eyes to see what Sticky was looking at.

There, in plain sight on the floor outside the crate, were his spectacles.

They must have come loose when Kate tossed him into the crate. She hadn't seen them fall — she was too busy throwing Constance over her shoulder, tumbling in after the boys, and pulling the top of the crate over them. But she saw them now, all right. And if Mr. Curtain hadn't been absorbed in his newspapers when he came in, *he* would have spotted them, too. But the moment he finished his task at the printer and turned around . . .

Kate could tell the spectacles were beyond her reach. She would need to consult her bucket. This proved a bit tricky, though — one arm she could not move at all; the other she had to thread around Constance's neck while pressing her elbow into Sticky's nose; and she had to bend her wrist backward at an unnatural angle that hurt like the dickens. A bit tricky, yes, but Kate managed it, and with a sharp tug (which brought tears to Sticky's eyes), she had her horseshoe magnet.

The spectacles had wire rims. Kate just hoped it was the proper kind of wire.

Mr. Curtain had turned the volume up on the television. A news anchor was saying something about the Emergency. Mr. Curtain giggled — actually giggled — as if he were watching a comedy show. He sipped his juice and returned to his work, humming again.

From her awkward angle inside the crate, Kate could see Mr. Curtain's wheels pointed toward the printer. Now was the time. She slipped her arm between two crate slats and stretched it out as far as she could. The magnet was still a few inches short of the spectacles. Gripping it as tightly as she could between two fingers, Kate stretched just a tiny bit further. The spectacles twitched. Then quivered. Then slid over to meet the magnet with a click.

Mr. Curtain's humming stopped. "Hey? Who's there?"

With a sharp squeak, the wheels whipped about to face the crate, into which Kate, a split second before, had drawn the spectacles. There was a long pause, a tap-tap-tapping of fingers on a hard surface, and finally a grunt. The wheels turned away.

A few minutes later Mr. Curtain had left the room.

The children piled out of the crate, stretching their stiff limbs and rubbing their bruises.

Reynie looked quickly about. "He took his juice, so maybe he's not coming back. Constance, will you stand guard? You know the code — if you hear someone coming, run in and warn us." He ushered her out the door before she could think to argue.

Sticky was already going through a stack of fresh print-outs. "These are government press releases."

"What's a press release?" Kate asked, looking over his shoulder.

"A kind of report sent to the newspapers to be printed," Sticky said. He scratched his head. "Strange, these are all dated from the *future*. One's from next week, one's from the week after, and so on for months — even years!"

"They're *planned* press releases," Reynie said, coming over to flip through the pile. "Articles Mr. Curtain intends to have printed in the newspapers. And they all have something to do with *him*. Look at the headline on this one from next week: 'ESTEEMED SCIENTIST AND EDUCATOR APPOINTED TO IMPORTANT POST.'"

Sticky groaned and took off his spectacles. "Will you read it aloud, Reynie? I'm afraid I need to polish these."

And so Reynie read aloud:

LEDROPTHA CURTAIN, the recently named Minister And Secretary of all The Earth's Regions (M.A.S.T.E.R.), had this to say about his new role: "The governments of the

world have established my position as that of an advisor
and coordinator in this time of crisis. Being a private man,
I accept the honor reluctantly, believing it my duty."

"That's preposterous!" Kate said. "There's no such position!"

"Apparently there will be. It says here that the governments have finally reorganized themselves in response to the
Emergency."

Sticky spluttered. "But the Emergency is made up — it's
something Mr. Curtain created! I can't believe every single —"

"That's it!" Reynie cried, staring intently at the paper. He
felt a wave of relief, quickly followed by alarm — as if he'd finally succeeded in translating hieroglyphics only to discover
he'd translated a curse.

"What's it, Reynie?" asked Kate.

"The Emergency is the first step," Reynie said, thumping
the paper. "Mr. Curtain thinks fear is the most important el-
ement in human personality, remember? It's why the Whisperer has so much appeal to Messengers — it soothes their
fears, and Mr. Curtain uses that to motivate them. So what if
he *created* a fear, a fear everyone would hold in common, a
fear the entire public would share?"

"The fear that everything is hopelessly out of control,"
Kate said.

"Exactly! Then his next step would be to *soothe* that fear
with just the right message. The Messengers all love the
Whisperer with a passion, right? Well, Mr. Curtain intends
to make it so that everyone in the world will feel the way
Messengers do!"

"Everyone will love the Whisperer?" Sticky said.

"No," Reynie said. "Everyone will love *him.*"

Reynie was putting it all together now. "So those journal entries — the places where he seemed to be talking to himself — 'Trust Ledroptha Curtain' and all that. They were rough drafts!"

"He's working on his new message," Sticky said, finally understanding.

Kate couldn't help but laugh. "You mean 'Ledroptha Curtain Stops the Hurtin' was an idea for a hidden message? That's so lame!"

Reynie handed another press release to Kate. "Look at this one: 'CURTAIN BEST MAN TO HANDLE BAFFLING AMNESIA EPIDEMIC.'"

"An *amnesia* epidemic?" Sticky said.

Kate had moved down the table to rifle through a stack of pamphlets, shaking her head in disgust. "And here's how he intends to pull it off." She handed each boy a pamphlet. Reluctantly Sticky put his glasses back on, and in grim silence they all read the pamphlet. It was an official advisory from something called the Public Health Administration:

Just what *is* Sudden Amnesia Disease (SAD)? SAD is an extremely contagious disease that causes total memory loss in those who contract it.

What's being done about it? Although the origin and cure of this disease have yet to be found, they're being investigated by a group of experts headed by none other than Ledroptha Curtain, the highly regarded scientist and our newly named Minister And Secretary of all The Earth's Regions. SAD cases are admitted for free care at the Amnesia Sanctuary on Nomansan Island, a state-of-the-art facility where patients live comfortably, under strict quarantine, while the cure for their disease is sought.

Am *I* a SAD case? Are my neighbors? A common first symptom of SAD is the belief that one hears children's voices in one's head. The onset of this symptom is most sudden, and once it has begun, it persists without interruption until amnesia sets in.

Reynie flipped to the next page, which showed a picture of two smiling Recruiters. They had their hands on the shoulders of Jackson the Executive, who was trying his best to look miserable and happy at the same time. The photo caption read: "Already feeling better! A SAD case jokes around with our friendly doctors."

Sticky had finished the pamphlet and hurried to the other table. "There are more over here, printed in dozens of languages!"

"I can't believe it," Kate said. "It doesn't make sense."

For Reynie it all made too *much* sense. The last piece of the puzzle had fallen into place. "This whole thing," he said bleakly, "the Helpers, the Recruiters, the Messengers — the entire Institute — it's all been one big experiment to make sure his plan can work. Mr. Curtain has been *practicing*. The Institute will become the Amnesia Sanctuary — he needs a place to put all the people who resist him!"

"People like us," said Kate.

"People *including* us," said Sticky.

Know Thine Enemy

"I still say it makes no sense," Kate said. "It can't *really* happen, can it? He intends to brainsweep everyone who resists him? Doesn't he have to put them in his Whisperer to do that? What about people in other countries?"

Sticky waved a handful of pamphlets. "He has Sanctuaries set up all over the world. The maps on the back show their locations."

Kate humphed, then frowned curiously. She had just noticed the edge of a doorframe behind the folded tables leaning against the wall.

"It *is* hard to understand how he'll manage it, though," Reynie said. "Sticky, remember when he told us the Whisperer was going to be a 'healing device' that would bring peace to thousands of troubled minds?"

"Even millions," Sticky said with a shiver. "I remember."

Kate had squeezed behind the tables and found a numeric keypad by the covered-up doorway.

"But how would that be possible? So many people brainswept in so short a time? That's a major operation — it would take ages to prepare for it." Reynie felt an unexpected burst of optimism. "Maybe we've gotten lucky! Maybe we're in time. If we can just figure out how —"

"Boys?" Kate poked her head out from behind the tables. "There's a door back here. You need to see what's on the other side." She spoke in an oddly strangled voice, as if she'd just seen a dead body.

Sticky's eyes widened. He shook his head. "I don't *want* to. Reynie, you look and then tell me about it."

But Reynie grabbed Sticky's arm, and together they went to look through the door.

"Oh," said Reynie.

"Oh, *no*," said Sticky.

"Are those what I think they are?" Kate asked. "They look like old-timey hair dryers."

"I'm afraid so," Reynie said.

The machines stretched in long rows — row after row after row — across a vast underground warehouse. An elegantly lettered sign that hung from the ceiling read: WELCOME TO MEMORY TERMINAL. Along one wall were stacked hundreds of crates. Reynie bent to inspect the nearest one. It was filled with bundles of paper and marked with an address in

China. The crate next to it bore the same address but was filled with machine parts — including, he noted, a red helmet and a blue one.

"It really *is* happening," said Kate. "I can't believe it."

"So what's in the crates?" said Constance.

They turned to find Constance standing in the doorway behind them.

"What happened to standing guard?" Sticky cried.

"You took too long!"

Sticky's eyes bulged, but Reynie cut him off before they could start arguing. "She's right. We *have* taken too long. We need to get out of here before it's too late."

And yet as they rushed out of the Memory Terminal and up the long secret passage, Reynie couldn't stop thinking, "But we *are* too late! Much, much too late!"

The night was rainy, the plaza deserted. The light in the distant woods had stopped flashing, and Sticky turned from the window. "They want us to wait for a reply. I guess it's a lot for them to think about."

It was a lot for everyone to think about.

None of the children spoke. They only waited.

An interminable hour passed. Constance fell asleep sitting cross-legged, and Kate repeatedly asked Reynie to thumb-wrestle her to pass the time. Reynie declined. Even thumb-wrestling felt beyond his ability at the moment. Everything did. He was hoping against hope that Mr. Benedict would find some way to save them — to save everyone — without requiring anything more from him. Reynie didn't think he was capable of more, not since the Whisperer. He was worried, deeply worried, that the Whisperer had revealed to him who he truly was.

At the window Sticky suddenly sat up straight. "Here's a message!" He adjusted his spectacles and stared intently toward the mainland. *"Know . . . thine . . . enemy."* After a minute Sticky climbed down. "That's it. 'Know thine enemy.'"

Kate looked hopefully at Reynie. "I don't suppose you know what he means, do you? Just right off the bat?"

Reynie shook his head. "No idea."

Kate sighed. "Then I suppose we'll have to wake up Constance. It's been so pleasant not to have anyone grumping and mumping for a few minutes."

The children woke Constance (who claimed she hadn't been sleeping) and put their heads together. What could it mean? Didn't they already know Mr. Curtain was the enemy?

"Why do they say it like that, anyway?" Constance muttered. "It sounds stupid."

"It's an old saying," said Reynie. "That's how it's usually said."

"At least in the early translation," Sticky said. "Originally it appears in a book by Sun Tzu called *The Art of War*. It comes at the end of the third chapter."

The others stared at him.

"Well, it does," Sticky said.

"I think we need more," said Kate. "We're in too big a hurry and have no idea what they're talking about. Let's ask for another hint."

The others agreed — it couldn't hurt to ask — so Sticky returned to the window and sent a follow-up question: *Which enemy?* But to this he received no reply. Sticky repeated the message and again got no reply. He was about to try a third time when Reynie stopped him.

"There has to be a reason they're not replying," Reynie said. "Are you sure the coast is clear?"

Sticky cringed. "I hadn't thought of that." He peered out the window. "The plaza's empty . . . so's the rock garden . . . the shoreline and the bridge are harder to see, but as far as I can tell they seem deserted."

"Let me look," Kate said, climbing up beside him and sweeping her eyes from left to right. "Sticky's right, it does seem clear." She took out her spyglass and scanned the view again. "Nope, no one out there that — oh, no!"

Kate jerked away from the window, and Sticky, alarmed, leaped backward. He tumbled onto Reynie and Constance — who luckily had covered their heads, expecting whatever it was to come crashing into the room.

"Sorry!" Kate whispered sheepishly. "It's all right. I thought he was staring right back at me. But he's too far away for that, of course. The spyglass makes him seem closer."

Frazzled, the others gathered themselves up.

Kate was looking out the window again. "He really is staring in this direction, though. Oh, it gives me the creeps. Surely he's not looking at our window? I have to remember it's dark in here. He can't see me."

"Who are you talking about, Kate?" Reynie asked nervously.

"A Recruiter. He's standing down under the edge of the bridge." She lowered the spyglass and squinted into the darkness. "No wonder Sticky didn't see him. Without the spyglass he just looks like a shadow among the bridge pilings."

"Maybe the message was a warning," Constance said. "To let us know an enemy was out there watching."

"That doesn't make sense, Constance!" Sticky said impatiently. "If they'd seen him there, they wouldn't have sent any message at all."

"*You* don't make any sense," Constance snapped. "They shouldn't have sent *you* at all."

"What's that supposed to mean? I don't know who you think you are —"

"Easy, you two," Reynie said. "A message broadcast just started, didn't you notice? It's making us cranky."

It was true. Though the messages were unpleasant as ever — and came more frequently now that Mr. Curtain had some sessions recorded — the children were getting used to them. Sometimes they didn't immediately recognize the reason for their bursts of fussiness.

Sticky took a breath. "He's right. Sorry about that."

"That's okay," said Constance, though everyone noticed she didn't apologize herself.

Kate was still watching the Recruiter. Exasperated, she said, "Why won't that man *leave*? Doesn't he know we have a secret message to receive?"

"Maybe he does," Reynie said with misgiving, "and is waiting to see it."

Sticky rubbed his head in agitation. "Do you really think so? You think we've been found out? They're spying on *us* now?"

"I don't know, but something seems extremely fishy about him standing in the shadows all alone. Recruiters are *never* alone — they're always in pairs. And he obviously doesn't want to be spotted. In fact, from this angle, we're about the only ones who could see him down. . . . Wait a minute."

"You think he *wants* us to see him, don't you?" Kate said, raising her spyglass again. "He really is looking this way! Just standing there not moving. And here's something weird I didn't notice before — his hair is wet, but his clothes are dry. What do you think he's up to?"

Reynie thought he knew. "Does he remind you of anybody, Kate?"

"Does he remind me . . . ? Of course! I can't believe I didn't see it!" She rapped her forehead with her knuckles. "It's Milligan!"

"Milligan's *here*?" Sticky cried, unable to contain his excitement.

Reynie grinned. "That's what they meant by 'Know Thine Enemy.' And that's why they didn't respond to our second message — they had to make sure we looked for him. Sticky, let's send a message that says, 'Enemy Known.'"

Sticky sent the message.

No sooner had he done so than the light in the woods began flashing a message with extreme rapidity: *Go at once. Hurry. Hurry. Hurry.*

The children leaped to their feat, their hearts racing. What in the world? Had they been found out? The boys threw on their shoes, Kate retrieved her rope from the ceiling, and Constance climbed onto her back. Sticky took one last glance out the window — "It's still flashing 'Hurry!'" — and the children flew from the room, down the darkened corridor, and out into the night.

They had stared out their window at night enough to know where the darkest shadows lay, and it was to the darkest shadows they kept. Avoiding the plaza, where they would be terribly exposed, they bolted quick as cats along the bottom of the hill by the dormitory, dashed across a stretch of crumbling shale, then made straight for the water. With a final scramble down a rocky incline, they came to the island shore. If they kept low they would not be easily seen; the incline would shield them from view of the Institute. Keeping low, then, and stepping carefully on the rocky shore, the children made their way toward the bridge.

It had stopped raining, but the night remained cold and windy. Before the children had gone half the distance to the bridge, the wind began to carry a strong, spicy scent to their noses. The odor of a familiar cologne. They stopped and looked around, seeing nothing. Then a shadow detached itself from the rocky incline and took on the general form — if not the exact appearance — of Milligan. He certainly smelled like a Recruiter, Reynie thought, but for some reason he seemed un-Recruiter-like. He was dressed in a fine suit; he wore watches on both wrists; and his hair, though quite wet as Kate had mentioned, was perfectly combed. So what was it?

It was the smile, Reynie realized, or rather the lack of one. He'd never been near a Recruiter who wasn't smiling, and certainly not one who looked inconsolably sad.

"I'm sorry not to have fetched you myself," Milligan said, "but this was the safer course. A Recruiter on the shore alone may or may not draw suspicion, but a Recruiter in the student dormitory most certainly would."

"What's going on, Milligan?" Kate asked.

"I'm to take you away," Milligan said.

The children were stunned.

"Away?" Reynie repeated. "You mean off the island?"

Milligan produced four black cloaks — no one saw from where — and held them out. "Put these on and draw them tight. They'll help conceal you. If we run into trouble, stay close and don't worry. I'll die before I let harm come to any of you."

"Don't worry?" Sticky said. "Don't *worry*? You're talking about dying and we're not to worry? What's happening, Milligan?"

"There's little time for explanation, Sticky. I can get you to the mainland, but we must make our way to the other side of the island, and it will be slow going."

"But *why* are we going?" Kate said.

"Your mission is completed."

Reynie felt an enormous pressure lift from his shoulders. Completed! That meant he wouldn't be tested anymore! No more worrying about failing everyone. He could leave the island without ever facing the Whisperer again. Yes, it was time to go: Just thinking of the Whisperer filled him with longing, even made him want to stay. . . .

"Completed?" Kate said. She seemed suspicious. "Does that mean Mr. Benedict has a plan now? He thinks he can stop Mr. Curtain?"

"You mustn't worry about that, Kate," said Milligan. "Please put the cloak on."

Kate tossed the cloak onto the ground. "You didn't answer my question. Does Mr. Benedict think he can stop Mr. Curtain or not?"

Milligan frowned. "It doesn't *concern* you anymore, Kate. The Improvement is much too close. Mr. Benedict wants you away from here, where you can be safe."

"I'm not budging until I get an answer," Kate said firmly.

"Can Mr. Benedict stop the Improvement or not? Tell us the truth!"

The other children were holding the cloaks in their hands, glancing back and forth from Kate to Milligan.

Milligan looked away over the water. He seemed extremely reluctant to answer. Finally he sighed. "No, children. We have no way to stop it. You'll have to go into hiding — we all will. We'll need to keep moving, keep ahead of the Recruiters . . . but Mr. Benedict believes he can keep you safe, and you have my word that I'll do all I can to protect you. Please, try not to worry. Mr. Benedict will never give up. That much I can assure you. He will work tirelessly, and perhaps in time he can find a way to counteract Mr. Curtain's messages — to clear all of our minds."

Kate was having none of it. "What about Constance?" she demanded. "What happens to *her* when Mr. Curtain boosts the power all the way? She's already hearing voices, you know!"

Milligan looked sadly at Constance. "I don't know, child. Nobody does. I'm so sorry — you're in danger no matter *where* you go."

At this, Constance sat down on a rock and covered her face. She seemed smaller than ever now — so small the harbor breeze might catch her up like a scrap of paper and carry her away, carry her into nowhere.

It was then Reynie knew they couldn't leave.

He shouldn't have needed Kate to show him, he thought. His desire to save himself had kept him from seeing it at first, but at least he saw it now. He felt it in his bones, and it felt perfectly awful, but there it was: They couldn't leave. Not just for poor Constance's sake, but for Mr. Bloomburg, and Milligan, and the Helpers, and all the future people Mr. Curtain intended to brainsweep, not least of whom was dear Miss Perumal herself. Mr. Benedict would never ask it of him, but he must ask it of himself.

"Milligan, please tell Mr. Benedict thank you," Reynie said. "But I'm staying."

Kate threw her arms around him. "Oh, I hoped you would say that, Reynie! Because I'm staying, too. We *have* to, don't we?"

Sticky seemed ready to cry. "You're staying? But . . . but . . ." He turned and gazed longingly toward the mainland. He had known they would say this. And he knew they were right.

"Sticky?" said Kate.

"I suppose we don't have much choice," Sticky said. "We don't have much *chance*, either. But we're the only one Mr. Benedict has got."

Milligan tried again, and then again, but the more he pressed the children, the more determined they became. Finally he gave up. "In that case, I'm to give you a message from Mr. Benedict."

"A message?" Constance said. "Why didn't you tell us before?"

"Mr. Benedict had a feeling you would choose to stay. 'That is exactly the kind of children they are,' he said. He hoped to discourage such a decision and carry you to safety. But if you adamantly refused — and *only* then — I was to give you the message."

"So what is it?" Kate asked.

"He said to remind you that every single one of you is essential to the success of the team — that now more than ever, you must rely upon one another in all things." Milligan took the cloaks back from the children. "What's more," he said, tucking the cloaks down the legs of his suit pants, "you must also rely upon me. Whatever develops, I'm here to help you. I'm staying on the island. When the time comes, this is the place to contact me."

"How do we do that?" Reynie asked.

Milligan pointed back the way they had come. "Not far from here an old drainage culvert empties into the channel. It's a good marker. To leave me a message, hide it in a dry spot within twenty paces of the culvert, and stack two stones upon it. I'll check the place often, and meanwhile I'll keep an eye on you as best I can." With that, Milligan turned to go.

"Wait a minute," Kate said. "Aren't you going to wish us luck?"

"Luck?" Milligan said, without turning around. "I've been wishing you luck from the moment I met you. What I wish for you now is a miracle."

He disappeared into the darkness. The children stared after him.

"He thinks we need a miracle," Sticky said in a bleak voice.

"Well, optimism has never been his strong suit," said Kate. "Or haven't you noticed?"

A Chess Lesson

Reynie woke before dawn, shivering and drenched in sweat. For the second night in a row he had dreamed an awful thing. This time, while his friends cried for help from somewhere far away — so far away they sounded like whining mosquitoes — Reynie had been sitting in the Whisperer, incredibly happy and content, grinning in triumph. Why triumph? He tried to remember. He was grinning because . . . Reynie shuddered, remembering: He had decided to join Mr. Curtain.

Reynie rubbed his temples. Just a dream, he told himself, though reality wasn't much better.

Nor did reality improve as the day unfolded. Classes, meals, studytime — all passed in an unpleasant blur as Reynie struggled to come up with a plan. For the first time since he'd set foot on Nomansan Island, he was dreading the meeting of the Mysterious Benedict Society that night. He had no idea what to do. The others were looking to him as a leader, and he could only look back at them as a failure. When the lights finally went out and the girls joined them, Reynie was cringing even before Kate asked her question.

"Okay, Reynie, what's the plan?"

Reynie shook his head. "I . . . don't have one. I'm sorry. I've tried, but my brain just goes round and round. All I can think is that we need to disable the Whisperer, but —"

"That's a *great* plan!" Kate said, excited. "How do we do it?"

"That's what I mean," Reynie said with a shrug. "I don't see how we can. The computers are below the Whispering Gallery, tucked away beneath two feet of metal and stone. There's no way. . . ."

"Mr. Curtain told you that," Kate pointed out. "Are you sure he was telling the truth? You were blindfolded, remember. How do you know the computers aren't sitting out in the open and you just couldn't see them?"

Reynie was surprised this hadn't occurred to him. "It's a good question." He considered a moment. "But no, as much as he emphasized security, I'm inclined to think he's telling the truth. Wouldn't you say, Sticky?"

"I'm afraid so," Sticky said.

"But Mr. Curtain needs *some* way to get to those computers," Kate pressed. "To work on them and modify them and all that. Don't you think?"

Reynie went from being surprised to being mortified. Shouldn't *he* have thought of this? "You're . . . you're right, Kate. He must have some way of getting to them. Which means *we* might be able to get to them, too. After all, we know the door codes now!"

"It couldn't hurt to take a peek," said Kate, standing up. "And the sooner the better. I'll go by myself — if I get caught, you three might still have a chance to figure something out. Now just tell me how to get there. I know I need to go through the secret entrance behind the Institute Control Building, but then what? Sticky?"

Sticky felt a powerful urge to make up a lie — to protect the Whisperer. Unbelievable, he thought. He tried again, but again he felt the urge. Only by clenching his fists and speaking through gritted teeth did he manage to tell Kate the truth. "It's just down a short passage and then up the tower steps."

"We need to go with you, though," Reynie said. "It's too dangerous alone."

Kate waved him off. "I'll be fine. It's really a one-girl operation, anyway."

You shouldn't let her go alone, Reynie thought. She ought to have help. But when he opened his mouth to argue, he found nothing would come out. A fog seemed to have rolled into his mind, and on top of that he felt bone-weary. He was tired, very tired, of always trying to do the right thing.

Kate set her flashlight on the television. "You'll need this in case I get caught."

"If you get caught —," Constance began.

"Don't worry, I won't give up my friends," Kate snapped. "Good grief, Constance, it's the last thing I'd do!"

In a vexed tone Constance said, "I *was* going to say, 'If you get caught, don't worry. We'll find some way to save you.'"

They were all moved by this — especially Constance, who'd said it herself — and Kate patted Constance's shoulder. "Sorry, Connie girl. Sometimes I forget you're not *always* a crab. Now let me take you back to the room. Reynie, Sticky — I'll let you know what I find out. Wish me luck!"

They wished her luck, and moments later the girls were gone.

With hardly a word between them, hardly even a glance, the boys slipped into their beds. They often chatted a minute or two before dropping off to sleep, but now both were afraid of betraying how strongly the Whisperer was affecting them.

Betray, Reynie thought. It was an ugly word, an awful thought. But as often happens with awful thoughts, he could not stop thinking it. Why hadn't he argued with Kate? He should have insisted he accompany her. Why hadn't he? Was it the broadcasts fogging his mind? Or was it that part of him didn't *want* to stop Mr. Curtain?

Reynie pressed his fists into his eyes. In his mind he began composing a letter.

> *Miss Perumal,*
>
> *Would you ever have thought I might choose a lie for the sake of my own happiness? The Whisperer's version of happiness is an illusion — it doesn't take away your fears, it only lies to you about them, makes you temporarily believe you don't have them. And I know it's a lie, but what a powerful one! Maybe I'm not who I*

always thought myself to be. Maybe I'm the sort of per-
son who will do anything *to hear what I want to be-*
lieve. . . .

Reynie was crumbling, on the brink of despair. Mr. Benedict had expected him to be a leader to his friends, to be smart
enough to devise a plan, to be brave. But he was no kind of
leader at all, he knew that now, certainly not brave, and Mr.
Benedict felt very far away indeed. More and more, Mr. Curtain seemed like the real man, and Mr. Benedict like a memory from a dream. And Miss Perumal, the only person who
always treated him kindly, had become an imaginary reader to
whom he wrote imaginary letters.

What has happened to you? he thought. He'd never expected
doing the right thing to be so hard. But it was. Too hard for
him, anyway. He was the wrong person for this task, the
wrong person in the wrong place.

Reynie squeezed his eyes shut, trying not to cry. But that
only made him see the Whisperer all the more clearly. How
was he supposed to resist the Whisperer when it was the one
thing that offered relief? What he needed was help — some
encouragement, some guidance, anything to bolster his resolve. The others all looked to him. Who was *he* supposed to
look to?

It had to be Mr. Benedict, Reynie thought. If Mr. Benedict
couldn't help him, then he was beyond help.

Reynie climbed down and went to the window. He gazed
out into the dark night. Kate was off somewhere risking her
neck. Sticky was murmuring in his sleep, having troubled
dreams. And Constance's dreams could be no less troubled —
she had more to worry about than anyone.

Reynie would send one message, one message only. He had never been superstitious, but he decided now that if he received no response to help him, he would give up. Just give up and take an easier path. He wouldn't have to try to be some kind of hero, wouldn't have to fail — and soon it would be too late to matter. There would be nothing he could do, no point in trying. It would be out of his hands.

Just thinking about it was so enticing Reynie almost didn't send the message. But then, squeezing his lips tight in determination, he signaled the words before he could change his mind: *Whisperer too strong. Please advise. — RM*

Reynie waited at the window, his heart hammering. He felt his entire future, indeed his entire character, depended upon the next few moments. *Send me something,* he thought. *Please just send me . . . just send me* anything.

He waited. Minutes crawled by. Why must they take so long? Perhaps they had nothing to offer him. Perhaps they were racking their brains for anything to say other than "good luck." Or perhaps they weren't even watching — perhaps the Recruiters had found them. Reynie couldn't know the reason, but the reason hardly mattered. What mattered was the empty night.

"I can't believe this is it," Reynie thought, with the strangest mixture of despair and relief.

But this was it. It was all over.

He was just turning from the window when he saw a distant flash, a pinprick of light among the trees on the mainland shore. Someone, at last, was signaling a response. Reynie heard his pulse pounding in his ears. He held his breath until the message was completed.

Remember the white knight.

Reynie let out his breath. A long, slow release. He didn't have to think very hard to know what Mr. Benedict meant by that. Though it seemed so long ago, he well remembered their conversation about the chess problem. The white knight had made a move, changed his mind, and started over.

"And do you believe this was a good move?" Mr. Benedict had asked.

"No, sir," Reynie had answered.

"Why, then, do you think he made it?"

And Reynie had replied, "Perhaps because he doubted himself."

Reynie stared out the window for a long time. Then he put down the flashlight and climbed back into bed. His heartbeat had steadied, his shoulders relaxed. In his mind he took out the letter he had just written to Miss Perumal, crumpled it up, and threw it away.

He would write her another.

The Mouse in the Culvert

As Reynie composed a more optimistic letter to his former tutor — indeed, even as, in his mind, he wrote the words "and now our hopes really *do* lie with Kate" — Kate was feeling less and less optimistic herself.

Her problem wasn't finding Mr. Curtain's secret computer room. Her problem was not getting caught.

At first everything had gone fine. Kate had flitted through the shadows behind the dormitory, and in no time had made her way down to the boulders behind the Institute Control building, kicked open the secret entrance, and darted inside the foyer. It was here that the problems began. The ceilings had no crawl space, and the air vents were too small to accommodate her. She had no choice but to move about in the open. And it *was* open in the passage, as a quick peek from the foyer proved — open and bright as day. Not to mention it was hardly a "short passage" at all. Lined with doorways, it stretched off into the distance, where it finally turned a corner. Why had Sticky said it was short?

Then Kate remembered the boys had been blindfolded. They must have *thought* it was short, because they'd only gone a little way before Jackson had led them through a doorway and onto the tower steps. Any one of these near doorways might lead to the steps, then. Should she try them all?

As if in answer, about halfway down the passage a door slid open and Jackson stepped out into the passage. Kate pulled back into the foyer and listened. No footsteps. She peeked out again. Jackson was leaning against the wall by the door, munching absently on a stick of licorice. He seemed relaxed, settled, as if he intended to stay there awhile. Kate smiled. She thought it pretty likely he was guarding the tower steps. Now she just needed to get past him.

Pulling back out of view, Kate eased her slingshot from her bucket, snugged a marble into it, then peeked around the corner again. She waited a long minute, then another. Finally the opportunity came: Jackson looked down to straighten his sash, muttering something to himself. It was now or never. Kate launched the marble down the passage.

The marble shot over Jackson's head, struck the stone floor in the distance with a satisfying click, bounced off the far wall, and skittered around the corner. Jackson spat out his licorice and barked, "Who's there?" Not waiting for an answer, he ran down the passage and around the corner, and Kate dashed to the door he'd been guarding. Next to it was a numeric keypad. She hadn't counted on that, but if Mr. Curtain hadn't changed the codes again. . . . Her fingers flew across the numbers.

The door opened. Kate leaped inside.

Only then did she realize she was in an elevator. An elevator? Of course! How else would Mr. Curtain get up to the Whispering Gallery in his wheelchair? He must not let his Messengers use it — he did like his secrets, didn't he? Probably enjoyed the thought of the children laboring up all those steps, too. As the door slid closed, Kate saw the tower steps through an open doorway across the passage. Jackson had been guarding *both* entrances.

There were only a few buttons inside the elevator. They were unlabeled, but it wasn't hard to guess that the top button would be for an entrance outside the Whispering Gallery, and the one below it — that would surely be the computer room. Kate stared longingly at the button . . . but of course she couldn't press it. She couldn't use the elevator. Jackson was sure to hear it. He was probably already coming back down the passage.

And so Kate improvised. She emptied her bucket, flipped it over, and standing atop it on her tiptoes, unscrewed the maintenance panel above her. She'd never worked so quickly in her life. In no time she'd tied her rope in place, gathered her bucket and things, and disappeared though the panel into the elevator shaft above.

No sooner had Kate replaced the panel below her than the elevator door opened. Kate held perfectly still. She heard Jackson grunt. The door closed again.

Kate flicked on her penlight. The elevator cables stretched high above her, disappearing into blackness. She took off her shoes and socks, slid the socks over her hands to protect them, then put her shoes back on. With her penlight clamped between her teeth, she started up, wasting no time. She had a very long, very difficult climb ahead of her.

It was a very long, very difficult way to go only to be disappointed. Despite the socks, the cable hurt her hands; the climb was exhausting; and when at last Kate came to a set of doors near the top, she found them impossible to pry open or peek through. Above them another set of doors (which must open onto the passageway outside the Whispering Gallery) proved equally immovable. Then, squeezing past the winch and machinery at the top of the elevator shaft (if the elevator had started just then, she'd have been killed), Kate discovered that a vent cover she'd spotted was welded shut. The vent was too tiny to climb through, anyway. She did manage to peer down through it, if only to make the following, discouraging mental notes:

In the foyer: two Recruiters, very big and dangerous-looking, both wearing shock-watches. Behind them: thick metal door, three manual locks in addition to an electronic keypad, one of the locks a combination. Air ducts: too small for Constance to fit through, even if greased. Ceiling: inaccessible. Windows: none.

No windows, Kate thought, and no hope for entry. She couldn't even get to the room *outside* the computer room, much less into the computer room itself. It was hard to resist a sigh. She'd had grand visions of sabotaging the Whisperer, destroying its computers all by herself. Ripping out cables, crushing components, stealing mysterious gizmos that could not be replaced. Not only would she be regarded as a hero, she would prove once and for all that she could do everything alone — that she needed no one's help. But now she saw she could do no such thing. Not this time.

Kate stiffened. In her disappointment she had let her mind wander, and only now became aware that one of the Recruiters was peering into the darkness in her direction.

"McCraig," the Recruiter said to his partner, "do you see something odd behind the vent there?"

McCraig pulled out a flashlight. Nothing behind the vent. "Probably a mouse."

"A *talking* mouse?"

"That's not coming from the vent, you idiot. That's the Executives coming up the steps. Got a new one taking the tour tonight, remember?"

Kate, who had pulled back just in time, also heard the voices. They were just on the other side of the wall.

"— part of your training," S.Q. was saying, his voice growing louder. "After I show you the ropes up here, you and I meet with Mr. Curtain so he can explain some things to you."

"Yes, you've already *said* that," said a testy voice. Martina Crowe. "But why are *you* coming to the meeting? You've been an Executive for almost a year now."

"Well, you probably haven't noticed," S.Q. said, "but I'm a little slow on the pick-up. Mr. Curtain sometimes has me sit in on these tutorials, to refresh my memory about certain things."

Kate heard a derisive snort, then Jackson's voice saying,

"Hold on, you two." She leaned and peeked through the vent again, but couldn't see him. The entrance from the tower steps was out of view.

"McCraig," she heard Jackson say to the Recruiter. "Everything fine up here? Nothing unusual going on tonight?"

"I'm telling you, Jackson," said S.Q.'s voice, "it was probably a mouse."

"We got mice, too," said McCraig. "Other than that all's fine."

"Jackson takes his guard duty very seriously," S.Q. said knowingly.

"Hey, it's Mr. Curtain who wants security stepped up," Jackson snapped. "You got a problem with Mr. Curtain, S.Q.?"

"Of course not! I was just saying . . ."

Kate didn't hear the rest. She was already easing her way down the elevator shaft again. She needed to beat Jackson back down so she could slip out. And then? What was this about a meeting with Mr. Curtain? Maybe the night didn't have to be an *entire* loss. The trouble would be finding a way to eavesdrop on his office. Too risky going into the Institute Control Building. But maybe she could find another way.

"And so you see, Martina," Mr. Curtain said, rolling out from behind his desk, "after the Improvement most people will be much happier."

"But not all," said S.Q. "Isn't that right, Mr. Curtain?"

"Quite right, S.Q. Unfortunately, there are *some* people whose natures incline them to be sad when others are happy."

Martina was smiling. "May I assume," she said in a sly tone, "that these poor souls would not only be unhappy —

which certainly is tragic enough — but might also . . . cause trouble? Am I right that brainsweeping will not only help them feel better, it will make them more *manageable?*"

"You understand perfectly," said Mr. Curtain with an approving look. "And S.Q., I believe that explanation should satisfy *you*, as well."

If the explanation had not satisfied S.Q., it had nonetheless created in him the strong impression that he *ought* to be satisfied, and so he laughed and said, "I see, yes. Of course."

Martina leaned forward in her chair. "One thing I'm still unclear on, though, is how brainsweeping works. It doesn't actually erase the memories?"

"Not at all," Mr. Curtain said. "Anyone who knows anything about the human mind understands that it never truly forgets anything. To completely erase memories is impossible. What *is* possible, however, is hiding memories from their owners. To use my favorite comparison, we sweep the old memories under a mental rug — hence the word 'brainsweeping' — and there they remain hidden away, with no one the wiser."

"And everyone happier," S.Q. said.

"Yes, S.Q.," said Mr. Curtain with a significant look at Martina. She was a brand new Executive, but already understood far more than S.Q. ever would. "Yes, my friend. Everyone's happier."

"Isn't it amazing?" S.Q. said to Martina. "I get goose bumps every time I learn it."

"It is much the same with fears, you know," Mr. Curtain said. "S.Q., do you believe you have it down now? Would you like to explain to Martina how the Whisperer deals with fears?"

"Oh, yes, of course I would," said S.Q., reddening. "That is, I *would*, but, um —"

"But you've forgotten?" Mr. Curtain snapped, flashing a sneaky half-grin at Martina. (Apparently he took pleasure in toying with S.Q., which no doubt explained why Mr. Curtain hadn't booted him off the island years ago.)

"Forgotten? Oh, no!" S.Q. cried in dismay. "No, I wouldn't say I've forgotten — you know, nothing is ever *truly* forgotten, you said so yourself, sir, ha ha —" He coughed. "It's just that, uh, you're so much more elegant than I am."

"I daresay that's true. Perhaps you also find me more *eloquent* than you. Very well, S.Q., I shall explain it, and you may nod along as always."

S.Q. nodded.

Mr. Curtain turned to Martina. "You recall how your fears seem to disappear when you're seated in the Whisperer, do you not?"

Martina's expression sharpened with hunger. "Absolutely," she breathed.

S.Q. nodded.

"Of course you do. Again, the magic is in the messages. My Whisperer rewards your cooperation by sending extremely high-power messages that *deny* your fears. A simple procedure. Fears lurk just beneath the surface and are easy to detect."

S.Q. nodded.

"So it's just a wonderful illusion!" Martina said. "That explains why the fears come back later. I've always wondered about that — when I'm in the Whisperer they seem to have gone away forever."

Mr. Curtain laughed. "Sadly, no. The only way fears *truly* disappear is if you *confront* them. But who in the world wishes to confront his or her worst fears?"

"Not me!" Martina said.

S.Q., already beginning to nod, checked himself and shook his head.

"Nobody does," said Mr. Curtain. "And now we are on the brink of offering the same peaceful contentment on a much grander scale. After the Improvement, you see, everyone's greatest fear shall be drowned out by a message much like the ones you receive in the Whisperer. It will be grand!"

"I can't wait!" S.Q. cried, unable to contain himself. "To think that so many people will be so happy!"

Mr. Curtain chuckled. "You don't have long to wait, S.Q. My modifications have gone much more quickly than I even hoped. I now fully expect the Improvement to begin the day after tomorrow — perhaps even sooner."

"The day after tomorrow!" Martina exclaimed. "I had no idea!"

"Yes, you're very lucky," Mr. Curtain said. "You're the last Executive promoted before the Improvement. It's a proud tradition, Martina. Several generations of Executives have come before you, many of whom were dispatched to the four corners of the world to prepare for the Improvement. In fact, many have become important government officials."

"What will *I* be doing?" Martina asked, her eyes shining with anticipation.

"You'll start by helping with the Sweepers," said Mr. Curtain. "You've been to the Memory Terminal, yes? S.Q. showed you the Sweepers?"

"We just came from there. They look exactly like the Whisperer."

"True, but they are much less powerful," said Mr. Curtain, "and much less sophisticated. The Whisperer, Martina, is a sensitive, delicately balanced machine that requires my strict guidance for its proper function. Only my Whisperer can bring about the Improvement."

Here Mr. Curtain paused, his face adopting an expression of fond reverie.

"So the Sweepers just bury memories," Martina said. "Nothing fancy."

"Correct," said Mr. Curtain. "They are much simpler tools than the Whisperer, hardly more sophisticated than metal brooms. Otherwise my Executives would be unable to operate them."

This time it was Martina who nodded and S.Q. who did not. In fact, S.Q. now wore an unusually serious expression.

"Um, sir?" S.Q. said timidly, raising his hand. "A thought just occurred to me."

Mr. Curtain raised his eyebrows. "That's remarkable, S.Q. What is it?"

"Shouldn't we be asking people's permission? I mean, if we're putting things in their heads, shouldn't we ask them first?"

Martina's jaw dropped with disbelief, but Mr. Curtain was long used to the workings of S.Q.'s mind. In fact, S.Q. had asked this question before, more than once, but had forgotten. With more amusement than impatience, Mr. Curtain answered, "If we ask permission, S.Q., then it doesn't *work*. Do you want people to be happy, or don't you?"

"Oh, I do!"

"Then the answer is no, we should not be asking permission. Do you see?"

Relieved, S.Q. nodded.

"And so, Martina," Mr. Curtain concluded, "you may now

anticipate the Improvement with pleasure. As I said, by the day after tomorrow we —" Mr. Curtain's attention shifted to the drain cover in his office floor. "How odd. I thought I heard something in the drain."

"Maybe it's a mouse," S.Q. ventured.

"What's that drain for, anyway?" asked Martina.

"Would you like to tell her, S.Q.?" said Mr. Curtain, still peering toward the saucer-sized grate. "I suspect that's something you *do* remember, grisly details being the most memorable."

"Oh, yes, sir!" replied S.Q., eager to prove his knowledge. He cleared his throat importantly. "You see, Martina, back in the early days, when the Institute was being built and a colony of workers lived on the island, this room was used as the butchery. There was always a lot of blood, of course, gallons of it, and the butchers would wash it down that drain. The drain connects to a culvert, which carried everything off to the harbor. They say sharks used to gather in the waters there, drawn by the scent of blood, and workers would fling mice out for them to snap up. . . ."

Here S.Q.'s face brightened. He'd suddenly remembered something *else*, and it was rare that he remembered two different things in so short a time. "You know what, Mr. Curtain? Jackson heard a mouse, too, not half an hour ago. We're having a real problem with them lately."

"The real problem," said Mr. Curtain, "is that we hear these mice but never see them."

Rolling to his desk, he took up a pot of hot water S.Q. had brought him for his tea. "It may be that our mice have grown better at hiding. However, it occurs to me that although the drainpipe is mouse-sized, the culvert is human-sized, and

would provide a perfect hiding place for some bold eaves-
dropper who managed to find its entrance." Even as he spoke,
he shot across the room and dumped the steaming contents
of the pot down the drain.

He waited, listening carefully, but not a sound reached
him save the gurgling of the hot water as it drained away.
"Hmm. Perhaps it was a mouse, after all, or the echo of harbor traffic. Pipes do have strange acoustic effects." For a moment he stared at the empty pot in his hand, somewhat lost
in thought, then said, "I do want my tea, however. S.Q., run
over to the cafeteria and bring me another pot of water. And
some pastries, too. Here, I'd better write it down for you."

The note Mr. Curtain handed to S.Q. had nothing to do
with tea or pastries. It read: *Go at once to the culvert opening on
the south shore. Bring Jackson along. If you find no one, scour the
sand near the opening for footprints. Hurry!*

S.Q. read the note, read it again, glanced up to express his
puzzlement, and saw Mr. Curtain lay a finger to his lips. Understanding dawned on him then, and tripping in his great
haste, he left the room.

Kate's ear had been to the pipe when she heard the splash —
she'd barely had time to jerk her head back before the hot water gushed out. Even then, a little splashed onto her neck, and
it was all Kate could do to hold in a gasp. Then she heard Mr.
Curtain send S.Q. away, and suspecting a trap, she beat a
quick retreat down the culvert to the shore.

As she emerged into the night air, Kate spotted two figures (S.Q. and Jackson, though in the dark she couldn't tell
this) burst out from behind the Institute Control Building

and race across the plaza for the shore. In moments they would be upon her. There was nowhere to go but the water. Kate plunged in and dove deep. It was shockingly cold — too cold for sharks, she hoped, for what S.Q. had said just before Mr. Curtain dumped the water was much on her mind. That butchery business was long ago; surely by now the sharks would be out of the habit of congregating here. She hoped. Anyway, she could hardly return to shore, so in the water she must stay.

Fortunately Kate was an excellent swimmer. Heading out into the channel, she stayed underwater as long as she could, emerged briefly to gulp air, and dove under again. When at last she surfaced and looked back, she'd put a good distance between herself and the shore, and saw to her relief that she wasn't being pursued. Perhaps she hadn't even been seen. Good. She would just need to swim down the coastline and find a safe, inconspicuous place to sneak aground.

Kate turned, looked at the water ahead, and gasped.

She'd seen what she expected to be the last thing she ever saw. A shape, triangular and black, slicing toward her through the dark water. Fear coursed through her body like an electric shock. She braced herself for the brutal, daggerlike teeth, and in that split second of waiting, managed to wonder if it would be the shark's bite that killed her, or if instead she would be snatched away, deep down, to drown in a bloody darkness.

In the next moment, she saw that the shark fin was only a rock.

The fear drained away, but the aftereffects of panic remained, sharpening Kate's senses. With her heart thudding like bass drums in her ears, she looked around. Jagged rocks pierced the water surface all about her. Amid the murk of night and the sloshing of a thousand tiny waves, most of them appeared to be moving. More than a few resembled shark fins. Perhaps a few even were.

"Good grief," she said, for she had no choice but to swim right through them. She'd have to be careful not to cut herself to ribbons on their sharp edges. And she'd have to hope none of them were actually sharks.

SACRIFICES, NARROW ESCAPES, and SOMETHING LIKE A PLAN

By the time she crept into Reynie and Sticky's room half an hour later, Kate was in a better mood. Which is to say, she was disappointed with her mission, miserably cold, soaked to the bone, and in a good deal of physical pain. But at least she hadn't been eaten by a shark. At the sound of squishing shoes and a strange, rapid little clicking sound, the boys awoke to see Kate giving their radiator a bear hug, her teeth chattering furiously, her clothes dripping water.

"Kate!" they cried in barely contained whispers. "What happened? Are you all right?"

"W-w-w-ell," she stammered, unable for the moment to continue.

Reynie threw his blanket over her shoulders, and when at last she grew warmer, Kate told them everything. (She omitted, however, the part about the imagined shark. No sense getting into all that.)

"Luckily I had my bucket secured with my belt," she said, "or I'd have lost it for sure. Even so, I did lose a few things, and my penlight is waterlogged. And my fingers were too numb to grip anything, so I couldn't climb into the ceiling. I had to sneak down the corridor. Can't believe I didn't bump into Jillson or somebody."

"I can't believe you managed to eavesdrop through that drainpipe," Sticky said. "How did you even think of it?"

"A lucky guess," Kate said. "Reynie mentioned that drain in the floor when he first told us about Mr. Curtain's office. Then last night Milligan pointed out the culvert to us. Drains and culverts — I put two and two together and hoped for the best."

Reynie had been rummaging for an extra towel. He handed it to Kate. "So there's absolutely no way we can get into that computer room?"

Kate shook her head reluctantly. She hated to admit it.

"All right," he said. "Nice job, Kate."

"Nice job? But I didn't accomplish a thing!"

"Are you kidding? Now that we know we can't reach the computer room, we won't waste time trying. And we don't have any time to waste — by the day after tomorrow we'll have no chance at all. We know that now, too, thanks to you. It's all crucial information."

Kate shrugged dismissively, but secretly she was pleased. She opened and closed her hands. The feeling seemed to be returning to her fingers.

Reynie was concentrating. There was no message broadcast at the moment; the storm system in his mind had moved out. "And what was that he said, Kate? About his Whisperer being a sensitive machine?"

"Sensitive and delicately balanced," said Sticky. "And it requires his strict mental guidance for its proper function."

"I *think* that's what he said," Kate admitted. "I tried hard to remember it just as he said it, but I don't have quite the memory you do."

"All right, we'd better report all this to Mr. Benedict right away," Sticky said, scrambling up onto the television. Instantly he groaned. "Jackson's out on the plaza with S.Q. — he's yelling at S.Q. about something."

"Sticky and I will wait them out," Reynie said. "Kate, you should change into dry clothes and go on to bed. No point all three of us staying —" Just then another broadcast began. They all grimaced. Reynie felt the storm system move into his mind again.

"Good grief, I hope this one doesn't keep me awake," said Kate with a sigh. "I'll go lay these clothes on my radiator and *try* to sleep, anyway. We only have a day or so to save the world. We'll need all the rest we can get!"

Sleep she did: Kate was so tired from her night's exertions that she slept through the wake-up announcement and was late getting ready for breakfast. Constance was no help, either. When Kate had returned in the middle of the night, she'd awakened Constance to fill her in, and afterward Constance was even sleepier than usual. So both girls were snoozing soundly when Jillson banged on their door. Kate dreamed she was back in the circus, being fired from a cannon.

"Up!" Jillson shouted, rapping again with such force that the girls' window rattled in its frame. "Helpers stop serving breakfast in fifteen minutes, girls!"

Waking with a start, Kate leaped out of bed, threw on some clothes, and snatched her shoes from the radiator. They hadn't dried much, unfortunately. Then she shook Constance awake — or at least into a groggy stupor. "Come on, Connie girl! We've got to get moving!"

Constance smacked her lips, blinked a few times, and said, "Don't call me Con —"

"Right, right. Sorry."

After a lot of hustling and cajoling, Kate got Constance moving, then quick-stepped it to the cafeteria with the smaller girl riding piggyback. She spotted the boys at their usual table and squished over to them. For some reason, Reynie's eyes widened at Kate's approach, and no sooner had she sat down beside him than he said loudly, "There you are! Let me pour you some juice, Kate!" With unusual awkwardness he grabbed a juice pitcher, lost his grip, and ended up sloshing an entire quart of juice all over Kate's feet. At a nearby table, a group of Messengers burst out laughing.

"Good grief, Reynie!" Kate said. "I can pour my own juice, all right?"

In an undertone Reynie said quickly, "Listen, Kate. Rumors have been flying all morning. They know someone was in the culvert and swam away to escape — your soggy shoes are a dead giveaway. Everybody saw me spill that juice, so now you have a reason other than harbor water."

"Yikes," Kate said. "Thanks, buddy. And wipe that grin off your face, Constance. You don't always have to enjoy it so much, you know."

As the girls wolfed down their breakfasts, Reynie and Sticky filled them in: After Kate left their room, they'd finally had the opportunity to send Mr. Benedict a report, but to their enormous disappointment, Mr. Benedict hadn't been able to reply. Jackson and S.Q. had returned to the plaza, this time with Mr. Curtain, who like Jackson was clearly furious with S.Q. about something and kept shaking his finger in S.Q.'s face.

"We wondered why S.Q. was in so much trouble," Sticky said, "and this morning we found out. Everybody's heard about it: Jackson and S.Q. failed to catch the spy, but they did find footprints in the sand at the culvert entrance, footprints leading down into the water."

"What?" said Kate, freezing with a forkful of scrambled eggs halfway to her mouth. "Oh, no! I meant to wipe away the prints, but then I didn't have time." She reddened, ashamed, and set down her fork. "I'm sorry, everybody. They'll match my shoes to the prints, you know they will. And then it's . . . Why are you both shaking your heads?"

"Because you have nothing to worry about," said Reynie.

Sticky broke into a grin. "S.Q. took care of the problem for us. Those big feet of his came in very handy for once. He found the footprints, all right, and followed them down to the shore, but in the process his own footprints destroyed yours! Destroyed them completely! That's why Mr. Curtain is furious."

"Ha!" Kate said, profoundly relieved. "Here's to good old S.Q.!"

"We're still in a tight spot," Reynie said. "Mr. Curtain will be watching everybody very . . . and, oh, don't you find these danishes splendid, Sticky? They go down wonderfully well with cold milk, especially the raspberry ones."

Sticky wasn't puzzled by the change of subject. He, too, had seen Jackson and Martina approaching the table. He was responding earnestly that he preferred the cinnamon rolls when Jackson drew up and said with a sneer, "George, forgive me for interrupting your *very* interesting conversation about breakfast foods, but Martina and I are making an inspection. No doubt you've all heard about the spy."

"We have," Reynie said, "and we can hardly believe it. Why on earth would a spy be at the Institute?"

Jackson knuckled Reynie painfully on the head. "If you would use your brain, Muldoon, you might figure a few things out. The spy obviously hopes to steal some of Mr. Curtain's secret technology, then sell it to someone who might use it for wicked purposes."

"That would be terrible," Kate said.

Reynie was rubbing his head. "Anyway, yes, we've heard about the spy."

"And yet one thing you probably have *not* heard about is this." Jackson reached into his pocket and drew out a marble. Kate's marble.

"The spy is a marble?" Reynie asked.

"Ha ha, young man. Ha ha. No, this marble happens to

have been found somewhere last night, somewhere — let me put it this way — somewhere it should not have *been*."

"That seems a reasonable way to put it," Reynie said.

Martina leaned forward, peering into Kate's bucket. "So Jackson and I are looking for the marble's owner. I don't want to point any fingers," she said silkily, "but it seemed to me Kate's bucket might be a good place to look. She has so many odds and ends in there, you know."

Reynie and Sticky tried to appear unconcerned, but their minds were in turmoil. Kate had mentioned losing a few things in the water last night, but she'd said nothing about the marbles and slingshot.

"Mind if we have a look?" Martina asked, already reaching.

"Not at all," replied Kate. Before Martina could actually touch anything, she dumped the bucket's contents onto the table: a magnet, a Swiss army knife, a spool of twine, a kaleidoscope, and a rope (which was damp, but you couldn't tell without touching it). No marbles. No slingshot.

"Oh," said Martina, with a look of bitter disappointment.

"Okay, then," said Jackson. "Just checking. We have other people to ask, so we'll leave you to continue your fascinating conversation. Come on, Martina." With some effort he drew the reluctant Martina away.

Kate winked. "I may not know when the Cenozoic Era was —"

Sticky was aghast. "Kate, we *live* in the Cenozoic Era. Sure, it began 65 million years ago, but —"

"What I was *going* to say," Kate continued stubbornly, "is that I may not know when the Cenozoic Era was, but I wasn't born yesterday."

"What in the world are you people talking about?" asked Constance.

"She just means to say she's not stupid," said Reynie. "So you got rid of the marbles and the slingshot on purpose, Kate?"

"Of course. I figured he'd find that marble, so I *had* to dump the others. I sure hated to, though. I won most of them in a game with a lion tamer."

"Poor Kate," said Constance, "she's lost her marbles."

Everyone but Kate was chuckling about this one when Martina and Jackson, halfway across the cafeteria, suddenly seemed to change their minds and returned to their table. An intimidating look of cruel pleasure on Martina's face dried up all their laughter and made them wait in silence for the explanation.

"Jackson forgot to mention something else," Martina said. "He just so happened to spit out a piece of licorice last night in the same place he found that marble. But when he looked for it later, it was gone."

Reynie felt Kate stiffen next to him. They were in trouble.

"Funny thing about licorice," said Jackson. "It's just the sort of thing to get stuck in the bottom of your shoe without your realizing it."

"I get it, I get it," said Kate, squirming in her seat. "So now you want to see the bottoms of my shoes."

"If you'd be so kind," Martina said with a wicked grin. She'd noticed Kate squirming and was delighted to think she'd frightened her.

"Well, sorry about the dripping, but Reynie just spilled juice all over them," Kate said.

"Oh, yes, we saw that," Jackson said. He let out an amused rattle of laughter that sounded like a sheep in pain.

While Jackson was bleating at her expense, Kate pressed something sticky, gritty, and cold into Reynie's hand beneath the table. She hadn't been squirming from nervousness — she'd been twisting her legs up to get at the licorice. As she lifted her sodden shoes now for the Executives to inspect, Reynie reached across under the table and pressed the hunk of licorice into Sticky's hand. The further away from Kate the better, he thought. Sticky had the same idea, immediately passing the licorice on to Constance.

Constance, unfortunately, did not understand what it was.

In horror the boys watched her raise the slimy, dirty, half-chewed glob of candy above the tabletop to examine it. Reynie's eyes swiveled to the Executives, who, having been disappointed in Kate's shoes, were now asking her to show her empty hands, then checking for stickiness under the edge of the table. He looked back to Constance and saw the realization hit her, her eyes widening with alarm. And then, an instant before Martina glanced up to see it, Constance popped the licorice into her mouth, chewed it up, and swallowed it.

"Eww, that was the most disgusting thing I've ever seen," Sticky said later, when the crisis had passed and the Executives were off harassing other children. Constance's cheeks, normally a rosy red, had turned a faint shade of green.

"Disgusting, yes, but heroic," Reynie said.

"We all have to make sacrifices," Constance muttered miserably.

"What we need to make is a decision," said Kate. "We need a plan, and quick. Does anybody have any ideas? I'm fresh out."

Constance only groaned and put her head in her hands.

"I do have one thing to say," said Reynie, then hesitated. He had intended to say that he couldn't face the Whisperer again — that the mere thought of it turned his mind to jelly, so how much worse would it be if he actually *experienced* the Whisperer again? Wouldn't he be certain to give up? This was what Reynie had meant to say. But now he found he couldn't. He was too ashamed.

Constance groaned again without looking up. "Reynie, you're the king of saying you have something to say, then not actually saying anything. Do you realize that?"

"Sorry," Reynie said. "I . . . I forgot."

He was not the only one at the table with troubled thoughts. Sticky felt the same way Reynie did, and Kate was still wishing she'd been able to sabotage those computers, to have solved the dilemma all on her own. (And having failed to do that, she was trying to pretend to herself that she hadn't.) Constance, meanwhile, was trying not to contemplate what might happen to her when Mr. Curtain boosted the messages to full power. Thus all the children were trying *not* to think of things instead of *trying* to think of things, and *trying not* being generally less productive than *trying*, they weren't coming up with ready answers.

In the midst of going round and round in his mind about not facing the Whisperer, however, Reynie did stumble against something which — if seen from a distance and not stared at directly — might resemble a plan. A hundred times he'd thought to himself, "I can't face the Whisperer again." But this time, for some reason, he had tacked on the word "alone." And this was how he stumbled against the planlike thing.

"Okay, everyone. I think I *do* have a plan now. Didn't Mr. Benedict tell us that we must rely upon one another in all things? That every single one of us is essential to the success of the team? We have to take into account that we need each other."

"That's the plan?" Constance said. "To give each other big hugs?"

Reynie ignored her. "I was thinking maybe if we faced Mr. Curtain and his Whisperer *together*, we could figure out what to do."

"You mean all of us in the Whispering Gallery at the same time?" said Constance doubtfully. "With Mr. Curtain there? What could we possibly do?"

"I don't know yet," Reynie admitted. "But there's Milligan, too, remember. If we contact him, we'll have him to help us."

"I say it's worth a try," said Kate. "We're running out of time. How do we manage it? Should Constance and I sneak in while you two are having your sessions?"

Reynie considered. "The door is controlled by a button on Mr. Curtain's chair, so you can't sneak in. But Sticky and I could press the button to let you in."

"There's at least one problem with all this," said Sticky. "We weren't to have another turn in the Whisperer for at least a few days, remember? By then it will be too late!"

Kate tried to think. "What would be good . . . What would be good would be if Mr. Curtain won the Nobel Peace Prize!"

Sticky spewed a mist of chocolate milk. "Have you gone off your . . . oh, hi there, S.Q.! What brings you by our table?"

S.Q. Pedalian looked down upon them dejectedly. "Hello, kids. I suppose you heard how I bungled that spy business. Wiping out the footprints and all that."

"You shouldn't feel bad," Reynie said. "I doubt anybody could have done a better job."

"It's nice of you to say," S.Q. said with a sigh. Then he took a deep breath just so he could sigh again. "But enough about pitiful me. I came over to ask about *you*, Constance. Are you feeling all right? You seem rather, well, green-colored."

"I'm afraid we gave her a stomach virus," Reynie interjected. "Sticky and I just got over it."

S.Q. looked sympathetic. "Oh, yes, the other Messengers told me about that stomach bug. It's a nasty one, eh? How *do* you feel, Constance?"

"Like I ate something revolting," said Constance. "I guess that's what I get for hanging around with Reynie and Sticky."

"Now, now," S.Q. observed, "nothing better for you than spending time with Messengers. Good influence and all that. I mean, stomach bug aside. Let's just hope not too many other people get sick. It would be a shame if classes had to be canceled. There's too much good stuff to review!"

They all heartily agreed with S.Q., thanked him for stopping by, and nodded as he droned endlessly on about the escaped spy and a good many other things, until finally his jaw was worn out, his mind was empty, and he went away.

"What we need," said Kate, as if they'd never been interrupted, "is for you boys to get your turn sooner. Isn't there any chance you could be called on tomorrow?"

"I'm afraid not," Reynie said. "Not unless every other Messenger suddenly fell ill."

"Too bad we can't *actually* give them belly aches," said Constance.

Sticky's ears perked up.

"Who says we can't?" he said.

BAD NEWS AND · BAD NEWS·

The children's plan was bold, ill-formed, and likely to fail, and all of them knew it. They also knew they must act now or never. "Tomorrow, then," Sticky said, hurriedly grinding a plant root between two rocks. When he was finished, Constance swept the powder into a small bag and handed him another root.

"Yes, tomorrow," said Kate, standing guard on the hilltop, a few yards up the path. "And let's hope it's not too late."

"I wouldn't want it to be any sooner," said Constance. "I

don't particularly look forward to tomorrow." She contemplated a few pulpy grains of crushed root clinging to her fingertips and resisted — for the twentieth time — the temptation to see what they tasted like. Sticky had warned her that wild chuck-root ("or *Euphorbia upchucuanhae*, as it's more widely known") was a powerful emetic. Constance had never heard the word "emetic," but for once she hadn't required an explanation. It was clear from their plan — and from Sticky's mischievous grin — that by tomorrow most of the students at the Institute would be barfing up their suppers.

Those suppers had yet to be eaten, however. It was the end of the school day, not yet suppertime, and the uneasy members of the Mysterious Benedict Society were the only children outside in the chill air. The other students were either in their rooms studying or watching television, but the moment class was dismissed Sticky had led his friends up here, just over the top of the hill beyond the gym. It was here, on the day they'd encountered Mr. Bloomburg, that Sticky had spotted the patch of wild chuck-root (along with various other plants whose Latin names he rattled off and the others promptly forgot).

"This should be enough," Sticky said, grinding up the last bit of root. He dusted his hands vigorously. Then considering what would happen if he absentmindedly touched his lips — then absentmindedly *licked* his lips — Sticky dusted them again. And a few minutes later, when the children were gathered on the hilltop, he dusted them again. "I'm actually starting to feel guilty about this, can you believe it?"

"Maybe it means you still have a conscience," Reynie said.

Kate snorted. "Or maybe it means you're sympathizing too much with the enemy. Personally, I don't feel the least bit guilty for sending a bunch of bullies on an emergency trip to the bathroom."

Sticky wiped his hands on his pants. "Don't let your feelings make you too ambitious on this one, Kate. If you overdo the dose, you might hurt somebody."

"And it isn't just Messengers getting the stuff," Reynie reminded her. "That would be too suspicious. It has to be everybody."

Kate rolled her eyes. "Who needs parents when I have you two? Don't worry, I won't kill anyone. And I promise not to enjoy it the tiniest bit if Martina turns green."

Guilty or not, they all smiled at the thought.

"So let me just review the plan," Constance said. "The other Messengers will get sick and won't be able to do their sessions with the Whisperer, so you boys will get your turn early. When you get called for your session, Kate and I will sneak away somehow and wait outside the door to the Whispering Gallery. Now, how exactly are we supposed to do that? What if we're in class?"

"We haven't worked that part out yet," Reynie admitted.

"Right," said Constance. "And then one of you will push the button that opens the door, even though the button is on Mr. Curtain's *wheelchair*. How are you going to manage that?"

"We haven't figured that part out yet, either," mumbled Sticky.

"I see. And then, after all this has been magically accomplished, Kate and I will rush inside, and the four of us together will somehow defeat Mr. Curtain, ruin his Whisperer, and make our escape unharmed — even though we're on an island, and the bridge is guarded by Recruiters. Any idea how this is going to happen?"

"No," the boys said dejectedly. Kate shrugged.

"Okay," Constance said. "I just wanted to be sure I understood the plan."

"Anyway, you can't count Milligan out," Reynie said. "He'll be there to help us."

Constance threw her hands into the air. "How do you know? You haven't even left the note for him yet!"

Reynie rubbed his temples. "I'm going right now, Constance. Okay?"

"Be quick, Reynie," Kate said. "I'll need all three of you to distract the Helpers while I doctor the food."

"How are we supposed to do *that*?" Constance asked, launching into a tirade about how ill-prepared they were, how little time they had, and how this plan was giving her a worse headache than the hidden message broadcasts did. "So I ask you *again*," she concluded, "exactly *how* are we supposed to distract the Helpers?"

"Just be yourself," Kate said with a sigh.

Reynie left the others arguing on the hilltop and hurried down toward the shore. He had insisted he be the one to hide the note. Kate would have loved to sneak down to the culvert again, but this was not a clandestine operation. It had to be done in the daylight. Reynie did take a route that made it difficult for him to be seen from the Institute grounds, but if he *was* spotted, he'd invented a good explanation.

In one pocket Reynie carried a note for Milligan that told him of their plan. In another pocket he carried a sketch of the island bridge, which Reynie had spent most of two class periods working on from memory. He was a fair artist and had felt modestly satisfied with the result until Kate glanced at it after class.

"Not good?" he'd asked, seeing her brow wrinkle.

"It's okay," Kate had said tentatively. "But the perspective's a bit off. See, if you just follow the line here . . . and darken those shadows there. . . ." In about two minutes she had produced a much better sketch than his own.

Reynie scowled. "I'll take yours," he said grumpily. "Wouldn't want you to have gone to all that trouble for nothing."

At the top of the sketch he'd printed the title, *Your Favorite View.* If he was caught, Reynie would say he'd gone to the shore for a better view of the bridge, so as to make the best possible drawing — the drawing, of course, being intended as a present for Mr. Curtain.

Hurrying along at the bottom of the incline, just out of reach of the lapping water, Reynie patted his pockets anxiously. Both pieces of paper were there. Good. *Now don't step in the water,* he told himself. *Wet shoes might draw suspicion. And be sure the note doesn't stick out when you leave it — cover it up completely with the rocks. And don't leave any footprints. It's a miracle footprints didn't sink us last time. Only poor old S.Q. spared us that disaster.*

Reynie found the culvert and marked off twenty paces from it. He looked around. Not a soul to be seen. There was no one on the bridge, the incline concealed him from the rear, and in front of him was nothing but water . . . and across it the mainland shore. It occurred to him that Mr. Benedict and his crew were probably watching him through a telescope right now. He stared toward the trees across the channel. No doubt they could see him. The question was whether he would ever again see *them*. Reynie gave a melancholy little wave — one part hello and one part goodbye — then bent and hid the note beneath two big rocks.

Be sure, Reynie reminded himself. Had he stacked the rocks carefully? Had he made sure the note couldn't be seen? Had he left any telltale footprints in the sand? Satisfied on all counts, he hurried back the way he'd come, anxious to put distance between himself and the note. As he left the shore and started up the incline, Reynie considered what to do with the sketch. He didn't think he'd been spotted, but he should save it just in case. If someone confronted him about it later, he would have his excuse in his pocket.

Reynie patted his pocket, but the sketch wasn't there! How could it not be there? Hadn't he put it in his left pocket? He reached into his other pocket and felt the paper. He must have had it confused. Or had he? He took out the paper to be sure, then stared at it in disbelief. It was his note! He had left the *sketch* under the rocks!

Now things were getting dicey. Kate needed his help, and it was almost time for supper. But they absolutely had to contact Milligan. *You can do it*, Reynie told himself. *You'll just have to run.*

Reynie ran. Down the incline, watching his step on the rocks, careful not to get wet, careful not to leave prints. Soon he'd made his way back to the two stacked stones. He glanced quickly around — shore, bridge, water. All clear. Exchanging the note for the sketch (unfolding the note to be certain this time), he put the stones back, checked one last time for footprints, and ran off as fast as he could.

Two minutes later Reynie was alone on the plaza, breathing hard. He saw S.Q. Pedalian appear from behind the Institute Control Building, but there was no way S.Q. could have seen him, and there was no one else in view. Reynie wiped his brow. That was a lot of excitement over nothing. He waved to S.Q. and hurried on, not wanting to get caught up in a conversation. No time for that. The others were waiting.

As it happened, S.Q. was in a hurry, too. All day long he had been tormented by his mistake. How could he have been so foolish as to wipe out the spy's footprints? Such a ridiculous blunder! And all day long he had thought maybe, just maybe, if he were to go back down there and take a closer look . . . S.Q. picked up his pace, feeling more eager with every step. He would skip supper and spend the entire hour searching. Wouldn't it be something if he *did* find the spy's footprint after all? Or some other clue? They had scoured the area pretty carefully before, but you never knew, did you? How wonderful it would be if he could redeem himself in Mr. Curtain's eyes!

And so it was that with longer and longer strides, S.Q. Pedalian hurried across the plaza and down the incline, toward the shore, toward the culvert, toward the place where Reynie, in his anxious hurry, had stacked the two stones just a little less carefully than he'd done the first time — toward the place where one corner of the note stuck out, flickering in the harbor breeze like a tiny white flag of surrender.

When suppertime came and the cafeteria roiled once again with rowdy students, the members of the Mysterious Benedict Society suddenly developed an apparent dislike for anything salty or sweet. They loaded up their trays as usual, to avoid suspicion, but carefully avoided touching their forks to anything but green vegetables.

"You couldn't have saved even *one* kind of pastry, Kate?" asked Constance, screwing up her face to swallow a Brussels sprout. She barely managed it, gulping it down with plain water rather than her usual orange-flavored soda. "These might as *well* be poisoned."

"Better safe than sorry," said Kate, through a mouthful of lima beans. "Anyway, I didn't have time to pick and choose, you know."

All around the cafeteria, children were stuffing themselves with their usual favorites — greasy foods, savories, and sweet treats — and guzzling chocolate milk and soft drinks. Reynie, meanwhile, speared a dry lettuce leaf with his fork and thought: *So far, so good.* Despite his bland supper, despite the nagging message broadcast in his head, and despite the uncertainty of his plan, he felt a stirring in his heart, a good feeling that might pass for hope. Kate had spread the powder, Reynie had delivered the note to Milligan, and neither of them had been caught. At least *some* parts of the plan were going as hoped.

It really was a good feeling. But it didn't last long.

Jillson appeared in the cafeteria, a jubilant grin on her face, and came straight over to their table. Without asking, she crowded herself into a seat between Reynie and Kate — her wide shoulders forcing them to draw their arms close together over their trays, like praying mantises — and snatched a cream puff from Kate's tray and said, "Hi, there, squirts!"

Kate frowned, but only out of principle. Privately she was delighted. "Help yourself," she said coolly.

"Thank you, I will," Jillson said, gulping the cream puff down. "Listen, I have good news and bad news, and I thought you kids would be particularly interested. You heard about S.Q.'s bungling the spy business, right?"

"It does ring a bell," said Reynie, who didn't like where this was going.

"Well, guess what?" Jillson said. "There's been a new development. S.Q. went back down to the culvert just now, to take one last look around. And he *found* something."

The children could only stare at her, stricken with dread. They were also confused. If S.Q. had found the note, then why weren't they already in trouble? Was Jillson toying with them?

"Now, as I said, there's good news and bad news," Jillson went on.

Feeling as if they'd just been given very bad news indeed, Reynie had to stop himself from asking what the good news was.

"The bad news," Jillson said, "is that what S.Q. found — a curious piece of paper — was destroyed before he could read it."

"That's . . . terrible!" the children cried, trying to cover their relief. It was too plain on all their faces, and they knew it.

Luckily, Jillson didn't notice. She placed a hand on her belly and frowned. After a moment she belched, smiled with satisfaction, and continued, "Don't worry, the good news makes up for it. The spy's been caught!"

The children looked at one another. *Caught?*

Jillson belched again and scowled. "Must have eaten too much pudding. Yes, caught like a rat in a trap. Turns out it was a man disguised as a Helper. Came out of nowhere, snatched the paper from S.Q., and tried to run away. But Jackson heard S.Q. shouting for help, and some Recruiters on the bridge had seen it happen, so in no time they had the spy surrounded. He tried to fight them off, but he was no match for *our* guys, I can tell you. He's in a classroom right now, under heavy guard."

Reynie felt as if he'd been kicked in the belly. They had lost Milligan. "Why . . . why are you telling *us* this, Jillson?"

"Well, I have to admit I was surprised. Martina had convinced me that *Kate* was the spy. She was disappointed to learn otherwise. But I thought you should know Kate's off the hook. The Helper confessed to everything. He's a lone operator, apparently. That means he works by himself."

Kate looked quite sick. "Did he say who he was?"

"We don't know his name, but he was on the island once before — years and years ago. When they took off the disguise, Mr. Curtain and some of the Recruiters recognized him at once. Oh, and get this: He *ate* that piece of paper! Chewed it up and swallowed it before anyone could read it. Said it was from his private journal and was none of our business. Very dangerous madman. Don't worry, though, they're taking him to the Waiting Room in just — oh! Here they come now!"

The children could barely bring themselves to look.

There was Milligan. His hands and ankles were cuffed, his feet dragged along in a defeated shuffle, and his ocean-blue eyes, sadder than ever, focused only on the ground before him. Though he kept his head bowed, the cuts and bruises on his face were easily seen. He was being marched across the cafeteria by a half-dozen Recruiters and Executives (including a very proud Martina Crowe) — none of whom showed any marks from a scuffle. Reynie wondered how this was possible. Jillson said he'd tried to fight, but if Milligan had really resisted, wouldn't his captors look as if they'd caught a tiger by the tail? Had he only pretended to struggle? But why? Unless . . .

Suddenly Reynie understood. Because S.Q. had glimpsed the note, Milligan had *chosen* to be caught. He'd wanted a chance to confess, a chance to make up a story about that piece of paper. A *note* would have suggested someone else had written it — another spy on the island — but a page from a private *journal* pointed only to Milligan himself. Yes, he had wanted to convince Mr. Curtain he was working alone, had wanted to take suspicion off the children. He had sacrificed himself for them.

As Milligan passed through the cafeteria, the whole place erupted in applause for the Executives and Recruiters, then horrible boos and jeers for the captured spy. The miserable man was led past their table — right past the grateful and heartbroken children he'd saved — but never did he look up or reveal any awareness of them.

"Boy, doesn't he look glum?" Jillson said.

Kate started to speak, but a catch in her voice made her words incomprehensible. She was thinking exactly what her friends were thinking. Milligan had said he would die before he let any harm come to them.

STICKY'S DISCOVERY

M *captured. Must face Whisperer tomorrow. Please advise.*

"Still no response," Sticky reported from the window.

The others waited in depressed silence. Although the "stomach virus" had spread like wildfire (already the bathrooms and the Best of Health Center were crowded with students), the success of their scheme had done nothing to boost their spirits. Not even the sight of Jillson hurrying down a corridor with her hand over her mouth, clutching a paper bag in case she didn't reach the bathroom in time — not even this managed to cheer them. Time was slipping away, and they'd been forced to abandon the hope that they'd nurtured in the backs of their minds: the hope that if things went terribly wrong, Milligan would be there to save them somehow.

After another interminable minute had passed, Kate said, "I'm sick of waiting. I say forget the plan and let's try to rescue Milligan instead."

Sticky was taken aback. "But he's under heavy guard — we wouldn't stand a chance!"

"We don't stand a chance either way, do we?" said Kate.

"That isn't like you, Kate," said Reynie, surprised. "I think the broadcasts are getting to you."

Kate frowned. "You're . . . you're right. I'm sorry."

"Wait, here comes a response," Sticky said. "What in the world? Can that really be it?" He began signaling with the flashlight again.

"For crying out loud, what are you *doing*, George Washington?" demanded Constance. (Though the others wouldn't have thought it possible, Constance grew steadily crankier as the Improvement drew closer.) "Did they send a message or not?"

"I'm asking them to repeat it." But when the message was repeated, Sticky was left scratching his head. "It's just an old saying: *Laughter is the best medicine.*"

"Are they joking?" Kate said.

"Maybe it's their way of saying for us to cheer up, to have hope," Sticky said.

Reynie didn't think so. "That's too lighthearted. They wouldn't expect us to feel like that, not with Milligan taken prisoner. It's a riddle of some kind — important advice. We just have to figure out what it means."

"For once I'd like a straight answer," Constance grumbled. "It's ridiculous that they do it this way — it isn't right!"

"They have to be careful, don't they?" Sticky said. "If they gave us a straight answer and someone else saw it, we'd be in even worse shape."

"How much worse shape could we possibly be in? I'm *tired* of being careful. And I'm tired of their dumb codes, and I'm tired of you all treating me like a stupid baby."

"Easy now, Constance," Reynie said, as calmly as he could. "We're all frustrated and upset, and I know you're scared —"

"Shut *up*," Constance snarled. "I'm sick of you, too! Who made you king, anyway?"

"Why don't *you* shut up?" Reynie snapped.

With that — the first time Reynie had ever spoken so sharply to her — Constance lapsed into furious silence. The others, disgruntled, turned their energy toward solving the riddle. But Sticky and Kate were not the best puzzle-solvers, and Reynie was lost in his mental fogbank. (And the Whisperer, high up in its tower, kept shimmering like a lighthouse beacon through that fog.)

After half an hour of useless guessing, the children had come no closer to an answer, and Constance abandoned her silence in order to mock their efforts. Reynie put his head in his hands. "Okay, Constance, I give up. Is that what you want? None of us can concentrate while you're being this way. I say we adjourn and get a few hours of sleep. Maybe a little rest will help."

Constance, who felt very desperate indeed, could not control herself. "Rest?" she sneered. "I thought what we needed was laughter. Isn't that what stupid old Benedict said? Well, hardy har har, that's the funniest thing I've ever heard."

"You're hopeless," said Kate, who'd been in an awful mood to begin with and now had lost all patience. "Reynie's right. Let's go back to our room." She scurried up her rope into the ceiling, and as she hauled Constance after her she whispered down: "We'll be back before dawn. Or I will, at least. If she's still acting like this, she can rot in our room, for all I care."

The gap in the ceiling closed.

Reynie and Sticky looked at each other. Everything seemed to be falling apart, and neither boy could hide his worry. It was written plainly on both their faces.

"If you think of anything at all . . . ," Reynie said.

Sticky nodded. "I'll wake you up. You do the same."

Fully dressed and fully miserable, the boys climbed into their beds, still going over the message again and again in their heads. *Laughter is the best medicine, laughter is the best medicine.* . . . By midnight, neither had come up with anything. By one o'clock, Sticky was whimpering himself to sleep. By two o'clock, Reynie was abandoning his last letter to Miss Perumal, starting over, then abandoning the new one as well — too anxious even to think about being anxious. His mind returned to Mr. Benedict's message.

"Why laughter?" he wondered for the hundredth time. "Why medicine? It's something . . . something that cures an illness or . . . or solves a problem, maybe, but what problem?"

But the answer remained maddeningly elusive. Reynie decided he would have to stay awake. There was no way he could sleep, anyway, not until he had figured out the message. Having made this decision, he sighed, rolled over to get comfortable . . . and fell asleep.

‿:‿

Some time before dawn Reynie awoke with a start. His mind had been working furiously as he slept. He swung down off his bunk and shook Sticky. Sticky opened one eye, then closed it to open the other, as if too afraid now to look at the world with both at once.

"Wha —?"

"Sticky, wake *up*."

This time Sticky blinked both eyes. "Hmm? What time is —?" He sniffed and rubbed his head, coming slightly more awake. "Oh, has something happened?"

"I have an idea about what Mr. Benedict meant," Reynie said excitedly. "I just don't think it's quite right yet. I think maybe it's half right. Let me tell you about it, and then you tell me what you think."

Sticky sat up, fully awake now. "I'm all ears."

But no sooner had Reynie begun than a knock sounded on their door, and S.Q. Pedalian, not waiting for a response, poked his head into their room. "What, already up? Good boys! You must have guessed all the other Messengers are down for the count, and Mr. Curtain needs you again right away. He's had to cancel half his night sessions thanks to this stomach bug. Good thing you two are already over it, eh? Can you imagine anything worse than not being able to go when Mr. Curtain summons you?"

The moment had arrived too soon! No one had expected such an early morning session. Snatching a pen from his desk, Reynie scribbled something on the palm of his hand.

"What are you doing?" S.Q. said.

"Just writing down something I don't want to forget."

"I do that sometimes," S.Q. reflected, "only I usually forget I wrote something on my hand, and I wash it off before I remember. What are you writing?"

"Remind me to tell you later," Reynie said.

"Right — now hurry and get dressed. Don't want to keep Mr. Curtain waiting."

The boys threw on their clothes and followed S.Q. out the door. In the corridor a few weak-kneed, pasty-faced students were making their way to and from the bathrooms, and a group of silent Helpers worked double-duty to keep the floors mopped. S.Q., cheerful now that he'd made up for his earlier blunder, smiled and patted the miserable students as he passed. "Hang in there! Chins up! Look on the bright side — it could always be worse!"

The trip to the Whispering Gallery didn't seem nearly long enough. The blindfolding, the walk to the secret entrance, the exhausting climb up countless steps — all of it seemed to pass in one excruciating instant. Then S.Q. was removing their blindfolds and pressing the intercom button. "Reynard Muldoon and Stic . . . er, George Washington here for their sessions, Mr. Curtain!"

Mr. Curtain's voice came through a speaker: "They must wait. Meanwhile, bring me more juice."

In his most authoritative tone (which was not very authoritative), S.Q. ordered the boys not to stir from that spot. After they assured him that such a thing would never have occurred to them, he hastened back down the steps.

"Let's run!" Sticky whispered.

"No, listen, we still have a chance," said Reynie. "You have to go first, Sticky, and make your session last as long as you can. If you resist the Whisperer at the very beginning, while you still have strength, you might be able to stretch out the session —"

Sticky's jaw dropped. "Resist it? But Mr. Curtain will suspect something! He'll notice it, you know he will. He'll send me back to the Waiting Room! He'll —" Sticky began to shake all over. "He'll turn the Whisperer on *me*! I'll be brainswept!"

"I know the risks," Reynie said. "But this is our only shot."

Sticky's horrified expression shifted into one of anger. "Why don't *you* go first, then? Why don't you be the one to resist it, if you're so brave?"

"I need to try to signal the girls," Reynie said. He grabbed Sticky's arm. "We can still do this, Sticky!"

Sticky looked doubtful, even suspicious. "How do you propose to signal the girls? How —?"

The Whispering Gallery door slid open and Martina Crowe came out, her expression pleasantly befuzzed. She was so content she almost didn't bother to sneer at them. Almost. But then she stopped and made an effort.

Reynie returned the sneer with his best fake smile. "Did you just have a session with the Whisperer? I thought you were an Executive now."

"I'm such a young Executive, I can still do Messenger work in a pinch," Martina boasted. "And this is definitely a pinch. I've never seen so many upchucking kids in my life."

"You haven't gotten sick?"

"Sick of being hungry, is all. I was so busy capturing that *spy* last night, I missed supper. That's the price you pay for being an Executive, doing the important work. Not that you boys would know anything about that." With an immensely self-satisfied and condescending expression, Martina walked on, saying over her shoulder, "Hurry on in, boys. I'm off to another duty. You'll notice I don't have to wear a blindfold, either."

The moment she was out of earshot Reynie whispered, "You have to trust me on this, Sticky. To give us a chance, you have to go first. It's our only hope."

Sticky's face was a mask of doubt.

"Boys, get in here!" Mr. Curtain called.

Reynie tried to make one last plea to his friend, but Sticky turned and plunged into the Whispering Gallery without looking back.

Reynie had no choice but to follow. Taking a deep breath, he walked into the Whispering Gallery . . . where his breath escaped like air from a balloon. There it was! The Whisperer! Reynie's eyelids fluttered. Stepping into its presence was like stepping into a warm bath. He wanted to take his seat in it and never climb out.

You have to fight, Reynie told himself, and with great effort he tore his eyes from the seductive machine to look at Mr. Curtain.

Mr. Curtain seemed tired but eager. "Welcome, boys. I trust you are fully recovered? You have your strength up?"

"Yes, sir," the boys said together.

"I hope so! Only a tiny handful of Messengers have recovered, and I've worn them all out. You saw I resorted to using an Executive — a rare thing, as older children are so much less effective. But I've been put off my schedule and am raging against the delay. If only this infernal stomach sickness hadn't emerged, my project would already be complete!"

"Sorry to hear that, sir," said Reynie.

"No matter, my young friend. The problem will soon be rectified, for I intend to finish right *now!*"

Reynie sucked in his breath.

"You mean . . . you mean . . . ," Sticky stammered.

"I see you're quite tongue-tied by the honor. That's right, George, you boys shall personally preside over the completion of my project. If all goes well, that is."

The boys forced weak smiles.

Mr. Curtain clapped his hands together. "Now, here is our task. First we shall have a last session devoted to old material — the last of the lessons. Then we shall have a session of entirely *new* material. Material hot off the presses!" Mr. Curtain waved his journal triumphantly. "I've just completed it."

Reynie tried to stall. "Shouldn't we take time to study it, sir?"

"No, Reynard, in this case simplicity is essential. My Whisperer is designed to soothe troubled minds, and nothing soothes the mind more effectively than a simple answer to a complicated problem."

"Mr. Curtain, sir?" Sticky asked. "Do you still plan to close the Institute?"

At this unexpected question, Reynie glanced sharply at Sticky. Was he stalling, too, or was it the opposite — had Sticky already given up?

Mr. Curtain chuckled. "Don't worry, George, I haven't forgotten you. The other students will be sent home tomorrow — I have chosen to answer a higher calling and will be serving the public in a much grander capacity — but I have you boys in mind as personal assistants, to be groomed as Executives as you mature."

"You . . . you really do want us, then?" Sticky asked.

"But of course I do," Mr. Curtain said, with an encouraging smile. "I could use you both! And the sooner the Improvement begins, the sooner you'll begin your new life. What better motivation to perform well, eh?"

Sticky's lip quivered.

"I'm here with the juice, sir," S.Q.'s voice called through the intercom speaker.

"Finally," Mr. Curtain grumbled, his smile instantly vanishing, as fake smiles often do. He pushed a button on the arm of his wheelchair.

Reynie, who had been watching Sticky in bleak despair, noted which button Mr. Curtain pressed. If Kate and Constance managed to come, he could open the door. But what were the chances of that? First Sticky would need to resist Mr. Curtain's invitation — and with the pull of the Whisperer so powerful, with Mr. Curtain now so likely to succeed, could Reynie hold out hope for this?

S.Q. brought their juice and tripped out again; Mr. Curtain sipped from his paper cup with an expression of eager contemplation, and then the moment had arrived. "Very well, Reynard, let's improve the world. You may take your seat in the Whisperer now."

Reynie stared pleadingly at Sticky, whose expression was impossible to read. What was going on in his head?

As it happened, Sticky himself did not know.

There had been times in Sticky's life when an important question would flummox him no matter how well he knew the answer; and times he had run away from his problems; and times when he'd felt himself paralyzed when action was most needed. He'd never understood this tendency of his — he knew only that he rarely lived up to expectation, and for this reason had clung so fiercely to his nickname. Any boy with a name like George Washington must surely have great things expected of him.

And yet, in these last days, he'd become friends with people who *cared* about him, quite above and beyond what was *expected* of him. With perfect clarity he remembered Reynie saying, "I need you here as a friend." The effect of those words, and of all his friendships, had grown stronger and stronger, until — though he couldn't say *why* he didn't feel mixed up now — at the most desperate moment yet, he knew it to be true. There was bravery in him. It only had to be drawn out.

So it was that Sticky stepped in front of Reynie and said, "May I go first, Mr. Curtain? I've been looking forward to this ever since my last session."

Mr. Curtain laughed his screechy laugh. "I daresay Reynard feels much the same, George. But let's not quibble. Reynard went first last time. You may go first this time. Take your seat."

At last Sticky met Reynie's gaze, which was now full of gratitude and admiration. With a quick nod, Sticky turned and climbed into the Whisperer. Immediately Mr. Curtain whizzed over to sit behind him, fitted his head inside the red helmet, and barked, "Ledroptha Curtain!"

The cuffs sprang up around Sticky's wrists. The blue helmet lowered.

"Sticky Washington," Sticky said aloud, closing his eyes.

Reynie watched his friend's face grow tense with the effort of resisting. He knew the Whisperer wanted Sticky's given name.

"Sticky Washington," Sticky repeated.

"Hold on, Sticky," thought Reynie, his eyes darting to Mr. Curtain's face, which seemed both tired and troubled. Had Mr. Curtain already sensed a problem? He was frowning with concentration, his eyes closed.

How long *could* Sticky hold on — knowing his resistance might betray him? Knowing all he must do to relieve his terror was cooperate? Knowing he was but moments away from that wonderful relief? It would be like trying not to scratch the most powerful itch anyone had ever known.

Reynie moved silently to the window.

"Sticky . . . Washington," Sticky said again, in a much weaker voice, and Reynie knew they hadn't much time.

Mr. Curtain's eyes were still closed. Now was his chance. Reynie waved his hand back and forth in front of the window. It was dark outside, but the room was well-lit — his hand would be visible from outside. Back and forth he waved, back and forth, back and forth. *Please, please, let somebody notice,* he thought. *Please, Rhonda, let it be true what you said. Through the telescope we appear to be only a few feet away. Through the telescope you watch the island constantly. Please let it be true. And please let your eyes be sharp.*

With one final attention-gathering wave, he placed his hand against the glass so that the message scrawled on his palm could be read, if only someone was out there to read it: *We need K & C here! Now!*

The Great Kate Weather Machine

Kand C, as it happened, were still in bed. It had been an awful night for Kate. Try as she might, she couldn't forget the look in Milligan's eyes as the Executives and Recruiters paraded him through the cafeteria. She slept poorly, in and out of a doze, constantly worried and miserable, and never once did she have a shred of an idea what to do.

Now it was almost dawn, time to rise, though rising hardly seemed worth the trouble. Worsening Kate's mood, if that was possible, was a distant, irritating beeping sound, the erratic honking of a faraway horn. A car alarm on the mainland, or some obnoxious kid fooling around with an air horn. It had been going on for several minutes now. Long honks, short honks, long honks again, on and on. Irritating, and irritatingly familiar, like something she was supposed to remember but couldn't. Almost like a code, she thought. Almost like . . .

"Morse code!" Kate said aloud, sitting bolt upright in bed.

A long honk, a short honk, a long one again, a pause. That would be a *K*. She listened intently. Here came some more. Oh, why hadn't she been studying her Morse code? Flying to her desk, Kate wrote the code down as it came. Short, long. Long, short. Long, short, short. A pause. That spelled *and*, she was fairly sure. Long, short, long, short — a *C*. *K and C*.

"Will somebody turn off that stupid alarm?" Constance moaned in her sleep.

"Shush! No, *don't* shush! Constance, wake up! We're being signaled!"

But Constance, lost in a sleepy fog, only buried her head under her pillow.

The code kept coming. Kate struggled to decipher it. "I hope the boys are getting this," she thought. "Sticky will know it for sure." After a pause the message started to repeat, and Kate studied what she'd jotted down: *k and c to flauto were now*. Good grief! It made no sense at all. "K and C" stood for Kate and Constance, obviously. But what did "flauto" mean? Was it Spanish? Latin? Again she hoped Sticky was listening — he knew every language in the book. Here came the message again. Kate paid close attention, careful not to mistake short for long or vice versa, making sure to recognize pauses. She came up with this: *k and c to flau tower now*. What in the world? What was a "flau tower" anyway?

"*Flag* tower!" she exclaimed, realizing her mistake. "Good gravy, Kate! The boys are in the flag tower already! Constance, wake up!"

"Quiet down!" came the muffled voice from beneath the pillow.

Kate threw on her shoes, fastened her bucket to her belt. Who knew how long they'd been up there? Who knew what sort of danger they were in? What if she was too late? She'd have to —

Kate stopped in mid-thought, staring at the tiny lump of bedclothes that was Constance Contraire. How could she possibly make it with that belligerent girl along? Kate would have to carry her, assuming she could even get her out of bed. What if Constance slowed her down so much she couldn't help the boys in time?

It occurred to Kate to leave her behind. An inviting thought — so inviting she almost did just that. She went to the door. Hesitated. Looked back. The plan had called for all four of them. That was what Mr. Benedict had said mattered most, and it was what they'd agreed upon only yesterday. All four of them. That was the plan. No way would *she* be the one to mess it up. In a flash Kate was at the bedside, shaking Constance like a maraca. "Wake up, Constance! It's an emergency!"

Even with the shaking and urging, it took Kate a minute to get Constance fully awake. Dawn had broken, daylight grew stronger by the second, and with it her fear that she'd be too late. By the time Constance understood what was happening, Kate had jammed her shoes onto her feet. "Get on my back!" she ordered, ignoring Constance's whining that her toes hurt (Kate had forced the shoes onto the wrong feet).

Constance climbed on — still grumbling — and Kate dashed from the room.

In the corridor they passed several students clinging miserably to paper bags, standing in line for the overcrowded bathroom. There were slick spots here and there on the floor that the Helpers hadn't mopped up yet, and Kate nimbly avoided these, trying not to think about them. When a queasy-looking Executive approached to ask their business, Kate cried, "Get back! She's about to barf her Brussels sprouts!" The Executive, who had already seen more of this sort of thing in one night than she cared to see in a lifetime, stepped aside without another word.

Faster and faster Kate ran, catching her pace, her bucket bouncing against her hip and Constance clinging desperately to her shoulders. Past exhausted Helpers with their buckets and mops, out of the dormitory, and straight for the secret entrance behind the Institute Control Building. With the help of Mr. Curtain's elevator, Kate figured they could be outside the Whispering Gallery in thirty seconds or less. "Provided we get lucky," she thought, "and the entrance isn't guarded." She rounded the boulders, kicked the door open, and burst through the foyer into the secret passage.

The entrance was guarded, unfortunately. And by none other than Martina Crowe.

Kate drew up short, trying to think of what to do.

Martina was so astounded by Kate's sudden appearance, she almost looked afraid, as if Kate had come to deal her some blow. But she quickly grew haughty. "How did *you* two get down here? You're in serious trouble now, do you realize that?"

Kate scarcely heard Martina. Her mind was racing. Could

she get past Martina? Alone, maybe, but with Constance on her back? Martina would call for help, and the Recruiters guarding the computer room would come running. All Martina had to do was hold Kate off a few short moments. No, they'd never make it. They would have to try another way.

"Well, what do you have to say for yourselves?" Martina snarled, advancing threateningly.

Kate bit her lip, clenched her fists, and for once, said nothing. Instead she whirled on her heel, hitched Constance higher on her back, and ran away.

Martina stared after the girls, extremely confused. It was not like Kate Wetherall to back down like that, not like her at all. And why had they come into the secret passage in the first place? They'd been in a hurry, clearly rushing toward some urgent business. Her face darkened as she contemplated the possibilities.

Just then Jillson rounded the corner. She'd spent a dreadful night in the bathroom making sounds like a sea lion, but now that she was feeling better she was coming to relieve Martina from guard duty. "Jackson told me to take over for you. If Mr. Curtain doesn't finish the job with Reynard and George, you may be having another session in a few hours. Go get some rest."

Martina wasn't listening. Her mind was awhirl with speculations about Kate. The wicked little snoop must know this was the way up to the Whispering Gallery, she thought. Why else would the girls have come here? And what had they been in such a hurry for? And . . . and what was that infernal *beeping* sound in the distance? Martina was finding it difficult to concentrate.

"Jillson, did you pass Kate Wetherall in the foyer just now?"

"And that little squirt Constance? You bet I did. I sent them straight back to their room. Some kids never learn. It'll be a brainsweep for those two, no doubt about it."

"They aren't going back to their room," said Martina. "Something's going on."

Jillson frowned. "Is that so? Do you think it has anything to do with that maddening honking sound? What *is* that, anyway?"

"You've noticed it, too, then. I don't know. It almost sounds like — no, it *definitely* sounds like a code. Yes, it's a code! *Morse* code. Jillson, you don't know Morse code, do you?"

"Why on earth would I? Nobody uses Morse code anymore. But you know, Mr. Curtain keeps all sorts of code books in his office cabinet. We could take a look. I have the cabinet key with me — privilege of a senior Executive."

Moments later the two of them were in Mr. Curtain's office, poring over a chart of Morse code, hastily scrawling a transcription of the distant honks.

"What's a 'flauta'?" Jillson asked, scratching her head.

Martina corrected the mistake. Not short short long, but long long short — not *U* but *G. Flag tower.* "I knew it! Let's go find Jackson. We have two more spies to catch!"

The spies in question were at that very moment hurrying down a corridor in the Helpers' barracks, where Kate had just burst into a storage room and snatched a ladder from an alarmed Helper. Now they were tripping and stumbling toward the exit. Kate stumbled because of the unwieldy ladder. Constance stumbled because it was her natural method of locomotion, and because her feet hurt from being in the wrong shoes.

"Come on!" Kate urged, panting for breath. "Can't you move any faster? Honestly, I can't carry you and the ladder both."

"Just leave me then! You don't want me along, anyway."

"We don't have time for this," Kate muttered, banging the door open at the end of the corridor and hauling the ladder out into the early morning light. Constance came tottering after her, struggling to keep up as Kate rounded the classroom building and charged onto the empty plaza.

The horn still sounded from across the water, insistently repeating its urgent message.

Kate was just thinking, *I wish they'd knock it off now, someone else is sure to catch on*, when the horn abruptly stopped. Unfortunately, even as it did so, two Executives emerged from behind the boulders on the hill to stare curiously toward the mainland. (One of them was S.Q., whose gangly frame Kate recognized even from this distance. The other, judging by the size of her head, was a tall-haired Executive named Regina.) They were too distracted at the moment to notice the girls. Still, this would never do. Constance was dragging behind. If the Executives spotted them, she was sure to be caught.

"Listen," Kate puffed as they crossed the plaza, "if the sashes come after us, I'll slow them down. You keep going. Head straight up the hill behind the Institute Control

Building — to that stone wall below the brook. I'll catch up with you there."

Constance stopped. "All the way up there? But I can't walk that far! I'm exhausted! My feet are killing me!"

Kate skidded to a halt. "You can't make anything easy, can you? Not even now, the most important moment of your life?" She dropped the ladder and reached into her bucket for the rope.

"What are you doing?" said Constance. "I thought we were in some huge hurry."

"Put a lid on it," Kate said.

Before Constance could think of a grumpy reply, Kate had tied the ladder to her belt and hoisted the smaller girl upon her back. "I'll just have to drag the stupid thing. It's going to make an awful racket, though, so hang on."

With that, Kate was off, faster than she would have thought possible herself, perhaps spurred on by the tremendous bang and clatter and scrape of the ladder dragging behind her. In the distance Regina began to shout — the ruckus had caught her attention. Kate glanced up the hill to see S.Q. tripping over his feet, and Regina tripping over S.Q., as they started out after the girls. "Bless those size fifteens," she thought. "Now we may just make it."

Kate made her way to the back of the Institute Control Building, hustled past the boulders and the drapeweed trap, and started up the hill. It was a difficult ascent. There was no path here, the slope was steep and slippery with gravel, and Kate — unlike her pursuers — was dragging a ladder and carrying someone on her back. Even so, Kate was halfway up before S.Q. and Regina even arrived at the bottom. She was just about to feel encouraged when Martina, Jackson, and

Jillson came swarming out the back of the Institute Control Building.

"Well, *that's* unfortunate," Kate said. She smiled and waved.

"Unfortunate?" cried Constance. *"Unfortunate?"*

"Don't you think so?" Kate asked, panting under her burden. Jackson sent S.Q. and Regina scurrying away — probably to notify Mr. Curtain — and started up the hill with Jillson and Martina close behind.

They were moving very fast.

Kate stopped glancing back and pressed on, hard, until she and Constance came to the stone wall. From below them they heard the rapid scraping of boots on gravel. Quickly Kate worked to untie the ladder from her belt — but after the long drag uphill, the knot had grown too tight. *Come on, come on,* she thought, unfastening her belt to slip the knot free. In her haste she missed her grip on the bucket and, to her horror, it slipped loose and tumbled several yards down the hill behind her.

"Leave it!" Constance cried, seeing her look of dismay. "There's no time!"

Constance was right. They would lose their narrow headstart. But even worse was to lose her bucket. And so, to the mocking laughs of Martina from halfway down the hill ("Fat lot of good that bucket will do you when we catch up with you!") she handed her rope to Constance and scampered back to retrieve it. Everything had spilled out, including her precious spyglass, but here Kate drew the line — she snatched up the bucket and left the rest behind.

"You lost your lead!" Jackson called. "You might as well wait for us there."

"Just wanted to give you a fighting chance!" Kate called back. With the ladder in place and Constance (fuming with disapproval) on her back, she began to climb. She was really sweating under her load now. The wearier she grew, the heavier Constance seemed. In a final determined burst, she scaled the last few rungs just as Jackson reached the ladder. She scrambled forward onto the high, sloping ground above the wall.

A few paces ahead, just above the rock wall, ran the brook Kate had spotted their first day on the island. It streamed along a shallow gully for some distance before finally spilling over the wall and running downhill. Kate stumbled quickly toward it. By the time she'd dumped Constance — rather unceremoniously — next to the brook, Jackson and Jillson were both on the ladder, and Martina was preparing to climb.

"What good is your bucket doing you now?" Jackson jeered.

"I'm glad you asked!" Kate said, bending over the brook to scoop the bucket full of water. Instantly it was as heavy as a bowling ball. Returning to look down into Jackson's icy blue eyes — he was only a few rungs from the top — she gave him a friendly wink.

And dropped the bucket.

Surprised though he was, Jackson resisted the urge to let go and catch the bucket. It didn't matter. The bucket caught him. It landed squarely on top of his head and sent him tumbling backward down the ladder, in the process knocking Jillson down as well. They landed in a wet, moaning heap at Martina's feet.

"Instant ton of bricks," Kate said with satisfaction. "Just add water."

There wasn't time to reflect upon the pleasing scene. Martina had been quick-witted enough to grab the ladder before Kate could haul it out of reach, and was waiting only for her dazed companions to climb to their feet again. Slinging Constance over her shoulder, Kate splashed across the brook (too tired now to leap it) and made her way up the last, steep stretch of ground to the tower wall.

"Ugh!" Constance cried. "Get your shoulder out of my belly, you big —"

"Listen," Kate said, setting her down and hastily forming a lasso with her rope. "I need to concentrate, so keep quiet, will you? We have to reach that window as quick as we can." As she spoke, she swung her lasso round and round, eyeing the flagpole that jutted out from the tower wall high above them, the Institute's red flag rippling gently beneath it.

Careful, Kate warned herself. *Don't let the lasso get fouled up with that flag.* It was essential she didn't miss — there'd be no time for a second attempt.

Kate concentrated, took aim, said a prayer, and . . .

"You don't really think you can lasso that *flagpole*, do you?" Constance blurted just as Kate flung the lasso upward.

The outburst nearly broke Kate's concentration, but her throw was true enough — with a perfectly timed twitch of the rope, she adjusted its path. The lasso dropped neatly over the end of the flagpole. Kate heaved a sigh of relief. "You call that quiet?" she asked, tightening the loop with a tug.

"It could have been louder," Constance replied.

"Thanks ever so much," said Kate, already tying the rope around the smaller girl's waist. "Now don't argue. I'm doing this so I can haul you up after me. I can climb faster this way."

Constance, of course, began to argue, but Kate had already completed the knot and begun scrambling up the rope. She didn't waste time looking back. She knew that at this very moment Martina was leaping the brook. She knew she had only a matter of seconds. And when at last she'd reached the flagpole, balanced atop it, and looked down to see Martina charging toward Constance far below, she knew that those seconds were not in her favor. As tired as she was, as fast as Martina was moving, she wouldn't have time to pull Constance out of reach.

It took only one of those seconds for Kate to think: *It has to be all four of us, but Constance can't handle them. You can handle them, though. It will be rough, but you can handle them.*

(Part of Kate believed this — a very important part, for Kate's sense of invincibility was the main thing that had sustained her all her young life alone. But another part did *not* believe this — and it, too, was an important part, for unless you know about this part it is impossible to understand how brave a thing Kate was about to do.)

With a fluid motion Kate slipped the lasso from the end of the flagpole. She gripped the rope tightly. Oh well, she thought. I sure hope the little grouch is worth it.

And with that, she leaped backward into empty air.

The rope fell across the flagpole like a cable over a pulley, and as Kate dropped downward, so Constance — much lighter by far — shot up out of the grasp of the astonished Martina Crowe. The tiny girl clung madly to the rope, her eyes bulging, but Kate could do little to calm her. As they brushed past each other, one going up and the other down, both to uncertain fates, Kate offered her breeziest smile and said, "Hang tight, Connie girl! And be sure to untie yourself when you get up there."

Then she descended into the waiting arms of three powerful Executives, all of them grinning with vengeful excitement.

STANDS AND FALLS

"**M**r. Curtain! Mr. *Curtain*, sir!" buzzed S.Q.'s voice through the intercom.

For Reynie, the interruption could not have come at a better moment. For what seemed an eternity now, he had watched Sticky alternately frown with effort and smile with relief, his tea-colored skin going almost as pale as honey, and perspiration trickling down his .cheeks like tears. But the frowns had at last faded away, replaced entirely by the pleasant, contented smiles. Sticky had made a great effort, but in the end he couldn't help it — he had stopped resisting.

Mr. Curtain, however, did *not* welcome the interruption. After a night with too few sessions, he'd finally got a Messenger into his Whisperer again, only to struggle unexpectedly. The machine had gone balky as an old donkey, losing Mr. Curtain's train of thought and sometimes misunderstanding him altogether. Usually the mental effect for him was of speaking into a telephone and hearing his own voice in the receiver. But *this* session had been like hearing himself through a staticky radio. It was the boy, it must be, and Mr. Curtain had just begun to suspect that George was an unfit Messenger after all — that in fact he might be untrustworthy — when the session improved. The boy's mind grew more receptive, the Whisperer's wrinkled messages straightened, and Mr. Curtain had at last settled into some real, productive work. He was just finishing the session when the interruption came.

"Mr. Curtain! Please, sir, it's an emergency!"

"Rats and dogs!" Mr. Curtain said furiously, thrusting off his red helmet. Behind him, the cuffs and blue helmet freed Sticky, who rose, wobbling, in a state of weak confusion. Reynie leaped forward to support him.

"What is it, S.Q.?" Mr. Curtain said, pressing the intercom button on his wheelchair. "It had better be important."

"It is, sir. Two students are trying to break into the tower!"

Reynie closed his eyes; his heart sank. The Executives knew what the girls were up to, and S.Q. was already outside the door. It was over, then. After all this, after Sticky had been so brave, had tried so hard . . .

"Two students?" Mr. Curtain was saying. "By students you mean children, do you not?"

"Um, yes, sir," came S.Q.'s uncertain reply.

"Do you mean to tell me you can't prevent two children from breaking in?"

"Um, well, sir, we're sure to comprehend . . . I mean apprehend . . . I mean we're sure to catch them soon. I just thought I should alert you —"

"Thank you, S.Q.," said Mr. Curtain, who did not sound at all thankful. "Consider me alerted. And by the way, unless you are presented with an *actual* emergency, I want no further interruptions, understood?"

"Yes, Mr. Curtain," came S.Q.'s reply. "Sorry, Mr. Curtain."

With a disgusted shake of his head Mr. Curtain exclaimed, "Children! Am I supposed to fear unarmed children? No doubt they're in cahoots with my prisoner. Unlikely agents, but no matter — they'll soon join him." He grew silent, staring intently at Sticky as if considering how best to cut him up and cook him. "George, I'm afraid I was not terribly pleased with your performance. No. In fact I was rather *dis*pleased. Reynard will take over for you now. We will see about you later."

There could be no doubt what Mr. Curtain meant by "we will see about you," but Sticky was too exhausted at the moment to be afraid. He only shook his head. He had done all he could.

Mr. Curtain gestured impatiently toward the cushions, and Reynie helped Sticky over to them. Sticky collapsed. Reynie turned to meet Mr. Curtain's gaze, and saw in those silvery lenses the reflection of his own uncertain, frightened face.

"The time has come, Reynard," said Mr. Curtain. "Unsatisfactory though your friend's session has been, we are nonetheless close — very, very close." Mr. Curtain coughed and wiped his pale, moist brow. As if to himself he mumbled, "I'm afraid I must pause for refreshment, though. But only for a moment. It can't hurt to savor the occasion, at any rate. A cup of juice, then. Do you hear me, Reynard? I shall have a cup of juice. After that, only a few minutes more . . . and then! And *then*! The Improvement will begin! Can you believe? I can scarcely believe it myself!" Mr. Curtain's face, though pale and drawn, quite gleamed with exultation. His dream was on the cusp of becoming reality.

Reynie glanced at the Whisper. Then his glance hardened into a focused gaze. He couldn't tear his eyes away. Didn't the Whisperer look inviting? Comforting? It almost seemed to be speaking to him — whispering to him all the way over here. *Was* it whispering to him? Whispering the unthinkable thing . . . ?

Don't struggle for nothing, Reynard. You can still join Mr. Curtain, be important, be a part *of something.*

But . . . but Mr. Benedict, Reynie thought. *He . . . he needs me to . . .*

Mr. Benedict! Is he the one who tricked you into joining him, who encouraged you to cheat on quizzes, who offered you 'special opportunities'? Or was that Mr. Curtain, who said cheating doesn't bother him, who rounded up poor unfortunates only to give them a better life, who has offered you a chance to be an Executive? How different are the two men? Not very, Reynard. The only difference is that one can offer you only suffering now, while the other offers you a way to belong — a way to relieve the loneliness.

Shaken, Reynie thought, *But . . . Miss . . . Miss Perumal.*

You can help her! You can warn her, tell her to keep quiet about the voices in her head. You'll have Mr. Curtain's ear — you can vouch for Miss Perumal. You can protect her!

Reynie clasped his hands to his head. *But would she want me to do that? At such a cost? No, she wouldn't. And yet . . . and yet . . . it's impossible! There's no way out!*

Mr. Curtain had finished his juice and was watching Reynard watch the Whisperer. "You've missed it, I see," purred Mr. Curtain. "Well, miss it no longer. Take your seat, Reynard. Take your rightful place."

Reynie's mind was so foggy. Had Mr. Curtain said "your rightful place"? Or was that his own mind? And who had been talking to him before that? Wasn't it the Whisperer? No, he realized. Unfortunately not. It wasn't the Whisperer at all. It was Reynie himself.

"Reynard!" Mr. Curtain prompted.

Reynie made his way toward the Whisperer. The session would go quickly — a few minutes, Mr. Curtain had said — and then it would be over. And then . . . he swallowed hard. What would happen to Constance? Would something dreadful happen to her when Mr. Curtain boosted the power? And what would become of the others?

He looked back at Sticky, slumped on a cushion in a posture of weary defeat. Despite his terror, in the face of the Whisperer's irresistible power, Sticky had resisted with all his might. He would never have done that if not for Reynie's urging, and now it had put him into disfavor with Mr. Curtain. Was Reynie really going to *help* Mr. Curtain? It would be a betrayal of their friendship! And Kate — to think of what they'd been through together, and the risks she'd taken. . . .

"Ledroptha Curtain!"

The cuffs clasped Reynie's wrists. The helmet lowered. Reynie closed his eyes, only to see the faces of his friends. He remembered the final question of Mr. Benedict's first test: Are you brave? Now, at least, Reynie knew the answer. He wasn't brave. He had only hoped he was.

Good, said the Whisperer. *What is your name?*

"Just get it over with quickly," Reynie told himself.

Welcome, Reynard Muldoon.

"Welcome," Reynie repeated. Yes. Welcome was such a — such a *welcoming* word. It made you feel a part of something. It made you feel . . . not alone. No, he was not alone at all. And yet . . .

Reynard Muldoon, what do you fear most?

In his mind's eye Reynie still saw the faces of his friends. Sticky, Kate, Constance — all watching him with concern. They'd been through so much together! Was he really going to betray them?

"You could never be more alone than if you betrayed your friends," Reynie said to himself.

Instantly the Whisperer's voice said, *Don't worry. You will never betray your friends. You are brave enough.*

Reynie was so startled he almost laughed aloud. The Whisperer was too perceptive for its own good! At the most important moment of all, it had given him just the encouragement he needed — the encouragement to help him fight it!

Let us begin, said the Whisperer.

Reynie was flooded with a terrific sense of well-being. *Real* well-being — not an illusion at all. He would not betray his friends. He knew that now. He had confronted his worst fear, and now it was gone. No need for the Whisperer to deny it — there was nothing left to deny!

Let us begin, the Whisperer repeated.

Reynie braced himself. Let the worst come. He would be brave enough to resist, and he would not be alone.

Let us begin, the Whisperer repeated, more insistently.

Not just yet, Reynie thought.

Let us begin.

First let me polish my spectacles, Reynie thought.

Let us begin.

Not without my bucket, Reynie insisted.

He heard Mr. Curtain muttering behind him.

Let us begin, let us begin, let us begin.

Rules and schools are tools for fools, Reynie thought.

And then, as if he had conjured her, Reynie heard Constance's shrill voice. It was perhaps the first time he had ever been glad to hear it.

"Help! Open up! Let me in!"

"Pah!" sputtered Mr. Curtain. "What is *wrong* with this infernal machine? And now another interruption! Where is that voice coming from?"

"From the window," said Sticky, who looked every bit as surprised as Mr. Curtain.

"The window?" Mr. Curtain said, thrusting the red helmet from his head and looking toward the window. Nothing was visible beyond it except blue sky. He grunted and lowered the helmet again. "Never mind. We'll just ignore it. I am going to finish this session if it's the last thing —"

"Open up! Open up! Open up!" shrieked Constance.

"That's going to be difficult to ignore, sir," Reynie said as Constance continued to shriek.

"This is outrageous! How am I to concentrate if . . . ?" Mr. Curtain's face twisted with frustration. "Very well, I'll have to address this. The window latch is too high for me to reach from my chair, however. George —" He glanced suspiciously at Sticky, then shook his head. "No, George, you stay where you are. Reynard, go and see what the trouble is."

The cuffs unclasped his wrists, the helmet went up.

Reynie needed no prodding. In an instant he was across the room and scrabbling at the window catch. He flung open the panes and looked down. Just beneath the window, the miniature figure of Constance Contraire clung desperately to the flagpole — Reynie's first impression was of a koala bear hugging the trunk of a fallen eucalyptus tree — her entire body trembling with effort, her eyes rolling with fright. She had good reason: The least slip would send her plummeting to rocky ground.

Nor, apparently, was the ground a safer place to have remained, for there Kate was engaged in a furious struggle. Reynie's heart swelled with pride and hope. It might be bad, but it wasn't over. The girls weren't captured yet.

"Well?" Mr. Curtain demanded from across the room. "What is it?"

Sticky was watching with a hint of new hopefulness.

Reynie kept his face turned away; he must not reveal his smile to Mr. Curtain. "It's those children S.Q. mentioned, sir. One appears to have been apprehended. The other is stuck on the flagpole outside the window."

Mr. Curtain seemed unsure whether to laugh or snarl. "Go ahead and haul him inside, then. This will be our last interruption."

"It's a girl, sir," Reynie corrected. "Sticky, can you help me?"

Sticky, having recovered a bit of strength, came over to hold Reynie's legs as he reached out and lifted the frightened girl through the window.

"Well, well, well, Constance Contraire," said Mr. Curtain with apparent satisfaction. "Just as I suspected. I knew all along you weren't to be trusted. In fact, I would have taken care of you long ago had it not been for —"

He gave a sudden start, whipping off his glasses to reveal bright green, horribly bloodshot eyes — eyes quite flaming with angry realization.

"Had it not been," he repeated, turning those eyes now on Reynie, "for *you*."

Mr. Curtain threw his silver glasses to the floor, as if without them he would have seen the truth much sooner. And then, to the children's great confusion and horror, the fearsome man unstrapped himself, rose from the wheelchair to stand at his full alarming height, and strode across the room to seize them.

Kate Wetherall, meanwhile, was fighting for her life. Martina Crowe had been hoping for just this sort of occasion, an opportunity to exact revenge for past humiliations. And now Jackson and Jillson, never the most delicate creatures to begin with, were equally determined to knock Kate about, having been embarrassed — not to mention bruised — by her bucket. Kate might be clever and quick as a fox, but she was a weary fox now, and one among hounds.

Still, she *had* managed to inflict some unpleasantness: In addition to the knot on Jackson's head, his pointy nose was swollen and red where she'd pinched it to encourage her release. Jillson's ear was ringing painfully — the result of a well-placed elbow. And Martina had been rebuffed by an

excruciating shin-scrape. The Executives circled her more warily now, looking for the right moment to renew their attack.

Kate crouched, watching them carefully, her lasso at the
ready. (For once Constance had followed Kate's advice —
had untied herself so that the Executives couldn't yank her
down — and the rope was now free). The others circled and
circled, eyeing the lasso, looking for a weakness. But it was
Kate who saw one first: Martina had taken an awkward step,
was slightly off balance. Kate feinted to the side — moving
as if to flee — and when Martina lunged to stop her, Kate
snared her ankle with the lasso and jerked her off her feet.
Martina landed in the dust with an angry growl.

It was an excellent throw, but it was also the beginning
of the end. Before Kate could let go of her rope, Martina
grabbed it and heaved. Kate was pulled off balance, and Jackson chose that exact moment to give her a shove — and no
gentle shove, at that. It was as if she'd been struck by a ram.
Kate went reeling, trying to catch herself.

But it was Jillson who caught her.

The next few minutes were wretched ones indeed. Kate's
ears were boxed, her hair pulled, her cheeks pummeled
with Jillson's boltlike knuckles. And though she writhed and
twisted, swung her fists, and kicked her feet, she could do
nothing to stop them. Kate had told herself she could handle
the Executives, but she'd been fooling herself — just as she
had fooled herself for so long. She couldn't do everything by
herself. She realized that now.

Kate stopped struggling. Why struggle? She was of no use
now to her friends, herself, or anyone. She was completely
overcome, helpless and alone. The bitter irony wasn't lost on

Kate: The moment she finally admitted to herself she needed help, there was no help to be found.

As if reading her thoughts, Martina hissed, "*Now* you realize how outclassed you are, don't you, Wetherall? I don't blame you for giving up."

"Don't kid yourself, Martina," Kate mumbled through bloody lips. "I'm just taking a nap while you yammer on."

This infuriated Martina, and as Jackson and Jillson redoubled their grips on Kate's limbs, the raven-haired girl prepared to unleash her most vicious attack yet. Stepping back to get a running start, she cried, "I'll kick you until you cry for mercy, Wetherall! I'll make you suffer until you beg me to stop! I'll beat you until you admit I'm the best! I'll —"

"You'll do no such thing," said an unfamiliar voice, followed by three successive *swit, swit, swits*, upon which Martina's eyes crossed, Jackson and Jillson sighed, and all three collapsed upon the ground unconscious, dart feathers blooming from their shoulders as if by magic.

Where Martina Crowe had been, Milligan now stood with his tranquilizer gun. Covered from head to toe in slimy black mud, his left arm in a sling fashioned from an Executive's blood-stained tunic, Milligan — wonder of wonders! — was grinning at Kate with joyous eyes. *That* was why his voice had seemed unfamiliar — it was too cheerful. She hadn't recognized it at all.

And yet. Staring at him all the while, Kate rose unsteadily to her feet. And yet . . . something about those eyes. There was something familiar about him, after all. Something . . .

"Sorry it took me so long, Katie-Cat," said her father.

"*You,*" Mr. Curtain repeated, looming over the children and
glowering in particular at Reynie. "You betrayed me! After all
I did for you — welcomed you to my Institute, soothed your
fears with my Whisperer, offered you a role in my Improvement — after all this, you chose to defy me?"

"I don't suppose you'd accept an apology," Sticky offered.
(A cheeky response for him, especially since he was too petrified by the sight of Mr. Curtain's towering figure even to
reach for his spectacles, though every bone in his body wanted
to give them a terrific polishing.)

Mr. Curtain laughed a terrifying, screech-owl laugh, and said, "Oh, no, I'm afraid not, George. But I thank you for reminding me how pathetic children are. Quick to follow, quicker still to flee. Yes, quite pitiful, and annoying as gnats, but certainly not a threat. To think you hoped . . . what *did* you hope for, anyway? To defeat *me*? But you're only children!"

Mr. Curtain erupted into laughter again, a long fit of convulsive screeching. Calming himself with some effort, he said, "Well, no matter. I needn't dirty my hands clutching your grubby little collars. I'll summon my Executives to bear you off."

Mr. Curtain turned to walk back to his chair. He paused, however, at the sight of Reynie Muldoon's penetrating stare. The boy's eyes shifted rapidly back and forth, as if calculating something with great concentration. Before Mr. Curtain could ask what the devil he was doing, Reynie said aloud, as if to himself, "Okay, so it isn't laughter."

"What are you blathering about, Reynard?" Mr. Curtain demanded.

Reynie hardly seemed to hear him. "With Mr. Benedict, it's usually laughter that does it. But if it's not laughter with you, then what? It must be *something*, otherwise you wouldn't strap yourself so carefully in. You're so afraid of losing control — but how, exactly?"

Mr. Curtain's eyebrows shot up. His entire head quivered like a struck bell. "I have no idea — what the devil are you — snakes and — I haven't time for your childish —," he sputtered.

"Yes, you're definitely afraid of *something*," Reynie said more forcefully, his eyes lighting up. "The chair, the straps, the reflective glasses — they're all there to keep your secret safe from the children. But why are you so afraid of children? Maybe that's why you keep saying we're so harmless. You're trying to convince yourself. In fact you're scared to death of us! You're like a tiger afraid of mice! Why else would you stand there shaking in your boots?"

"It's not from *fear*, you insignificant speck of dust!" roared Mr. Curtain, his face livid with rage. "How dare you! I'll crush you all like the gnats you are!" And with that, he sprang forward . . . only to drop in a green-plaid heap at the children's feet, where he promptly began to snore.

Reynie's breath escaped in a whoosh of relief. Then he nodded. "Laughter usually puts Mr. Benedict to sleep. With Mr. Curtain, it's anger. Quick, Sticky, let's tie him up with our sashes."

Sticky released Constance's hand, which in his fright he had unconsciously seized, and loosened his sash. "So *that's* the reason for the chair and the glasses. When he gets really mad, he goes to sleep, but he doesn't want anyone to know!"

"All those times he seemed so furious and then suddenly got quiet," Reynie said, knotting his sash around Mr. Curtain's ankles, "I always thought he was getting ready to kill me, but really he was just asleep!"

"Um, fellows?" said Constance. "He's awake."

The boys jumped back. Sure enough, Mr. Curtain's eyes were open and looking wildly about. When they fell upon Reynie's face, they narrowed with hatred. "Oh, that's right," he said, yawning. "I was on my way over to kill you. But what's this? Sashes? Surely you don't think mere ribbons could restrain me?"

Reynie's face fell. "I sort of hoped they would."

"Then you are even more foolish than I perceived you to be," said Mr. Curtain, and spreading his arms and legs with one powerful thrust, he ripped the sashes in two.

"If we're so foolish," Constance shouted before he could rise, "then what does that say about you? You made the boys Messengers even though they always intended to betray you, and we've tricked you again and again. We even know about your narcolepsy, though you tried so hard to hide it. If we're foolish, then you're the greatest fool of all, since we're obviously much smarter than you!"

For a moment Mr. Curtain trembled violently, unable even to form words in his fury. Then his eyes closed and he sank back upon the floor.

"That was fun," Constance said.

"That was *close*," Sticky said. "But now what? There's nothing else to tie him up with."

"How about this rope?" cried a familiar voice, and to their surprise Kate Wetherall suddenly leaped in through the open window.

She was a welcome sight, but a terrible one. Her cheeks were scratched and bleeding, her lips were swollen, her clothes were torn, her hair stuck out in all directions, and on top of this she was streaked with mud. Yet she seemed cheerful as ever they'd seen her, her bruised, black eyes shining with happiness and her bloody lips spread in a terrific grin. As she knelt to bind Mr. Curtain's hands and feet, Kate eagerly told them what had happened.

"Your father!" Sticky cried. "I can't believe it! So that's why Milligan disappeared all those years ago — he was captured on a mission!"

"But why has he disappeared now?" Constance demanded. "Shouldn't he be here?"

"He said he was going for help. I didn't take time to ask for details — I thought you'd need me."

Reynie nudged the slumbering Mr. Curtain with his toe. "It's good you came when you did. Otherwise he'd have throttled us when he woke up."

"So now what?" Constance asked.

Reynie was already moving toward the Whisperer. "I've been thinking about what Mr. Curtain said. That the Whisperer is a sensitive — how did he say it, exactly, Sticky?"

"A sensitive, delicately balanced machine that requires his strict mental guidance for its proper function."

"Exactly, and we also know that its computers are modeled on Mr. Curtain's brain. Well, if it's so sensitive and delicate, and if it's like a brain, we ought to be able to confuse it. Maybe we can trick it into shutting itself down!"

"That's your plan?" Constance asked doubtfully.

"Any machine can be turned off," Reynie said, "if only you know how. So let's figure out how." He pulled Mr. Curtain's red helmet down onto his head. Instantly he heard the Whisperer asking his name.

"Ledroptha Curtain!" he barked, just as he had heard Mr. Curtain do.

You are not Ledroptha Curtain, came the reply.

Reynie took a deep breath. He had to trick the Whisperer, had to think just as Mr. Curtain would. Concentrating with all his might, he tried to imagine what a genius he was, and how pleasant life would be once he was known as MASTER Curtain, and what a nuisance children were.

"I am Ledroptha Curtain!" he declared again.

There was a pause. Could the Whisperer be hesitating? Was it uncertain? *I must control it*, Reynie thought, which definitely reminded him of Mr. Curtain. Focusing on these words, he redoubled his concentration. *Control it*, he thought. *Control it, control it, control it.* The pause stretched out. In his mind he thought he could hear a clicking sound, like the tumblers of a lock. This really might work!

Then the Whisperer said, *No, you are not Ledroptha Curtain.*

An awful chuckle sounded from across the room. Reynie ducked out of the red helmet. Mr. Curtain had opened his eyes. His face showed evident mirth. "Surely you didn't think you could fool my Whisperer. How typically juvenile. I'm afraid my Whisperer is foolproof, Reynard. Or perhaps I should say childproof — they amount to the same thing."

At that moment S.Q. Pedalian's voice came over the intercom. "Mr. Curtain? I hope this qualifies as an actual emergency, sir. I don't want to disturb you. But I just received a report that some Executives have been knocked out with tranquilizer darts, and Kate Wetherall was seen climbing through your window. There's a ladder by the brook, but it's too short. Shall we send for a taller one and follow her in?"

Mr. Curtain smugly lifted an eyebrow. "Reynard, be a good lad and tell S.Q. you wish to surrender. This will be the most efficient course. You are soon to be captured, regardless."

"We're not done yet," Reynie said determinedly, climbing into the Whisperer's seat.

S.Q.'s voice came over the intercom again. "Mr. Curtain, sir? Since you haven't responded, we're sending for the tallest ladder we can find. We'll come to your aid at once!"

"Poor Reynard," Mr. Curtain said. "The Whisperer won't activate the *blue* helmet unless *I* am wearing the *red* one. So you see, your idea may have been good — for a child — but ultimately fruitless."

"He's trying to trick us!" Kate warned. "He wants us to put him into the Whisperer!"

Reynie had sat beneath the blue helmet, just in case it might work. But about this, at least, Mr. Curtain had told the truth — the helmet wouldn't come down. He stood and poked his head up into it. Nothing happened.

"This is really very amusing," Mr. Curtain said.

Reynie turned to his friends. "I have to try it."

"Splendid!" Mr. Curtain cried.

Sticky grabbed Reynie's arm. "If you're sitting in the Whisperer, he can *brainsweep* you. That's how he does it. You won't stand a chance!"

"Maybe not," Reynie said somberly, "but if we don't stop him now, he'll never be stopped. I'll do my best to resist. If he brainsweeps me, one of you has to take my place. He's already tired — maybe we can wear him out."

"How very touching," Mr. Curtain said. "Willing to be brainswept are you, Reynard? I applaud your sacrifice. That is, I would if my hands were not so crudely bound."

The others looked uncertainly at Reynie, who smiled as bravely as he could and said, "What choice do we have?"

Sticky and Kate agreed. It was the only thing to do.

With the three of them working quickly together — Constance had retreated into the corner looking more frightened, stubborn, and miserable than ever — they lifted Mr. Curtain (who only smiled, offering no resistance), strapped him into his wheelchair, and rolled him into position beneath the red helmet. Then shaking hands and wishing each other luck, they fitted the helmet over his head.

"Ledroptha Curtain!" he roared in delight.

Reynie's vision seemed to flicker. Did he have something in his eyes? He blinked and looked again.

Mr. Curtain was smiling triumphantly at him. "Obviously, Reynard, you were unaware of the extent of my improvements. You needn't be *seated* in my lovely Whisperer to experience its most powerful effect. In this room you are all quite within range."

In horror Reynie's mind flashed back to an entry from Mr. Curtain's journal, the one that began, *"As of this morning, the messages are transmitting directly. To my great satisfaction, the Whisperer is now capable of..."* They hadn't seen the last part, but now — too late — Reynie realized how it must have ended. If Mr. Curtain could broadcast messages directly into people's minds, he could brainsweep them in the same way! He had only to focus on them!

Again Reynie's vision seemed to flicker, this time for a little longer. Everything simply disappeared, as if the lights had gone out. It came again — a wave of complete blankness. Mr. Curtain was doing it to the others, too: Sticky stood blinking and clutching his head, utterly stunned, and Kate was turning round and round, as if seeking her invisible attacker.

"What . . . what's happening?" she cried. "What do we do?"

"He's trying to brainsweep you!" Reynie shouted. "Fight it! Think of everything you love and hold on to it!"

You have to *fight*, Reynie commanded himself. Think of Miss Perumal. And your favorite books. And Mr. Benedict. And your friends . . . You have to . . . hold on. . . .

"As you can see," Mr. Curtain was saying, "my machine is capable of much more than whispering. It is capable of *shouting*! And I'm afraid the final effect is — how to put it? Quite deafening."

It *was* like shouting, Reynie thought, an overwhelming shouted silence, above which you could hear nothing else. Nothing else. . . . His eyelids were drooping now. Reynie pinched himself, but he hardly seemed to feel it. He slipped to his knees. It was impossible to fight. Impossible to resist. What could they do? Reynie couldn't think straight at all. There was nothing they could do . . . nothing they could do . . . nothing they could . . . nothing they . . . nothing they . . . nothing . . . nothing . . .

"What's *this*?" Mr. Curtain exclaimed. He cackled with pleasure. "Well, well, *well*!"

Reynie forced his eyes open. Mr. Curtain was beaming as if he'd been given a marvelous, unexpected present. Sticky had dropped to his hands and knees. Kate was leaning against a wall, trying to hold herself up. And Constance . . . Where was Constance?

The sound of metal cuffs snapping into place drew Reynie's gaze back to the Whisperer, in which — was it possible? — *Constance* had just taken a seat.

Now Sticky and Kate were staring, too, their mouths hanging open.

Constance Contraire?

Already the blue helmet had lowered onto the tiny girl's head. Her eyes were squeezed shut, her mouth set tight and grim. She looked as cranky and unhappy as they had ever seen her. "Reynie Muldoon!" she shouted, and Mr. Curtain's delighted grin shifted into a frown.

The waves of blankness began to subside.

"Why . . . ," Kate said, shaking her head to clear it. "Why did she yell your name?"

"The Whisperer asks for your name," Reynie said. "Constance is resisting it."

"Sticky Washington!" Constance shouted, and Mr. Curtain quivered with irritation.

"That's the first time she ever used my nickname," Sticky said. He sat up on his knees. "But why has the brainsweeping stopped?"

"Mr. Curtain must be focusing all the power on *her*," Reynie said in a wondering tone.

"But why would he need to do that?"

Reynie leaped to his feet, having realized the answer.

"The Great Kate Weather Machine!" Constance shouted, and behind her Mr. Curtain said, "Bah!"

"Because she's resisting!" Reynie cried. "And *no* one can resist like Constance!"

For a moment Constance and Mr. Curtain both trembled violently, as if caught in an earthquake. Perspiration poured down the face of man and girl alike. And then, in a voice so loud it hurt everyone's ears, Constance exclaimed: "I . . . don't . . . CARE!"

This was followed by a crazed string of negatives: "No! I won't! I will not! You can't make me! Uh-uh! Never! *No!*"

Mr. Curtain hissed. "*Bend*, you obstinate child!"

"NEVER!" Constance shrieked. And indeed it seemed she never would. Mr. Curtain's face had gone quite purple, and drops of perspiration fell from the tip of his lumpy nose like water from a leaky faucet. It was a fierce battle. The children's admiration soared. This was Constance's great gift —

the gift of stubborn independence — and she was bringing it to bear with all her might.

For all her valiant resistance, though, the child was, after all, only a child. As the minutes passed, Constance's voice grew more cracked and strained, her cheeks redder and redder, her strength closer to failing. She could not hold out forever. Indeed, she seemed ready at any moment to fly apart like a broken doll.

"Can't we do something?" Sticky cried. "It's killing her!"

Yet what could they do but stare helplessly at the poor girl? If they could remove her somehow, one of the others could take her place. But Constance was shackled into place. The children watched in growing despair as the brave child grew weaker and weaker, her voice softer and softer, until at last her cries of defiance were scarcely more than mumbles.

And now Mr. Curtain's voice came to them. It, too, was weak, as if the struggle had taken as great a toll on the man as it had the child. But it was smug, nonetheless: "As I told you, and as you now see for yourselves, children, my creation is foolproof." He smacked his lips and forced a feeble smile. "A few moments more and I believe you can say goodbye to little Miss Con —"

A loud booming sound interrupted him. The children jumped. Had the Executives come to break down the door? But no, the booming sound didn't come from the door. It came from behind the *wall*, and was quickly followed by a muffled voice: "Katie! Are you in there, child?"

"Snakes and dogs!" growled Mr. Curtain. "Who is that? And how did he get back there?"

"Milligan!" Kate shouted as they all put their ears to the wall. "Where are you?"

"In a passage behind a hidden door, but the door opens from the inside. Is there a lever or switch of some kind?"

"The wheelchair!" cried Reynie, dashing to Mr. Curtain's chair to study its buttons. "I should have known you'd keep a secret exit. When it comes down to it, you're not even half as brave as a child."

Reynie was hoping his words would infuriate Mr. Curtain into sleep, but Mr. Curtain had prepared himself and was not so easily goaded. "You're right. I give up," he said slyly. "If you promise not to hurt me, I'll tell you which button to push. It's the middle one there on the right arm."

"Sure it is," said Reynie, who recognized the button. Pushing it would admit the Executives. He studied the other ones. "Let's see, this one's for the intercom — I saw you push that one, too — and these levers are obviously for the wheels and brakes, so that leaves . . . this one!" He held his finger above an inconspicuous silver button.

"You're right," Mr. Curtain said with a dramatic sigh. "That's the one."

Reynie grinned. "You want me to think you're trying to trick me. But you can't trick me *that* way, either."

Mr. Curtain scowled, Reynie pressed the button, and an electronic keypad popped into view on the wall above Kate's head.

"Well done, my miserable young spies," said Mr. Curtain haughtily. "You've found the keypad. What a pity you don't know the code."

"Try 3507," Reynie said.

Kate reached up to enter the code. "Oh, no! There aren't any numbers! It's all letters!"

Mr. Curtain smiled an oily, self-satisfied smile. "You must

have got that number from one of my Executives. I admit I'm impressed. However, I'm afraid not even my Executives know the code to my secret exit."

"Maybe we can guess it," Sticky ventured.

Mr. Curtain shook his head as if he pitied them. "Do you not see the pointlessness of your efforts? Even if you managed to escape the island, you would have accomplished nothing. Moreover, you can be assured my Recruiters would come for you. You would be captured by nightfall, and by morning you would be calling me your master. You will be under my complete control!"

"*Thank* you!" Reynie burst out, his face brightening.

Mr. Curtain was startled. "Thank me?"

"You've given me an idea! Aren't you always saying that control is the key?"

Mr. Curtain snorted with contempt, but from the look of fury in the man's eyes, Reynie felt he'd struck the right note. "Kate, try the word 'control.'"

Kate poked the keys deliberately, calling out the letters as she typed: "C-O-N-T-R-O-L."

Nothing happened.

Over the intercom came S.Q.'s voice: "Mr. Curtain, sir! We've found a ladder and should have it outside your window in two minutes!"

Mr. Curtain chuckled. "Reynard, you pathetic fellow, did you honestly think you were smarter than I? Did you truly believe you could guess my code? 'Control,' indeed. Oh, *bravo*. Bravo, bravo. Three cheers for Reynard Muldoon!"

"I thought we'd try English first," Reynie said thoughtfully. "But since you're so proud of your home country, I think we'll also try Dutch."

Mr. Curtain's jaw dropped. Then, trying to cover his consternation, he said, "As if you could *possibly* know —"

Reynie interrupted him. "Sticky, how do you spell 'control' in Dutch?"

"Same as in English," Sticky replied. "Only with an *E* on the end."

"Here's hoping," Kate said, reaching up to tap the E key.

"Snakes and dogs!" howled Mr. Curtain, before falling into a peaceful sleep.

As the hidden door slid open and Kate was swept up into Milligan's good arm, Reynie and Sticky rushed over to help Constance. The cuffs and helmet had not retracted. Constance's eyelids were fluttering, and still she murmured, so quietly it was difficult to hear her, "No . . . no . . . no . . ."

"We have to get her out!" Sticky said.

"Don't worry, we will," said a woman's voice.

The boys turned to discover Rhonda Kazembe and Number Two standing right behind them. And then, before they could express their amazement, into the room strode Mr. Benedict himself.

"Mr. Benedict!" Reynie cried. "We were trying to confuse it — that is, Constance was, but —"

Mr. Benedict nodded. "You've done wondrously well. *Wondrously* well. Now how is dear Constance?"

"Awful," said Sticky. "Just look at her."

"Yes," said Mr. Benedict, kneeling beside Constance, "this machine has come close to breaking her will. The brave child, she's very nearly used it up all at once."

"Very nearly?"

"Oh, she'll quite recover." In a much louder voice Mr.

Benedict said, "Constance Contraire! You've done it, child! The Whisperer is deeply, profoundly confused — you can stop fighting now!"

The little girl stopped mumbling, smacked her lips, and opened her eyes. "What took you so long?"

"Do you see?" Mr. Benedict said with a fond smile, tousling her hair. "She'll be fine. Constance, dear, please climb down from the chair now. We must hurry."

"But she *can't* climb down," Reynie said, indicating the cuffs.

"What do you know about it?" Constance replied grumpily, sliding her tiny wrists free of the metal bands and slipping her head out of the helmet.

The boys gaped.

"You mean you could have gotten out any time you wanted?" Sticky asked.

"It would take some pretty small cuffs to hold *me* tight," she replied.

Despite her bravado, however, Constance was so weak she toppled forward when she tried to stand. Mr. Benedict caught her, held her by the shoulders, and looked her squarely in the eyes. "I am so proud of you, Constance. You've been very brave indeed. Thank you for your great efforts."

Constance beamed with pleasure.

There was no time for anything: not to express their shock at Constance's having *chosen* to remain in the Whisperer despite the agonizing struggle, not to seek explanations for the arrival of Mr. Benedict and his agents, not even to tell Mr. Benedict what had happened. Fortunately, he and his agents seemed to know exactly what to do. Already Milligan had lifted the slumbering Mr. Curtain out of his chair and laid him — more gently than anyone thought he deserved — onto the floor. Already Rhonda was ushering the children toward the secret exit. And already Mr. Benedict (allowing himself only a moment to stare into the sleeping face of his brother, who had chosen such a dreadful path) — already he was taking Mr. Curtain's place in the wheelchair and reaching for the red helmet.

"Mr. Benedict, there's no time!" said Sticky. "They'll come through that window any moment!"

"There's time, Sticky, but not for everything. Thanks to you children, this machine is disoriented, and I must strike while the iron's hot. Hurry now, all of you. Make your escape as quickly as you can."

The others were dumbfounded, including Number Two, who had shadowed Mr. Benedict to the wheelchair and seemed at a loss what to do. "You mean you're staying behind? But they'll catch you! They'll *kill* you!"

"Why else am I here if not to do this now?" he told her soothingly. "Milligan, please take my brother with you. We must separate him from his machine. If I fail to disable it, you must do everything in your power to keep him away from it."

"You know I will," Milligan said, shaking his hand. With his uninjured arm, he scooped up Mr. Curtain, still bound by Kate's rope, and threw him over his shoulder.

"Now, don't worry about me, children," Mr. Benedict said. "Above all else, you must make your escape. Go at once! Milligan, allow no one to linger. Not even you, dear Number Two. Hurry now! Go!"

ESCAPES AND RETURNS

Down, down the winding passage they went, through darkness and spider webs and dripping water, until at last they emerged into a cold wind, brilliant sunlight, and the sound of waves breaking on rocks. They were on the far side of the island, the side opposite the bridge. In the distance a flat-bottomed motorboat lay beached on a strip of sand scarcely wide enough to accommodate it. Together the little group scrambled through scrub brush and gravel down to the boat. Milligan dumped Mr. Curtain onto the sand, then began helping Rhonda and Number Two usher the children into the boat. Kate had just climbed over the gunwale, with Rhonda and Number Two scrambling in after her, when Sticky pointed and cried, "He's getting away!"

Milligan whirled. Kate's rope lay in a tangle on the sand, and Mr. Curtain was running with surprising swiftness back the way they'd come. Already he was almost to the secret passage. In an instant Milligan had pulled out his tranquilizer gun and fired — but it was too late; Mr. Curtain had gone too far. The dart whizzed behind him just as he disappeared into the secret passage.

It was a terrible misfortune, and for a moment Milligan seemed his old grim self. With a severe expression he turned back to the children. "No time to chase him. My duty is to see you to safety, and for that we must leave at once." Laying a hand on Kate's shoulder as he prepared to shove off, he murmured gently, "Remind me, though, to teach you a better knot."

"What if Mr. Curtain stops Mr. Benedict before he can disable the Whisperer?" Sticky asked.

"We'll go into hiding," Rhonda said gravely. "Those are Mr. Benedict's instructions."

Milligan launched the boat and steered them out into the channel, where the children eyed the rocks that jutted up here and there on all sides.

"Um, Milligan, aren't these waters supposed to be dangerous to navigate?" asked Reynie as the boat whizzed past a sharp rock, missing it by inches.

"Oh, yes, fearsome dangerous," said Milligan with a smile. "Many a boat has capsized here. But I haven't been secretly swimming in the channel every night for nothing. I know these rocks well. You've nothing to fear."

The strange sight of Milligan's smile eased their fears of drowning, but it also chafed Constance, who blurted, "How can you possibly smile knowing Mr. Benedict is back there? He's sure to have been captured already, and now Mr. Curtain will see to it that he's killed!"

"Don't fret, child," Milligan said, squinting against the spray as he steered their boat between two boulders. The mainland was rapidly approaching. "I intend to return for him the moment I've ferried you to safety. I would never abandon Mr. Benedict."

"But you won't stand a chance! You're injured, and they'll be ready for you! Mr. Curtain will —"

The distraught girl was interrupted by the boat's rushing up onto sandy shore. Before she could continue, Number Two had carried her off to the waiting station wagon. The others quickly followed, and soon Rhonda Kazembe was cranking the ignition and pulling the car onto the road. Milligan sat near an open window with his tranquilizer gun at the ready. "Just drop me near the bridge guardhouse," he directed Rhonda, "then take the children away."

"But Milligan," asked Sticky, "how will you escape? For that matter, how did you ever escape in the first place? I remember that Waiting Room — there was no way out!"

"No way but down," Milligan replied. "I eventually realized that where there's mud, there's water, so an underground stream must run somewhere below the room."

"But . . . but how?"

"No great matter," Milligan said. "I had only to hold my breath a few minutes to dig down through the mud into the stream, drag myself upstream, then dig through more mud and, oh, about a foot of clay. After that it was only a question of tearing out a few stones, prying apart a few boards, chiseling out some mortar, bending the bars of a metal grate enough to squeeze through (that's how I broke my arm), then incapacitating the guards and using their keys to unlock my shackles. Really, it's quite simple once you know the trick."

The children blinked.

"More remarkable," Milligan went on, in a voice so happy he almost sang, "more remarkable by far was what happened while I was doing it. Down there in the mud, holding my breath and digging away, I realized that the feeling I had — that I must get back to you children, that I must reach you no matter what the cost — was exactly the same feeling I'd had when I first awoke out of blackness years ago with the name 'Milligan' ringing in my mind. Thinking of this, I realized for the first time that it was a child's voice that had been saying my name. And just as *this* realization struck me, so too did the cold waters of the underground stream, and into my mind flashed an image of a mill pond, a lovely place perfect for swimming. I could picture a girl swimming in that pond — so young it was hard to believe she could swim at all, much less splash and dive about like an otter — and in my mind's eye I drew her near to me, heard her laughing, and, as I took her hand to lead her home, heard her ask me, 'Daddy, may we come to the mill again?' To which I replied, 'Of course, Katie-Cat. Of course we'll come to the mill again.'

"Mill again — *Milligan*. Do you see? It wasn't my name at all. It was my last, unkept promise to my daughter. I had only to realize this, and all of my other memories came flooding back. The best moment of my life," he finished, with an affectionate look at Kate beside him.

Kate was trying to fight back tears and failing miserably. The station wagon was approaching the island bridge now. She'd been so thrilled to get her father back. Was she really expected to give him up again to another dangerous mission? Not just dangerous — hopeless. No, she wouldn't have it, and with a ferocity that surprised even her she declared, "You can't go, Milligan! I won't let you! How can you possibly leave me again?"

Milligan flinched as if he'd been stung, his own eyes suddenly brimming with tears. "Oh, Katie, it's the last thing I want to do, but how can I possibly leave Mr. Benedict? Without him we'd never have been reunited!"

"Then I'm going with you!"

"No, no, that would never do!"

"It will *have* to do!" Kate retorted fiercely as Number Two stopped the car near the guardhouse.

"Hush, both of you!" cried Reynie, surprising everyone. He was pointing at the bridge, upon which now Mr. Curtain could be seen in his wheelchair racing toward them. An entire troop of Recruiters ran alongside him, shaking their cuffs, their shock-watches glinting in the sunlight. The rocketing wheelchair zigzagged recklessly, forcing the Recruiters to jump this way and that to avoid being knocked aside, and the two Recruiters in the guardhouse (who must have radioed the island the moment they spotted the station wagon) had come out to stare first at Mr. Curtain, then at the car, uncertain what was expected of them.

"Kate, I love you, but you *must* leave with the others!" Milligan commanded. He reached for the door handle. "Rhonda, see that she does. I'll lure them off by heading back for the boat. Perhaps I can cut behind them. Number Two, drive like a fiend and never look back!"

"No!" Reynie shouted, just as forcefully, and Milligan checked himself with a start. "Stay put, Milligan! Number Two, don't drive away. Just trust me. *Please* trust me. We have to wait and see!"

It was a tense moment. And a curious one, too — for every person in the car, adult and child alike, realized just then that they trusted this eleven-year-old boy quite without reservation. If Reynie Muldoon asked them to do something, if he promised them something, they would do what he asked and believe every word.

Number Two looked at Milligan, who looked back at her. He nodded. She nodded. They waited.

At the near end of the bridge Mr. Curtain came to a sudden screeching stop in his wheelchair — so sudden that he almost flew out of it, despite the straps — pointed at the station wagon, and cried, "It's a trick! Those are decoys! The others must still be on the island!"

The Recruiters were scratching their heads. "But, sir," one of them protested mildly, "they look just like the ones we're after!"

"Fool!" Mr. Curtain shouted in his most terrible voice. "Do you really believe they would escape the island only to come right back to the bridge? These people are meant to distract us. Back to the island at once! That's an order!"

The Recruiters flinched and spun on their heels.

"You, too!" he snarled at the Recruiters in the guardhouse. "Forget the decoys! We need all hands on the island!"

The Recruiters saluted uncertainly and left their posts, hurrying to catch up with the others. For a moment Mr. Curtain watched them go. Then, quickly unstrapping himself, he rose from the chair and trotted toward the station wagon.

"What's he doing?" Rhonda said.

Milligan lifted his tranquilizer gun and drew a bead on the man, now only a few yards away.

"Don't shoot!" Reynie warned. "Don't you see? It's Mr. *Benedict!*"

Milligan lowered the gun, amazed. Mr. Benedict's performance had been most convincing. In all their years together, he had never seen him look so angry or speak so unkindly.

"Thank you, Reynie, for saving me from that dart," said Mr. Benedict with a wink and a clipped version of his dolphin laugh. He paused with his hand on the door handle, having noticed that Mr. Curtain wasn't in the car. His eyebrows rose. "But if my brother escaped, then how did you know who I was? How could you be sure?"

"To be honest," Reynie replied, "I knew it the moment I saw how badly you drove that wheelchair!"

"Hmm, yes. It's one thing to snarl and bark orders, quite another to steer that wicked contraption. However, I do think I would have got the hang of it with just a bit of practice."

"We're very glad you're safe, sir," said Number Two from behind the steering wheel. "But may we please leave now and save the congratulations for later?" She was nervously eyeing the troop of Recruiters, who had realized their leader was not among them. One by one they were turning to gawk and point at the station wagon. Some had started back across the bridge.

"By all means, Number Two," said Mr. Benedict, climbing into the car. "Let us fly!"

For Every Exit An Entrance

Every night the moon made its slow passage over Stone-town, and every night Reynie Muldoon gazed up through the window of the drafty old house, remembering the moonlit meetings of the Mysterious Benedict Society. There was much to remember about that time, and much to tell, but the moon in its nightly travels would dwindle, disappear, and fatten again before their stories were entirely told. There was too much to do, too little time for storytelling.

Mr. Curtain had escaped the island, along with several Recruiters and a few of his most trusted Executives. So reported the government officials Mr. Benedict had persuaded to raid the Institute. These officials had never believed him before, but their former skepticism had crumbled under the weight of new developments. For one thing, Milligan's memory had returned, and with it a number of top-secret government passwords. For another, Kate, unbeknownst to anyone, had swiped a pamphlet from Mr. Curtain's press room, not to mention Mr. Curtain's *journal*, which she'd nabbed on her way out of the Whispering Gallery. But most important of all, the Whisperer was no longer broadcasting Mr. Curtain's messages. Their mind-muddying effects were daily diminishing, the Emergency was fading, and minds long closed to truth were opening again, like flowers craving sunlight.

These days a steady stream of agents and officers flowed through Mr. Benedict's doors, gathering details and scribbling furiously in notebooks (and often getting lost in his maze). They wanted to catch Mr. Curtain, though for this Mr. Benedict held out little hope. Mr. Curtain, he said, was too smart to be outfoxed by adults. Only children could have accomplished it.

Still, there remained the important problem of all those who had been robbed of memories: the "recruited" children; the secret agents who'd been retrained as Helpers; Mr. Bloomburg, of course; and a good many of the Executives, who not so long ago had been hapless orphans in search of purpose and a home. It would be Milligan's task to lead the search for all the unfortunates who had ever set foot upon Nomansan Island; it would be Mr. Benedict's to restore their memories. Already Mr. Benedict was hard at work modifying his twin's invention with the aim of reversing its brainsweeping function — instead of covering up old memories, it would coax them into the open again — and when pressed, Mr. Benedict admitted he thought it rather likely he would succeed. To those who knew him, this meant there was no doubt he would.

Mr. Benedict firmly insisted, however, that modesty had nothing to do with his opinion that the children had been the real heroes in this adventure. It was they, he argued, who took the risks to discover Mr. Curtain's dark secrets; they who overcame Mr. Curtain in the Whispering Gallery; they who primed the Whisperer for shutdown; and they who figured out how to unlock the secret exit — something that could only have been done from the inside.

"How did you even know about that secret exit, Mr. Benedict?" Kate asked one night, some weeks after their return. Though everyone in the house had been talking nonstop, it had mostly been to government agents, not to one another, and their own curiosities had yet to be satisfied. This night happened to be the first that they all sat down together with no one to interrupt them. Everyone in the dining room cradled a mug of steaming hot chocolate, for autumn had now given way to winter, and everyone — even Constance Contraire — wore an expression of profound relief to find themselves alone together at last.

"Again I must defer the credit," said Mr. Benedict. "It was Milligan who found it."

Everyone looked to Milligan, who was seated at the table beside Kate.

"I just felt sure Mr. Curtain would have built a secret escape route for himself," Milligan explained. "So after I joined you on the island, I searched every night under cover of darkness. Even then I was lucky — I only found the entrance the night before I was captured."

"It's always about entrances and exits with you, isn't it, Milligan?" Kate teased.

Milligan laughed — it was a hearty, booming laugh — and everyone at the table jumped. They were still getting used to his laughter. After all these years of acting like the saddest man alive, Milligan now acted as if he were the *happiest* man alive — and perhaps he was. Having so long ago exited his life as a father, he had now, at long last, entered it again.

Milligan reached over and plucked Kate's chin, which for the first time in weeks was not greasy with ointment. (Her cuts and bruises were long since healed, having been constantly overattended to, not only by Milligan but by everyone else in the house as well.) Kate beamed, swatting playfully at his hand. The next moment she realized the marshmallow was missing from her hot chocolate. She looked up to see him pop it into his mouth.

"You thief!" she said, giggling.

Milligan gave her a wink and a fresh marshmallow.

At the other end of the table, meanwhile, Reynie was preoccupied with a curious question: What should he call the person beside him? He was seated next to Miss Perumal, of course. They'd been reunited at last — with much hugging and great quantities of tears — and she sat by him now with one hand resting on his shoulder. But would he continue to call her Miss Perumal? What *would* he call her? This is a pressing question for all children who find themselves with a new parent, and so it was for Reynie, whose absence had impressed upon Miss Perumal how dear to her he was: At their reunion, she had lost no time asking what he might think of her adopting him.

At first Reynie had been unable to answer her, only threw himself into her arms and hid his face.

"Oh dear," Miss Perumal had said, bursting into a fresh bout of tears. "Oh dear, I hope this means yes."

It had, of course, meant yes, and the two of them sat now with the odd sense — very much like that experienced by Milligan and Kate — of having been family for ages, yet somehow having only just met. An odd sense, but extremely pleasant.

"Mom" didn't feel quite right, Reynie decided. Why not use the Tamil word? He'd heard her refer to her own mother as "Amma," but whether this meant "mom" or "mother," he wasn't sure. Reynie felt a flutter of happy anticipation. He would ask Sticky.

At that moment, Sticky happened to be the only unhappy person in the entire group. He was trying valiantly not to show it, though. Instead he pressed Mr. Benedict with another question: "But how did you finally disable the Whisperer?"

"I only finished what you children had already begun," replied Mr. Benedict. "I persuaded the Whisperer that I was Curtain, then gave it orders that more or less baffled it out of operation. But had Constance not already thoroughly discombobulated it, and had I not possessed a brain so very much like my twin's, we might never have succeeded."

"Three cheers for Mr. Benedict's brain!" cried Kate. Everyone laughed and cheered.

"And three cheers for Constance," said Mr. Benedict, then grew thoughtful as the others cheered and Constance blushed. "That reminds me. Constance, my dear, would you please step into the kitchen and retrieve the small box on the table there?"

Constance nodded and went into the kitchen.

"I can't believe it," Sticky said. "She went without even grumbling. It's almost like she's growing up."

"That is precisely to the point, Sticky," said Mr. Benedict, with a nod to Rhonda Kazembe, who went to a cabinet and produced an enormous birthday cake that had been hidden inside.

"Thank goodness," said Number Two. "I'm starved."

Constance returned to find the others beaming at her and pointing to the cake. She blushed yet again. "But my birthday isn't until next month!"

"Who knows what the next month brings?" asked Mr. Benedict. "I say let us eat cake now!"

Constance shook her head bemusedly, though clearly she was delighted, and as she clambered back into her chair she handed him the little box he'd sent for.

"It was the three cheers that reminded me," said Mr. Benedict, opening the box and shaking out three birthday candles. "I'd forgotten to put the candles on the cake."

"Three birthday candles?" Reynie said. "*Three* birthday candles? Constance is only *two years old*?"

"Two years and eleven months," the girl said defensively.

The children gaped.

"But . . . but . . . ," Sticky began, then closed his mouth and shook his head.

"Why, that explains everything!" Kate said, with a feeling of great relief, as if a nagging question had finally been answered, though she'd never realized she'd had the question in the first place.

Reynie laughed with delight. "So *that* was what Mr. Benedict meant when he said you were more gifted than anyone realized. I thought he was just referring to your incredible stubbornness!"

"Who's stubborn?" Constance said, frowning.

"A toddler," Sticky murmured to himself. "No wonder she was always so sleepy, so cranky, so stubborn. She's two!"

"I am *not* stubborn," insisted Constance, who had overheard. Then she corrected him: "And I'm almost three."

The next day, although the house once again teemed with agents and rattled with the noise of a thousand phone calls, Mr. Benedict found it necessary to abandon the projects for a time and attend to important matters of a more personal nature. He tracked Sticky down in an upstairs hallway, where Number Two was rubbing Sticky's bald head and nodding.

"Yes, I concur," she said matter-of-factly. "Your hair is definitely coming back."

"Finally," Sticky said.

Number Two noticed Mr. Benedict and frowned. "What on earth are you doing out of your chair? Why didn't you call for one of us?"

"I apologize, Number Two. I was distracted by an urgent matter and will return at once. Sticky, will you please accompany me? I have something to discuss with you."

"Make sure he sits down, Sticky," Number Two called after them.

Together they went into Mr. Benedict's office, where Mr. Benedict obediently sat at his desk and said, "Sticky, I won't beat around the bush. Your parents are here."

"My — my parents? *Here?*" Sticky said, glancing around as if expecting to see them hiding behind furniture. It was only a nervous response. He had no idea how he felt about the news.

"I'll explain," said Mr. Benedict. "Let us begin with what

you already know. After you ran away your parents did, for a time, get caught up in the sudden downpour of riches. In fact they made so much money they were wealthier than most people, wealthier by far than they had ever been. Though they did look for you, their efforts grew halfhearted —"

"You're right," Sticky interjected miserably. "I know this part."

"Not entirely, my friend. Their efforts were halfhearted, I say, but this, more than anything, was because they were afraid of you."

"Afraid? Of *me*?"

"Indeed, they were afraid of their inability to give you a proper home. When you ran away, Sticky, your parents were bitterly ashamed. You were already so much smarter than they were, and they had already made such a terrible mess of things. If you wished to run away, then perhaps — or so they thought in their anguish — perhaps it was for the best. Perhaps you were better off without them."

"Better off?" Sticky echoed, remembering that long-ago phrase of his father's, the phrase he'd partly overheard. He'd thought his father meant *they* were better off without *him*.

"These were their thoughts at the time. You must also realize they were being influenced by Curtain's hidden messages. 'The missing aren't missing, they're only departed,' remember? A most pernicious message indeed. And yet *despite* this, Sticky, your parents became perfectly morose. Despite their desperate hopes that the money would help them forget you, they soon understood no amount of riches could fill the hole you'd left in their lives. They realized they needed *you*, even if you didn't need *them*. And so they've spent all their money looking for you, in fact have gone deeply into debt and are now quite poor.

"It may also interest you to know," Mr. Benedict continued, "that your parents began their search *before* we disabled the Whisperer. So determined were they to bring you back, you see, their minds began to resist the broadcasts. Only a powerful love could have mounted such a resistance."

Sticky was having trouble taking it all in. "And they found me? You didn't call them?"

"They found you. I could have kept you hidden, perhaps. But once I was convinced of how earnestly they sought you, once I had grasped their true feelings, I allowed you to be found."

"So you think I should go with them."

"It's what *you* think that matters, Sticky."

"Well, but how do they seem to you?"

"Quite wretched, I should say, and sick with longing for their lost child. They made a terrible mistake and will always regret it. When I told them you were safe, your parents' relief overwhelmed them. They wept and wept. Nor had they stopped weeping when I took my leave of them. I believe they're still weeping, in fact — I saw Rhonda bringing fresh tissues."

Sticky's eyes brimmed with tears. "And they really said they needed me more than I needed them?"

"That appears to be their take on the matter. What is your own opinion?"

The tears spilled over and ran down Sticky's cheeks. "May I see them?"

"You had only to ask, my friend," declared Mr. Benedict,

rising to shake Sticky's hand. His eyes shone with emotion. "They're waiting for you in the dining room."

Sticky flew from Mr. Benedict's study toward a reunion so joyous and tearful and, eventually, so full of happy laughter, that soon the dining room was crowded with all Sticky's friends, and with Milligan and Rhonda and Number Two, and even a few unfamiliar officials drawn by the commotion. It was a splendid, uproarious, spontaneous celebration, with hugs and handshakes and kisses all around, and eventually Milligan produced the remains of last night's birthday cake and Rhonda whipped up a frothy fruit punch. Even the officials, at first irritated by the delay in their investigations, got caught up in the frenzy, and before long they had shed their coats and ties, one of them had put on a record, and dancing broke out.

This had been going on for some time when Number Two suddenly looked about for Mr. Benedict. "Mercy!" she cried, and flew from the room. She found him exactly where Sticky had left him after their warm handshake; only instead of standing Mr. Benedict was sprawled facedown across his desk, papers scattered all about, snoring like a freight train with an expression of pure happiness on his face.

"Mr. Benedict is adopting Constance, eh?" Kate said to Reynie. "That's good news. And a good fit, I'd say. He certainly enjoys her lame jokes."

They had completed their snow fort and were building up a supply of snowballs for the coming attack. Across the courtyard Rhonda, Constance, and Sticky were engaged in the same activity. Peeking over the top of the fort to observe the other side's progress, Reynie said, "Yes, everybody's finding their family, it seems. You have Milligan. I'm to have a mother and a grandmother. Constance gets two sisters and a father —"

"Two sisters?"

"Oh, yes, it turns out Mr. Benedict adopted Number Two and Rhonda long ago. Though Rhonda believes it's more apt to say *they* adopted *him*. In fact, I think that's how Mr. Benedict put the question to Constance: 'Would you be willing to adopt us as your family?' Constance told him she'd have to consider it, but was inclined to accept."

Kate snickered. "'Inclined to accept.' What gumption. Hey, you're making those too big. Try to make them about this size." She displayed one of her perfectly formed spheres to Reynie, then scooped up more snow with her new bucket (a gift from Milligan — it was exactly like her old one).

"Kate! Reynie! Are you ready for ignominious defeat?" shouted Rhonda from across the courtyard.

"Defeat? We know not the word!" Kate shouted back, then whispered to Reynie, "Actually, 'ignominious' is the word I don't know."

"Shameful," Reynie said.

"Hey, I can't know *every* word, Mr. Smarty. For crying out loud, how —"

"No, 'ignominious' means shameful."

"It does?" Kate said. She frowned with passionate defiance. She was as happy as she had ever been. "The beasts! We'll see about that. Do you remember our strategy?"

Reynie rolled his eyes. "How could I forget? You barrage

them with snowballs while I run out and gather all the ones they've thrown, so as to keep our pile from running low."

"Yes, and repack them to the proper size while you're at it," Kate said.

"Would you mind terribly if I threw an occasional snowball myself? That *is* part of the fun, you know."

Kate sighed. "I hate to waste a snowball, but I suppose there's always the chance you'll hit something. Fine, you can throw some."

"Much obliged," Reynie said.

Moments later the courtyard erupted into a melee of flung snowballs, scurrying children, and peals of laughter. More laughter sounded from behind the windows of the house, where all the adults, including Miss Perumal and the Washingtons, sipped apple cider and watched the gleeful battle below. Mr. Benedict laughed so hard, in fact — a great, long, series that sounded like an entire *school* of dolphins — that Number Two hurried over to snatch the hot cider just as he went limp in sleep. He awoke minutes later only to laugh himself to sleep again, and so he continued, laughing and sleeping and laughing again, all afternoon, until at last he slipped into a prolonged slumber. When he awoke a final time to Number Two's gentle shaking of his shoulder, Mr. Benedict saw that the day had grown noticeably darker.

"It's dusk and we've called them in twice already," Number Two told him. "Can't you urge them to come inside at once? Dinner's growing cold."

"Soon, Number Two, soon," said Mr. Benedict, casting an affectionate look first at her, then at the giddy, happy children beyond the window. "Have a snack, why don't you? Sneak a bowl of the stew — I won't tell anyone — but let's give them a few minutes more. They'll be so cold that even lukewarm victuals will seem piping hot to them. Just a few minutes more, Number Two. Let them play. They *are* children, after all."

And this was certainly true, if only for the moment.

Dear Reader,

It has come to my attention that certain individuals wish to know my first name. If you are one of these, and if you are acquainted with the code, then I assure you the answer lies within your grasp.

Best regards,

Mr. Benedict

Acknowledgments

Many good people helped this book along the way (in not a few cases by buoying its author), and they deserve far more than an expression of my gratitude, but here they shall have at least that: I would like to thank Sara Curtis, for encouraging me before I began; Mark Barr, Todd Kimm, and Lisa Taggart, for their thoughtful and valuable comments on early drafts; Eric Simonoff and Kate Schafer, for spectacular agentry; Megan Tingley, Nancy Conescu, and Noel De La Rosa, for their faith in the book and dedication to making it better; Mary O'Connell, Chris Adrian, Diane Perry, Nicola Mason, Michael Griffith, Brock Clarke, Kenner Estes, and Shannon and David Collier-Tenison, for their generosity of spirit; Elaine Price, for minding the front while I minded the books; my wife, Sarah Beth Estes, for her helpful opinions on multiple drafts, not to mention braving fire and rain; and my son Elliot, for being Elliot—which is to say, for making everything fine.